RAGING STORM

Richard Nesbitt

For Sue
Best wishes

Copyright © 2018 Richard Nesbitt

All rights reserved.

ISBN: 1981770135
ISBN-13: 978-1981770137

Dedicated to the Brotherhood

of the

United States Marine Corps

Semper Fi

Also by Richard Nesbitt

ANGEL

CHOSEN

GOOD COP BAD COP

MOB RULES

Raging Storm

1

It was an idyllic place to die. Far better than he deserved.

Lying prone and motionless in a thicket of brush behind a large Fraser Fir, I peered down towards the valley. The undergrowth was wet with dew and the morning air already thick and humid. The sun, a small, orange slice, was peeking over the eastern horizon. Long, drawn out shadows pointed upwards against the slope of the mountain. Overhead, with wide stretched wings, hawks circled an updraft against an azure backdrop. A low mist had settled to blanket the valley below.

It was a damn better place than he deserved.

The spotters scope I used was a luxury. Retailing for six thousand dollars, it was one of the best pieces of equipment a hunter could own. The instrument offered an advantage that few could afford. But, the cost of my equipment was not the issue. The fact that I was a hunter was the issue today. In fact, if such things were ranked, I would be counted as one of the best hunters on earth. I'd spent many years honing my skills and there is no substitute for experience.

I'd left my camouflaged truck in a ravine six miles from my current position. If somebody stumbled upon it, it would not seem unusual. Hunters were common in the Smoky Mountains and deer season was in full swing.

I had approached up the western side of the mountain the previous day. With my face covered, I'd hiked with great caution as I ascended the small peak. Upon reaching the top, I'd donned a ghillie suit and spent the better part of the evening low crawling. It had taken a full seven hours to traverse the final leg of the journey. Yet it was imperative that I be the master of my surroundings. To see and to hear everything, long before I was either seen or heard. The quarry demanded no less.

The surrounding hillside was coming alive as the sun continued to rise. Birds sounded and there was a soft crunching of undergrowth. The wildlife had begun their daily task of survival.

I was well camouflaged in my ghillie suit which accommodated the local fauna and flora. As was the purpose, I blended in with the surroundings. I was invisible.

The front door of the cabin was 1,100 meters below and faced east. It was now completely bathed in brilliant, morning sunshine. The Nikon scope was so powerful that I could see the direction of the grain on the wooden door. Parked roughly fifty feet from the door was a black Chevy Suburban.

Next to me lay a Barrett .50 caliber sniper rifle. Wrapped

in the same fabric as the ghillie suit, it too was invisible. At the end of the long barrel was a fat, nine inch silencer. When the time came, there would be no sound from the hillside. There would be no muzzle flash against the bright sunlight of the morning. The only sound at cabin level would be the impact of the large projectile. I would most likely not have time for a second shot but that was fine. I rarely needed a second shot.

Time passed and I waited. Patience was the game. In prior hunts, I'd lay in place for days at a time. It was the discipline, the difference between success and failure. The cabin door opened.

I raised my head a fraction and looked up from the spotting scope. Shifting three inches to my right I transferred my eye to the high powered scope of the rifle. With the cross hairs fixed on the cabin door, I watched as a burly man stepped outside into the hazy sunshine.

One of the bodyguards, the man had thick black hair that looked unwashed. He was short but powerful looking. Very strong with a wide back. The man looked to his left and then to his right. He then looked up the mountain slope towards where I lay. He paused, scanning the hillside. In the man's left hand was a pair of binoculars. I watched as he lifted and placed them in front of his face. His eyes swept the hillside.

As I lay, watching him perform his security ritual, the man froze. Bringing his other hand up to focus the binoculars, he kept his gazed trained upon one spot. It looked as if something had caught his eye. From the great distance between us it looked as if he was staring right at me. I remained still, understanding the man's motives. It was an old trick designed to prompt panic in a less skilled hunter. His goal was to make any would be assassin think that he'd been spotted. I waited the man out, knowing that I was completely concealed. Finally, the bodyguard turned and walked towards the black SUV. Opening the door, the man tossed the binoculars onto the passenger seat. He then slid behind the steering wheel.

I brought the cross hairs back to the cabin door as another large man walked out. He was very tall and very wide. His shoulders were as broad as his torso was long. As with the other man, he also had greasy, dark hair but this man's face looked as if it had beat upon with a crowbar. Several jagged scars ran in deep, pock marked crevices. His nose looked flat and smashed. The entire upper ridge of his brow looked twisted. This would not be somebody you would want to engage in hand to hand combat.

The man stood in place and looked about with deadly seriousness. A shorter, heavyset man followed and stood behind him. This man had the look of wealth with zero class. A gold chain and diamond studded pinky ring sparkled in the sunlight. Over a stretched, white T-shirt, his track suit hung limp from the sides of his bloated belly. He had a cigar clenched between his teeth and it appeared as if he hadn't shaved for several days.

The target.

The man who had made his living through extortion, racketeering and murder. A ruthless thug who had climbed the ranks of organized crime. Now on the run from a pending indictment.

The bodyguard held his spot. As his smaller colleague had done, he performed a quick scan of the surroundings.

The short, fat man waited. Smoke rose from his stub of a cigar.

I looked for my best chance but the man was shielded by the large frame of his bodyguard. The only clear shot was the left side of his head. From 1,100 meters it was too far to risk a miss. Any movement or variation in the wind could mean a miss. And they would scramble back into the safety of the cabin. The mission would be compromised. The mission would fail.

The decision made itself.

Inhaling in a slow and steady manner, I trained the cross hairs on the larger man's chest. The bodyguard would have to go too. I exhaled softly and then held my breath. Applying a slow and gentle pressure to the trigger, the sniper rifle burped with a soft thump.

Travelling at 2,799 feet per second, the large round found its mark. Both the bodyguard and his boss flew backwards. The large caliber bullet passed with ease through both of their midsections. The door frame and outside wall of the cabin splashed a crimson red in a splotched, random pattern. Their bodies fell as one, the larger man coming to rest atop his former employer.

The remaining bodyguard launched himself out of the SUV and sprinted to the cabin. He skidded to a stop in front of the two fallen men and crouched low to examine them. Through the scope, I watched his panicked face as the man spun around to look back up the hillside. He reached under his jacket and produced a pistol. It was a foolish thing to do.

I pulled back the bolt and the empty shell casing flew out, landing in the brush. Pushing the bolt forward, I chambered another round.

The man continued to scan the hillside. He should have sought cover. I had little choice. If I allowed him to live, the mountain would be swarming with men before long. A second round left the barrel.

The man rocked back on his heels, his arms flying wide. His pistol sailed out and away to the right, skidding to rest in front of the cabin. By the time the man landed backwards on top of the other two men, he had also left this world.

I chambered another round and watched the front of the cabin. I waited to see if there was anybody else who might run out, someone I had not accounted for.

After a half hour of inactivity, I pulled back the bolt of the rifle. The unused round popped out and landed in the underbrush. I pushed a button on the side of the Barrett which released the magazine. Picking up the fallen round, I snapped it back into the magazine. With the chamber empty, I slid the bolt back in place and then slid the magazine back into the breach. I found the two spent shell casings and placed them in the front cargo pocket of my suit.

Sighting in on the kill once more, I saw that flies were already buzzing around the corpses. Soon the animals would arrive. I did not want to see what would remain of these men if they weren't discovered for a few days.

Mission complete, I began the arduous task of backing up the steep hillside. All the while I kept my eyes on the cabin below. Once I felt sure that there was no risk, I stood and hurried my way to the top of the small mountain. When the summit was finally crested, I began a brisk walk back down the opposing slope.

If I reached the truck by nine o'clock, I figured I could be in Atlanta before noon.

Raging Storm
2

I needed to stop for some coffee as my eyes were closing. Exhausted, I struggled to stay awake and that's not a good thing when you're barreling down a highway. A road sign loomed, telling me that I was two miles from an exit. Among the other restaurants and gas stations being advertising on the sign was a Love's truck stop. Perfect.

I eased my pickup into the slow lane and took the exit ramp. Making a right, I drove the 0.3 miles the sign had promised, and turned into the gas station. I pulled into a parking spot on the left side of the building. It was chilly outside and the crisp air felt refreshing as I stepped out of the F-150. I stretched, extending my arms high above my head.

"Can I ask you a question, sir?" A voice sounded behind me.

I jumped, spinning around with my fists raised. There stood a older man with a weather beaten face, disheveled clothing and a patchy, Irish beard.

"Sorry!" He said. With wide eyes, he looked as

frightened as I had acted.

I stood six foot two inches tall and weighed two-hundred and twenty-five pounds. With almost no body fat, I was an intimidating presence. Whipping around like an idiot and assuming a fighting stance as I had, I was surprised the guy hadn't bolted.

Jesus, where did he come from? I asked myself. I was tired and had neglected to check my surroundings. That was unlike me. I looked the man over, he appeared homeless.

"It's cool, man," I said. I offered him a weak smile. I felt like an idiot. "You just startled me. Not your fault."

"Uhhh, okay," he said. He was still a tad wary. He decided to press on. "Can I ask you a favor?"

I knew what was coming but stood in silence, waiting to hear him out.

"I hit a patch of bad luck and can't get home. I'm trying to get enough money to buy gas. Do you have any change you could spare?"

I looked at the man and did my best to size him up. He had a red veined nose and puffed, bloodshot eyes. With his hair disheveled, it looked like he'd had a rough night.

"Where's your car?" I asked.

"Uh, what?" The man answered. It was clear that he had not expected to be questioned.

"I asked where's your car? Let's push it to a pump and I'll fill the tank for you."

"It's-it's down the road a piece," he replied with a stutter. "I don't want you to go to any trouble. Some spare change would help."

"Are you an alcoholic?" I asked, changing tact.

The man, looking perplexed, stared at me and shuffled his feet. He was unsure how to respond.

"Do you really need money to get gas or do you just want to buy a bottle?"

He looked around, eyes darting left and right. He searched for an exit from this unexpected conversation.

"Take your time," I said. My voice remained level and calm. "Honesty is the key here."

"Well," he said. "A drink would warm me up."

He looked like a child who had been caught swiping a cookie.

"Well then why not say that? Or don't say anything at all. You do know that bullshit line about needing gas is obvious, right?"

The man remained silent. He looked around the station. There were other cars pulling in and I knew that all he wanted was to get away from me to put the bite on a softer touch.

"I'm sorry to have bothered you, sir," he said. He hung his head and turned to walk away.

"Wait," I ordered.

Stopping, he turned back to face me. I fished in my pocket and came out with a small wad of bills. Peeling off two twenty dollar bills, I thrust them toward the man. His eyes lit up.

"Are you serious?" He asked.

His hand crept forward, unsure whether I was messing with him or not. I could read his thoughts. Was I was one of those assholes who liked fucking with people? Was I going to pull the money away at the last second? When I didn't move he closed his hands around the bills.

Yanking them out of my grasp, he thrust them into his own pocket.

"Thank you," he said.

"My name's Ryder," I said. I extended my hand, this time with only an open palm.

"I'm-I'm Micky," he answered. We exchanged a handshake. It had been a long time since anybody had treated him like a human being and it showed on his face.

"Try honesty next time, brother," I said. "It works more often than not."

Giving him a warm grin, I turned and walked towards the doors.

"I will. Thank you again."

I raised my hand to acknowledge him.

The warm blast of air felt good as I entered the store. I made it over to the wide array of coffee dispensers and found the Colombian blonde. A lot of people grab the darker blends thinking they are stronger. But the lighter the color, the less the bean has been cooked and thus the more caffeine remains in it. I chose the blonde.

Next, I eyed the wide variety of snacks that adorned the racks. I settled on a honey bun. It was a rare indulgence but I knew the sugar would give me a quick boost and the caffeine would do the rest. I walked to the counter and placed both the coffee and pastry on the counter. The redhead working the register smiled at me with more warmth than she had the last customer. Her name tag read Heather.

"Howdy, stranger," She said.

"Hi." I answered.

"Two dollars and eighty-nine cents, please."
I went into my pocket again. This time I grabbed a five and handed it to her. She smiled again. Her eyes were pretty.
She made change and handed it to me making more hand contact than was necessary. And then she locked eyes with me and smiled again. It appeared that insignificant things like my wedding ring didn't matter much to her.
"Thanks," I said. I turned from the counter.
"You're welcome."
Her voice giggled with a lilting flirt.
"Come back anytime, handsome."
I ignored her and walked back outside through the door which a trucker held open for me. I nodded my appreciation and walked over to my truck. Five minutes later I was heading south again on Hwy. 23. Ten minutes later the honey bun was gone. The empty wrapper lay crumpled in the passenger side drink holder. I sipped my coffee as I drove.
The thoughts came back. They always came back.
Why did I have so much to drink that night? Why?
Debbie had driven us home from the party. Sasha and Hunter were asleep in the back seat. It had been a fun afternoon with a large group of friends at a beach house. The kids screamed and played in the sand while the adults barbecued and drank. And played horseshoes and drank. And swam and drank.
Debbie had laughed when I stumbled getting out of the water. It wasn't like me to drink that much but it had been a carefree day. In truth, it had been an excellent day. A great day with great friends. Strange how that

works. You have one of the greatest days you can remember and then just like that you don't ever get to have a great day again.

I had consumed too much. But I was a happy drunk. I was always a happy drunk. Before that night in any case. And my wife looked hot. Delicious. I wanted her in the worst way. I'd run my hand up her thigh as she tried to focus on the road. Underneath her sun dress. Up to her panties. I traced my finger around her underwear, doing my best to tease her as I inched closer. Shooting me a sideways look, Debbie narrowed her eyes in mock consternation as she drove. She squeezed her thighs together to halt my progress.

"Stop," she'd said. Her voice was a rose petal. She gave me that smile. That smile that could melt an iceberg. She had that familiar twinkle in her eyes. "Wait until we get home and get the kids to bed."

I'd felt good. Very good. Leaning back in the seat, I contented myself to watch her as she drove. I ached for her and knowing that it was only fifteen minutes to the bliss that was her warm, naked body felt good. Felt perfect. The day had been perfect. She was perfect.

But I would never make love to her again.

In that peaceful, joy filled moment I hadn't known that. It's funny how everything can change in a split second. How your entire life can flip upside down so unexpectedly. So cruelly. And that it can stay that way forever. Forever destroyed. Forever alone.

And in my head I heard that damn song. That goddamn John Waite song, Missing You. That fucking song. I used to love that song. It was her song. Our song. Now it tortured me. Now it followed me everywhere and mocked me at random and unexpected moments.

'Every time I think of you, I always catch my breath...'

I could hear it now. It was in my head. I wanted it out. I felt the moisture gathering in my eyes when the phone rang.

It rattled me and I sucked in a big gulp of air. Then I closed my lips to a small pucker and let it rush out. I rubbed at my eyes with my thumb and forefinger, pinching out the wetness. I grabbed the phone from the passenger seat. It was him.

"Yeah," I said after sliding the green bar to the right. It wasn't a question, it was a greeting.

"How did it go?" The man asked.

"It went well."

"Was it clean?"

"Yes. But I had to cancel the help. It was unavoidable."

"I understand. But it's one hundred percent?"

"Yes. One hundred percent. Nothing on the news yet I gather?"

"No. It could be a while. Days even."

"Quite possibly."

"Listen," the man said. As always he spoke with authority. "Forget Atlanta. I want you to go to Hilton Head. Use the house there."

"What's up?" I asked.

"Nothing. I want you to go lay on the beach for a week. You've earned it."

"Done."

"Thanks, Ryder. You made the world a little better place."

I remained silent, not needing his praise or the obvious attempt to work me. I knew what I was doing. His validation wasn't necessary and to be honest, it kind of irritated me.

"Talk to you soon," I said.

"Goodbye," he answered.

I thumbed the red button ending the phone call.

I knew Hilton Head well. I would continue on to Atlanta and then grab I-75 south to I-16 east. That would take me into Savannah and from there Hilton Head was a mere 45 minute drive.

I focused on the road, trying to hold back the advancing hordes. I tried to barricade the gate. To block the horrible memories that tormented me. The memories that launched attack after attack, haunting me without mercy. I forced myself to think of something else. I went over the latest mission in my head step by step, reliving each detail as best I could. It was fresh in my mind. It was a distraction. It helped me turn it off.

I won this battle as the thoughts receded, beaten back to the far corners of my mind. But there they would regroup and plan their next assault on my sanity. It never ended.

I pushed down on the accelerator, feeling a simmering rage below the surface of my psyche. I grit my teeth and stared down the highway as the miles ticked by.

The coffee had cooled enough so that I was able to chug the last few swallows in one long pull.

I felt my energy returning.

Raging Storm
3

After pulling my truck into the garage I exited the vehicle. Grabbing my bag from the back seat, I walked through a door and into a spectacular great room. The eastern facing walls were large sheets of glass that spilled into the Atlantic Ocean. It was breathtaking.
The house sat atop a small bluff which served to obscure the beach view. The design had been purposeful. From most spots in the room, and the entire house, it appeared as if you were on a ship looking out across a tranquil sea. Only when you approached the glass could you look down upon the beach. Behind the home was a sprawling party deck with stairs that led down to a private, wooden path. This cut through the dunes and wisps of sea grass, leading out onto the sand.
I turned to the right and made my way to the master bedroom. Throwing my duffel onto the bed I went to the dresser. In the top drawer I found the bathing suit I'd left the last time I visited. Stripping off my clothes, I donned the suit. I stopped to grab a beach towel from a folded

stack which sat atop a hand carved, driftwood side table. I flung the towel around my neck, hanging on to each side with both hands.

Walking out the side bedroom door, my feet met the warm wooden deck. The sun was still high although in the western sky. It was not quite four o'clock. The salt air smelled intoxicating and the onshore breeze felt refreshing. It tempered the heat that beat down from a cloudless sky. I was still extremely tired and hadn't planned on running until the song came back again. It came at random times and always uninvited. And when it happened, I always felt the need to move. Fast.

'Every time I think of you, I always catch my breath...'

I bounded down the steps and broke into an easy jog between the dunes and towards the ocean. Leaving the wooden path, I felt the hot sand with each step and made for the damp, hard packed surface at the water's edge. Once there, I turned left, heading north and trying to outrun the noise in my head.

'And I'm still standing here and you're miles away and I'm wondering why you left...'

I increased my speed, and tried to recall the beach runs my platoon used to do on the other side of America. Camp Pendleton is located on the Southern California coast. Between tours of duty in Iraq and Afghanistan, I'd spent many years there. First Recon Battalion, First Marine Division was still a home away from home for me. I kept in contact with a lot of my brothers. Or at least I used to before that life changing night. I hadn't been very social in the past few months.

'And there's a storm that's raging...'

I tried to think of the war. My first tour. My first kill. Anything. It was no use. It was alive in me, kicking me. Winning the battle for my mind. For my sanity. That night was back again. And it wasn't going anywhere. Debbie had pulled into our driveway. She put the car in park as I hit the little black remote on the passenger visor. Our top of the line garage door opened with a whisper. Debbie turned in her seat to stare at me. Her eyes sparkled. I yearned for her. She was so close. The moment was so close. Get the kids to bed, I thought squinting my own eyes to give her the look. She read my mind and there was that smile again. God she was beautiful.

She opened her door and I opened mine. We stepped out of the car and opened the back doors at the same time. Debbie unstrapped Sasha from her car seat as I unbuckled her older brother. Hunter pushed against me with his little hands. He grimaced, eyes closed. He didn't want to be disturbed.

"Come on, champ," I'd said. He gave up and let me slide my arms underneath him. I lifted and backed out of the vehicle, my son in my arms.

Debbie had Sasha pressed against her shoulder as she walked through the garage. She pushed open the door and entered the dark house. I remembered wondering why Boomer hadn't run out to greet us, jumping on two legs, clawing at us to shower him with love. That wasn't like him not to welcome us home. I probably would have given it more notice if I hadn't been drunk and preoccupied with my wife.

I followed Debbie down the hallway on the right side of

the house. She turned left into Sasha's bedroom as I turned right into Hunter's. I started to lay him in his bed.

"I gotta go pee, daddy," he had said.

I sighed. A delay.

"Okay, pal," I answered.

I lowered him down and, as his feet hit the carpet, he scampered back into the hallway and made a beeline for the bathroom. He closed the door. He didn't use to do that. He was getting to be a big boy and now required privacy.

Debbie appeared before me.

"Come on," she whispered. I could hear it in her voice. She was ready too.

"Hold up, Hunter's going potty. Be right there."

I leaned over and kissed her. She kissed me back and then with a giggle, headed towards the other side of the house. She turned back to shoot me a sexy look as she rounded the corner.

"Hurry up or I'm starting without you."

I laughed. She always said that. And it always made me bite my lower lip.

I waited with painstaking patience for my son to finish in the bathroom. I imagined Debbie getting undressed and jumping in the shower.

The memory was so achingly vivid.

ENOUGH!

I roared internally as I took back control of my head. I cursed at myself, snapping out of it. I was back now, away from the demons and on the beach, running at almost full speed. I'd had enough of the damn thing winning! Enough of the torture! Why can't I stop reliving it?!

I ran straight into the water, legs kicking high as I tried to make it as far as I could. Finally, the water got too deep and I tripped, falling over with a large splash. I lay there for a few seconds, face down in the warm water, and then turned and pushed back with my heels. I pushed until I was shallow enough to sit with just my head above the small ripples. There was almost no wind now, the waves virtually nonexistent. I sat in the water and felt the emotion sweep over me. It was always like this. When I couldn't stop the memory from coming. I lowered my head and cried. Silently, no weeping. Just tears running down my face. I missed them so badly.

'And there's a heart that's breaking down this long distance line tonight...'

I sat in the ocean without moving for the better part of an hour as the sun continued its westerly descent. The shadows of the palms grew long. Finally I knew I needed to move. Exhausted, I picked myself up and headed for the beach house. I needed sleep.

Raging Storm
4

The ringing of my cell phone woke me. I looked over at the clock on the bedside table, shocked to see that it was 9am. I rarely slept that late.
Swinging my legs out of bed I grabbed for the phone and looked at the tiny screen. It was the man. I took the call without hesitation.
"Yeah," I said.
"I need you to go to Jacksonville."
No greeting, no bullshit. Straight to the point as always.
"What's up?"
"Let me work on some details. Call me when you're on the road."
"Done."
I clicked the phone off and sat there for a brief second. So much for a week in the sun. I rose and walked to the bathroom. Turning the shower on full blast I stepped to the mirror and waited for the water to warm. I placed both hands on the counter and leaned forward to gaze at my

reflection and into my eyes. I wasn't sure how I'd gotten here, or if it was even the right path, but I knew that it felt good. I had become a killer but I was unapologetic. Nothing I did could ever erase what happened. I knew that. But I was a fighter. I was dealing with my pain the best way I knew how and with every mission I made the world a better place. I couldn't give a damn what the law said about my actions. Where was the law when I needed it? Goddamn hypocrites. Politicians can start wars that kill millions, and usually for bullshit reasons. They snap their fingers and send men off to kill. And the more men you killed, the heavier your chest got with medals and ribbons. Yeah, it was all bullshit. They could play their manic violins and what did we do? Nothing. We danced to their tune. Puppets on a string. Well to hell with that. I refused to be a puppet. Not anymore, not after what happened. What I was doing saved countless lives. Saved innocent lives. And I wasn't going to apologize for that.

Steam began wafting over the glass encasement of the shower. Stepping out of my boxers and into the warm water, I washed my hair, scrubbed myself and brushed my teeth. Toweling off I felt refreshed. After getting dressed I went into the kitchen and microwaved a sausage and egg Hot Pocket. Twenty minutes later I was in my truck heading west on 278 towards I-95 south. I knew of a gas station right off the highway, and I planned on filling the tank and getting a nice hot coffee there. My phone synced to the trucks Bluetooth so I pressed a button on the steering wheel and stated my command.

"Call the man."

He'd told me from the very beginning that he didn't want names. He preferred anonymity.

I'd met him one evening after attending one of my court ordered group therapy sessions. The group was for the family members of victims of violent crimes. It was here that we could vent our anger and find support among other people who were in similar situations. People who felt powerless and hate-filled. Their loved ones were victims of rape, assault and muggings. There were even a few, like myself, who had had family member's murdered. I did not want to be there, but as it was one of the things keeping me out of prison I attended. I would go and sit in silence. Meeting after meeting, week after week, putting in my time. And then, one day, the group's leader pulled me aside. He told me that my participation was mandatory. If I refused to speak, he would have to report my inactivity to the judge.

So, I got up in front of all those other heartbroken and angry people and told them what had happened that night. How it had gone down. I told them all the gory details. What happened next surprised me. Although I hadn't planned on sharing shit, once I started, it all came pouring out. I told them everything. Starting with how I'd cut my career in the marines short for her because she couldn't take me leaving anymore. She couldn't live with me going off to fight for six months at a time. I gave it all up for her. And it was nothing I regretted. I would have given my life for her. For the kids. And when she needed me most, when my children needed me most, I failed them. I had gotten drunk that day. I was sloppy. I got them killed. It was my fault.

After describing that life changing evening, I went on to explain how I'd had a tough time coping afterwards. I told them how I'd been in a local bar trying to drown myself with Jack Daniel's. I told them about a guy who had played that damn song on the jukebox. Debbie's favorite song. He was just some guy. I didn't know him. And he didn't know what playing that song did to me. But I didn't care.

You don't know how desperate I've become...

Fuck no, I remembered saying aloud to the patrons of the establishment. Not tonight.

In a drunken fog, I went over to the jukebox and unplugged it. At the time, I thought it had showed amazing restraint because I'd wanted to put my foot through the fucking thing. In any case, this hadn't pleased the guy who had plunked down money to hear his songs. I remembered him calling me an asshole or something close to that. The rest of the incident was a blur. I woke up in a jail cell. The guy who had played that tune woke up in the hospital. Along with two of his buddies. I guess they thought they'd had the odds in their favor.

They'd been wrong.

I'd always been a good fighter, even when hammered. As a marine, I'd had a lot of practice against a lot of other guys who were also damn good fighters when they were drunk. Practice makes perfect.

The judge was sympathetic. He knew my story. He knew my entire story. He knew my name. The prosecutor had wanted to try me for three counts of attempted murder and assault on a police officer. Two police officer's actually. But it didn't stick. I explained that if I'd wanted those guys dead, they would have been trying me for three counts of manslaughter. Because it would have happened. I guess the judge believed me.

The judge dropped the resisting charges. And then he convicting me on three counts of aggravated assault. With intent to cause bodily injury. He gave me a two year sentence, a sentence he suspended provided I go to group therapy meetings. That and stay out of trouble.

That was it. I finished speaking and stared out at the group. Some were looking at me with sympathy. Others simply looked at me. I walked back to my chair to the low murmurs of how sorry they were. A few gentle slaps on my shoulder as I passed.

On my way out the door that night, the man had stopped me. I had noticed him before. Always sitting in the back. I'd caught him looking my way a few times. I'd never heard him speak to the group. He asked me to have a coffee with him. There was something very authoritative about him. Very in charge. He reminded me of my Commanding Officer in Recon. He told me that he had a proposition for me. I agreed to listen and he laid it all out.

Sitting in a coffee house, the man opened up. His wife had been taken from him by a fucking rapist psychopath. The assailant had jumped in her car and forced her to drive to a seedy part of town. Then the animal had raped her and cut her throat, leaving her to die in an alley. They'd never caught the guy.

The man told me the story in a very low and ominous register. I could see the fury bubbling beneath the surface. He was angry. And he wanted to do something about it. He wanted to do something about the scum that preyed upon society.

And he had a solution.

A solution that intrigued me immensely. Yeah, he laid it all out. He had the financing, connections and anything else I needed.

And I had the expertise. The skills.

He asked me if I was interested and I agreed without hesitation. I was more than on board.

Our unholy union was formed.

Over the next couple weeks we met a few times. The man had given me a debit card that was linked to one of his corporate accounts. He said I had unlimited access. He also gave me one hundred thousand dollars in cash. Holy shit, I'd said at the time.

I worked for him now. And I could quit any time I wanted. He was very adamant about telling me that. Anytime I wanted out he would understand. And I could keep the money.

I had access to things like the beach house in Hilton Head as well as a few other perks. A few days after receiving the cash, an extremely expensive arsenal had arrived on my front porch. In discrete packaging. I had given him a wish list of every weapon I wanted and he never batted an eye. I got everything. The dude didn't play. And although I had my own truck, the F-150 I was now driving had appeared in front of my house one night. The keys were lying on the front seat with a note telling me not to use my own vehicle.

At our final face to face meeting, the man told me it would be the last time we would meet in person. Not a good idea anymore, he had said. It didn't matter. Everything was in place. He handed me a phone that he said was untraceable.

It came with GPS and all the other bells and whistles. This was to be our sole form of communication from this point on. It was better that way.

And then I went to work.

The man supplied me with intelligence and logistical support and I more than knew what to do with it. The job in the mountains two days ago had been the fourth mission. And with each one I felt like I was saving the world. Or at least a small part of it. The people I eliminated would never harm another soul. It felt good.

The phone rang through the trucks speakers. Click.

"Where are you?" The man asked.

"Almost on 95."

"Good. Jacksonville is only a couple hours south. When you cross the Florida state line, there is a Visitors Center not too far down the road. Pull in there and I'll call you with more details."

"Target?"

"A scumbag named Trevor Pinter. He's about to walk scot free on a murder rape charge. The victim was twelve years old."

"About to?" I asked. "How do you know?"

"I've got an inside source."

"Why?"

"Technicality. The arresting officers fucked it all up."

"Guilty?"

"Guilty as sin. Smug little bastard was smirking as he left the courtroom yesterday. He knows that he's going to get away with it. The judge is reviewing the case any minute now."

"Okay."

"I'll send you a picture and find out where he's going to hole up afterwards. There are a lot of upset people. Bullshit death threats. The whole shebang. He won't go home."

"Got it."

"Sit in the Visitors Center and wait for my call. I'll be as quick as I can."

"Will do."

The man ended the call.

I tossed the cell phone onto the passenger seat and ten minutes later, turned into the gas station. After getting gas and coffee, I got back on 278 West and then made an almost immediate left onto the highway.

I-95.

Southbound.

Raging Storm
5

The Florida Welcome Center was packed. I found a spot in the back, close to where the truckers parked their semis, and settled in to wait. It was a little after noon and I hoped the man would get me the intelligence before too long. I wanted time to plan. I took every job seriously, leaving nothing to chance. Every angle was carefully weighed and considered.

If the target stayed close to home, as I was sure he would, there was a chance I could finish this today. If all went well, I would be back on my "vacation" before long. But only if the job allowed. I would not permit myself to be sloppy just so I could get back to the beach sooner.

I used my smart phone to pull up news about the case. Sure enough, Trevor the scumbag had been sprung on a technicality. And he looked every bit the weasel. There was a video of him coming down the steps of the courthouse. Flanked by security and what looked to be his lawyer and parent's, he was a scrawny little fuck. No more than five foot seven inches. His blonde, shoulder length hair was in a pony tail. It was a pathetic attempt to look presentable. The suit he wore looked expensive and custom tailored. I read the entire article. Wealthy, divorced parents. Over privileged. Bullied in school. Loner. All the calling cards consistent in your run of the mill sociopath. A small crowd was being held in check by the police. I wondered why it was that he deserved protection when his victim had not received it? There was a middle aged man crying. He was being restrained by two burly officers. You could see it on the cop's faces. They wanted to let him go, to let him take care of unfinished business but they had a job to do. Sometimes doing your job sucked. It was the girl's father. It had to be. Poor bastard. The look on his face was all too familiar. I'd felt his pain. I'd lived it. I was still living it.

At the bottom of the web page was a picture of the girl. Big blue eyes. Blonde hair. Cute, little pushed up nose. She was the picture of innocence. A young girl with her entire life ahead of her. A child. A child destroyed by a twisted psychopath. By a monster.

There was no doubt in my mind that she would not be Trevor's last victim. I doubted she was his first. You could see that. You could see it in his smug arrogance. He had a taste for it. It would always be a part of him.

Trevor's mother and father looked happy. Happy that their baby boy wouldn't have to pay the price for his horrific crime. What kind of people were these, I wondered? I would turn in my own brother if he did something like this, no question, no hesitation.

Yeah, you could see it. He would definitely do it again the first chance he got.

The thought caused my teeth to grind.

I read the entire article a second time and let the image of Trevor Pinter burn into my brain. Like most warriors, I had a soft spot for children. And I took a very special interest in bringing justice to those who would hurt them. I was of the firm belief that child molesters should at the very least, qualify for the death penalty. Who the fuck would oppose it? Nobody who has ever lost a child or had one raped by one of these dirt bags. That was a fact.

The earlier hits had been jobs. Jobs I enjoyed, but just jobs. I considered them necessary steps to ridding the world of vermin. Like a doctor removing a malignant tumor, it was strictly business. Something that needed to be done. But this? This one was going to be different. I was looking forward to this.

Looking up from the phone, I scanned my surroundings. I watched people of all sorts as they pulled into the welcome center. I watched as they got out of their vehicles and stretched. Eighty percent of the people stretched. I watched as parents corralled and safely herded their kids towards the restrooms. I saw the happy faces and wondered how many were on vacation. The visitors center was on the southbound side of the highway. I-4 was less than a couple hours south. Once on I-4 heading west, Disney World was only another hour. And beaches were everywhere in Florida. Lots of out of state plates. Lots of happy looking people.

I couldn't help but think of Trevor's victim. I wondered how many times she and her family had been to Disney.

How many times had they enjoyed a family outing to the beach? Like the last outing I'd had with my family. I looked down at the girl's picture on my phone. I could see the joy on her little face. I could hear her happy laughter. That was forever gone. Stolen by a sick bastard.
The girls' photo dissolved as the phone hummed. It startled me.
The man.
I thumbed the button on the steering wheel again.
"Yeah." I said..
"Got a pen handy?"
"Yes."
The man gave me an address which I scribbled onto a piece of scrap paper. I then typed it into my GPS and saw that it was only about an hours' drive.
Perfect.
"Feel free to have fun with this animal," the man said.
"How so?"
"Use your imagination. Leave a message if you want. I wouldn't mind hearing that he suffered a bit."
"Yeah," I said. "I read up on the case. I understand."
"The story omits a lot. He made it last a long time. You don't want to know."
I felt my jaw tighten.
"I understand."
"Let me know once you get there. Get me a tag number if there are any cars in the driveway."
"Will do."
"Good luck."
The phone clicked as the man hung up. I tossed it onto the passenger seat and put the truck in drive. Rolling out of the

Welcome Center, I continued south on I-95 through Jacksonville. Gripping the steering wheel with white knuckles, I heard the man's words ringing in my ears.
'He made it last a long time.'
I stared straight ahead, looking forward to finding this piece of garbage.
And there's a storm that's raging through my frozen heart tonight...

Raging Storm
6

As the target was only an hour south of Jacksonville, it had been a short trip. After getting off I-95 and making my way over to Hwy 1, I drove south. After a few twists and turns my GPS had me on the Vilano Causeway heading east towards Vilano Beach. It was just after 2pm and the sun was blazing overhead.

I sat on the Francis and Mary Usina Bridge which connected the island beach town to the mainland. It was a beautiful day and traffic was thick with people heading to the beach. Many of the vehicles had surfboards strapped to roof racks. There were Salt Life window decals on a great majority of them. Shirtless men and bikini clad women rode bicycles and passed cars on the downside of the bridge.

As this was the southern tip of the island, most of the eastbound traffic took the sharp bend to the left. They would drive north up the coast, hoping to find parking. I turned the opposite way, making a right onto Coastal Highway. The locals never went this way as they knew there was no legal parking available. Those who rolled the dice often returned to find their cars had been towed. Besides the neighborhoods, there was also a shopping center. It was here that I would leave the F-150 while I went on foot to find Ferrol Road. 143 Ferrol Road to be exact.

I pulled into a strip mall which was home to a Publix Supermarket and a few smaller shops. I parked as close to the grocery store as possible. People who illegally parked here always put their cars as far away from the store as they could. They thought that this would make them look less conspicuous. The exact opposite was true.

I got out of the truck and walked into the grocery store. No matter how big the grocery chain, there were always specialty items when located close to, or on the beach. In short order I found the tourist section. There were lotions, clothing, toys and a wide assortment of other beach accessories. I grabbed a beach towel and floppy sun hat. Then I spotted some cheap black sunglasses which were a blatant rip-off of Ray Ban Wayfarers. Into my basket went a Vilano Beach tank top, medium sized bathing suit and some sandals. I also grabbed a small paperback spy novel. Using the man's debit card, and feeling like an idiot, I paid for the cheesy items. I then headed to the stores men's room. Ducking into a stall, I quickly changed. Exiting, I glanced at my reflection in the mirror and couldn't help but smirk. I looked like a ridiculous tourist. Which is exactly what I was going for.

I walked out of the store with my other clothes piled into the Publix's shopping bag. Going to my truck, I unlocked the door and threw the bag inside. I clipped my karambit, a small but special type of combat knife, onto my waistband. It would go unnoticed as my un-tucked T-shirt covered it. I then placed a couple other things in the large pockets of my swimsuit.

Locking the truck, I headed back towards the smaller stores. If parking security saw me, they knew that I'd already shopped. They would now think I was heading towards one of the other establishments to shop some more. They wouldn't mess with my truck.

Once under the covered walkway, I turned left, passing by each storefront, and headed to the end of the strip mall. I crossed into the side parking lot and then eased my way back towards the Coastal Highway sidewalk. The streets were lined with tall, green palm trees. The houses were almost all one story ranch homes.

After a few minutes walking, I found Ferrol Road and made a right, away from the ocean. I started strolling up the road, the towel flung over my shoulder in a casual fashion. I looked as if I'd just left the beach. As the neighborhood was small, it didn't take me long to find the house.

There was a car in the driveway.

I grabbed my cell phone and texted the license plate to the man. Then I continued walking as if I belonged there. I made it to the end of the block and turned left. I decided to walk down to the ocean to wait for the man to get back to me. I didn't make it there before the phone rang.

"Yeah," I answered.

"That's his father's car. He's here."

"Okay. Thanks."

"Head back to Hilton Head afterwards. Sorry about messing up your vacation. This was one I couldn't pass up."

"Absolutely my pleasure," I said. I meant it.

Clicking the red button, I slid the phone back into my pocket.

Crossing along the public access path which cut through the dunes, I walked onto the beach. I had to wait for nightfall anyway and besides, Trevor might be here. I scanned the area. There were not as many people at the southern end of the island, again because of the lack of parking.

I grabbed my phone again and opened the texts. Finding the pictures of Trevor the man had sent me, I studied his face and his hair. It's much easier to spot somebody if you look for their hair.

I began a slow walk northwards, walking with my feet in the fast moving surf that rushed up with each crashing wave. Holding my flip-flops in my hand, I pulled my floppy hat low, taking in each person I passed. I didn't have to go far.

The sonofabitch was actually here. I couldn't believe my luck. Trevor Pinter was here. Wading in waist deep water and body surfing the beach breakers without a care in the world. Within a minute I would be right in front of him. As I continued past, I looked to the left and saw an older woman sitting on a folding beach chair. She was watching him. I recognized her from the video I'd seen of them leaving the courtroom. It was his mother. She did not look as happy anymore. I guess the smiles from the earlier video had been for the press.

But Trevor was still smiling. In fact, he looked downright giddy.

Doing my best to elicit no emotion, I watched as he frolicked and dove under small waves. You would never guess that only this morning he'd been in a courtroom beating a murder rap. A child's murder rap. A child's rape and murder rap.

I forced a stupid, carefree smile onto my face as I walked past the piece of shit. If he noticed any anger or hostility it might get his radar up and send him deeper into hiding. I had to look non-threatening. But he never even glanced in my direction. Trevor was busy celebrating his freedom.

I thought of the young girl he had slaughtered, the beautiful little life that hadn't even started yet. I thought about all that he had stolen from her, the fact that she would never get to grow up. Never graduate high school. Never have a first love or go to college. Never present a grandchild to her aging parents. I thought about the tragic blow it dealt to all her family members, not to mention her mother and father. The gut wrenching feeling was all too familiar to me.

Fighting the urge to dash into the water and choke the life out of him then and there, I continued walking. When I was about fifty yards down the beach, I made my way up onto the warm, dry sand and spread the towel. I settled in to wait. To wait and to watch as the child raping murderer enjoyed his last day on earth.

Raging Storm
7

I waited and watched from a distance as the monster swam and enjoyed the hot sun and the cool Atlantic Ocean. He played as if he didn't have a care in the world. The courthouse was a million miles away. He had gotten away with it.

It's a funny thing how mob mentality works. There were a few dozen people at the courthouse who'd wanted to tear this bastard limb from limb. And perhaps a few would have tried had the police not been there. But mostly people only vented. They screamed and yelled and pulled their hair out and cried. And that was it.

Of course the father wanted revenge. And he deserved it. But he would do nothing. Except to go home and cry and scream and maybe get drunk. If things went the way that they typically do, he would let it consume him until he was sure that he'd go mad. He would become distant, moody and quick to anger. He would pay a heavy price emotionally. And then more and more time would pass.

And he would see the light at the end of that very long and dark tunnel. One day he would find a way to make peace with it. He would apologize to those he hurt. They would forgive him. He would always have a burning hatred towards Trevor for what he did to his little girl, but he'd find a way to move past it. He had other people who depended on him, he'd tell himself.

Maybe it was better that way? After all, this is the way society should work. Leave law and order to the professionals.

But I found it much too slow.

In the marines, I learned that I could shoot. Except for a few shots with a .22 rifle when I was a teenager, I had never fired a gun before. The instructors told us that they'd rather teach a young recruit with no shooting experience at all. That way they didn't have to undo bad habits, mistakes or improper methods. They often told us that the worst marksmen were the country boys. The guys who'd grown up with a rifle in their hands. Those fellows thought they knew everything there was to know about marksmanship.

No, I had been green. And I knew it. So I'd listened in class and I'd paid attention during snapping in drills and on the range. I listened to the instructors who had expert badges on their chest. I wanted one of those in the worst way. I wanted those crossed rifles.

So I was attentive. I was studious. And it turned out I was good. Damn good. The best in my platoon actually. Out of seventy-two guys in my unit, I was the only one wearing the crossed rifles at the end of basic training. All the rest sported Marksman or Sharpshooter badges.

It gave me a sense of pride. A lot of the other graduates came up and looked at it, touched it in envy and praised me. It felt good to be the best at something. I wanted more.

The next step for me was infantry training school or ITS. Once again I paid attention and learned everything I could. I was tops in my class in tactics and also in demolition. Meaning, I was good at blowing shit up. Upon graduating ITS, I finally made it to my infantry unit and immediately put in a request for recon. With my weapons skills and top physical fitness scores, they gave me a shot. And from twenty-six candidates, I was one of only three accepted.

I was now part of Special Forces which meant even more training and, once again, I paid close attention. I learned my craft from the best in the world. I became a very deadly man, both with weapons and with my hands. And I used those skills fighting some of the vilest scum ever known to man, the Jihadist's in Iraq and Afghanistan. These were the cowards who threw homosexuals off of buildings. They stoned women to death for minor infractions like daring to show their face in public. They also took pleasure in mutilating their victims and in beheading. They were the ultimate bullies and sadists and I took pleasure in every one I killed. After racking up an impressive body count, my reputation grew. I was one of the top snipers in the Marine Corps. Yes, I could shoot. But I didn't plan on doing any shooting today. No, this was going to be a hands on mission.

I turned my attention back to the rapist, child killer. Trevor was toweling off. His mother was standing, and folding up the beach chair. They were leaving. I followed from a safe distance although losing them was not an issue. I knew where they were going.

It was after five so darkness was still over three hours away. I didn't care. Patience was something I had in spades. It was an absolute necessity in my profession. At the end of their block was a small park. It was perfect. Kids played on an elaborate jungle jim and people walked dogs. There were several benches situated under palm trees for shade. I chose one facing Trevor's house and waited, pulling out the paperback to use as a prop. I was a man enjoying the warmth of the afternoon, sitting on a park bench, reading a novel. Nothing to see here.

Two hours later, the front door opened and there were Trevor's parents. They walked down the small, paved path to the driveway and stood in front of their car. Trevor came out. He followed them to the driveway. I watched as his mother hugged him. Even from the distance, I could see she was crying. She grabbed his face and planted a big kiss on his lips and then got into the passenger side and closed the car door.

Trevor turned to face his father who spoke to him for several minutes. The man looked serious and I'm sure he was lecturing his son on final chances. The need to turn his life around and other such nonsense. Little did he know that he was wasting his time. Finally they embraced. And then the older man walked around the car, got behind the wheel and backed out of the driveway. Trevor watched them drive away and then headed back into the house. Moments later I watched as the blinds on each window closed. Trevor had secured the perimeter. He was holed up.

Nightfall came. Darkness blanketed the area and the park had emptied. People began leaving their homes, showered and ready for a night stroll or a walk into town. There was a lot of hand holding and happy chatter. It had been a nice day and now a fun evening lay ahead. I waited until the residential streets cleared. There was no more foot traffic as everybody who was planning on going out had already done so.
It was time.
I walked towards Trevor's house. Passing it, I continued down the sidewalk and then, made a left onto the lawn between his and his neighbor's house. I walked towards the back of the houses staying on the edge of both property lines. Walking was important. There are many things you learn when you are in the business of espionage or subterfuge. One of them is that suspicious behavior always looks suspicious. It's that simple. Sprinting towards the back yard would have looked funny. People don't do that. But anybody seeing me calmly heading towards the back of the home would think nothing of it. Could be I lived there, or was visiting. Don't act suspicious and you won't appear that way.
Walking through the thick, spongy St. Augustine grass, I was now between the homes. I turned to my left and went to a side window to peer into Trevor's home

through the small cracks in the blinds. I could see into the front room of the small house.

There he was. Sitting on a couch. He wore boxers. Nothing else. He was watching a TV which I could not see from my vantage point. On the side table next to the couch were three cans of beer. And a gun. It looked like a 9 mm or a .45. I couldn't tell from the limited view I had. It was most likely his fathers. I doubted the scumbag even knew how to use it. But it told the story. Trevor was nervous. He was right to be.

I went from window to window, peering in to see if anybody else was home that I may not have known about. There was nobody, the place was empty except for Trevor.

Going into my pocket, I retrieved a pair of surgical gloves. I leaned against the side of the house and pulled them on. I then went to the back of the home. To the back door. I grabbed the knob and twisted slowly. Very slowly. Locked. Okay.

Plan B.

I checked the position of the karambit which sat clipped onto my shorts. It was exactly where it should be, to the front of my right hip. The clip was a hard plastic sheath. Locked in it was a 4 inch, curved blade with a handle that curved to fit ones hand. It had a finger hole cut at the top. You put your pointer finger all the way through the hole and then closed your fist to grip the handle. It was a perfect weapon for getting in close. The ring made it almost impossible to knock the knife out of your hand. The curved blade, sharpened to a razor's edge on both sides, was ideal for slashing or stabbing. It had never failed me and as close combat knives go, it was my absolute favorite. I almost always carried one.

I also had a silenced .40 caliber in my cargo pocket which was a very squat little pistol, only the size of my palm. I didn't think it would be necessary but if Trevor managed to get to his piece, it was a good back-up.

In the end, after dismissing many different ideas, I chose the simplest solution. I walked to the front door and knocked.

The TV went silent.

After several moments, Trevor spoke. He stood on the other side of the door.

"Who is it?" His voice sounded nervous.

"I am so sorry to bother you," I said in the most amicable, harmless voice I could muster. "My car will not start and my cell phone is dead. Can I please use your phone to call Triple A?"

Trevor paused. There was no window in the door.

"What's wrong with it?"

"My car?" I asked. "God, I don't know. I'm an idiot when it comes to cars. Just a dead battery I think."

"Where are you parked?"

"Down the street. Nobody else answered their front door. I'm really sorry to bother you."

"You don't live around here?"

"I live in Jacksonville. I have my daughter this weekend and took her to the beach."

"You're not supposed to park on these streets unless you're a resident."

"I know," I said. I did my best to sound apologetic. "I guess karma got me."

Another pause. Trevor was thinking.

"I will call a tow truck for you. What kind of car do you have?"

"Oh my God, would you? That would be great. I have a black Volvo. I'm right here on your street. I'm not sure what it's called."

"Okay. I will call. Good night."

"Thank you so much. Could I ask you for one more favor?"

I could almost hear him sigh on the other side of the door.

"What?"

"Can my little girl use your bathroom?"

This got a very long pause. I stayed quiet.

"Uhhh, what?" Trevor finally asked. His voice cracked.

"She really has to go," I said.

Another pause.

"Come on man, have a heart. She's nine years old and if she pees her pants she's going to have to ride all the way home that way. I don't have any extra in the car."

Another longer pause.

"I will wait out here. She'll be quick."

You could almost feel Trevor's sick mind working.

"Have her stand out on the lawn so I can see her from my living room window," Trevor said. The nerves were evident in his voice. "I'm sorry but there's been a lot of crime in this neighborhood."

In every deal, fear of loss is the determining factor. The salesman will drop his price if he fears the buyer might walk. The buyer will go up to the salesman's price if he's afraid he might lose the deal. It was basic psychology. I decided to get the principle working for me.

"Look man, never mind. I'll go down the street. I'm pretty sure we passed a Publix on the way in. Sorry to have bothered you."

"No!" Trevor cried. There was a brief pause before he continued. "I mean it's fine. But just her, okay?"

I heard the dead bolt click open.

"Hey, you're the best. Thank you so much."

Trevor turned the knob and cracked the door half an inch. I saw his head come into view as he looked down, searching for my daughter. He didn't even look at me. Checkmate, scumbag.

I pushed off with the ball of my foot and pivoting my hip, whipped my right shoulder into the door. It caught Trevor completely off guard, slamming into him. He went crashing into the rear wall of the foyer and fell in a heap on the floor. I followed, slamming the door shut behind me.

Trevor's eyes were giant saucers of terror as he scrambled to his feet. I had the karambit out and held it in my right hand. Rushing forward, I grabbed him by the throat with my left hand. I pinned him against the wall. He struggled but I was half a foot taller and outweighed him by at least 80 pounds. In a flash the curved blade rested against his jugular.

"No, please don't!" Trevor choked. His eyes bugged wide as I squeezed his windpipe.

I glared at him, my body trembling with controlled fury. "Did Ashley plead with you like that you piece of shit?" I hissed through clenched teeth.

"I didn't do it! Ask my lawyer! Please!"

"Did she? Did she beg for her life, you maggot?"

Trevor began to cry and I felt a warm liquid splash against my leg. Jesus Christ! The son of a bitch was pissing on me.

"Answer me you fucking cockroach!" I growled.

"Please!" He sobbed. "Stop!"

"Did little Ashley plead for you to stop?!" I tightened my grip on his throat.

"Mommy!" He cried.

I'd had enough.

I pushed his chin upwards and with a quick snap of my wrist, thrust the blade into the thickest part of his neck. Trevor let out a sharp gasp and I felt him convulse. His body clenched up. I pushed deep, making sure the entire blade was buried.

Then I yanked my arm back and the sharp knife sliced, opening the entire left side of his throat. As I did so, I jumped aside to avoid the first long stream of blood that shot out of his severed carotid artery.

I let him go and Trevor, eyes bulging, grabbed for his throat and went to his knees. He was in shock and said nothing. He clutched at his neck and looked up at me, disbelief in his eyes. And then he slumped forward as his brain, deprived of blood and oxygen, shut down.

A dark crimson pool of blood formed a small lake on the old linoleum floor. Trevor pawed at the ground, his arms flailing as his nerve endings fired. And then he was motionless. He died with his eyes open.

I look down at my legs which glistened with his urine.

"Shit!" I muttered under my breath. I knew I couldn't

wipe it off yet. I couldn't leave anything behind.
I looked at the TV which Trevor had paused when I'd knocked. He'd been watching The Disney Channel. Sick fuck.
Looking down at his body, I remembered the man's words and made a decision. I would send a message to every pervert out there. It would only take a second.
I squatted low and rolled Trevor onto his back as blood continued to pulse from the slash wound. Yanking the top of his boxers down, I grabbed his genitals and pulled them towards me. The steel blade of the karambit flashed again.

Raging Storm
8

An hour later I was back on I-95 heading north. Back towards Hilton Head. With any luck, meaning no traffic snarls, I would be back in the beach house by one in the morning.

I felt good. A calm settled over me and for once I didn't hear that damn song in my head. I was always calm after a mission. After a kill. Something took over and I rode it, knowing that other guys weren't as fortunate. Some guys let it eat them up. I didn't. The way I saw it, I killed people who had it coming and believe me, there is such a thing.

Take Trevor for instance. He'd raped and murdered a twelve year old and had gotten away with it through a flawed legal system. But I fixed it. The man and I fixed it. How many children would never have to fall prey to his twisted desires? What I did today saved some young lives. That was the way I saw it, and in fact, that was the way it was. There were children who would get to live their lives, grow to adulthood. Children who would someday have families of their own because of what I'd done. It was that simple and I felt great in that knowledge.

I got off on exit three shortly after crossing the Georgia state line. Finding a gas station, I filled the tank and then went inside and surveyed the grub. None of it looked too appealing. There was a fast food place a ways down the road so I got back in the truck and soon found myself in the drive thru lane. I didn't eat burgers and fries very often but tonight I would indulge myself.

I pulled back onto the highway and enjoyed the tasty, albeit unhealthy meal.

Finishing the last bite, I took a long last pull on my soft drink to wash the taste down. Wiping my mouth with a napkin, I thumbed the button and placed a call to the man.

"How did it go?" He answered. No greeting.

"It's done."

"Good. Where are you?"

"On the road, heading back to Hilton Head. Unless you've got something else?" I laughed.

He laughed as well. It may have been the first time I ever heard him laugh.

"No. Go enjoy your time off."

"Thanks. By the way, you'll like the little touch I left. It should shake a few people up."

"Excellent," he answered. "I look forward to hearing about it."

The phone clicked dead.

I drove in silence and continued to think about the day. I had done the world a favor. I couldn't care less if the law didn't see it that way. I'd bet that if you polled one hundred people, ninety-five of them would have no problem with Trevor's demise. Of course, there's always that small percent of the population who are bleeding heart idiots. That is, until somebody they care for falls victim to a deranged psychopath. That has a way of changing somebody's mind right quick.

Traffic thinned as the hour grew late. I moved along steadily, keeping my speed at 75 miles per hour. It was good to be moving. That was my mantra for life these days.

I just had to keep moving.

Raging Storm
9

I only got about six hours sleep but it was enough. I'd always been like that. Between six and seven hours was perfect. Any more than that and I felt logy.
After a small breakfast of steel cut oatmeal and half a grapefruit I went for a long run. A good, hard training run. It had been a while since I went all out and it showed. I was going to pay for last night's bacon cheeseburger and fries. Staying in peak physical shape is a strange thing. You stop working at it for even a week and you feel it. I pushed myself, checking my time on my wristwatch.
My lungs were burning as I hit my fourth six minute mile. And that's the moment it began.
The song started playing in my head. The thoughts came for me. They were back. That horrible night was back and this time there was no stopping it. I couldn't help it. I couldn't stop it. I pumped my legs all the harder.
And if I can't bridge this distance, stop this heartbreak overload...
Hunter needed to pee so Debbie went ahead of me

towards our bedroom. We were both very ready to have a little alone time. Hunter had closed the bathroom door which was a new thing. I waited to take him back to bed. The toilet flushed. Good boy, Hunter. The door opened. "Did you wash your hands?" I scolded with a smile. And then my world changed forever. Right then. I can still see Hunter's face. Like it happened five seconds ago.

I saw the shock in my son's eyes before I even heard the scream. Or at least that's how I remember it. It was a blood curdling scream. It was a scream that will haunt me forever. I turned and bolted towards the other side of the house. I made it to the family room and saw my wife. And I saw a man hitting her. Hitting my wife.

Things went red.

The closest thing to a weapon I could find was a table lamp so I grabbed it as I sped towards the two. I threw my arm back and as I came within range, smashed it down upon the intruder's head as hard as I could. He crumpled to the floor. I remember straddling him as my wife ran for the bedroom. I roared, smashing at his skull over and over with the heavy base of the shattered lamp. He had been hitting my wife. I swung the lamp back overhead and brought it down again.

And then my world went black.

I had been so busy venting my rage on the intruder, on the man who had been hitting Debbie, that I had gotten sloppy. I hadn't check my six. I hadn't check my three or my nine either. I didn't see the scumbag's partner lay me out with the butt of a shotgun.

As those horrific, vivid memories were playing in the

theater of my mind, I flew down the beach. Faster and faster. My legs burned and my lungs were on fire. Fuck a six minute mile. I wanted to go faster. Faster and harder until my heart gave out and I could join my family.

And there's a storm that's raging through my frozen heart tonight...

When I came to, Debbie, Hunter and Sasha were all there. They were all staring at me with wide, frantic eyes. Their ankles and wrists were bound with duct tape, their arms behind their backs. I saw a man lying on the carpet, his head was stove in. Blood had pooled around it. As I struggled to comprehend the unreal scene in front of me, a man kicked me hard in the side.

"You motherfucker!" He screamed. "You killed my brother, you motherfucker!"

I looked up at him. A white man. A big white man. Lots of tattoos. Prison ink by the look of it. He had the wild, strung out look of a meth head, eyes bloodshot and darting with madness. In his hands was a shotgun. A Winchester. I knew the model. Standing behind him were two other white men. They also looked pissed. But nothing like the guy who was screaming at me.

I tried to move but soon discovered that I was also bound. I was trapped and helpless. I experienced a panic like I'd never felt in my life, not in combat, not in any hairy situation I'd ever found myself in. Not in anything. I wasn't afraid for me. I could handle whatever they did to me. But my family.

"They're just kids," I pleaded. I'd never begged a man for anything in my life. Not ever. Never thought I would.

I begged then. I remembered every heart ripping detail.
"Please. Kill me. But let them live."
"We were just going to take your TV!" The man screamed. He kicked me hard in the ribs again. "Your stereo! Your wife's jewelry! You didn't have to kill him!"
"I didn't know," I said. I remembered trying to speak to him in as calm a voice as possible. I thought that might bring him down a bit. "He was attacking my wife. I didn't have time to think."
"Shut the fuck up!"
"Come on, Danny," one of the others said. "We gotta get out of here."
"Did you really just call me by my name, you retard!?" He screamed.
The man said nothing. He looked away. It was obvious that he was not the alpha. The dead guy's brother was in charge.
"Come on, dude," the third man said. "We gotta go."
"Go start the car," he answered. He turned to the man who had called him by his name. "Grab the stuff and go."
They both listened and moved. Quickly.
The large psycho was now alone in the room with us. He knelt down beside me and growled.
"You killed my brother."
"It was an accident. I'm sorry." I could feel each heartbeat.
"No you're not. But you're gonna be."
Time slowed to a crawl as the next thirty seconds seared into my brain forever. I knew that if I lived to be one

hundred the next few moments would always seem as if they happened yesterday.

The man rose to his full height and took a step towards my wife and children. He flashed me an evil smile as he leveled the shotgun at Debbie.

I remember them screaming. I screamed too. No words, but a desperate, guttural wail. My brain couldn't process this. This wasn't happening. It was a nightmare. An unbelievable nightmare.

The shotgun roared. I heard the high pitched shrieks of my children. My wife made no sound. Her screaming had stopped. Forever. I heard him pump the shotgun and watched him point it towards my two small children.

"NOOOOO!!!" I screamed. It came from a darker place than I ever knew existed.

The shotgun roared again. And again. And again.

There was no more screaming. Not from my wife. Not from my kids. Never again from my kids.

I thought I'd experienced hatred in the war. Watching friends die. Dealing with the worst elements of humanity, people who were devoid of dignity or honor. People who murdered innocents to advance their twisted agendas. I thought I knew rage. I knew nothing about it. Until that moment.

I lost any form of rationale consciousness. I had tunnel vision. It was a red tunnel. There was only him. He turned and sneered at me.

"Now you're sorry, motherfucker." he said.

And then my arms weren't bound anymore. It was like some terrible, cruel joke but at that moment, I had my arms again. Later I would come to realize that I'd ripped through the duct tape in a super charged adrenaline rush. A rush fueled by insanity. That is the only way to describe it. Insanity. Why hadn't I been able to do that a minute earlier? I would never forgive myself for that. Never.

I heard sirens.

The large, tattooed, white man heard them too. He smiled at me. He fucking smiled. And then he pointed the shotgun at me and he pulled the trigger.

A loud click.

A reprieve. A chance.

He was empty.

My feet were still bound with duct tape but it didn't matter. I bent my knees, got my feet planted and sprung. I launched myself at him like I had been shot from a cannon.

I had two weapons. My hands. And they went straight for his throat.

I grabbed the maggot and saw terror in his eyes. The same terror that my wife had had in her eyes. He swatted at me with the shotgun. The cold steel hit my face. It may as well have been a feather. I didn't feel it.

The sirens were outside now. They were here.

I ripped the man downwards and brought him to the floor with me. I was on top of him in a nanosecond. My fingers locked on to his windpipe and I crushed. His eyes bulged and I watched as his face turned red.

And then purple.

Above my hands, I saw a large vein pulsing in his neck and I bent over and clamped down on it. I pressed my face into his neck and bit down with all my strength. I felt his skin rip open. Whipping my head back and forth I tasted the warm, salty blood spew into the back of my throat. The man tried to scream but it came out as a strangled gurgle.

I heard the front door slam open and policemen yelling, but I couldn't make out what they were saying. I continued my deadly onslaught.

I didn't feel the tasers barbs enter my skin. I didn't even feel the juice. The taste of the man's blood was my last memory.

I woke up some time later in the hospital.

Alone.

Forever alone.

And as fast as it had begun, the high definition head movie was over and I was back, racing along the beach. I wasn't sure how long I'd been running but I had been going at such a frantic pace that my body seized up. I stumbled and crashed in a tangled heap onto the sand. The only sound was the whooshing of blood between my ears. The world was spinning and I clung to the earth to avoid falling upwards into oblivion. I felt myself blacking out and I was thankful for it.

And if I can't bridge this distance, stop this heartbreak overload...

Raging Storm
10

I spent the next two days sleeping, running and thinking too much. I had the house for another few days but I didn't want to stay any longer. I wanted to go home. Back to my house in Tampa. Back to our house. As much pain as it caused me to be there, it was still where I felt the closest to them. I almost needed it.

Calling the man from the truck, I told him that I was heading home. He didn't question me. He understood. He wished me a safe journey and said he'd call within a few days.

The drive was uneventful, traffic was light and within six hours I pulled into my driveway. I got out of the truck and grabbed my bags. I looked at the house. My house. Our house. That's all it was to me now. A house. It wasn't a home, not anymore. It would never be a home to me again.

The man had said he'd call within a few days so I was a little surprised to hear my cell phone ring.

"Hello," I said.

"Are you home?"

"I just now pulled into the driveway. What's up?"
"We've got a rare opportunity. The target is in D.C.."
"I'm listening," I answered.
The man went on to tell me about a major player in the drug game. The target was an American who worked hand in hand with the Mexican cartels. He was responsible for tons of cocaine entering the country. He also had a hand in sex trafficking and prostitution. He was as dirty as they come, the man explained although he kept up a great facade of a successful businessman. The man continued, explaining that the target looked like a dignitary. He traveled in all the right circles. With judges and politicians in his pocket, he was considered untouchable. Intelligent and wily, the target exercised an overabundance of caution. His whereabouts were rarely known. But there was credible intelligence that he would be in Washington D.C. tomorrow evening. And that he would be dining at the Ritz Carlton.

"There's a first class plane ticket waiting for you at Tampa International. United Airlines flight 735 and it leaves at 9:00 tomorrow morning. You have a reservation paid for at the Park Hyatt which is only a block from the Ritz Carlton. The target will be meeting guests at 6 pm for dinner in The Quadrant Lounge right inside the Ritz," he said.

I could hear the urgency in his voice.

"Security?"

"He will have bodyguards but they will most likely be off to the side, sitting by themselves but watching. Can you handle that?"

"Is it crucial that this happen tomorrow?" I asked. I

ignored his question.

"Yes," he said. "This piece of garbage never has his plans leaked. We may never get another chance like this and believe me, he is worth it. He's responsible for countless deaths and untold suffering."

"Okay," I said. "Consider me there."

"Good, call me when you're in your hotel room."

"Will do."

"Thanks, Ryder," he said. He ended the call with a click

That was odd, I thought. He'd never said thanks before. This guy must be near the top of his hit parade.

I woke up early the next day and got to the airport in plenty of time. It was a smooth flight and I enjoyed the pampering of first class travel. After landing in Washington, I took a cab to the Park Hyatt. After checking in, the bellhop escorted me to a suite overlooking the Potomac River. It was a beautiful view. But this wasn't a pleasure trip.

I called the man and he answered after two rings.

"I'm in my room," I said.

"Okay, excellent. My intelligence confirms that the target is still on for dinner at six. Make your way over to the Quadrant and get the lay of the land."

"I know what to do."

"Yes, my apologies. Of course you do," he said.

"I will text you a picture of him. Good luck."

The man ended the call and within a few seconds, my phone buzzed with the incoming text. I opened it and got my first look at the man I was going to eliminate later this afternoon. He was as advertised and looked nothing like how one would expect a major criminal to look. In fact, he looked like your run of the mill, successful businessman. I guessed him to be in his fifties. He had graying hair which was neatly cut. Wearing a tailored suit that looked expensive, he resembled a politician or a banker. Nobody would ever suspect that he was a drug kingpin, a pimp and a murderer. I studied his face, burning it into my memory. Then I opened my suitcase and got out the disguise I had packed. I laid it out on the small table that sat in front of the balcony.

I had a few hours to kill so I settled in for a nap. I contacted the front desk and requested a wakeup call for 4pm. I also set the alarm on my cell phone. This would give me plenty of time to get ready and be at The Quadrant by 5pm, a full hour before the target arrived.

The room phone rang at exactly 4pm. I lifted it from its cradle and dropped it back down. It had been a great nap, I felt refreshed and ready for the mission.

Taking a quick shower, I walked out to the table and donned my disguise. Then I tucked a few tools of the trade into my pockets, left the room and walked one block to the Ritz Carlton.

I found the Quadrant bar, entered and paused, looking around. There was a long, well stocked bar ahead that ran half the length of the room on the right hand side. Beyond that were smaller tables in a lounge area and both a ladies and men's room behind that. To the left was the main dining area with many, linen covered tables.

It was ideal and a planned formed in my mind.

The hostess greeted me with a warm hello. I requested a

table close to the restroom, telling her that I wasn't feeling great. She showed me to a small, corner table that was close to the lavatory as I'd requested. I gave her a weak smile and thanked her.

As soon as she walked away I got up and went to the bathroom to have a look. There was no men's room attendant. That was good. I had assumed this since The Quadrant was more of a lounge and not a full scale restaurant. There was the standard common area with three urinals separated by marble dividers. There were also three sinks. But what interested me the most was that the two toilets had their own full length, wooden doors. They were two separate, albeit small, rooms. This was also not surprising as The Ritz Carlton is about as swanky as it gets. There was no way to peek underneath as is typical with standard bathroom stall doors. No, these were top shelf. I walked into one, it was very roomy. I couldn't have asked for more.

I walked over to look at myself in the mirror. I had done a good job with the disguise. I had on a blonde wig, giving me a goofy, Ted Koppel appearance. I also sported a well-trimmed beard that had been easy enough to glue on. I wore a shirt with a built in paunch to make me appear overweight and pants designed with the same idea. I also wore thick glasses which were only clear lenses. I looked every bit like the typical K Street lobbyist or businessman. It was perfect urban, high society camouflage.

I walked back into the dining area and took a seat at my small table.

"Hello, sir," a soft voice said. A petite, yet buxom,

brunette with a nametag that read Marcy smiled down at me. She held a notepad and a leather bound menu.
"Hi Marcy," I answered. I used a Texas accent, or at least as good a Texas accent as I could muster. It was a spur of the moment decision. Marcy sounded like she was from New York so she'd never know the difference. I grimaced, placing my hand on my stomach.
"Are you all right, sir?" She asked.
I smiled up at her.
"Got a touch of the old green apple quick step, I'm afraid," I said with a laugh.
"Oh, I'm so sorry," she said. Her face registered a genuine look of concern. "There's a gift shop just outside the bar. If you want I'll go get you something?"
"Well, you are a sweetheart," I answered. "But I already took something. I'm hoping it kicks in soon."
"Okay, I hope so too."
"I'm not sure I should even be eating to be honest with you. What would you recommend for an upset stomach?" I laughed again, having fun with the accent.
"Well, we have an excellent chicken salad sandwich that is on very thick rye bread. It comes with fries or potato salad. The bread might help your stomach."
"That sounds great. I'll do that. But just the sandwich, please."
"Very good, sir. And to drink?"
"Dewar's on the rocks. In fact, make it a double. Let's see if we can't drown this thing." I chuckled again and she joined me. She had a pretty laugh.
"I love your accent," Marcy said. "Do you mind me asking where you're from?"

"Amarillo, darling" I answered.

"Wow," she said. She looked puzzled. "Is that in Georgia?"

"Not too far off, Marcy. Texas. But you were close."

She beamed, proud to have gotten it almost right.

"Well it's charming, you sound like a movie star. I'll be right back with your drink." Marcy walked away to an enclave in the bar which housed a computer screen. She punched my order into the system. Everything was computers these days. Would it have been so difficult to go tell the chef that I wanted a lousy sandwich?

She had just finished that task when my target walked into the lounge. He was early. It was easy to spot him, he looked exactly like his picture. I made a point of looking in the other direction, picking up my spoon and staring into it. I pretended to pick at something in my teeth. In reality, I was using the reflection. I watched the hostess lead the target and his two guests to a table on the far side of the room. I did not see any bodyguards following him and none of the other diners qualified. Believe me, I would know.

This was almost too perfect. Too easy. I heard a nagging voice in the far recess of my mind. It was trying to tell me something. I wasn't listening. Nerves, I told myself. Nothing more.

Marcy was back in a flash with my drink. First rule of being a good waitress was to get the people their drinks. Nobody cared about waiting on their food so long as they had their libations. She set the drink in front of me. "Thanks, Marcy," I said.

"Your sandwich should be right out." She smiled at me.

"Thank you," I answered.

I settled in to watch. The man had arrived with two other well dressed men. Strange, that there were no bodyguards. Chances are he'd given them the night off. Maybe they positioned themselves outside the door, watching to see who entered? After all, they were in the Ritz Carlton, what could happen?

I paid attention to what their waitress brought them. My target had ordered Heineken. That was good. A couple of those and nature would call.

Marcy brought me my sandwich. I thanked her and then picked at it slowly.

And waited.

Raging Storm
11

I sat for a good forty minutes watching my target speaking with the other two men at his table. They drank and picked at appetizers. From time to time they shared a laugh. I wondered whether the other men were dirty too.

Their waitress placed a third round of drinks down when the target stood and pushed back from the table. I knew where he was heading. After placing a fifty dollar bill on the table, I rose and shuffled into the bathroom well ahead of him.

I walked to one of the empty toilet stalls, pulling the door closed behind me and waited.

Seconds later I heard the door to the restroom open. Footsteps.

I waited until I heard splashing at the bottom of the urinal and then pushed the door open a crack. The man was standing with his back to me. He was taking care of his business. I flushed and exited the tiny private toilet. Walking behind him at a casual pace, I made it to the sinks and turned on the water. I then took an extra two steps to the bathroom door and very quietly twisted the steel lock. Nobody was getting in. I hoped my luck would hold and nobody would try for the next minute. I went into my pocket and came out with a garrote. Two small wooden handles with an unbreakable strand of wire fastened between them. Holding the handles tight, I took the few steps necessary to get behind the man. I placed a foot between his legs and looped the wire over his head and around his neck in one fluid motion. As he started to cry out, I crossed my hands with a snap and pulled back for all I was worth. The wire sunk into the man's flesh as he made an instinctive grab with both hands to try and free himself. I stepped backwards, pulling, and dropped to one knee. By design, he came with me.

My muscles strained as I held the death grip tight. The man couldn't make a sound as the thin wire pinched off both his vocal cords and his arteries. It only took seconds with no blood flow to the brain until he swooned and blacked out. I held on, waiting for the lack of oxygen to stop his heart. It happened with a jolt and the man's feet kicked outward in a violent spasm. And just like that he was lifeless.

As a precaution, I kept the pressure on for another fifteen seconds. I then looped the garrote back around and over his head. I had to tug to get the wire out from where it had bitten into the skin. The man's face was a swollen crimson, his eyes bugged and wide open with the vacant stare of death.

Grabbing under his armpits, I moved quickly, pulling him into the toilet enclosure. I spun his body around, lifting him onto the toilet and then stooped to tuck his feet back. I needed them out of the way so I could close the door. I then locked it from the inside, stepped out and pulled the door closed. I tested it. Locked.

I strode to the mirror and checked my disguise. My wig had slipped during the struggle so I straightened it. I then walked to the bathroom door, unlocked it and exited the bathroom. Job complete.

As I walked back into the lounge, I held my stomach and did my best to look miserable. Marcy, standing by the bar, noticed and offered me a sympathetic smile. I gave her a weak wave and pointed to my stomach. I then gestured that I was leaving and I pointed to the money on the table. She hurried over.

"Are you all right, sir?" She asked. "Can I call a cab for you?"

"No thanks, Marcy," I said. I grimaced as I held my stomach. "I'm staying here at the hotel."

"Well I hope you feel better, sir."

"Thanks. I left some cash on the table. Keep the change."

"Good night, sir and thank you."

"Good night."

I turned and walked out of the restaurant and into the lobby. Taking my time, I ambled down the hallway bypassing the elevators. I then made a left and exited the hotel. The air was crisp and I took in a deep breath and shuffled off in the opposite direction of my hotel. This was for the benefit of any surveillance cameras.

After walking a good ten minutes, I stepped into a shadowy alley. I removed my paunch shirt, wig, glasses and beard. I had worn a jogging suit on underneath which had helped with the appearance of being overweight. I put the eyeglasses in my pocket as they would have fingerprints on them. The rest of the disguise I tossed in a dumpster. Donning a folded ball cap and sunglasses pulled from the pocket of my sweatpants, I stepped out of the alley. I wound my way through the busy streets taking a long, roundabout route back to the Hyatt.

I was happy with the outcome of the mission. It had gone smoothly. Clean.

That scumbag would never poison another person with his drugs. His days of running prostitutes was over. He would never again bring misery to another human being. I felt no remorse.

I wondered how long it would take before they forced open the door of the stall to find his lifeless body. But it didn't matter.

I was a ghost.

.

Raging Storm
12

I woke as the first rays of sunlight bathed the room in a warm, burnt orange glow. I never closed the thick curtains in hotel rooms as I wanted to see the sunrise. Plus, those double lined, leaded drapes made it look like midnight all day long if you kept them closed.

I swung my legs out of the comfortable bed and walked to the bathroom to relieve myself. Standing in place, I turned my head to gaze at my reflection in the mirror. As always I felt nothing but satisfaction. One more bad guy gone. Good.

Task completed, I flushed the toilet and went back out into the room. I wondered if my mission had made the news so grabbing the remote control, I turned on the TV. I flipped around until I found a cable news channel and then tossed the remote aside. Going to my suitcase, I grabbed the shirt and pants I would wear on the flight home and laid them on the bed. Then I walked back to the bathroom to turn the shower on.

I was about to start brushing my teeth when I heard the news anchor mention the Quadrant Lounge. There was my answer. I walked back to stand in front of the TV and sure enough, there was a photograph of the man I'd taken out. The name below the picture read Bradley Wakefield. And below that it said that he was the founder and CEO of World Tech, Inc.

A computer software company.

My mind balked. I squinted my eyes as if they might be playing tricks on me. That had to be a mistake. It didn't make sense. This wasn't right.

And then I lost my hearing. My head filled with the large whooshing sound of my heart pumping blood into my brain. I could see the anchorman's lips moving but could not hear a word he was saying. I felt dizzy and, reaching behind me to feel for the bed, sat down.

There on the television screen. Right next to the man I'd killed. Right next to Bradley Wakefield. Right next to the man I'd strangled in the men's room of the Quadrant Lounge.

Was a picture of The Man.

The Man.

My benefactor. The guy who had sent me on this mission. I've felt the crippling paralysis of fright before. I've experienced the icy clutch which makes it seem like any movement whatsoever would be the end of you. You freeze.

It felt like that now. I caught my breath as a horrible roadmap opened in my mind. Dots were being connected faster than I wanted them to be. A cold dagger of dread had been thrust into my entire being and I looked down to my hands to notice they were shaking.

It was only a matter of seconds before my hearing returned. Although I wished it hadn't. As I sat, rooted to the bed and listening to the report, the story grew clearer and clearer. And then it became crystal clear. With the subtlety of a cannon shot, the picture came into focus. And even though it was right in front of me, my mind was still unable to accept it as reality. There was no way that this could be true. If it was, then I was –

I couldn't even complete the thought. The truth was too horrible to accept.

The person I had killed last night was not a drug kingpin. He was not a criminal. He owned a company that put him in direct competition with the man. They were both wealthy business owners and they were competitors. Both were vying for the same large, government contract. The anchorman spoke the words I already knew but dared not accept. With Wakefield gone, the government contract would most likely go to the other firm.

The Man's firm.

I learned his name for the first time. I learned who my boss was.

William Kenealy.

And he was the President and CEO of Global Securities Initiative Inc.. A software giant, they developed, among other things, applications utilized by our government.

I couldn't believe it. This was not possible. This could not be happening.

As the anchorman continued to lay it all out, the undeniable, horrible truth came into focus. There was no getting around it. No amount of rationalization could square it.

I was an assassin. I was a cold blooded murderer.
Oh Debbie, I thought, what have I done? What the fuck have I done? The temperature in the room felt as if it had dropped below zero. I felt chilled to the bone.
In a twist of irony, as I began thinking about my wife, they showed a still shot of Wakefield's wife. Sobbing and bathed in the red and blue glow of police cars, she stood outside the Ritz Carlton. The picture, taken sometime last night, was heartbreaking. Her name was on the bottom of the screen.
She was being held by another man. Brother? Friend? One of her husband's business partners? I had no way of knowing. But what I did know was that I had done this to her. I had caused this pain. I looked into her heartbroken face and felt my stomach turn. I had done this to another innocent human being. I had caused this woman the same type of agony that I'd felt for months now.
I began to feel nauseous. The enormity of my crime was beginning to crash down upon me. I had not only forever altered her life, but everybody who ever knew or cared for Bradley Wakefield. If he had kids, and I was sure he did, I'd made them fatherless. If he had any brothers or sisters, they too would agonize over his death.
I was a monster. An absolute monster.
I thought of the man who now had a name.
William Kenealy.
Anguish began to darken, pain giving way to a fury which I felt coming from the bottom of my soul, the very core of my being.
The ruthless bastard. The heartless motherfucker. I felt my teeth grind as a blinding hatred enveloped me. How long

had he planned this? Had he been devious enough to set this up from the very beginning? Had every job been leading to this?

And then another thought. Was I truly this big a fool?

I needed answers. I had to know.

I rushed to the bedside table on wobbly legs, grabbing for my cell phone. Picking it up, I went to recent calls. It was strange reading it now.

The Man.

With a trembling hand, I hit the button and placed the call. The phone rang and rang. I finally gave up and ended the call. And then I texted him.

Call me!!

Raging Storm
13

I wasn't sure how much time had passed. After watching the story on every news channel I could find, I'd turned the TV off. I sat on the edge of the bed in numb silence. I felt nauseous and questioned every decision I'd made in the past month. What the hell had I done? Who was I to play executioner to this man's whims? How could I have been so blind to have fallen for this? For everything.

I thought about killing myself. I couldn't take the guilt. It was too much. The poor guy had been taking a piss. A piss and I…

I couldn't even finish the thought. My body began shaking and I felt my sanity slipping away.

The phone rang, startling me so that I flinched. My cell phone. The man.

I grabbed it and with a trembling hand, hit the green bar. "Start explaining, you piece of shit," I said. My voice quivered as I struggled to restrain my emotions. I needed to stay in control until I had answers.

There was a pause. What was he waiting for?

"Who is this?" The man finally asked. He sounded as calm as always.

"You know goddamn well who this is, you fucking asshole!" I screamed. So much for restraint but I couldn't help it.

"No, I honestly don't. I got a strange text from a strange number and I called."

"William Kenealy, is it?" I asked. It was a rhetorical question. "How the fuck did you think you were going to get away with this?"

"I really have no idea what you're talking about," he said with half a chuckle. "Is this some kind of sick joke?"

"All along you wanted me to kill this guy. You played me from the beginning, didn't you?"

"What?" He continued the act.

"You planned this guy's death before we even met, didn't you, you sick son of a bitch!?"

"Are-are you saying you committed a murder?" He stammered in feigned shock.

The guy deserved an Oscar. As I listened to him play the game we both knew he was playing, it was almost more than I could stand. I felt my fury grow but did my best to stay level headed.

"You made a big mistake," I said. I spoke in a soft, menacing tone, backing it down a bit. "You forgot who I am. What I can do."

"Look, buddy. I'm getting tired of this. If you committed a crime my advice would be to turn yourself in."

"FUCK YOU!!" I roared.

"You sound disturbed," he said. His voice dripped with condescension. "Let me give you some advice."
He paused.
"Are you listening?" He asked.
"You motherfucker," I said. "I'm going to get you if it takes me the rest of my life."
"Listen and listen well my friend. You've made a mistake contacting me. A very big mistake. My advice to you is to walk away. Walk away and forget this ever happened."
"I know your name, you bastard. I know who you are."
"That's the best advice I can give and I strongly recommend you take it. Understand?"
"You son of a bitch," I hissed.
Click. The call ended.
I roared and threw the phone as hard as I could. It hit the wall and exploded into several, irreparable pieces. My chest heaved and my heart pounded so that I could feel every beat. Not knowing what else to do, I ran to the bathroom and jumped into the shower. The need to feel clean was overwhelming and I stood for a half hour as hot water poured over me. My mind raced a million miles an hour.
This was a nightmare, a doomsday scenario that I couldn't come to grips with. I had taken the life of an innocent man. I was a monster. I was a murderer. There was no way that I could ever come back from this. I wanted to cry, to weep for the man I'd killed but I couldn't. I was still numb with shock. And as the shock subsided, in its place grew a cold fury. And It came from a very deep, very dark place and it enveloped me

completely.

I felt the overwhelming urge to get out of this hotel room. Out of Washington. I needed to get home. I needed to get home, to think of my next move. I had to figure out a plan. There was only thing I knew with absolute certainty. Whatever I did next would include William Kenealy.

That was for damn sure.

Raging Storm
14

After a very rough flight from Washington back to Tampa, I made my way to the short term parking lot. The truck was gone. I didn't search for it. I knew the exact spot I'd parked in and it wasn't there. In truth, I hadn't expected to find it. The man was going to tie up loose ends.

The man...what a laugh.

William Kenealy. He had a name now. I had his name. But it wasn't enough. There were more questions than answers and I'd always hated that. I had to know. I didn't care how bad a situation was so long as I understood it. But in this case, there too many goddamn questions running through my head.

I hurried to the front of the terminal and hailed a cab. A thought struck me like the slap of a frozen glove. My house. If he took the truck what would he have done to my house? The weapons were there. Both my weapons, which I'd owned for years, and the small arsenal he'd given me. And the cash. Almost one hundred thousand dollars.

Although the temperature in Tampa was in the mid eighties, I felt a cold sweat run down my back. Had Kenealy ransacked my wife's home? Had Debbie's home been violated a second time?

Everything was growing dark. The day. The situation. My mood. Although I would soon have my answer about the house, the larger picture was still out of focus. The more I tried to make sense of it, the more I realized how little I knew.

I gave the cabbie an extra twenty to take liberties with the local speed limits. He did not disappoint. We entered my neighborhood and instead making a right towards my street, I asked him to turn left. I had him pull in front of a house I knew to be empty. And that's where I got out. After paying the man, I grabbed my suitcase and began a slow walk. I walked past the house, down the street and towards a thicket of trees that offered a view of my home. Night had fallen and thick cloud cover obscured the light of the stars and moon. There were no lights on in my home. I huddled down in the bushes and waited. I could see in the front windows and I watched for any type of movement. I didn't have a gun. I felt naked without one. There had been a 9 mm in the truck but that was now long gone.

After almost an hour, I decided to move. I couldn't sit here all night. I began the short walk towards my house. I expected anything. Gunfire. Arrows. Wild dogs. Nothing was outside the realm of possibilities in my twisted, confused mind. I kept low and stayed close to

my neighbor's house, making my way to the backyard. Setting my suitcase down in the grass, I went to my back slider and peered inside. My eyes had adjusted in the dark and my night vision was at full go. I scanned the rooms.
Nothing.
Okay, I thought. I have to go in. There might be an ambush waiting for me. I might get killed. But the bright side is that it would be over. And I would be with my family again.
You don't know how desperate I've become…
I went into my pocket and found my keys. Sliding the house key into the door, I unlocked it. I half expected a hail of bullets to greet me but there was nothing. No sound. No activity. I slid the door open and entered my home, a bundle of nerves and paranoia. The entrance was right off the kitchen and on the wall was a security keypad that blinked a small red light. I punched in my code and the light went to a steady green. The kitchen was dark. I left the light off and walked over to a drawer. I kept a Glock G36 inside the drawer underneath some papers and other assorted crap. If somebody opened the drawer they would never see it unless they searched. It looked like the junk drawer found in every kitchen.
The gun was there. I checked that the clip was full and it was. There was also a round in the chamber which was the way I always kept my guns. Round in the chamber, hammer back and safety on. My insecurities vanished tenfold as I was now armed and ready for anything. Flipping the guns safety off, I moved room to room, sweeping the house. In each room I closed the blinds or

curtains if they weren't already closed. After clearing the entire house, I finally turned a light on. I went back to my bedroom and made for the far left corner. Digging my fingers under the baseboard, I pried back the carpet and pulled. I then peeled back the foam pad to reveal the hidden safe I'd had placed there many years before. The safe resembled a wall locker lying on its side, the door staring straight up. I had run a wire to the unit when I'd installed it as there was an electronic keypad. I punched in the code and the door unlocked with a soft click. Pulling it open, I let out a sigh of relief. It was all there. The Barrett, the assault rifles, the ammo, the money, everything.

I sat there. On the floor, next to the safe. And I thought. I tried to make sense of it. If they had come here, it didn't show. They didn't flip the house. Everything was in place. Not that they would have thought to peel the carpet back, but still, I couldn't figure it.

Home now and safe, my nerves began to settle although I still felt numb and detached. Everything that had started to make sense again had been shattered. I thought that I'd found a kindred spirit, a man who understood my pain. My anger. A man who could help me heal. Yes, I'd chosen a dark path but for an honorable purpose and even though I was taking lives I hadn't looked at it that way. I was saving lives.

I was now certain that all the jobs leading up to the Washington hit had been legitimate. That's how he got me to let my guard down. Kenealy knew I'd do a little digging, at least on the first few missions. And I had. That was why he'd orchestrated a rush job on this last one. He gained my trust and then he used me. Used me to commit cold blooded murder. It was a calculated hit. I recalled our last phone conversation. Kenealy told me to forget it. It had never happened. He had to get the truck back as it was most likely registered to his company, but maybe he was allowing me to keep the rest? Maybe he intended to simply let me be? He knew there was nothing I could do. I couldn't go to the cops. Maybe he was just content to let me live in peace now that my usefulness had run out? Was it possible that the words he had spoken during that last, angry conversation had been true? Forget it, walk way, he had told me. It never happened. Go about your life.

For a brief second I considered it. I could simply walk away. I would have to look over my shoulder for a while but perhaps it was for the best? I could put this ugliness behind me and try to repair my shattered life.

Then the stubborn streak I possessed went into overload. Hell no. I wasn't on board with that. No fucking way. Kenealy was going to pay. Now that I felt the nerves dissipating, I felt the anger return.

And there's a storm that's raging through my frozen heart tonight...

I grabbed a few items from the safe and then closed it up, putting the carpeting back in place. After going back outside to retrieve my suitcase, I locked the house down. I had grabbed three IR motion sensors from the safe and set them at the most likely entry points. I synced them to my watch. If anybody tripped the sensors, my watch would vibrate. Tomorrow I would take extra precautions. But tonight I had to close my eyes.

I slept with the Glock under my pillow. But I didn't sleep well.

Raging Storm
15

I stumbled through the next two days in a surreal and guarded daze. I was super vigilant and treated everywhere I went as I would a war zone. I expected an ambush around every corner but none came. My nerves were on edge. But, in a way it was almost a rebirth. I reverted back to my days in combat. My senses were fine tuned and I was one with my surroundings.
I began doing serious research on Kenealy. And the more I learned, the angrier I became.
William Kenealy. Owner and CEO of G.S.I, Inc., a major, global conglomerate with some massive government contracts. Married to his college sweetheart. Yes, she was still very much alive. I found a picture of them at a recent charity event. She was wearing a stunning, gold gown with a plunging neckline and was a very striking woman. Around her neck lay a large, diamond necklace that had to be worth more than the average American made in a year. Kenealy, in an equally

impressive tuxedo, smiled for the camera as he played the role of good citizen.

As I read up on the firm I learned that it was founded by Kenealy's grandfather shortly after World War II. Decades later, the successful company had fallen to Kenealy's father. And then, in turn, to Kenealy. The motherfucker hadn't even built it himself. He had inherited his wealth and position.

I continued reading up on Kenealy and his wife. They had three grown children, the oldest being in his early thirties. He was listed as a vice-president in the company directory but was obviously much more than that. He was a Kenealy and would take over the company some day. I saw a picture of the privileged, silver spoon asshole and disliked him immediately. He had the smug look of entitlement that is common among those who get handed success without earning it. He'd graduated Yale, like his father before him. A legacy, he most likely hadn't earned admission into the Ivy League either. He was a member of the lucky sperm club.

Next in their bloodline was a twenty-eight year old daughter in her final year of Law School. Also Yale. I wondered what she had done in the interim as she was a few years older than the average third year law student. After a bit of digging I learned that she'd joined the Peace Corps after getting her Bachelor's Degree. Now it made sense. She had spent a few years giving back. I guessed it was her way of thanking the universe for the good luck she'd received through her privileged birth. She was pretty. Not stunning, but pretty. She looked like a nice person, if one could make such a judgment from looking at a picture.

The third and youngest of the Kenealy children was a bit of a mystery. He had enlisted in the army after graduating from a very prestigious private high school. It must have made his father cringe that he was a mere enlisted man. There was little else I could find on him. The kid had gone off the grid. He must have been the black sheep that every family seemed to have. Those were usually my favorite people. In any case, it was obvious he'd given his father a big middle finger as soon as he reached adulthood.

'Screw Yale, screw the business and screw you, dad.' I could picture it.

I found an older picture of the entire family posing in front of a large Christmas tree. While the rest of the Kenealy's were beaming, the youngest had a forced smile that could have frozen water into ice. Yeah, I liked him.

With a heavy heart, I Googled the man I'd killed in D.C. and gathered as much information about him as I could. Bradley Wakefield. Very successful guy. All the right pedigrees including a Harvard MBA. All the typical things that rich guys tended to have in common.

I looked even deeper into his company's history and saw what I had suspected. Kenealy and he were no strangers. They had been in fierce competition for years, each amassing fortunes in the same field. In fact, on the surface it looked as if this guy had bested Kenealy more times than he'd lost. That would explain Kenealy motives for wanting him dead.

I found a picture of Wakefield posing with his wife at a

golf outing from the previous year and felt my stomach turn. They looked like a very happy couple. She was very pretty with her hair pulled back in a pony tail under a white Titleist visor. He had a golf club in one hand and held her hand with the other. Their smiles seemed very genuine. These were good people. I could sense it.
The guilt was almost unbearable.
Reading further, I discovered that they had two adult children. I could imagine their faces as they learned of their father's murder. They would still be in shock and pain and think about him several times a day. I knew that pain only too well.
Wakefield and his wife had five grandchildren. Five youngsters that would never get to sit on their Grandpa's lap or play with him in the backyard. Thanksgiving's had been forever altered in the Wakefield family. The oldest son would most likely take over the patriarchal duties such as carving the turkey. Perhaps he would even take over the company. But, no matter what else happened, I knew that I had changed that family forever. I had thrust upon them a horrible loss that they would carry forever. I did that.
I did that to that family.
I hated myself at that moment. It was not an unfamiliar feeling. I'd been dealing with self loathing on a pretty large scale after allowing my own family to die. But, as time passed, I'd begun to forgive myself. Not completely, but little by little. I came to the realization that getting a buzz on at a party was normal. There was nothing negligent about that. I was living my life like everybody else. I was not responsible for what those

animals did that night. How could I have possibly known what awaited us that horrible night? I was not responsible. I kept telling myself that. I knew that it was important I accepted that.

And it looks like I'm losing this fight…

But I *was* responsible for what I did to Wakefield and his family. There was no way to excuse it. Kenealy had been a virtual stranger to me yet I had killed on his command. How could I have been so blind? I had allowed my anger and my pain to skew my judgment. My need to lash out, to right the wrongs of this world had allowed me to become his pawn. I had been a dupe, a highly trained and lethal fool.

I did my best to shake those thoughts and focus on the evening. Tonight I would take the first steps towards understanding and payback. It was group therapy night and although I was still under a court order to attend, tonight I actually wanted to go. I had questions that needed answers.

I arrived early. After getting coffee, I chose a seat in the back and waited. I watched as the broken hearted filed in to take their places. I was attentive but said nothing as I listened to one sad tale after another. These groups were supposed to make us feel less alone. That there are others who understand what we experienced. But the truth is, hearing first hand all the pain and loss only served to make me angrier.

The session ended and people began to leave. I waited for the crowd to thin and then approached the group leader.

"Hey Michael," I said.

"Hey, Ryder. How are you?"

"I've been better, man. I've been a hell of a lot better."

"I'm sorry. Is it anything you'd like to discuss? I have a bit of time."

I looked to the door and saw that the last of the group members were making their way out into the warm, Tampa night. I reached in my pocket and pulled out a picture of Kenealy.

"Do you remember this guy?" I asked. I held up the picture.

He squinted and gave it a long hard look. Finally he looked back at me.

"Yeah. I do."

"Did he ever talk? Before I arrived in the group?"

"Why?" He asked. He furrowed his brow. "Are you having a problem with this man?"

"God, no," I answered. I laughed a little to lighten the mood. "He just looks familiar. I was wondering if you knew him."

"Nope."

"So he never talked?"

"Not that I recall. He just sat in the back and listened. It's different for everyone, you know."

"Yeah, I get it. Do you remember his name?"

"I don't think I ever knew it. This is an anonymous group, Ryder. A lot of people even use fake names. They come here to…"

He hesitated, searching for the right words.

"…feel connected to something. You know? Like they're part of a group. Part of a group that can relate to their unique experience."

"So there's not a lot of court ordered people?"

"Well, obviously I couldn't point them out if there were but I will tell you that in this current group, you're the only one. Most of the others just wander in and out. Not a lot of long timers."

"Great. Nice to hear I'm the lone fuck up."

"That's not a bad thing, Ryder."

"Feels bad."

"Well. If you're worried about confidentiality, don't be. Not only would I never disclose information about a group member, it would be illegal if I did."

"So this guy never asked you about me?"

Michael looked me up and down. Now his radar was up. I could see that he was growing suspicious.

"What's going on, Ryder?" he asked. "Is there a problem?"

"No, no." I answered. I tried my best to sound nonchalant. "The truth is, I thought I recognized him from my military days and just wondered if you could help me fill in the blanks."

"Oh," he answered. I wasn't sure if he believed me. "He looks familiar, like somebody I knew from Afghanistan or Iraq."

"Sorry, Ryder. I don't know anything about him."

"Can you tell me how long he's been coming to the group? Is that against the rules?"

"No, I guess not. But I don't really remember. He just showed up one night. In fact, now that you mention it, it was right about the time you started coming to the meetings."

"Seriously?"

"Yeah. I think so."

The motherfucker, I fumed inwardly.

The son of a bitch had played me like a Stradivarius. Kenealy must have seen my story in the news. He'd probably started hatching his plot the same day. The papers spoke about my war record and my time in the Special Forces. How my family had been slaughtered in front of me. How I'd attempted to kill three men in a drunken bar fight which was utter bullshit. The papers had also mentioned the fact that I'd received a suspended sentence. That I was to attend group therapy.

Kenealy was smart. He knew that I was distraught, an emotional wreck. He knew that a man like me would be longing for payback. Of any kind. A chance to lash out at the bad guys of the world. And he was good, playing right into my emotions. I thought back to the first night he had approached me. Over coffee I heard the story about his wife getting raped and murdered. The guy had almost managed to squirt a few tears. He was very good. Or I was very stupid. Or a little of both. Yeah, I was going to go with that for the time being, a little of both. But we'd see. I wasn't finished with William Kenealy by a long shot.

I thanked Michael, shook his hand and headed out the door into the crisp, cool evening. There were a million stars out. A full moon too. I headed to my truck and tried to think of my next move. I wanted to talk to the son of a bitch. Face to face. Watch him squirm. Although I couldn't do anything legally, I sure as hell could put the fear of God into him. Let him know that he'd better watch his back. Get him shitting his pants on a daily

basis, never knowing when or where I might strike. At the very least I could fuck with him a bit. It was something.
I headed for home.

Raging Storm
16

I awoke that morning with a plan. I'd do the last thing the bastard would expect and go to him. Right to his company. Confront him. Let him know that he messed with the wrong guy. I doubted I'd get the chance to actually meet with him, but it was the right play. Rattle his cage a bit. Shake his tree. Let him know that this wasn't over.

G.S.I.'s corporate headquarters were here in Tampa. It made sense. MacDill Air Force base was here and it was Central Command for all operations in the Middle East. This would be the perfect spot to run his empire and stay close to the action. Golf outings, dinners at Bern's Steak House, wining and dining. Outside of Washington, it was a great place to court the military's top brass.

As with most things these days, the address was simple enough to find online. I made my way over and as suspected, the building was massive. It took up an entire city block, with five stories of glass offices. The parking lot was bordered with a high, thick hedge. Whether on foot or in a vehicle, there was only one way in or out and a guard shack and gate protected it.

I pulled my truck down a side street, drove for a few blocks and parked against a curb. Walking back along the sidewalk, I approached the building. I could see a uniformed man inside the shack at the parking lot entrance. A vehicle pulled up to the gate. Hoping it was enough to distract the guard, I bent and cut through a small gap in the hedge. Although there were quite a few people coming and going, nobody appeared to notice. I hoped.

I strode through the parking lot like I belonged there and made it to the front door. I got lucky as a small group of women were exiting. As I didn't have the security pass needed to open the front door, it was perfect timing. The women smiled and I gave them a courteous nod as I held the door for them.

Entering the building, I walked across the impressive atrium. The buffed, marble floors shone like mirrors. There was a magnificent fountain spewing water in the center of the lobby. To the left, a rounded staircase wound its way to a landing on the third floor. The ceiling was as high as the building, with natural light pouring through the glass top.

I traversed the grand lobby towards a large reception area against the far wall. The company name and logo were affixed in big, bold letters behind the big, half-moon shaped desk.

Global Security Initiatives, Inc.

Above the company name was one of those maps of the entire world, like a globe cut in half and spread out.

Through the world map were the letters **G.S.I. Inc.**.
Arrogant prick, I thought.

"May I help you?" A pretty receptionist looked at me with no small amount of suspicion. It was her job to buzz visitors in through the door and it was clear that I was a visitor.

"Bill Kenealy, please," I said. I gave her an easy smile. Like we were old buddies or businesses partners.

"Do you have an appointment, sir?"

"I do not, Kathy," I answered. I'd read her name badge. "But Bill and I go way back. He told me to drop in any time I was in town."

Her eyes moved up and down. She gave me a thorough once over, none too happy with this breach of protocol.

"Uhhh, yeah," I said. I attempted to placate her. "There were people leaving as I approached the door. Otherwise I would have rung the buzzer. Sorry."

I gave her the biggest, friendliest grin I could. Nothing to see here, just an old friend stopping by.

"One moment, please," she said.

Very professional. Very attractive. Blonde hair pulled tight in a ponytail. Soft brown eyes, which were just the right amount of crooked.

Debbie had brown eyes.

Every time I think of you, I always catch my breath...

She picked up the phone. "What is your name, sir?"

"Ryder Dunham."

Kathy punched some buttons on the phone a few times and waited. She didn't wait long.

"We have a gentleman here to see Mr. Kenealy. A Mr. Ryder Dunham."

She frowned as she waited.

I interlocked my fingers with my arms hanging low in front of me. Rocking on my heels, I did my best innocent guy impersonation. All I needed to do was start whistling to complete the dumb fuck look I was going for. I heard a male voice on the other end of the line but couldn't make out what he was saying.

"Yes. Yes. Yes," Kathy spoke as she listened. "I see. Okay." She hung up and shot me an awkward smile. "Mr. Kenealy is in a meeting but it should end shortly. He has agreed to see you if you care to wait?" She stood and walked around the desk. Great figure. She could have been a swimsuit model.

"Sounds good," I said.

"Follow me please."

I followed as she led me towards the back of the beautiful atrium and down a narrow hallway. We walked past several doors finally coming to one marked Guest Reception. Kathy stopped and swiped her ID badge across a glowing red bar which was next to the door. The light turned green with a click. Opening the door, she led me into a beautiful waiting area. There were three couches and several easy chairs. All rich leather. A large flat screen TV adorned the far right wall. There was a full kitchen with a bar and an espresso machine that looked like it was part of the space program. A refrigerator, granite counter tops and food preparation area completed the kitchen. There were also three tables situated next to a beautiful fish tank. The tank held every type of tropical colored fish you could imagine. There were more than you could count. A noticed a pair of small Tiger Sharks swimming around the large, pink coral formations.

"Make yourself at home, Mr. Dunham. You will find bottled water in the refrigerator and coffee at your disposal. Unless you'd like something stronger?"
"No," I answered. "Water will be fine."
"Would you care to watch television?"
"No thank you, I'll just read a magazine."
"Very well, sir. Please let me know if you need anything else."
I smiled again as she turned and left the room. The door closed with a heavy, metallic click. I didn't like the way that sounded. There are good clicks and bad clicks. That was a bad click. I walked over and tested the door.
Locked.
Shit.
It was then that I noticed the pass bar, requiring a badge, on this side as well.
Shit, I thought again. Locked in.
I didn't like this. Not one bit. Taking a closer look around the room I noticed black bubbles in each of the four corners of the ceiling. Cameras.
I wondered how many people were watching me right now. Was Kenealy one of them? I began to realize that this wasn't the best of plans. No, this was not good at all. Every instinct in my body was screaming to get out.
I knocked on the locked door. No response.
"Kathy," I spoke.
Nothing. I knocked again.
"Kathy!" I yelled this time.

Nothing.

Shit. This was bad.

Think, I scolded myself. You got yourself into this mess now get yourself out.

I knocked again, hoping for a break.

"Kathy!" I yelled again. Louder.

"Shut the hell up in the there!" A man's voice barked. It surprised me so much I jumped.

"Uhhhh…I think you people have mistaken me for somebody else," I said. Stay calm, I told myself. "Open the door and I'll show you some ID."

"Save it. Our head of security will be with you shortly so why don't you sit down and shut up!"

Oh boy, was this ever a bad idea. And I'd walked right into it.

"What the hell are you talking about?!" I yelled back. Still playing innocent. Not too bright.

"I said shut up in there! And don't even think about breaking anything because we're recording your every move."

He sounded like a real asshole. I didn't like him.

I examined the ceiling again. It was a standard eight foot, drop tile ceiling made up of several square tiles. If you pushed one up, you'd find a mess of wires running on top.

With a growing sense of urgency, I formulated a plan. Jumping up, I punched the ceiling tile that lay in front of the door. It lifted up and fell back in place. I jumped again and this time when it lifted I got my fingers under it and pushed. The tile slid back on top of the others. I now had a ledge to grab a hold of. I jumped again, this time grabbing the ledge which was the top of the door frame. I did a half pull up, raising my head above the tiles and took a look. Although it was dark, I could see the cables and wires running along the top.

I pulled myself all the way up, locking my elbows so that only my legs were hanging into the room. I had both hands on the top of the wall frame and looked like a gymnast preparing for a dismount. I could see the same square tiles on the other side of the door. They would be right above the hallway Kathy had led me down. That would also be right above the asshole standing guard. Although I wasn't looking forward to this, it was the only way out. The alternative was much worse. I knew that my situation was getting more desperate with every passing second. There was no more to think about. Here goes.

Pushing with my arms, I launched myself into the space over the hallway. As I did so, I twisted around so that my butt would land on the thin tile. I'm sure it looked pretty funny when they watched the surveillance tape afterwards. Out of thin air I came crashing through the ceiling and landed on my backside. Right beside a very surprised and wide eyed security guard. Too bad, I'd been hoping to land on top of him but at least he was alone. That was a break.

"Hey!" He shouted. He spun around to tower over me. There wasn't a second to waste so sweeping my right leg in a vicious, low kick, I took out both his legs. He crashed down beside me in a heap. His hand went for the pepper spray attached to his belt.

"That won't work on me," I said. I scrambled to my

feet.

The guy must have practiced this shit at home in front of a mirror. Like a quick draw artist, he had the mace from his belt and was spraying it before he even got to his feet. And he scored a direct hit. Right in my face. The son of a bitch was the Wild Bill Hickok of mace.

As getting gassed is a regular part of recon training, I knew how to handle it. But this must have been some high grade stuff because it burned like hell. And it pissed me off.

I knocked his arm away and pivoting my hips like a boxer, drove my right fist squarely into his chin. I made solid contact and he folded like a cheap suit, dropping straight down as his eyes glazed over. I grabbed the mace that he'd wielded and started running, bursting into the atrium. Another pair of security guards were hustling down winding staircase.

"Lock it down!" One of them yelled.

I noticed Kathy speaking with another woman by the fountain. She spun around and raised a hand to her mouth in shock.

Sprinting past the two ladies, I ran towards the door and a very shocked businessman who had just entered the building. Unfortunately the door had closed behind him. He gaped at me with wide, panicked eyes.

"Buzz me out!" I ordered giving him my hardest look.

The guy stood there, frozen in fear. Kathy was now moving fast, trying to get back behind her desk to hit some type of lock-down switch. I whipped my head to the right. The two security guards were streaking across the lobby towards me. Turning back to the man in front of me, I raised the can of mace and pointed it at his face. "Swipe your card or die!" I screamed. It was a desperate bluff as mace is painful, but not lethal.

The guy grabbed the badge on his belt and blindly stabbed in the direction of the pass bar.

"Don't!" One of the guards screamed.

The businessman, wide eyes still fixed on me, kept missing the mark so I decided to help him out. I grabbed his wrist and shoved his hand into the security strip. The light turned green and I kicked the door open, sprinting outside. I had a good thirty foot head start on the two security guards.

Dashing to the left I got to the edge of the parking lot in mere seconds. I looked behind me to see that the guards were no longer in pursuit. They were on their walkie talkies.

I dove through the hedges and tore down the street heading for my vehicle. Thinking better of that, I made a right and went the opposite direction. I kept pumping my legs, putting as much distance as I could between myself and G.S.I. Inc..

After a few blocks I finally slowed to catch my breath. My heart was a trip hammer, about to beat out of my chest. Doing my best to walk in a normal manner, I circled back the long way, on the opposite side of G.S.I Inc. and waited to hear sirens, to see law enforcement fanning out. I hugged the curb, ready to dive into nearby bushes.

But they never came.

Why, I wondered. Why the hell not? Of course they would call the cops. Who wouldn't? It was a normal thing to do. Especially seeing as how I'd clocked that guard. But there was nothing. A golf cart came into view and I jumped behind a large palm tree. The cart said G.S.I., Inc. and there were two security guards scanning the area but they never did turn down the street I was on. I finally made it back to my truck. Looking around to see that nobody was watching, I climbed in, started the engine and eased away. Before long I was miles away from Kenealy's corporate headquarters. My heart rate slowed to a normal pace.

And then it started to dawn on me.

Kenealy wasn't going to call the cops. Not now. Not when he could handle this himself and do with me as he pleased. He probably had plenty of goons working for him. Goons who would be more than happy to take me into the Everglades and feed me to the gators. He must have had tons of military contacts. I wouldn't be at all surprised if he knew some hard cases. One thing was for sure though, he didn't want me talking to the cops. He was handling this in-house.

I drove home knowing that my mission had backfired and backfired big. It was I who had shaken a hornet's nest. If Kenealy had meant what he said, if he was serious about allowing me to forget the whole thing. To walk away. It was a safe bet that I'd ruined that.

Okay, I thought. Fine.

Bring it.

Raging Storm
17

Kenealy didn't waste much time.
They came for me that night. Three of them.
At four in the morning. The best time for a sneak attack.
REM sleep was usually deepest right around that time.
Your victim would be at his most vulnerable, disoriented and unfocused. However, I'd had that trained out of me in Recon. I woke up ready. Always. So did every other S.F. trained man.
Besides, it didn't matter. They hit the wrong room.
That fact aside, it was well planned. They entered through the slider in the back and went straight for the master bedroom. They most likely pulled public records and got hold of the plans to my house. Had the lay of the place.
What they had no way of knowing was that I had those three IR sensors strategically placed. Small, invisible beams of detection. Special ops, high grade stuff. Set to vibrate the watch on my left wrist.
Even so, they might have gotten me had I been sleeping

there. But I never did. Not anymore. I couldn't. It was her bedroom. Our bedroom.

After gaining entry they wasted no time. The sensors vibrated my wristwatch. I woke up. Seconds later I heard the door to the master bedroom kicked open. I heard the thumping of their silenced weapons as they shot up the bed. Our bed. Her bed. That pissed me right off.

I rolled out from beneath the covers, dropping in silence between the wall and the bed. This would provide a small bit of cover if they made it this far.

But I was betting on that not happening.

My hand closed around the shotgun laying under the bed. Just as quickly I decided against it and grabbed the AS Val instead. A Soviet weapon, it was a favorite in Special Forces circles. Very quiet, very deadly. A member of the sturdy and reliable Kalashnikov family the AS is short for Avtomat Special'nyj. That translates to Special Automatic Rifle. The Val is the description of the shaft or the long, fat silencer. It fires a 7.62, subsonic round. Deadly silent. Deadly period.

I knew they would be wearing night vision goggles. I would have been. Dark house. Unfamiliar surroundings. It was a no brainer. But night vision goggles have one fatal drawback. Light. The goggles work by drawing in and magnifying even the slightest bit of light. Starlight, moonlight, a distant street light, it didn't matter. So if somebody throws a switch and lights up a room, that also gets amplified and believe me, it's blinding. I've had it happen. It causes temporarily blindness and all you can do is react by ripping the damn things off your head. It then it requires squeezing one's eyes shut and allowing darkness to calm down the pupils. It hurts like hell and that's from a normal sixty watt light bulb. I had something a little better than that.

Flash bang grenades do two things. They produce a blinding flash of magnesium light over one million candela strong. That alone is excruciating to the naked eye. Add night vision amplification and it's enough to cause an instant migraine and even burn one's retinas. The second half of the grenades name comes from the one hundred and seventy decibel bang it produces. This startles and disorients your victim for a couple seconds. And in close combat, seconds meant life. Or death.

I had three of these beauties under my bed. But I would only need one. My hand closed around a grenade and I wasted no time moving to the bedroom door. Flipping the safety off the Val, I crouched low. A tactical advantage this bedroom offered was the direction in which door opened. By cracking it only a bit, I was able to look out into the family room without having to look around the door. Less exposure. Through the small sliver I could see the master bedroom and since I'd had no exposure to light, I had full night vision. I could see very well. I waited.

The three men exited the master bedroom a moment later. They came out stacked, meaning one behind the other and in a tight group. They wore all black, gloves and skull caps to boot. Of course, as suspected, they had on night vision goggles. It must have been very upsetting to find my bullet riddled bed empty. And I guarantee they were not happy about having to fall back on phase two of the operation. The sweep. Sweeping is a dangerous business which leaves you vulnerable to the unknown. But that's the game.

They began.

Single file, low, one behind the other. I could see that they were former military, almost certainly Special Forces. Their next move would be to fan out and form a 180 degree perimeter sweep as they closed on this side of the house. They did not disappoint. One of the men hugged the back wall by the sliding glass door. The next stayed low and came up the middle and the third man headed left towards the front. They were well trained. The problem for them was that I knew right where they were and they had no idea where I was.

Oh, that and the little surprise I had waiting for them in my right hand.

They moved quickly so I had to as well. I could not let them see the grenade being tossed. That would give them a split second to rip off their head gear and I'd lose the edge. So I didn't toss it. I pulled the pin and rolled it out the door. Then I turned and shut my eyes. Cradling the Val, I placed two fingers in my ears.

Whoomp! Even through closed eyes and with my back turned, the flash was brilliant.

The men cried out in pain. I stepped through the door in a crouch and leveled the Val at the man in the middle. With two quick squeezes I put a couple rounds into his chest. He dropped. The man on the right, who had by now ripped off his goggles, was next. Chances are he didn't hear the silenced Val take out his friend. His ears would still be ringing from the bang of the grenade. He had dropped to lay prone and was in the act of raising his

weapon to fire blind when I placed a single shot. It went through the top of his skull. So much for the carpet.
The third man had done the same, dropping to the ground while ripping off his goggles. Yet, he managed to get off a spray and pray, raising his gun and letting loose a volley of lead. But he had two major problems. The first being that he put his rounds about ten feet to my right and never even came close to hitting me. The second was that he emptied his clip in doing so. He hadn't taken it off full auto after he'd shot up my bed. It was a mistake, but at the end of the day it wouldn't have made a difference. I had him. As he scrambled for a fresh magazine I rose to my full height and stepped towards him.
"Don't," I said. I kept my voice low and even.
The man stopped. He was beat and he knew it. He looked up at me, blinking and trying to clear his blurred vision. The entire fight had taken less than ten seconds.
"Can you see me?" I asked.
"Yeah, kind of," he answered. He had a British accent. And he was very relaxed. Pro all the way.
I took a step to my left and hit a switch. The family room light came on and I examined my house guest. He was a middle aged, white man. Strong jaw line. Excellent shape. Brush haircut. Definitely former something. I would bet he'd seen tons of action.
I knew his weapon was empty so I wasn't stressed. Still, I knew he would have at least one backup piece on him.
"Who sent you?" I asked. I knew, but it was always polite to ask.
"Doesn't work that way," he said. Still cool. He wasn't

going to give an inch.

"Aw c'mon, please?" I asked. I didn't mind toying with him a bit. He came into my house to kill me. Debbie's house.

I stood staring down at him, my assault rifle leveled at his head. He remained on the floor, propped up on his elbows. His lips were pursed tight. He breathed through his nose. I could see his resolve. This was not a stupid man. He was going.

And he knew it.

He looked me dead in the eyes. Fear completely masked. No begging for his life. No quick plea bargains. This was a ballsy motherfucker. Under different circumstances, I would have loved to have served with him. Unyielding courage went a long way with me.

"Not going to tell me, huh?" I asked.

"Not going to happen, mate" the man answered. He was resigned to his fate. "Either let me go or-"

My Val burped and a single round smashed into the bridge of his nose. Where it exited is anybody's guess because the back of his head blew off. The entire thing. Bits and pieces of it coated the far wall.

All in all it was a good death. A soldier's death. No pain. No drawing it out. He never saw it coming.

Instantaneous.

I inhaled as much air as I could and blew it out in a long, slow breath. I repeated that several times. I wanted my adrenaline rush to fade as soon as possible. I had to think.

Was there a fourth man? A getaway driver? Almost certainly not. This wasn't a bank robbery. No, it was a three man hit team. Very standard for a creep and destroy.

I surveyed the room. Three tango's down, I thought to myself. Funny how you revert right back to military jargon.

Nice try, Kenealy you bastard.

I thought of *the man* and fell my heart rate spike again. Ruthless, cold blooded son of a bitch. This changed things. Now I knew. I was number one on his hit parade. I was a very big loose end. Walking back into the guest bedroom I grabbed my cell phone and made a quick call. The police arrived in record time. Three dead men is not a routine call. They even sent a SWAT team. I waited for them on the front porch, sitting in one of the chairs that Debbie had picked up at an outlet store. She'd loved these chairs. I stayed in only my boxers and kept my hands very visible. They came in right. Strong and very authoritative. Had me assume the position. Cuffed me. Did a quick assessment of the house and learned that I was indeed the owner. A detective approached as I sat on the lawn. He bent down and undid the cuffs himself.

"Sorry about that, Mr. Dunham."

"Why? You did it by the book."

"Well thanks for understanding. Want to run it down for me?"

I gave him the scenario. How it had played out. It was his job to be suspicious. He started asking his questions.

"Mr. Dunham," he began.

"Call me Ryder."

"Okay, Ryder. What gives? This was no simple home invasion. These guys are mercenary's by the looks of it."

"Were mercenary's," I said.

"Yeah," he said. He paused, narrowing his eyes a bit. "Were. Something you want to tell me?"

"Such as?"

"Such as who did you piss off?"

"I wouldn't have any idea. This caught me by surprise."

The man looked at me like I was full of shit. Of course he was right. But he couldn't prove it.

"Ryder," he answered. "If this is you surprised, I'd hate to see what you can do when you're prepared."

I shrugged, giving him a half smile.

"Why did you sleep in the guest bedroom?"

"Because I don't sleep in the master bedroom."

"Why?"

I hesitated, searching for the right words.

"You know who I am, don't you? You know about my wife and kids, right?"

"Yeah," he said. His demeanor changed. "And I'm incredibly sorry, Ryder.

He got it. I nodded my appreciation.

"That's why."

"Still," he continued. "Why the arsenal? It seemed like you were ready for something like this."

"I *was* ready."

"Okay, but the question remains why?"

"Because you're either ready or you are not ready, detective. I always choose to be ready."

The man sighed. Not the answer he was looking for.

"Were you expecting trouble?"

"No. But I wasn't expecting trouble the night my family was slaughtered either."

"Okay," he said. "Okay. And you have no idea who these guys were?"

"Not a clue. Maybe the guys who killed my family hired them as payback. I got two of them that night and the other two are most likely headed to death row."

"Possible, but I'd say unlikely. These guys look expensive."

I shrugged a second time.

"So that's it? That's all you're going to give me?" He asked.

"I got nothing else, detective," I answered. "I'd tell you if I did."

He gave me the look again. Knew I was full of shit.

"You got someplace you can go? Somewhere to stay?"

"Yeah, right here. This is my house."

"The dead guys don't bother you?" He asked.

"Well," I began. "I assumed you guys were going to take them with you."

He couldn't help chuckle.

"Yeah," he said. He extended his hand. It was not a departing handshake. It was one of respect. I shook it.

"It's not like I'm going back to sleep anyway," I said. "I'll brew a pot of coffee for you guys."

"I can't have you in the crime scene until we finish up."

"But they never got as far as the kitchen," I said.

"Rules, man. Rules."

"Okay. Tell your boys to feel free to make some anyway. But bring me a cup if you do, detective."

"Dan," he said. "Captain Dan Suto."

"Pleased to meet you, Dan."

We shook hands again.

"Likewise."

"I guess I'll wait out here then," I said.

"We'll try to be quick."

I looked at my watch. It was closing in on five in the morning. I took a seat again and waited. I had some thinking to do. I had a feeling that tomorrow was going to be a very hectic day.

Raging Storm
18

As soon as the cops left I started packing.
Kenealy had declared war and I was a sitting duck here. He had underestimated me but I had also gotten very lucky. It could have easily gone the other way. I went back to my floor safe in the master bedroom and emptied the contents into a large duffel bag. I still had most of the money the man had given me. I also had the weapons, something that I hoped would come back to haunt him. In light of what he'd planned, I wondered why he'd given me so much. Was it to earn my trust? Did he think I would join him? Maybe he planned on getting it all back once he'd zipped me up? Who knows? I felt nothing for the three guys I'd killed. Nothing at all. They had come to murder me so it was fair play. They'd made one hell of a mess out of my house but I suppose it didn't matter. Chances were I'd never be back here. I actually found that comforting in some small way. It was time to leave it behind. The things that had made it a home were gone. My beautiful wife. Sasha. Hunter. Gone forever. Now the house was no more than a torture

chamber for me, a place to wallow in my misery. It was here that their ghosts lived and for me was an unhealthy thing. It had driven me to the brink of madness, to a dark place. It had caused me to make some horrible choices. It was time to leave.

As I packed up I kept a 9mm in my waistband and the lethal Val within easy reach. They wouldn't come now, there was no way. There wasn't time to put together another team, and even if there was, they knew I was onto them. But even with that knowledge, I was taking no chances. I wasn't going to get ambushed again. Kenealy would most likely know by now. The hit team would have had orders to report back. To give their handler a situation report. When they failed to check in it would raise red flags. If these guys monitored police scanners, and I would have, then they'd already know that I'd capped all three of them. I had to admit that it felt good knowing that Kenealy would be starting to get a little nervous. A crew like this wasn't cheap. They were as professional as they come and I'd eliminated them. If that pompous asshole didn't have a healthy dose of respect for my abilities before, he sure as hell would now.

I loaded a suitcase with the basics, underwear, socks, and some shirts and pants. In my duffel, alongside the weapons and cash, I threw some boots and sneakers. I also tossed in some cammies and both my black ops and ghillie suits. Then I went into the bathroom and packed my toiletries into a black shaving kit. As an afterthought, I threw some disguises together. I grabbed a couple hats and some dark sunglasses. Searching though a

Halloween box in the garage, I found a personal favorite. The ball cap with the long hair sewn into the sides and back. Easy to don, it changed ones entire look immediately.

After I finished packing, I steeled my resolve. I had something to do and I knew it was going to rip my guts out. I took a slow and final walk through my house. Through my family's house. As hard as it was, I had to say a final goodbye.

As I headed down the hallway towards the kid's bedrooms I broke down. I felt all the pain of that night returning. Every bit of it. I'd spent months trying to fight the pain. Trying to be tough enough to handle it. Now I gave up. I stopped trying to be a hard ass and I let the tears fall.

I started in Hunter's room. My little man. My dude. My Hunter.

I never got to take him to a ball game or teach him how to throw a hard slider. I never got to help him buy his first car. I never had a chance to watch him grow into a man so I could have a beer with him. I would never teach him how to treat women with respect and avoid those unworthy of it. I stood there and cried thinking about the type of kid he was, always full of curiosity and life. I cried for the type of young man, and then grown man, he would never be. It wasn't fair.

I took my time and walked to Sasha's room to start the entire process over again. Sasha was smart. Smarter than Hunter. Smarter than me. She had an intelligence that might have cured cancer someday. She may have wound up on the Supreme Court. Or she may have been the best damn mommy God ever put on the planet. All great accomplishments. None of them easy. Now, because of a couple whacked out meth heads, she would never be anything. Nothing but a memory. A beautiful, precious memory. I stood in the center of her room, surrounded by stuffed animals and wall stenciled ponies, and I wept. I didn't go back into the master bedroom because that's not where I remembered Debbie. I remembered her in the backyard tending her flowers and in the kitchen making dinner. I remembered her on the couch, the four of us watching a kid's movie. I remembered her in her art room, painting. On the beach. In the playground. On the dance floor.

I remembered holding her and looking into those beautiful brown eyes. Those eyes that could destroy me every time. That smile that could melt me no matter what type of day I'd had. I remembered her body, her absolute perfection as a woman. I remembered the way her hair smelled, fresh strawberries after a rainfall. I remembered how soft her lips were.

Every time I think of you, I always catch my breath...
But more than anything, I remembered always knowing that I was one lucky son of a bitch. At least I knew it, I thought to myself as the last of the tears streamed down my face. I always knew it. And I told her often. I was happy for that. I had no regrets about the way I'd loved her. I would take that with me always.

And now it was time.

I grabbed my gear and my suitcase and headed to the door. Turning around, I gave the place one final look. "I love you," I spoke aloud. I like to think that wherever

they were, they heard me.
I turned and walked out, closing both the door and a large chapter of my life, behind me.
Forever.

Raging Storm
19

I wasn't sure where to go as I hadn't left with a real plan. The only thing I knew was that I couldn't stay at my house. They would come again.

I drove with no destination in mind for about a half hour. It felt good to simply move. Finally, with nowhere else to go, I made my way down Dale Mabry Highway. Dale Mabry is a major artery that runs north and south through Tampa. If you drove far enough south, the road ends at the gates to MacDill Air Force base in South Tampa. A mile or so before getting to the base you could find any number of seedy strip motels. These were often weekend homes to young military men. Teenagers, fresh out of basic training, who wanted to get off base and live a little. I had been one of those young idiots once.

My thoughts drifted back to Camp LeJeune. Jacksonville, North Carolina. Home of Marine Corps Infantry Training School and the second marine division. We were all very green and very naive. Fresh from boot camp, most of us had only been out of high school for a few months. On Friday nights we'd hit the town, get one of those cheap motel rooms and hit every dive bar and strip joint we could find. And once out there we got a crash course in life. Real life. There was no shortage of dirt bags. Bikers, drug dealers, hookers and other predators were everywhere. And they all seemed to be looking to score off young, dumb victims sporting fresh high and tight haircuts. They knew we had a pocket full of cash and almost no street smarts. A bad combination. It was a place where you grew up real fast. Trial by fire, lots of scrapes and even a few trips to the emergency room.

Yeah, this would be a good place to squirrel myself away while I figured out my next move.

I paid cash for the room. The desk clerk didn't even look up. My guess was that he didn't want to ever have to pull somebody out of a line-up. Keep your head down and your mouth shut. It was how you survived in this environment.

The room was clean but I didn't want to think too hard on the sheets and microscopic creepy crawlers in the mattress. Some things are best ignored. Dropping my gear on the floor I headed to the bathroom. I needed a shower in the worst way and the towels seemed clean and surprisingly soft. These cheap motel towels usually feel stiff, like they starched them.

As soon as I jumped in I noticed the water circling the drain had traces of red and pink in it. Splatter from my earlier house guests. I hadn't even noticed. I didn't care, the hot water felt good and I stood there forever. One of

the great things about motels is that the hot water never runs out.
I'd finally had enough. I got out and stood toweling myself off in the mirror. Gazing at my reflection, I tried to figure out how my life had gone so wrong. I reexamined every decision I'd made since losing my family. Why didn't I take the time to mourn them properly? If only I had done that and gotten some counseling, I could have had a shot at a somewhat normal life. As hard as it was to even think about, someday I could have even met a woman who I could care about again.
But I hadn't gone that route. I had allowed myself to get duped by a murderous con man. The guy did a serious number on me. Not that I didn't blame myself as well. I'm a buck stops here kind of guy and I committed the acts with free will. But Kenealy was also culpable. He'd pulled the trigger and stuck the knife in as much as I had. And now he'd sent men into my home to kill me. He had declared war.
I stared into my reflection, into my eyes, and took mental inventory. I had no kids. I had no wife. I had no home. I had nothing to live for except one thing. Revenge. And it was enough. It drove me. For now.
I finished drying off and threw on a pair of sweat pants. Grabbing the remote control, I hoped it worked and pressed the button. The TV flickered to life. Good, I thought. I turned to one of the local stations and began watching a rerun of Wheel of Fortune. I solved one of the puzzles and watched as the day's winner blew the big money round. Tough break pal. But at least you have

a family to go home to. Stop it, I ordered myself.
The local news came on as I reached for a coupon that sat on the end table next to the bed. I read the offer for a large pizza from a mom and pop pizzeria down the street. They delivered no charge. Sounded good. I grabbed the phone, dialed the numbered and ordered a large pepperoni and sausage pizza. I had to walk over to the dresser and grab the key to tell them my room number. Too many thoughts in my head. Cash or charge they asked me. Cash, I answered, hanging up the phone. It would be a half hour they told me. Good enough, I was starving.

Stepping to my duffel, I was fishing a twenty dollar bill out when I heard his name come out of the television. William Kenealy.

I froze.

Stopping, half bent over, I strained to listen, certain that I'd imagined it. And then, for the second time in less than a week I was to learn of my old benefactor's betrayal on a hotel television. The anchorman's words cut through me like a knife.

"…founder of Global Securities Initiatives. Since the murder of World Tech CEO, Bradley Wakefield, three nights ago in our nation's capital, Global Securities is considered to be the front runner for the multibillion dollar defense contract..."

I dashed back in front of the bed to stare wide eyed at the television. There, in all his smug arrogance, stood the miserable prick. Taped earlier this morning, he was in the parking lot in front of G.S.I. with several microphones in his face. His face bore a look of great

concern and sadness. The scumbag was doing his best to look the victim. At that moment they superimposed another picture on the left side of the screen. I stared into the familiar face. It was the same face I'd stared into only moments before in the motel mirror.
Mine. Holy shit.
They rolled security footage of me breaking out of G.S.I.'s lobby yesterday. The bruised face of the guard I'd knocked out was up next. I could feel my heart pounding as I listened to the story unfold. Kenealy stood in front of the press and the words that came out of his mouth made me want to vomit. It was too surreal to grasp. He said that I had approached him on the street a month ago and offered to kill his business rival. That I'd offered to do it for one hundred thousand dollars. The twist was not lost on me.
"I didn't take it seriously. I thought it was just the ravings of an idiot looking to make a quick buck," Kenealy said. He looked out at the group of reporters and rambled, doing his best to appear flustered and upset. "I get all types of crazy propositions from people. I should have reported it. I know that now and I'll have to find a way to live with it. My heart breaks for Brad's family. But not for one second did I believe he would actually do it."
"It would appear that Mr. Kenealy was wrong," the lead anchorwoman spoke as they cut back to the studio. "And that the suspect, Ryder Dunham, came to collect…"
The rest of what she said got drowned out by the sound of blood rushing to my head. I felt my world, the little that remained, being torn apart. I took a deep breath and

forced myself to listen.

"…police are seeking Mr. Dunham for questioning. If you spot the suspect, do not approach him as he is considered to be armed and dangerous. Call local police and…."

I grabbed the remote and flipped through the channels. I was looking for a national cable news network. It didn't take long to find one.

Time stopped. I could hear every pounding beat of my heart as I realized that my life would never be the same. I had thrown it all away. It's funny the thoughts that go through one's mind in such an instant of clarity. My first impulse was suicide. I thought to myself, why bother? Screw it. Game over. Go join my family on the other side. And then the fighter in me growled at myself and I felt anger flood into every pore of my being. Hell no. If I was going, then at the very least I was taking that bastard with me.

My picture was in large frame on CNN. I was being sought for questioning in the murder of Bradley Wakefield. The national news outlet had picked up the feed from the local affiliates in Tampa. This story was big. Kenealy came on the screen and I got to hear him tell his lies for a second time.

I stopped listening.

The son of a bitch.

I raced to the window and eased the curtain back an inch. Nothing yet. It wouldn't be long though. Unless maybe the desk clerk wasn't watching TV? Who else might have seen me enter the motel? I had to act. Time was not on my side. I felt a rising panic.

I ran to my duffel and pulled out one of the rudimentary disguises. The baseball cap with the long hair sewn into it edges. I also grabbed a pair of dark Oakley's.

Jesus Christ, I thought as the enormous weight of the situation crashed down on my head. I stumbled sideways as a wave of vertigo struck me.

Jesus fucking Christ.

Catching myself, I bent at the waist. I placed one hand on the bed and the other on my knee. I breathed. Slowly, I ordered myself. Breathe. Breathe. I stayed in this position and waited for the rush of nerves to subside. Then I got down to business.

I hadn't had a chance to unpack so there wasn't much to do. I threw on a shirt and my sneakers. After that the shades and ball cap. Throwing the duffel bag over my shoulder, I grabbed for my suitcase. I made it to the door and stopped. I had a thought.

Putting the bags back down I rushed over to the end table where there was a notepad and pen. I jotted a quick note and left it there.

Going back to the door, I cracked it open and peeked out. There was nothing unusual, a few people walking on the sidewalk. No police presence. Not yet. I left the room and headed for my truck. Throwing my bags in the back I jumped in, fired up the engine and backed out of the spot. My senses were screaming and at any second I expected ten police cars to surround my vehicle. It didn't happen.

I forced myself to drive like a normal person. I didn't want to bring any attention to myself. I headed north on Dale Mabry. After a few blocks I realized that I had to get off the main roads. I started cutting through neighborhoods. What the hell, I chastised myself. I knew better than to take the main roads. By now, every cop in Tampa as well as the F.B.I. would be looking for my truck. I had to get another vehicle.

I spotted a convenience store and another idea struck me. I pulled in and parked behind the building. Walking head down, I entered the establishment and found what I was looking for near the front. Pre-paid cell phones. Burners, as they're called on the streets. I grabbed five of them and approached the cash register. A large woman in her twenties rang me up. She looked at me with obvious suspicion. I guess I looked pretty shady with the ball cap and Oakley's on. Also, buying five burners at once tends to get people's radar up. Screw it, I thought. I would be long gone if the woman decided to get civic minded. The phones were thirty dollars each and were good until the prepaid amount ran out. But, I wouldn't use each more than a couple times if that. I left the store and got back in my truck. I still had to get another vehicle and I knew exactly where to go.

As I drove I rationalized what I had to do next. There was no other way. I was already a murderer, so I guess I could live with being a car thief.

Raging Storm
20

I made my way towards the Brandon Mall which is roughly ten miles east of downtown Tampa. Directly off of I-75, it was the ideal place to secure another ride. If I had taken the normal route from South Tampa it was about a twenty minute drive. Winding through the back roads, it took me almost an hour.

I drove into the large mall parking lot and made my way to the side with the restaurants. Pulling into a spot near the back, I waited. I knew that employees had to park as far away from the mall as they could. This was so as not to occupy the choice spots that patrons enjoyed. This was what I was waiting for. If I caught somebody as they were coming in to work, I knew I'd have hours before they noticed their vehicle missing. In theory. Sure enough, within fifteen minutes a man drove up, parked and got out of an older model F-150. He wore a Cheesecake Factory uniform. It was the best I could hope for.

I waited until he walked out of sight and then pulled into

the spot next to him. I put my truck between his and the mall so if he looked out during a break he wouldn't notice that I'd borrowed his ride. Again, in theory. Reaching into the bed of my truck I transferred my bags into his vehicle. I kept a jimmy in my glove box as well as a small tool kit. Grabbing the jimmy and a screwdriver, I popped the lock. As it was an older model truck, it did not have an alarm which was the first break I'd had in a while. I slid behind the wheel, jammed the screwdriver into the ignition and gave it one good sharp rap with my palm. It went in to the handle. Twisting the screwdriver, the F-150 roared to life. I checked the fuel gauge and saw that I would have to fill the tank. It would have been nice to have had a full tank but expecting two breaks in a row was asking too much.

Giving my old truck a mental salute and thanking it for many years of service, I drove away. I found a gas station situated right before the on ramp to I-75 and filled the tank, paying cash of course. My entire life would be cash from this point on. I also grabbed a large coffee along with some snacks and a couple hours later I was passing Gainesville. I continued north and then jumped on Interstate 10 West towards Tallahassee. Pulling into a rest area, I broke one of the phones out of its packaging. I searched through my pockets and came up with Captain Dan Suto's business card. He'd given it to me as the police had wrapped up their work at my house this morning. Although that seemed like a week ago, I hadn't expected to be talking to him this soon. Turning on the phone, I punched in his number. After several rings, I got his voicemail. Shit. I left a long message.

"Dan, this is Ryder Dunham. By this time you've no doubt heard the lies that Bill Kenealy is spreading about me. I met him in the group therapy meetings the court ordered me to attend. He asked me if I was interested in a good job. I flew to Washington because I was supposed to meet a man there to discuss a security position. Kenealy put me up in a swanky hotel although I doubt you'll ever find any connection between that room and him. The guy who I was supposed to meet with in D.C. was a no show so I flew back. I went to Kenealy's office yesterday to ask him what the hell had happened when they illegally detained me. Kenealy is trying to frame me for the murder of this Wakefield guy so I guess we know who sent the hit team. I hope you can believe me. I will call you back on a number you will not recognize as I'm using burners for obvious reasons. Please answer."

I ended the call. It was the best explanation I could give. I made another call. This one from memory. After two rings a familiar voice answered.

"Hello?"

"Rob," I said with relief. "It's Ryder."

Rob Crawford was one of my closest friends. We did three tours together, one in Iraq and two in Afghanistan.

"Holy fuck, Ryder! Where the hell are you, man!?"

He didn't ask how I was. He asked where I was. He knew.

"Rob, listen to me, man. It's not how it looks."

"Dude, you didn't have to tell me that. I already knew. Where are you?"

"I'm still in Florida, but I'm heading your way. Can you put me up?"

"Man, I'm back in the barracks, brother. Susie and I split up. I tried to call you a couple times after..." He hesitated not wanting to say it. "...after what happened."

I had gone completely dark after Debbie and the kids murder. I didn't answer calls and I didn't make any. I'd crawled into a deep hole filled with self pity, self loathing and vodka. And it had led me to this unholy time in my life. I should have called my brothers. I should have reached out to them, leaned on them. I should have done a lot of things.

"Yeah, bro," I said. "I get it. I'm sorry."

"Fuck your sorry, man. You got nothing to be sorry for. Just wish you'd have let me help. I can't imagine what you've been through."

"Yeah. I was in a pretty fucked up place."

"What can I do, man?"

"I need a place to lay low. Something completely off the grid. You got anything?"

He thought for a second. "Yeah, I think so. How fast can you get here?"

"Couple days."

"Cool. Call me when you're an hour out."

"I will. And dude, not a word to anybody. Not anybody. Not even the unit."

"Come on, man. Did you really have to say that?"

"Yeah," I said. "I kind of do, man. This guy I'm up against is a heavy hitter. If he knew we were talking he'd take you out too. He already sent a team for me."

"I notice you're still around."

"Yeah," I answered. "But I got lucky. Listen to me, this guy is dangerous. And he is big time connected. No leaks."

"Fuck him," Rob said. He laughed.

"I'm serious, Crawdog."

He stifled it.

"I hear you bro. Goddamn, this shit's got you shaken."

"You don't know the half of it, buddy."

Rob paused. I could hear him thinking. "Well, drive three miles over the speed limit, stay in the middle lane and keep your ass low. I'll keep my phone on. See you in a couple."

"Yeah, brother," I said. I felt the old comradery. It was nice. The nicest feeling I'd had in a while. "See ya."

I hung up and stepped out of the truck, dropping the phone to the pavement. Smashing down with the heel of my shoe a few times, the thing broke apart. I had to make sure that the battery was no longer giving any juice to the circuitry. This done, I picked up the smashed pieces and walked them over to one of the many trash cans in the rest area.

I figured while I was here I would I would take care of some business. After using the facilities, I climbed back in the truck and headed west again on I-10. I planned on driving until I hit Texas. Then I would find a safe place to crash. I would need a new ride. This one would be on the cop's hot sheet soon. After that I would keep driving. I would stay on I-10 until it connected with I-5 north in California. From there it was less than two hours to

Oceanside and Camp Pendleton.

When I was researching Kenealy, I learned that he had a mansion in Malibu. Right on the cliffs, it overlooked the ocean. The place was worth a fortune. He had told the reporters that he was going to hole up there until I was no longer a threat. Still playing the victim, he claimed concern for his families safety. He would hire extra security and ride out the manhunt in his California enclave.

But I'd understood what he'd meant. It was an invitation. He was daring me to come for him.

So I headed west. I wasn't going to disappoint the man.

Raging Storm
21

The previous evening, I'd pulled the truck down a lonely country road. Parking off the beaten path, I hoped law enforcement wouldn't stumble upon me. I had planned on making it as far as Texas but after the sun went down my eyelids started closing. So I settled for Louisiana. It was the end of a very long, very stressful day and exhaustion had worn me down.

Sleeping in the back seat of the F-150, I woke with the first morning light. While in combat, I slept in some of the most hostile, uncomfortable places on earth. The back seat of a pickup truck was like a five star hotel by comparison. Despite the stress I was under, I slept well. I knew that there was an All Points Bulletin out for me and by now the truck would be on their radar as well. I needed a new vehicle. I would become a car thief for the second time in as many days at a mall in Baton Rouge. My plan was to repeat the same formula as yesterday. One of my philosophies in life is that if it ain't broke, don't fix it.

The only deviation was that this time I left the stolen truck in the back of a McDonald's parking lot. From there I walked a block to the mall. I hoped it would take the McDonald's manager a full day before he noticed the abandoned truck and call the law. Once that happened I knew it would only take a few minutes for the cops to learn that it was stolen. And once they spoke with the Florida authorities, they would find out who the suspect was.

Me.

In any case, the fast food restaurant was the right play. I didn't want to leave this stolen vehicle parked right beside the next one I planned on stealing. That would make it far too easy to follow my trail.

Before dumping it, I went through the drive thru and loaded up. I stuffed myself with two grand slam breakfast's and a large orange juice. Then I grabbed my bags and strolled to the mall.

Once there, I stood by the entrance of Sears and tried to make it look as if I was waiting on a ride. It didn't take long until I spotted a guy in a frozen yogurt uniform parking his Chevy Malibu near the back of the lot. I had been hoping for another truck but the Chevy had four wheels, and that was enough. Besides, I planned on grabbing another one tomorrow so it didn't matter. Besides, I told myself, car thieves can't be choosy.

After jimmying the lock and starting the engine, I drove my new loaner to the opposite side of the mall. I parked behind a tractor trailer. Ripping a new phone from its packaging, I fished Detective Suto's card from my wallet and called again. This time he answered.

"Hello?"

"Detective, it's Ryder Dunham."

"Holy shit. Where are you, Ryder?"

"Seriously?" I asked.

"You're goddamn right I'm serious," he answered. He sounded as stressed as I felt. "It just so happens that I believe you. I want to help."

"So you wouldn't grab me if you had the chance? Wouldn't arrest me?"

"Look, Ryder. You've been around so I don't have to tell you that you're facing some pretty serious charges. Of course I'd have to arrest you."

"Uh-huh," I said. "Well there you go."

"But after that I'd help you get to the bottom of this. Don't you want to clear your name?"

"Well," I said. "It's not my number one priority."

"And what is?"

"Staying alive. As you already know, somebody wants me dead."

He changed direction with his next question.

"Why did you leave your house, Ryder?"

"What do you mean?"

"I mean, you told me you were going to stay there. We go back a few hours later and you're gone. Why?"

"Why did you go back?"

He paused. What could he say?

"Orders, man."

"Yeah, I get that. By I have my own orders to follow."

"Such as?" He asked.

"Call it the will to live. I figured if I stayed there

Kenealy would just send another team. Of course, I had no way of knowing about his bogus press conference at the time. I only learned about that in the motel room."

"You don't know for sure that it was Kenealy who sent that team," he said.

"No," I answered. "*You* don't know for sure it was Kenealy. I have no doubt."

"Okay. Why?"

"Because he had Wakefield killed. I'm assuming you got my voicemail and the note I left? That pretty much says it all. He needed a patsy so he set me up to take the fall."

"Can you prove that?"

"If I could prove it I would let you arrest me. Until that time, I can't afford to sit in a jail cell, Dan."

The detective remained silent. I let him. When he spoke again it changed everything.

"Ryder."

He hesitated.

"The FBI has the video from the Ritz Carlton in Washington."

The unbelievable stress I'd been carrying doubled in the space of that second. Like one hundred pounds sitting atop each shoulder, it was almost crippling. Of course. After Kenealy fingered me for the Wakefield hit they'd be able to match me to the tapes, disguise or not. They had experts who would see through that getup in about five minutes.

That was the ballgame.

There was no way I was coming out of this clean now. I was a wanted man. Wanted for murder. And in fact, I was guilty. Guilty as hell. Through all the haze and emotional carnage I had a moment of clarity. I realized that this was how it should be. I deserved to go down for what I did. Murderers belong in prison. I deserved it and would be fine with whatever my punishment was. But the permeating thought, the one that cut through all the rest was this.

William Kenealy was coming with me. I swore to God at that very moment, he was coming with me.

"Ryder?" Suto's voice snapped me out of it.

"Detective," I said. My tone had changed. He heard it. I heard it. "All I can tell you is that it's not how it looks. Kenealy is just as guilty."

"Damn it, Ryder. Tell me what happened."

"I'm sorry. I am so sorry. Please tell Wakefield's family that-"

I couldn't finish. What could I possibly say that would make a difference to them? Nothing. Nothing at all.

"Wait!" Suto shouted. But he knew. I was already gone. I hung up and got out of the car. Once again I used my heel to smash the phone into a lot of very small pieces. When I was sure the battery was out, I kicked the entire thing down a nearby drain. Then I grabbed Detective Dan Suto's card and tore it up. I scattered those pieces to the wind and tried to ignore the obvious metaphor.

The sun was shining bright as the morning grew late. The sky was a perfect blue. White, billowy clouds floated past, eastbound. I stared into space for a very long time. I thought about how big the universe was. And how very small I felt at the moment. I took a deep breath and tried to clear my head. I needed to focus. I had to be on my game.

Donning my ball cap and sunglasses, I got into the car and drove out of the mall. I made it to the highway and continued west.

Raging Storm
22

The rest of the cross country journey was uneventful. Good weather all the way, no rain and only a handful of menacing storm clouds. After leaving Louisiana, I had driven all day. I kept the speedometer at an even seventy-five miles per hour and stayed in the slow lane. I'd spent the night in El Paso and upon awakening the next day, grabbed another vehicle from the Sunland Park Mall. I got lucky and found another truck. All I had left was a ten hour drive to Oceanside, California. It was a drive I'd made many times in the past decade, but never in a stolen, Dodge Dakota.

After cruising through Tucson, I jumped on I-8 which took me into San Diego. From there it was just a short drive north to Oceanside. The time had flown as the guy I'd boosted the truck from had an impressive collection of CD's. I enjoyed all six of The Door's studio albums and worked my way through a good chunk of Led Zeppelin's catalog. Before I knew it, I was within an hour of Camp Pendleton. I called Rob and he answered after the first ring.

"Hey brother," he said. It was his customary greeting. "Been waiting on your call."

"I'm here, man. They cut you loose yet?"

"Yup. Got liberty an hour ago. How far out are you?"

"About an hour."

"You want to meet at the Sport's Page?"

"No good, man," I answered. "Too many familiar faces."

"You're right, sorry," Rob said. He thought for a second. "Hey, you remember that old strip mall right across from it?"

"Yeah."

"First off, may I assume you're driving something borrowed?"

"That is an accurate assumption."

"Okay. Park near the street, there won't be any cameras there. You can get in with me and we'll go grab a beer and catch up. I'll fill you in on where you're staying."

"Sounds good, man. I should be there by six. Cool?"

"Absolutely. See you soon." He ended the call.

I continued on and felt an easy familiarity as I passed through parts very well known. I'd spent many years of my life at Pendleton and , knew the surrounding areas like the back of my hand. There were so many memories.

I made it to the strip mall which sat across the street from the Sports Page, one of my favorite old bars in Oceanside. Pulling into the lot I did a quick scan for cameras. As it was a very old plaza, there were none. No sooner had I parked than I looked up to see Rob's Jeep pull in. Same old Wrangler he'd had for ages, Rob loved the thing and treated it like it was his child.

Rob Crawford is about as hard corps as they come. He'd wanted to be a marine since he was five years old. His father, who had served in Vietnam as a marine grunt, had instilled in Rob a deep sense of service and duty. He was a shining example of the pride that came with being a member of the most elite fighting force in the world. As gung ho as he was, it was almost a given that Rob would join the Special Forces.

I joined the marines two years after Rob. Once I'd made it through Infantry Training School, I got stationed at Camp Pendleton. I wasn't with my unit a month before a billet opened and they were accepting requests to try out for recon. With the expert badge and the highest possible marks on the physical fitness test, I got my shot.

Thirty five guys competed for two open slots. I kicked ass and got chosen. It was one of the best days of my life.

Once I got to Battalion Recon, I got busy trying to be the best in my platoon. I had my sights set on making Force Recon which was the best of the best. One of the marines I'd looked up to was Rob. He had already made Force Recon and he impressed me right away as a very intense guy. He took the job very seriously. Most of the guys in recon were intense but they weren't career marines. They were going to do their time, have some adventures and get out. Not Rob. He was in it for the long haul. He was a lifer, a guy who wanted a career in the Corps and there was no questioning his commitment. Standing five foot ten, Rob weighed only one hundred and eighty pounds but every bit of it was muscle. The guy was a bulldog and the type of marine you wanted on your side. Whether it was in a bar fight in town or a firefight in Fallujah. He was loyal to a fault and would die to save a fellow marine or anybody else for that matter. His only drawback was a bit of a short fuse, but he made up for that with a big heart. He'd give you the shirt off his back. Rob was also part clown and his mischievous smile always hinted at a pending joke. He had been one of my groomsmen when I married Debbie and he'd had my back in more than one close encounter with the enemy.

I hadn't seen him in almost a year and it felt good to see his Jeep pull up. I saw that familiar smile flash before he even came to a stop. He rolled down his window and gave me a loud marine corps greeting.

"Oohrah, devil dog!"

I shook my head and chuckled. Stepping out of my borrowed vehicle, I strode towards my friend as he jumped out of his Jeep. We threw our arms around each other in a fierce bro hug.

"Holy shit, man," I said. I slapped him hard on the shoulder. "You look good, brother."

He took a second and sized me up.

"Jesus Christ, Ryder," he answered. "I wish I could say the same. You look like you have the weight of the world on your ass."

"That obvious, huh?"

"I'm just fucking with you, man. You look great."

"Yeah. Bullshit. Help me grab my shit," I said.

"Cool."

We transferred my bags, tucking them into the back of

his Jeep.

"Hey, you got a pen, man?"

Rob fished a pen out of his center console and handed it to me. I leaned back in the truck so as Rob couldn't see me and peeled a couple hundred dollar bills from my pocket. On one of them I wrote-

-Thanks for the loaner, sorry about that. Great tunes-

I then tucked the bills in the bottom of the ashtray and closed it tight. I hoped that whoever towed the truck wouldn't find them but at least it felt good to try and make it right.

I ran around the front of the Jeep and jumped in the passenger seat.

"Where to?" I asked.

"I know a new place, not far from here. There's always a lot of honey's and almost no jarheads. It's more of a rocker hangout."

"Yeah, that's cool man but I'm not really in the market for any honey's," I said. I looked out the window, away from his gaze.

"Damn. I'm sorry, Ryder," he said. "That's not what I meant. Sorry."

"Dude, life keeps going. Don't change for me."

The place was only a short drive. After parking we went inside and spent an hour catching up as we enjoyed a burger and a few beers. I talked in vague generalities when it came to Kenealy. Ducking questions, I finally told him that I would explain that mess another time. He accepted it without hesitation.

"So here's the plan," he said. "I'm going to catch a bus back onto base and you're going to drive my jeep up to

Oxnard to my parent's place. The clicker on the visor will open the garage door and the door into the house isn't locked. They're in Michigan for the summer so you can stay there for at least four months."

"I won't need it that long, knock on wood. But forget the bus, man. I'm at least going to drive you back on base, Rob."

"The hell you are. There are cameras everywhere at those gates, plus what are you going to do, come in and say hello to the old platoon? I thought the plan was to lay low?"

He was right. I grimaced but nodded at him.

"Yeah. Okay."

"My dad has an old Ford pickup truck in the driveway. The keys should be hanging on the wall in the kitchen. It's yours for as long as you need it."

"Dude, are you sure? I don't want to mess with another man's truck."

"Says the guy who recently stole a few," Rob said. He snorted and laughed.

"That was different asshole, and I didn't hurt them. The owners will get them back."

"He's got a for sale sign in it anyway so it's no big deal."

The waitress came with the bill which Rob grabbed.

"Hey man, at least let me get that," I said.

"Hell no, this ones on me."

Rob stuck a credit card on the tray and handed it back to the waitress.

"Thanks, Rob. I got the next one."

"Dude, you've got bigger things to worry about."

The waitress walked away and Rob continued.

"So once you get there, make yourself at home. You take my parent's bedroom and when I come up this weekend, I will stay in my old room."

"Dude, are you sure that's cool? It would feel kind of funny sleeping in your folk's bed."

"It's cool, Ryder. Plus, it's only a two bedroom house so it's either that or the couch."

"Okay," I said.

"There's a laptop in the office, feel free to use it. The password is oohrah1978."

"Oohrah1978?"

"Yeah, you got a problem with that?"

I responded with another laugh.

"Help yourself to whatever's in the pantry," he continued. "But there won't be shit in the fridge because they always empty it before taking off for the summer."

"Rob, are you sure about this?" I stared at him. I did not smile. "I mean, this is a lot to ask."

"You didn't ask, I'm offering. Plus, my parent's love you. They think of you as their own son. So fuck yeah, I'm sure."

"Thanks, brother. I can't tell you how much I appreciate it."

"Listen, you just start putting a plan in place to deal with your situation. Let me know what I can do to help."

"Oh, I already have a plan. I'm going to hit that motherfucker where it hurts."

"And where's that?"

"You let me worry about that. I don't you involved any

more than you already are."

"Dude, that's total bullshit."

"No, it's not. This guy plays for keeps. The less you know the better."

Rob stared at me as the waitress returned with the check for him to sign. After doing so, he downed the rest of his beer and I did the same.

"All right, asshole," he said. "I'll let it go. For now."

"Thanks," I said.

"Now get going, it's about a hundred and fifty mile drive and traffic's going to suck going through L.A."

"Man," I said. I shook my head. "I can't thank you enough for this, Rob."

"Dude," he answered. "Semper Fi, right?"

"Yeah," I said. "Semper Fi."

The Marine Corps motto. Semper Fidelis. Always Faithful.

We exited the restaurant and after a quick hug, Rob walked to the bus stop at the corner. I fired up his Jeep and began the trip to my new hideout.

For the first time in a long time, I felt good.

Raging Storm
23

After getting to Rob's parent's house I wasted no time. I put my gear away and took a few minutes acquainting myself, getting the lay of the place, and then I went to work. I wanted this over as soon as possible. I planned on hitting Kenealy before he had time to organize an adequate defense. There was no way that he'd expect me to come for him this soon. In fact, he probably thought that I'd never come for him at all. He most likely figured that I'd hole up somewhere in Florida and try to keep from getting arrested. At least that's what I hoped he would think.

I got a good look at his property from public records. It was easy if you knew where to look. Then I went to Google Earth to get a bird's eye view. The entire layout was incredible. It was awe inspiring. A huge mansion, he had tennis courts, a pool and every other thing you'd expect a very wealthy guy to own. And it was set only one hundred years from the cliffs overlooking the Pacific Ocean. I could only imagine the panoramic views from the place. All in all it consumed several acres of

California coastline and had to be worth a fortune. But the terrain was perfect for what I had in mind.

I noodled out a plan, picking the insertion spot. Then I mapped three different escape routes should I need them. The most important thing I had on my side was the element of surprise. It was everything. I double checked the gear in my large, camouflaged backpack. Ghillie suit, camouflage, weapons, some tools of the trade and night vision goggles. Satisfied, I brought it all out to Rob's father's truck. Sure enough, the truck had a For Sale sign in the back window that read $8,000 Or Best Offer. Below that was a phone number. I took the sign out of the window. I didn't need people calling Rob's dad saying that they'd seen the truck driving down the road and making offers on it. That might be tough for Rob to explain. I walked to the side of the house and found the garden hose. Watering a small patch of dirt between the hedges I soon had a bit of mud. I smeared this over the back of the tailgate making sure to obscure part of the license plate.

I got in, cranked it up, and worked my way to the Pacific Coast Highway. I headed south. It was a nice drive and I watched surfers peeling left and right breakers as I skirted the coastline. After about an hour I found the place I was looking for and pulled into the Sycamore Canyon Campgrounds. I was in full hippie disguise and even flashed the guy at the gate a peace sign. He grinned as he handed me the change for the twenty I'd given him. As suspected, there was a camera at the gate recording each vehicle that entered. This is why I'd covered the license plate with mud. If stopped, it would appear as if I'd been off roading and I could explain easily that away. But this way, they would get nothing except the fact that I was driving a Ford F-150. And there were hundreds of thousands of them on the roads. I drove the truck to the far end of the massive park. It was a few hours before nightfall but that was how I'd planned it. Arriving after dark might have aroused suspicion.

I knew that the trek up the steep canyon would be difficult. But it was nothing I hadn't done many times before and in worse conditions. Afghanistan had some back breaking mountains so this would be nothing.

I locked the truck and grabbed my gear from the back. Inside the large camouflaged backpack I had three weapons. A karambit combat knife, a Sig Sauer 9mm pistol and the Barrett .50 caliber sniper rifle. I'd broken the rifle down into two components, the lower receiver and upper receiver. This way it fit into the pack. Walking around with a large sniper rifle in the hills of California would not have been a great idea.

Earlier that day I'd gone into Oxnard to do a little shopping. I bought the most contrived, obvious hiking clothes that I could find. Tan cargo shorts with creased pleats and a braided belt. The shirt was a breezy, multi-pocketed button up job with ventilated side mesh. I felt like an idiot but it had the desired effect. I looked like I was straight out of a Hiker's World catalog. As always, I wore the dark sunglasses and my long hair ball cap.

Grabbing the compass out of my pocket, I got my bearings. I started heading up the canyon towards Kenealy's property line. It was only a couple miles away but I would go slow. I wanted it dark by the time I got there.

After hiking for some time through scrub and sand washes, I came upon a menacing barrier. Between deeply planted posts sunk every ten feet, ran razor sharp concertina wire. Strung at six inch intervals, there would be no squeezing through this obstacle. Not without slicing one's self to ribbons. Signs, nailed to each post, warned hikers that this was government land. Trespassers would face federal prosecution. Another sign warned of motion detection and roving patrols. These would persuade even the cockiest of 'blaze my own trail' granola muncher's to turn around.

Government property my ass, I thought. But I knew it served its purpose. There were always a few hard cases, those who viewed fences as a challenge. Those who might consider trespassing on private property would think twice before doing so on government land. Big Brother had a way of scaring people.

Removing a pair of wire cutters from the pack, I made quick work of the bottom four strands of wire. I then low crawled under with no problem. Creeping to a thicket, I took off my backpack. After assembling the Barrett, I donned the ghillie suit. I slid the pistol and the karambit into one of the suits hidden pockets. Now the real work began.

Stashing my pack in the thick foliage, I took out my compass and plotted an azimuth to where I wanted to set up. Having looked at the Google Earth shot of the property, I knew precisely where I'd have the best angle and line of sight.

I stayed low and crept up the ravine, winding my way to where the hill crested. I paused to take a good look. The terrain, although patchy and rugged was for the most part flat. It swept west towards the daunting cliffs and mighty Pacific Ocean. And there, rising above it all sat Kenealy's mansion. It was magnificent.

I lay prone and became part of the terrain. Low crawling at a painstaking clip, I inched toward the predetermined location. In my right hand, I gripped the Barrett. As with the job in the mountains, it was also swathed in camouflaged rags meant to match the surroundings.

If I'd simply stood and walked, it would have taken me ten minutes. Crawling, it took an hour and a half. It was the discipline.

I finally arrived at the spot. The mansion was seven hundred yards ahead and to my right. Also ahead, but to the left, I could see the edge of the cliffs and the big blue sheet of forever beyond that. From Kenealy's back yard, bathed in moonlight, it had to be breathtaking.

There was a very slight breeze blowing in from the west, but nothing serious enough to alter a shot. When the time came I would calculate a quarter inch of drift. The Barrett round was so fast, it would negate most of the gentle wind from seven hundred yards. Much like the slope on a putting green, if you hit the ball hard it took the break out of the putt. Still, there would be a slight amount of right pull. A quarter to a half inch would compensate for it.

I found a small mound of earth which would not only offer perfect cover, but also serve as a built in rest for the rifle. I got in position and took off the night vision goggles. It was not practical to try and use with them with a sniper rifle as they kept ones eye too far from the scope. As I sighted and adjusted focus, the spectacular mansion rounded into shape.

I couldn't believe what I saw. Fucking Kenealy, I thought.

In front of the house I counted three roving guards, each of them sporting a small machine gun. Uzi's by the looks of them. I also spotted two Doberman's and my heart skipped a beat. I fucking hated dogs. Not as pets, but as adversary's. Ruthless, hard core motherfuckers, they freaked me out in combat. Always went right for the throat with no regard to their own safety.

I went into my built in leg pocket and pulled out the Sig 9mm. It had a silencer attached. I laid it on the ground next to the rifle in case one of the pooches made it this far.

I scanned the windows with the powerful scope. Kenealy had to be home. The guards and the dogs told me that much. I took my time, scanning every solid inch of the place. I wanted to know it intimately. A small palace, the house looked even bigger than the twenty-five thousand square feet cited in the tax records. He'd most likely made some modifications and hadn't let the county know about them. It wasn't as if he would worry about such a triviality.

In the front of the house was a circular driveway adorned with a fountain. There was a limousine and a Bentley convertible parked alongside a row of statues to the left. This guy wasn't rich, he was filthy rich. And he'd not only inherited it, but maintained it through murder and, most likely, a wide array of other crimes. I felt my jaw tighten as I thought about it.

I settled in for what could be a long night. I would leave when sunrise was an hour away if I couldn't get my shot tonight. No matter how good the camouflage, I would be way too exposed in daylight.

Having been a very successful sniper in more than one war zone, I knew what it took to deal with the rigors a long hunt. It was impossible to sight in non-stop. I would scan the perimeter at regular intervals, taking short breaks to keep my muscles from tightening up.

I blew out a soft breath and lowered my forehead to the ground to rest my neck.

And that's precisely the moment that the earth exploded in front of me.

Raging Storm
24

Dirt blasted up, pelting my face with chunks of small rocks. Something struck my left eye, the pain instant and excruciating. I was grateful that the eye had been closed, otherwise I might have lost it forever. As I flinched with the shock, a large piece of my sniper rifle smashed into my forehead. A second round had slammed into the upper receiver. It destroyed the weapon, hammering it into my skull.
I saw stars and the brilliant flash that comes with taking a sharp blow to the head. My world spun and the attack seemed a foggy, distant thing. It took only a second before I regained my senses and training took over. I rolled to my left and the mound I'd been in front of disintegrated as another bullet crashed into it. I had to move. Fast. Standing would be suicide so I began to roll as fast as I could in the direction of the cliffs.
I heard the distant whine of the Dobermans. I stopped rolling and looked towards the house. Flashlights were bobbing up and down as men ran, closing the distance between us. I also heard the gas powered motors of off

road vehicles roar to life by the house.
Luckily, they were still several hundreds of yards away. Rounds began splashing in as men began firing in my general direction. They were shooting from the hip as they advanced, laying down grazing fire. Sweeping the ground and hoping to score a lucky hit. I turned my head and scanned the dark horizon. The cliffs were roughly fifty yards to my left. I knew from studying the terrain earlier that it was at least an eighty feet drop to the beach below. But there was nowhere else to go. I had no choice.
Things went from bad to worse. I heard the panting of the first dog closing in fast and realized that the 9mm was back where I had been lying.
Shit.
My hand shot down to the suit pocket. It closed around the karambit. Fighting panic, I pulled it out and unsheathed it. The dog was almost on top of me. I could see him now. His eyes were open wide, ears laid back and fangs bared. He closed on me. Twenty feet. Ten. Five. Pushing back, I made it to a sitting position as he leapt. Offering my left forearm, the dog barreled into me like a freight train. His teeth clamped down as he struck. The ghillie suit absorbed most of the force, but it still hurt like hell. As his jaws closed, I brought the karambit around and plunged it into his side. Together, we rolled backwards from the force of the impact. I pushed him away, yanking the blade out and prepared for his next attack. The Doberman, yelping in great pain, regained his feet and spun to face me. He continued to cry out as he stared at me. I held the blade out. And to my

surprise, he turned and ran off. His high pitched howls fading as he got farther away.

The approaching men must have temporarily lost sight of my position. I could still hear them firing, but there were no rounds coming close to me. With little time left, I got to my feet and crouched low, sprinting towards the cliff. As I approached the edge, I heard the second dog. He was almost on me, his rapid breathing was terrifying and I knew he was about to leap. I could see the edge of the cliff looming. Spinning around, I pushed backwards as the thing dove. Its momentum carried it over me. I could feel the heat of the damn thing. I hit my back and slid, feeling my shoulders go over the edge of the cliff. I grabbed at the earth forcing myself to a stop. The dog wasn't so lucky. It was the thing of nightmares how eerily silent it was as he sailed into the abyss. No barking or whining. He made no sound at all. A few seconds later I heard him hit the bottom with a dull thud. With labored breathing, I rose up to see the flashlights were getting very close. The men would be on me before long. A powerful beam of light found me and I dropped, hugging the ground. They had my position. Only a couple hundred yards away they would be here in half a minute. The dirt erupted around me and I heard the whine and snapping sound that bullets make when they pass very close by. I had no choice.

The cliffs in California have finger draws and cuts caused by erosion and rain runoff. While steep, they provide a crevice, something to grab. If I got lucky and found one it might slow me down. It was the best I could hope for. If I hit a sheer drop it would be like jumping off an eight story building. End of story. But there was neither time nor choice in the matter.

I saw one such grade about twenty feet behind me and frantically crawled towards it. I prayed that none of the lead flying towards me would find its mark.

Going over the side, I fell a good ten feet before slamming into the steep ridge of a finger draw. I bounced and as I did, plunged the tiny, four inch karambit deep into the crusted earth's surface. It slowed me down just enough that I was able to spin my body so that my feet were now leading the fall. I hit another jutting edge of earth and spun again. Now my head was closer to the bottom than the rest of me. I used the knife, my fingers and the toes of my boots to dig in, to create friction, anything to slow myself down. I tumbled and slid and bounced and before I knew it I was at the bottom in a twisted mess of legs, arms and ghillie suit. But I was alive.

I lay still, breathing heavily and wondered what the odds of doing that twice were. Lights appeared on top of the cliff. They shined down towards me and I thrust back with my legs, getting as close to the wall of earth as possible. Bullets started slamming into the ground in front of me and I realized that it might be a good idea to move. Keeping as close to the cliff wall as possible, I started running south.

I left the men atop the cliff and didn't look back until I was one hundred yards down the beach. I clung to the protection of the wall. Dropping to my knees in the soft sand, I struggled to catch my breath. My heart pounded so hard I thought I would have a heart attack then and there. I took deep, gulping breaths of air as I waited for my body to calm down. They couldn't follow me down the cliff. There was no way. At least, I don't know anybody who would be crazy enough to try. Unless their lives were at stake. I was okay. I had made it. Somehow. I would work my way back to the truck. I was going to make it, I thought.

And that's when I heard it.

In the distance. A sound that made me freeze. The all too familiar whumping sound of helicopter blades.

Shit. New problem.

Big problem.

I immediately began tearing my ghillie suit and boots off as the sound grew louder. I had a T-Shirt on underneath the camouflage but I left that on. It was dark olive drab and would not give me away. I saw the light of the helicopter as it flew down the coastline. The large, swinging spotlight swept the sand and the base of the cliff wall.

There was nowhere to go and the thing would be on top of me in less than twenty seconds. I yanked my last boot off and keeping low, sprinted like a madman for the surf. As soon as I entered the water, I was pretty much up to my waist. The Pacific gets deep fast, at least in this part of California. I dove under the spray, feeling the power of the incoming swells throw my body around like a rag doll. Holding my breath I took great, powerful strokes and headed for deeper water. When my lungs couldn't take anymore, I rose up and took a desperate, deep breath. Bad idea as the next wave hit me directly in the face as soon as I opened my mouth. I coughed, choked and then vomited salt water. While I retched, puking my guts up, I watched, dumbstruck with fear, as the chopper trained its light on the spot I had just left. The pilot must have spotted my ghillie suit because he hovered in place and lowered for a closer look.

And then my heart went into my throat as the thing did a very slow and scary turn towards me. They knew I'd made for the water. There was only one thing that would happen now and sure enough, it happened. The blades tilted, rear end of the chopper flaring up. The spotlight hit the water as the death machine accelerated, heading straight for me. I took another deep breath and went under the water again. This time I headed north.

I heard the blasting of the gunships 30mm cannon as the projectiles churned up the water behind me. Swimming for my life, I pushed as hard and as fast as I could. When I couldn't last another second I surfaced. This time I turned my head towards the shore to avoid catching another wave in the face. The last thing I needed was to swallow any more of the Pacific. Taking another quick breath I dove under again, swimming like I never had before.

The cannons continued to fire, tearing through the water. Whatever a 30mm round hits, it destroys. If you get shot in the arm, it tears your arm off. They use the damn things against armor. One of those big rounds would have finished me. After another gulp of air I dove again, pumping my arms and legs for all I was worth. Before long the chopper was in the distance, sweeping the beach and the surf as it headed south. The sound of gunfire stopped. I kept swimming but angled in towards the beach.

When I finally made it to the sand I flipped onto my back, exhausted. I needed to give my aching, screaming muscles a break. The pain was excruciating but after a long, cold rest, I felt my body calming down. I could no longer hear the helicopter so I stood and made it to the base of the cliffs. I started a slow jog north. In a few minutes I came parallel with the state park and spotted a few campfires in the distance. Almost home, I told myself.

I jogged around the base of the last cliff. As the land opened up I headed east into the parks scrub and forest. Almost out on my feet, I fell into a thicket of brush and stayed put.

What the hell had happened? How in the hell had I been compromised? A thousand questions tore through my mind. I rested long enough to feel a second wind before realizing that I'd better get to my truck as soon as possible. If they didn't already know I'd gained entry through the state park, it wouldn't be long before they figured it out. I was tempted to find my way back to the barbed wire to retrieve my pack, but it wasn't worth the risk. I had hidden the trucks key under the wheel well. Everything else I could replace. Still, it had been an expensive evening. I lost everything. The Barrett, my Sig 9mm, the Ghillie suit. I'd even let go of the karambit as I swam for my life. I had another one in my duffel bag, but it pissed me off because that one had been my favorite.

I grinned as I made my way through the park. Here I was upset about a goddamn knife. It started to dawn on me. I was the luckiest son of a bitch on the planet. It was a goddamn miracle I had survived that. I made it to my truck without further incident. Before long I was heading up the Pacific Coast Highway towards my Oxnard hideout.

Raging Storm
25

As I made my way north, the adrenaline rush faded and I felt myself crashing. My right leg began to ache. It felt broken. It might be. I drove in silence and tried to make sense of what the hell had happened. Most of it I could piece together. What I couldn't figure was how the motherfucker had a Huey gunship? How the hell was that even legal?

One thing was for sure though, that was a well planned and well executed assault. By Kenealy. He must have had a sniper in place for some time.

Waiting. For me.

I wondered how long the sniper had laid in place, scanning the perimeter. And I never heard a shot. The fact that he had a silenced weapon mattered. It meant he was a professional. Ordinary people didn't have silenced sniper rifles. I knew one thing for sure, if I lived to be one hundred, I would never figure out how he missed me. Other than that dirt pile. Hiding behind that small dirt mound had saved my life. I could only surmise that the shooter had been positioned very close to the house if not in it. From 700 yards I could understand the shot dipping a bit but a good sniper would have adjusted for that. Still…a head shot is not an easy mark from 700 yards.

No mattered how many ways I looked at it, in the end all that mattered was that the shots had missed. And on top of that, before the sniper had even fired his first shot, the dogs had been set loose. They were on me too soon after the initial impact. It had been coordinated.

I shuddered as I thought about the dogs. Fuck, those things were fast. Crossed seven football fields like it was nothing. I thought about the first dog. He ran away. I never heard of a dog running away. I couldn't say exactly where my knife had gone in but it must have sliced into the biggest damn nerve. The poor thing was in horrible pain. And the second dog came at me too fast. That was a Doberman's main flaw. They were good attack dogs but they tended to jump for their prey. A German Shepherd would have slid to a stop as it was grabbing me. Or it would have barreled into me, but it wouldn't have gone airborne like that. It was bad luck for the Doberman that there was a cliff there. I actually felt bad for the dogs, they didn't know right from wrong, they were only doing what they'd been trained to do.

So what was my excuse, I asked myself? I knew right from wrong, but I'd still decided to become judge, jury and executioner. What the hell did I think would happen? Of course innocent people would get hurt. How did I not know that back then? I felt the shame return. I couldn't help it. I couldn't stop beating myself up. But I deserved it. I'd killed a man. An innocent man. Made his wife a widow. Like I'd been left a widower. My actions had caused irreparable pain.

And it looks like I'm losing this fight ...

The thought fueled my hatred. Both for myself and Kenealy. I didn't care what happened to me, I was going to even the score with that son of a bitch. It was now my sole reason for living.

I arrived at my new, albeit temporary, home and pulled into the garage. Getting out of the truck, I limped into the house and walked straight to the master bath. I gingerly stripped out of my boxers and T-shirt and looked at myself in the full length mirror. Good God, what a fucking mess. Torn up from head to my toes, I had a slew of deep scratches and a few rather nasty gashes.

I examined my leg, pressing down on the inside of my shin where the calf muscle meets the tibia. I ran my fingers against the bone and didn't feel any break or crease. Not that I would have been able to diagnose a break but I couldn't exactly go and get an x-ray. I'd jammed it damn hard when I hit the bottom of the cliff. But I could walk. It was most likely nothing more than a deep bruise. I moved closer to the mirror to examine my face. The earth that had slammed into my face with the first shot had left many small nicks and cuts. I also had a very nasty welt from the Barrett smashing into my forehead. The rifle had taken the full brunt of the second shot and that alone had saved my life. It hurt like hell but it was better than catching the round in the face, I told myself. That would have pretty much wrapped things up for Kenealy as far as my sorry ass was concerned. I could imagine him talking to the cops.

'Yes, officer. I can't believe this psycho came all the way from Florida for me. Thank God I hired extra security.'

'Well, Mr. Kenealy,' the officer would respond. 'You are one hell of an American hero for taking this bastard out. You'll get the highest civilian decoration for this.'

'Shucks, officer. It weren't nothing...'

They'd probably invite the asshole to the White House. I turned the shower on and got right in, not waiting for the water to heat up. After my swim in the frigid Pacific this was nothing. The water warmed as I tried to make sense of it.

If Kenealy had his own mercenaries, his own snipers, then why the hell was I necessary? Why the entire charade in Florida? Why go through all that? The only reason that made any sense was what I'd told Captain Suto, Kenealy wanted me as a fall guy. It wasn't enough to simply kill Wakefield, he needed a shooter. He needed to provide a murderer. Otherwise, there would always be an element that considered him a suspect. He had to remove all doubt that he was innocent. There were too many things I had to guess about, but one thing made a hell of a lot of sense. This guy was smarter than shit. He'd outsmarted me at every turn. And I was surviving due to dumb luck.

Escaping from GSI, Inc.? Luck.

Sleeping in the guest bedroom and surviving a three man hit squad? Luck.

Having a trained sniper miss a fairly easy shot? Incredible luck.

Falling off a fucking cliff? Having a Huey gunship on my ass? Living to talk about it? Dumb ass luck mixed with damn good training.

As I pondered these thoughts I knew one thing for sure. My luck was going to run out. That was a mathematical certainty. And one more thing was also a certainty. I would never underestimate William Kenealy again. There was no way I was going to go after him head on like that again. He was two steps ahead of me and had been since the first time I saw him in group therapy. He was one smart dude. Okay. From this point forward, I was going guerrilla. Full on harassment operation. I recalled one of my favorite quotes from Sun Tzu's book The Art of War.

"Let your plans be dark and impenetrable as night, and when you move, fall like a thunderbolt."

I needed rest. And then I needed to form a plan. But most importantly, I needed to stop reacting and operating on an emotional level. I had to slow down and stop going for the jugular. It wouldn't work with this guy. There was one thing I was damn certain of, I had the upper hand when it came to what I could do to fuck his world up. He might have some skilled boys, but I had the advantage of invisibility. They had no way of knowing where I was. But I knew exactly where they were. And I had nothing left to lose except my life. And they could have it. As long as I got that bastard first.

I got out of the shower and toweled off. Going through the medicine cabinet, I saw that Rob's parents had a pretty good stockpile of meds. I found some antibiotic cream and applied it to every cut and scratch that I could find. Damn near went through half the tube. I found some ibuprofen and took four of them. They would help with both the swelling and the pain. After putting a few band aids on the deeper cuts, I walked to the bedroom and my duffel bag. Throwing on a fresh pair of boxers, I climbed into bed. I was asleep the second my head hit the pillow.

Raging Storm
26

My eyes flew open as I awoke in a panic. There was somebody in the house.
How, I thought, still coming out of the stupor of sleep? There was no way they could have followed me. My first thought was a weapon. I instinctively turned to my right. Nothing. I didn't even have a piece near the bed. I had abandoned the 9mm on Kenealy's property in my desperate flight for life. Goddamn I was getting complacent. I listened and heard footsteps. I hear drawers opening and water running. Pots and pans rattled with the sound of somebody choosing a skillet or a pan from a bottom cupboard.
I relaxed.
Nobody was going to come for me and then decide to whip up some breakfast first, I thought with a smile. I swung my legs out of bed and walked to the bedroom door. Twisting the knob, I pushed it open a crack and peered out.
There stood Rob in his parent's kitchen. I could see grocery bags on the counter. He had his back to me and

was measuring out scoops of coffee.

"Hey asshole," I said. I opened the door and stepped out of the bedroom. "You scared the crap out of me."

Rob laughed, keeping his back to me.

"Sorry, bro, I thought you might need the sleep," he said. As he turned around I saw the smile on his face. Until his eyes locked on me. Then he froze.

"Dude! What the fuck happened to you?!"

"That bad?" I asked.

"Are you fucking kidding?" He said.

I walked to a rectangular mirror which hung from the living room wall. Besides the scratches and cuts, my face and body now showed ugly purple swelling and bruises. My left eye was bloodshot red from the peppering it took and my right leg was swollen and turning purple. The left side of my torso looked like Mike Tyson had used it as a heavy bag.

"Yeah," I said. I spoke slowly, nodding my head as I performed the inspection. "Falling off a cliff isn't as much fun as it sounds."

"Ryder, are you all right?"

He wasn't playing, there was heavy concern in his voice. He dropped the coffee spoon and stepped towards me.

"You might need to go to the hospital."

"You may be right. But obviously I can't do that."

"What happened?"

"Keep making that coffee and I'll tell you."

"Dude, forget the coffee, you need help."

"Rob," I said. "It looks a lot worse than it is. Seriously."

Rob grimaced, realizing that the discussion was over. He continued to ladle the coffee grains into a paper filter and then placed it into the Mr. Coffee machine. Hitting a red button, the water started to heat and black liquid began to fill the carafe.

I took a seat on the couch and grabbed the remote control. The TV came to life and I found the local, all day news program. I wanted to see if Kenealy had reported our little altercation. I doubted it.

Rob, true friend that he was, brought me a steaming cup of joe.

"I was going to make a big breakfast. You up for that?" He asked.

"Shit yes. I'm starving, man."

"Cool. You chill and we'll talk over breakfast."

For the next twenty minutes I flipped channels. I checked both the local and national news. There was no mention of Kenealy. No mention of last nights activities. I wasn't surprised. He didn't want the authorities to know I was here. Didn't want the interference. He would deal with me himself. Or so he thought.

Perfect.

The small house filled with the mouth watering aroma of bacon, eggs and buttered toast. Rob was making enough to feed a small platoon. I realized that I hadn't had a decent meal in many days and planned on stuffing myself until I couldn't move.

"Let's go, troop," my friend ordered as he set the plates on the table.

I walked over and sat across from him. As we shoveled the food down, I looked over at my good friend. My thoughts went back in time to a firefight that Rob and I had been in during the battle for Fallujah.

I had just breached a house and was sweeping the first floor when a group of three insurgents burst out of a side room. They were firing AK-47's at me. Falling to a prone position, I returned fire and dropped one of them. The others two scrambled for cover. I did the same. I found my way into a back room that was their version of a bathroom. It had no toilet, only had a hole in the floor. I kicked the door shut with my foot and got as low as I could. It was my own tiny little death trap with no exit. I remembered thinking that this was a very bad and very stupid decision. I was at a serious disadvantage and the enemy knew it.

The two remaining insurgents started firing into the room. Round after round tore through the thin door. As was trying to get as low as I could when my world rocked with a deafening explosion. They had tossed a grenade against the door. It had disintegrated. The damn door was gone. Things had gone from bad to worse in the space of a second. The next grenade they tossed would come right in the room with me. To make matters worse, another two bad guys who had been on the second floor joined their buddies. I heard them running down the stairs, the excitement evident in their voices. I remembered thinking about Debbie and wishing I could see her one more time.

I was a dead man. And I knew it. But I would take a couple with me. I grabbed a fragmentation grenade from my flak jacket, pulled the pin and tossed it out into the main room. It exploded but didn't seem to have any ill effect on the bastards. They kept shouting back and forth in Arabic, thrilled to have a marine trapped like a rat. It was going to be a good day for them.

It had been foolish of me to enter without backup but going house to house got monotonous and I'd made a mistake. Making mistakes in combat generally led to very poor health. And this mistake would have been no different if Rob hadn't showed up with Pete, another of my platoon members. I heard him call my name from outside the house. He was trying to figure out where I was. I yelled back, screaming that there were at least 4 of the enemy in here with me. Rob called out, telling me to keep my head down. And then the tough bastard stood up right in front of a large window. He started shooting into the main room with the intention of drawing their fire.

The four insurgents unloaded in his direction. The sound of their AK-47's was deafening in the small house. After a few tense seconds, the shooting wound down. I lay there, not daring to move. Hopefully, they would think I was dead.

Things got eerily quiet and I could hear the bad guys reloading. With their focus now on Rob and the front of the house, it was their turn to make a mistake. They neglected to watch the back door. Like I said, making mistakes in combat rarely ends well. They were so concerned with what was in front of them they never saw Pete enter from the back. Standing only ten feet behind them, he started banging away with a large caliber, belt fed machine gun. The ones who were not immediately torn to pieces tried to make it to a door on the far side of the room. Rob was waiting for them. They ran right into his fire. It was over as fast as it had started.

It was a close call for me. Too damn close.
Rob found me lying on the floor of my little tomb.
"Dumb ass," he had said. He smiled down at me.
"Fuck you," I'd answered. "What took you so goddamn long? If I'm gonna keep flushing out bad guys you're going to need to respond a little quicker than that."
He laughed and extended a hand, pulling me up to my feet.
"Sorry," he'd said.
Rob and I had experienced quite a few firefights together. We'd slugged it out with some very determined bad guys on more than one occasion, but that time was the scariest. Pinned down, outnumbered and moments away from death, Rob had saved my life. If he hadn't exposed himself like he did, they would have carried me out of that house in a body bag. I owed him. Big time. But it's nothing I wouldn't have done for him either. That's the way it worked. War creates a brotherhood that is indescribable. It is almost impossible to understand if you haven't experienced it firsthand. Ask any veteran who's seen combat.
Now, the same fearless guy who had faced down four armed insurgents, sat across from me and watched me eat. He looked at me in a way he never had before. He was waiting. Waiting for answers, for an explanation. I guess I owed him that much.
"Dude," I asked. "What are your plans for the next couple days?"
"You're looking at them, amigo. I plan on hanging out with you and I even gave some thought to getting hammered drunk tonight."

My face clouded over. I thought back to the night that had changed my life. Rob didn't know how close to home that statement hit. Hammered drunk had gotten me into this mess. I looked down at my plate. I couldn't maintain eye contact.

In your world I have no meaning, though I'm trying hard to understand...

Of course I'd been drunk since the night of Debbie and the kids murder. I was blind drunk the night I put three guys in the hospital. That had set me on a collision course with anger management and William Kenealy. Meeting Kenealy had changed my life all over again and none of it was good. All because I couldn't open up. Couldn't get all the bad shit out. I had opted for getting drunk and hating myself. First I hated myself for failing my family. And then I hated myself for killing an innocent man. It was all a shitty mess. I looked up and struggled to control my emotions as Rob looked on with concern and love. Love for a comrade who's in pain. Love for a brother.

"Tell me," he said.

"I don't know where to begin, man."

"Yeah, you do."

I felt my eyes fill with wetness. I forced myself not to blink, not to let the tears roll down my face. I couldn't have that. I had to be a fucking hard-ass. I shook my head and pursed my lips together. Fuck me, I thought, where was this coming from?

"Dude," Rob said. He spoke in a soft tone. "It's me, man."

"What do you want to know, Rob!?" I yelled.

I lost control and great, salty streams of pain rolled down my face. I gave up the tough guy act and let loose.
"You want to know how I let some whacked out meth heads get the drop on me and murder Debbie and the kids right in front of me?!"
I watched Rob's face change. His pained expression mirrored my own.
"Do you want to hear how I had to watch some motherfucking junkie point a shotgun at my Sasha!? My little Sasha! Do you want to hear how her tiny head came apart?!"
"It's okay, man," he said. He grit his teeth and tried not to break down with me. "Keep going."
"Hunter turned away!"
I was sobbing now.
"The tough little guy tried to roll away and the heartless prick shot him through the back!"
Rob nodded, listening intently. He remained quiet, knowing that more than anything else I needed to get this shit out.
"Dude, I begged this scumbag,"
I cried. The tears were going good now and I didn't even try to hide them. "I begged him to kill me. To torture me. To fucking saw my head off. I didn't care. Me, man. Me. I begged."
I lowered my head and cried. I mean, this was the last thing I'd expected. I guess it was time. Maybe it was seeing Rob again. I don't know but I fucking lost it.
"I can't even imagine, bro." His voice was soft. Sympathetic.
I wiped my eyes as my mood turned a darker shade.

"Afterwards, I just wanted to kill. To destroy all the bad in this fucked up world. To crush anything that could that to innocent children. I started drinking way too much. I got in a bar fight. Nearly killed three dudes. Three dudes who didn't deserve the beating I gave them. They weren't looking for trouble. I didn't have to do what I did to them."

"Dude, shit happens."

"Awww, fuck that, Rob!" I glared across the table at him. "Don't you do that! Don't you give me a pass!"

"Shit." He paused to emphasize his words. "Happens." He glared back at me, determined to combat my self-loathing with his own grit.

"Yeah, man. Shit happens. It sure as hell does. Because of that, I got a two year suspended sentence and had to go to this whiny fucking group therapy bullshit."

"That bullshit can help, brother."

"Yeah, well it sure helped me. Helped me get set up by this asshole Kenealy."

"And we're going to fix it, Ryder! We're going to find a way. He had to make a few mistakes. He can't make this frame stick."

"Frame!?" I laughed through the pain as I stared at him. "Frame?!"

Rob's eyes narrowed.

"Man, is that what you think?!" I yelled. "Rob! I did it. I killed the guy!"

Rob leaned back in his chair. He seemed genuinely shocked.

"I killed a bunch of guys! I became a hitter for this psychopath!"

Rob stared at me. He didn't know how to process this so he remained silent and thought for a while. I sat quiet and let him.

"Ryder," he said. "You told me on the phone that you didn't do it."

"No, I didn't" I answered. "I said it's not how it looks."

Rob looked down at his plate and shook his head. He was trying to wrap his head around this new information. His good friend, his wartime buddy was a murderer. And now he knew.

"I killed in the war, and it was all right. I killed because the enemy were evil fucks who needed killing. And after Debbie and the kids were murdered…"

I looked at my friend and shook my head. It was no use. I couldn't pretend. Not anymore.

"You know what?" I said. "That's all bullshit. I'm not the first guy who had loved ones murdered. It happens all the time. That doesn't excuse what I did. I'm a killer, man. I'm guilty as sin."

"Ryder," Rob said. Speaking in a slow and methodical monotone, he needed to get a handle on this. "Start at the beginning. What happened when you met this guy? Tell me everything."

I spent the next half hour laying it all out. What Kenealy had proposed. How we were ridding the world of some horrible people. People who preyed on others. People who raped, killed, sold drugs to kids, you name it. I went into detail on each hit. I told him about the weapons, the truck, the house on Hilton Head. Everything. I wrapped it all up by describing my botched assault at his mansion the previous evening.

When I finished, I got up from the table. I walked over and fell onto the couch. I could no longer sit across from Rob. I couldn't face him. I was done. Empty. Drained. Not quite six months after I'd lost my family, I was now a murderer on the run. And I'd involved one of my best friends.

I made the decision then and there.

"Call the cops, man."

Rob, who had sat in silence, digesting everything, looked at me with a puzzled expression.

"What?"

"Dude, this is the end of the road. And now I've dragged you into it. But you can set it all straight by calling the cops. I'll tell them you didn't know, that after I told you what I'd done you turned me in because you're a solid citizen. You'll be a hero."

"Ryder," he said. "Please don't take this the wrong way. But fuck you."

I laughed. I couldn't help myself. Rob did not share in the laugh. He continued to glare at me.

"The shit you did in Washington is fucked up. No doubt. But it sounds like all those others needed to go. The scumbag who raped and murdered that little girl? Good! I hope you made the motherfucker suffer!"

I stared at him.

"You've got yourself convinced you're some fucking boogey man. That you're some monster running through the countryside like Frankenstein. Like you deserve to have villagers chasing you with torches and pitchforks, but it ain't like that. I'm not saying I agree with the route you took, but the fact is you saved lives. You saved more than you took. And you definitely saved more children from that piece of shit in Jacksonville."

I looked at the floor and said nothing.

"Dude, you got played," Rob continued. "No doubt. But there isn't a fucking guy in our unit who doesn't wish he could take out some of society's trash. You did it. It might be wrong, but it sure as hell feels right."

I let out a huge breath of air. I had only been awake an hour yet I felt exhausted. And my body ached with the beating I'd taken. I was spent, both emotionally and physically.

"Ryder," he continued. "This world is a better place because of you. That is a fact. The guy in D.C. is collateral damage. That's cold blooded and I'm sure it's a demon that will chase you for the rest of your life. But the fact is, you are better to society as a free man."

I looked up from the carpet to lock eyes with him.

My brother.

"So once again," he said. "Fuck you. I'm not calling the cops or anybody else. You and I are going to figure out how to fix this. Got it?"

"Rob, I'm too tired to get anything right now. I need to rest up for a while."

"I understand. You take care of getting better. Everything else you leave to me. My folks will be in their summer place in Michigan for another four months. That's more than enough time to handle this shit."

"There's nothing to figure out," I said. "My only goal is to kill that motherfucker. That's it."

Rob pushed away from the table and walked to the couch. Stopping in front of me, he extended his hand. I sat looking up at him for a moment and then grabbed it. Yanking me up off the couch, he pulled me close, wrapping me in a fierce bear hug. I squeezed back. We held each other and I felt the bond of brotherhood that I should have trusted six months ago.

"Dude," I choked up as I felt myself losing it again.

"Fuck that, man. No need to even say it."

He shoved me and I fell back onto the couch. Walking back to the table he grabbed the dirty plates. I could see his wheels turning. He was always more analytical than me. Rob was planning now.

"Okay, first thing we need to do is get you some cash. And you don't go anywhere without that fucking disguise on. Hell, I didn't even recognize you. But you'll need some things from time to time. Groceries, ammo, booze. I have a few thousand dollars in my savings account. It's yours."

"Uhhh, Rob?" I said.

"Yeah?" he answered.

"Cash isn't going to be a problem."

That stopped him in his tracks and he looked at me with a goofy question mark on his face.

I smiled.

I'd forgotten to tell him about the money.

Raging Storm
27

I woke up early the next morning with a splitting headache. Not that I cared a whole lot. Last night had been exactly what I'd needed. Rob and I had grilled thick, rib-eye steaks. To accompany corn on the cob and baked potatoes. I had an old family recipe for grilling potatoes. You slice the potatoes into several staggered pieces without cutting them completely off. Then you stuff each open wedge with butter, ground garlic and onions. Wrap them twice in tin foil and throw them on the barbecue for a good hour. You grill the steaks right next to them. It was delicious and the best meal I'd had since that beach party. The last night I still had a family. The last time I had real purpose in life.

I *ain't missing you, no matter what I might say...*

We'd also enjoyed several blended, Patron margaritas and almost a case of beer. Everything had gone down very easy. Rob and I traded stories about what had been going on in our lives. Meaning the last couple years, before the night I'd lost my family, we'd already covered that. This time we discussed happier memories. It'd felt great unloading yesterday. I wasn't embarrassed to have cried in front of him. Once again, if you served in a combat unit, you understood how close you became with one another. For years, we did everything together. Ate, worked out, hell even showered. It was a fraternity that defied accurate description. He was more a brother to me than if he'd been born to my parents.

I threw my legs out of bed and with that simple motion, felt a bit better. That very human impulse to move forward, to get on with it can make a difference. The swelling had gone way down, but I had always been a quick healer. It seemed the unburdening had been therapeutic both emotionally and physically.

In any case, after years of hard drinking with my recon unit, I knew the best way to deal with a hangover. I walked to the dresser in which I'd deposited my clothes and dug out a pair of shorts and a T-shirt. Then I threw a pair of socks and a set of running shoes on and walked into the family room. I chuckled under my breath when I saw that that Rob was still passed out on the couch. In the exact spot I'd left him last night when I'd staggered into my bedroom. Staying as quiet as possible, I walked to the fridge to grab a bottle of water. I downed it in one long drink. Then I let myself out the back door.

After stretching my hamstrings, quads and calves, I started a brisk run in the cool morning air. It felt exhilarating. For the first time in a long time, I enjoyed the simple pleasure of the wind and the rising sun on my face. I headed west toward Mandalay Beach Road which ran parallel with the coast. There were very few people out as California was just waking up. But I was already out, racing through it.

Once thing I knew with certainty, I needed to get back into shape. Serious shape. If I was going to take on Kenealy and his army of mercenaries, I needed to be at my peak best. As the debacle atop the cliffs two nights ago had illustrated, you never knew when you'd get pushed to your limits.

I felt good considering the amount of alcohol I'd consumed and after the third mile, broke into the next gear. My runners high kicked in and I felt like I was flying. I did a quiet count as I ran past the palm trees planted at staggered but equal distances. Whatever the previous time was, I tried to lower it between the next set of trees. My lungs ached but my legs felt strong. This was surprising considering how bad they still looked.

I thought about Kenealy and how he must be feeling this morning. I'm sure he'd been less than pleased when his men failed to drop my bullet riddled corpse at his feet the other night. He'd known I was dangerous but now he also knew that he'd missed his window. I would not make the same mistake twice and I'm sure he knew it. It had to be at Def-con five at the mansion.

Now I would take control. I had tried to match him head on and had almost died. Never again. But now Kenealy knew I was here and that I was gunning for him. It had to have him rattled.

He was out of aces. He'd guessed right that I would go to his mansion, but it hadn't worked out for him. Now I held all the cards because I was invisible. And I was going to get in serious shape. The shape required for a

deadly op. No more alcohol. The right food. Twice a day training regimens. Weight lifting in the evening and hard core cardio in the morning to get the day started.
I pushed myself even harder. The palm trees started ticking by. I felt alive. I didn't even have a hangover anymore.
I thought of Debbie.
Every time I think of you, I always catch my breath...
For the thousandth time I apologized to her silently. I failed you by becoming something you would have hated. But you have to see why I did what I did. What if somebody had taken out those meth heads who murdered you? You and the kids would still be alive today. Surely, that had to count for something, I debated, locked in a silent plea to my deceased wife.
It was no coincidence that I had these skills. No coincidence that I was the man I was. Whatever had gotten me here was what it was. And I was here. Maybe Rob was right. Maybe this wasn't a bad thing. Police can take out evil men. Governments can take out evil regimes and leaders. It was as great a sin that sympathetic, weak judges put scum right back on the street. Freed them so they could continue to inflict pain and suffering on innocent people. The cold hard fact was that some people needed to go. Maybe my mistake was not in doing what I did, but in letting my anger blind me. Blind me into following the directives of a murderous criminal. Except for the last job in Washington, I didn't regret any of them. Killing Wakefield was a horrible tragedy. And although I'd thought it was the right thing to do at the time, that did not excuse it. I would have to

find a way to live with that. I couldn't change what I'd done any more than I could change what happened to my family. But I would find a way to live with both.
I pushed harder. My lungs were screaming, my legs on fire. Sweat poured down my face and I could almost taste the spent tequila as it trickled into the corners of my mouth.
I was in the home stretch. Two hundred yards from the house I broke into a sprint. When I burst through the gate and into the back yard of the house, my heart was pounding out of my chest. I bent at the waist and tried not to puke. Or have a stroke. Forcing myself to take slow, steady breaths, I began pacing the backyard. Every four or five steps I stopped to stretch.
I made my decision then and there. I would continue what Kenealy and I had started, only this time I would gather the intelligence. Not somebody else. Me alone. And my first mission was none other than that rat bastard. I had failed two nights ago, but the next time would be different. I would take my time. I would come up with a plan and then execute it. It was the very least I could do for Bradley Wakefield. That might square the ledger with him in some small way. But I had to be honest with myself. After what Kenealy had done, this one was for me.
I continued pacing the yard, cooling down and stretching. When my heart rate dropped to a normal tempo, I walked back into the house.

Raging Storm
28

I snuck in so as not to wake Rob, but he was already up, sitting on the couch. I laughed as he stared at me with bloodshot eyes, his skin a pasty greenish hue. He looked like death warmed over.

"Oh, hell no," he said. His voice was a weak, sickly rasp. "You did *not* just do a fucking run!"

"Come on marine!" I clapped my hands together. "Go sweat that poison out!"

Rob, remaining silent, extended his arm and offered me a single finger. He slumped into the couch as his eyes rolled back in his head.

"Dude," I said. "You're the one who's still in the Corps. Don't tell me a goddamn civilian can kick your ass."

"I had a lot more tequila than you did, asshole," he said.

"I don't know about all that, amigo. Sounds to me like your panties are riding up on you a bit."

There was that finger again. I chuckled and made for my bedroom.

"I'm gonna shower and get ready for the day. We got some shit to talk about, brother."

I stepped into the room and closed the door. Stripping down, I tossed my drenched clothes into the hamper and walked to the bathroom. I turned the shower on and got in immediately. The cold felt great. I let it wash over me. After all my time training in the chilly Pacific Ocean, there was virtually no cold water that I couldn't handle. I scrubbed up and then shampooed my hair. After rinsing off, I killed the water and grabbed for the towel. I dried myself and then stepped in front of the mirror to brush the little hair I had straight back. I then walked back into the bedroom and threw on a pair of shorts and a V-neck shirt.

Walking back into the family room, I noticed the couch was no longer acting as a hospital bed. Rob was in the kitchen making a pot of coffee. I swear the guy would die if coffee was illegal. I pulled up a bar stool and sat, folding my hands on the counter in front of me. Rob poured me a cup and then himself one. He slid the mug to me like an old west bartender. It stopped right in front of me.

"Nice trick."

"Luck," he said. The raspy voice was still present but he attempted a smile.

Rob flipped a switch on the coffee machine and the red light went out. He turned to face me.

"What do we need to discuss?"

"I've been thinking. Kenealy is a double dealing scumbag, correct?"

"It would appear so."

"Then there has to be others. Others like me that he used."

"That would stand to reason."

"So, I'm going to find somebody."

"How?"

"Well," I said. "I guess I'll start with Google."

Rob laughed.

"Brilliant," he said.

"I'm serious, man, I'll bet if I go back far enough I'll find some info that I can exploit."

"Could be. And I have a contact at HQ who has a bro in intelligence. The guy's stationed in D.C.. Maybe he can slide us a little knowledge?"

"That may not be a good idea. Kenealy has some serious juice in Washington. Your boy might raise a few eyebrows if he starts asking the wrong people questions."

I drank the black coffee and felt its warmth spread through my torso. Any remnants of a hangover were gone. I felt good.

"Listen man," I said. I looked with appreciation at my friend. "Last night was great. Great food, great drinks. It was fucking good to hang out with you again, brother."

"Roger that," he said.

"But that's going to be it for a little while. I've got to get back in shape. I have a feeling I'm going to have to be at my best to take this son of a bitch down."

"I understand and no argument here. I'm not as young as I once was. This shit is getting more and more painful."

"Bah," I said. "You always were a lightweight."

This time he verbalized his obscenity as he turned to leave the kitchen.

I laughed.

"Where you headed?" I asked.

"Might go lie down for a while," he answered. "And since you asked, I'm also giving some thought to puking."

I laughed again and then made my way to the small office. It was an add-on with Red Oak hardwood floors, and what looked like some type of Ash veneer on the walls. There were several built in wall shelves cram packed with history books from World War II to Vietnam. There were also several plaques and framed awards adorning the wall. The one that caught my attention was the Silver Star. I read the citation. It was an awe inspiring story.

Rob's dad had single-handedly held off an enemy assault as his comrades were awaiting an airlift. Manning an M-60 machine gun, he provided cover as the enemy surrounded his unit. Although hit three times, he didn't stop until all the dead and wounded were aboard the chopper. If not for his heroism, the company commander wrote, they would have been overrun. I remembered Rob telling me about it.

I couldn't help but think of the irony. The government makes a big deal about handing out medals and ribbons if you're good at killing for them. But if you take out predators, child rapists and killers on your own they call you a murderer. Well to hell with their accolades. None of it mattered to me anymore. The worst thing I could ever experience in my life had already happened. I had no more downside. I wasn't afraid of dying, and to be honest, I almost looked forward to it. It was the only thing that would reunite me with my family.

In your world I have no meaning, though I'm trying hard to understand...

Sitting down behind the mahogany desk, I lifted the lid of the laptop and signed in. It was a good computer. Very fast. As soon as I got online I went to Google's home page and started searching. I already knew about the companies origin. Founded by his grandfather, later passed down to his father. Kenealy took over in the 90's when his father retired. It wasn't long after he took control that he'd been the subject of a federal investigation. Accused of attempting to bribe a government official, the matter never made it to court. The man he had allegedly tried to bribe recanted. He claimed that he may have misunderstood Kenealy's intentions.

I wondered what type of leverage Kenealy had used. My guess was it was either a threat or a payoff. There were several news outlets who voiced that same opinion but as there was no proof, the story faded away. I continued to scan and read different articles until I came across a link that caught my attention.

Global Securities Employee Sentenced To Twenty Years

I clicked the link and began to learn about a man named Randall Ducey. An upper level manager, he was with the company for many years. Netted in a sting operation, Kenealy hung him out to dry after the indictments came down. GSI stood accused of consorting with a South

American government. A government that the United States was not on good terms with at the time. After Ducey's arrest, Kenealy made a public statement.
"I am deeply saddened and shocked to hear of my employees wrong doing. Improprieties committed in the name of the organization will not be tolerated."
Bullshit.
Ducey entered a plea deal to avoid a life sentence for violation of the espionage act. He got twenty years. Eligible for parole in half that. I noticed the date. He had already served five years. I crossed my fingers and hoped that he wasn't in a prison somewhere on the east coast. After a quick search I found the information I was looking for. I caught a break. Ducey was doing his time at the California Institution for Men in Chino, California. Otherwise known as Chino, the prison was only about thirty five miles east of L.A.
Perfect.
I immediately searched for information on the prison and its visitation policies.

Raging Storm
29

Yesterday I'd spent a good deal of time learning as much as I could about Randall Ducey. The dude was unbelievable. A wunderkind. Number one in his high school class and a perfect 1600 on his SAT's. Yale degree and rumored Skull and Bones member. Harvard MBA, a beautiful wife and three adorable kids. How the hell had this guy managed to wind up in Chino?

I needed to get inside this guy's head. The fact that he jumped the Yale ship and got his Masters degree at Harvard told me something about the man. He liked status. He collected achievements. It wasn't enough to attend Yale. He wanted Harvard on his resume as well. Or at least that's the way I smelled the wind blowing. I could be wrong. Maybe Harvard had a better business school? What did I know? Either way, this guy was one smart cookie.

After looking into company records, I learned that Ducey had joined GSI Inc. in 2004 and was on the fast track for upper management almost immediately. His name attached to several high profile deals that netted the company millions. His intellect would have caught the eye of William Kenealy. A man as smart as Ducey would be a very valuable asset to any organization. That made his felony status all the more a mystery. Violating the espionage act? Crooked business deals involving a South American official? This didn't fit the profile. Ducey was a straight shooter, I'd bet my life on it.

I climbed into the F-150 and got on the 101 East out of Oxnard, following it all the way to Burbank where it became the 134. That went into Pasadena where it turned into interstate 210. I exited at San Dimas and from there it was just a short drive south to Chino. This was one bad ass prison full of some bad ass dudes. How Ducey had landed here and not some cushy, country club prison, was the million dollar question.

As I pulled up to the first security checkpoint I checked my reflection in the rear view mirror. I had on a wig that made me look like a burned out surfer who was still chasing the ultimate wave and the ultimate buzz. The guards were used to shady characters coming to visit their shady guests, so I did my best to fit the bill.

I'd had a fake California drivers license made which was easy enough to score if you know the right people. Thankfully, Rob did and had the entire thing expedited yesterday. All I had to do was e-mail a picture of myself and the license got delivered this morning. My name was Kevin Simmons and I was from Redondo Beach. It was completely bogus of course, so the one hiccup would be the magnetic strip. If they swiped it, it would come up as a user error. The best I could hope for would be to bluff my way in. I would tell the guards that I wore the strip down in the salt water while surfing. That sounded lame but then again, lame was what I was going for.

I pulled to a stop and offered the guard a stupid smile. He gave me the once over and asked for my ID. I handed it to him and he glanced at it for a nanosecond before handing it back to me.

"Drive through this gate and make a right," he said. "You'll see a sign that says Visitor Parking. Understand?"

"Got it, dude," I said.

"Do you have your V Pass?"

I reached over to the passenger seat and grabbed the letter that I hoped would get me into the prison.

"Right here, man," I said. I adopted the stoner accent and smiled at the man as I extended it out the window.

"Not me," he said. "You'll give it the guard at the door."

"Righteous, dude. Thanks."

The man turned back to the magazine he was reading with a disapproving look on his face. He didn't seem to have a very high opinion of Kevin Simmons.

I drove through the gate and made the right that led into the parking lot. Pulling into an open spot, I parked and killed the engine.

The V Pass.

To visit an inmate in the California penal system, you have to fill out forms and get clearance. It's a lengthy process. Unless you know somebody. Again, that's where Rob came in real handy. He'd stayed in touch with a guy who had gotten out of the Corps and became a prison guard. He didn't work at Chino but all the California prisons used the same database. It was a simple matter of putting my fictitious name in the system and then green lighting it. In a matter of minutes I had an electronic V Pass e-mailed to me.

The brotherhood is a strong thing.

I got out of the truck and headed towards the building facing the parking lot. Upon entering, I walked towards a podium where two guards stood.

There were several people in front of me and I waited my turn. Finally a guard motioned for me to approach.

"V Pass and ID, please." he said.

"Sure thing, dude," I said. I gave him a goofy smile and handed him both articles.

The man typed something into the computer and I watched as he read. He then looked at my ID and then back to me. I continued to grin like an idiot.

"Here you go, Mr. Simmons," he returned the documents to me. "Please empty your pockets and put anything metal or electronic into the basket."

I pulled my cell phone out of my pocket along with the little bit of cash I had on me and the truck keys. Dropping them in the basket, I looked up at him.

"Your belt too, please."

"Not wearing one, bro." I lifted my Hawaiian shirt to show the tied drawstring of the swim trunks I'd worn.

"Are you wearing a bathing suit?" The guard asked. He looked amused.

"Yeah, man. The thing online said no jeans or blue button up shirts. But I'm bummed I had to wear these deck shoes. My sandals are wondering what's up."

I laughed at the joke. The guard did not.

"Uh, yeah. No open toed shoes. Thanks for reading it.

Most people don't even do that."

"No problemo, amigo. Now what?"

The guard looked at me like I was a moron.

"Now you walk through the metal detector to where the other officer is standing."

I looked over and a cute female corrections officer raised her hand and wiggled her fingers, waving at me.

"Oh," I said. I walked over to the large portal.

"Now?"

"Well," the woman said. "I'm ready if you are."

I walked through the machine. Silence.

"Okay, you're good to go. Grab your things but at no time take them out of your pocket during your visit. Do you understand?"

"I do," I answered. I took my possessions.

"You are here to see inmate 345723-1 Randall Ducey?" she asked.

"How did you know that?" I feigned shocked amusement.

"It's on your V Pass, darling."

Of course I knew that but I kept up the charade. People tended to relax around idiots.

"Oh yeah."

"Through that door. Walk down the row and take a seat at window 7. Got it?"

"Cool."

I walked to the door and opened it, stepping through to the next room. There was a long wall with ten chairs in front of very thick glass. Each window had a divider for privacy. The windows had several small holes drilled into a softball sized circle. This enabled the inmate and

his guest to converse. The holes were far too small to push anything through. There were two guards positioned in the room, one as I walked in and the other at the far end. Walking past the first chairs I looked to my left and through the windows. I saw a guard on that side as well. The room was full of people talking. I walked past a woman who was in tears and made the mistake of looking at her. The tattooed and hairy inmate on the other side of the glass shot out of his chair.
"What are you looking at?!" He shouted.
I saw one of the guards approach him and whipped my head back around to break eye contact. I didn't want any part of that.
I came to window 7, as it read on the top of the pane, took a seat in the chair and waited. A few moments later a man appeared in front of me. He looked every bit the college boy type. Clean cut, spectacles, pressed prison blues. He looked like he belonged in this place like a nun belongs in a brothel.
He stared at me and remained standing. He appeared to be thinking.
"Hey Randy," I said. I lifted a hand in greeting.
He didn't respond.
"You don't know me," I said. "But I'm hoping that you might want to talk."
Dead silence as he stared me down. I fidgeted in my seat, starting to feel a little uncomfortable. I waited a few moments, allowing him time to think. He didn't even appear to be doing that anymore.
"At least give me a chance to explain," I said. I was afraid that he would leave.

"You don't have to explain, Mr. Dunham."
I felt my pulse quicken and froze.
"You know me?"
I looked him in the eye, trying to keep my angst in check. If he wanted me as a cellmate all he had to do was call me out to the guards.
"I'm in prison, Mr. Dunham. I'm not in a tomb."
"I'm-I'm sorry?" I was starting to get very nervous.
Ducey rolled his eyes and gave me a look. Exasperation. He finally took a seat.
"We have television. And newspapers, Mr. Dunham."
"Yeah, I guess I didn't consider the fact that you might put two and two together. Sorry."
"Putting facts together is what I do, Mr. Dunham. Or at least, what I did."
"Well then, Randy, I guess I don't have to tell you that we may have a common enemy. That is to say, I assume you and the man I'm referring to are not on great terms."
"It's Randall."
"Excuse me?"
"My name is Randall, since you have chosen to address me so informally. My parents did not name me Randy."
"Uhmmm, yeah. Sorry again, Randall. Ooops, I mean, if you'd like I will call you Mr. Ducey?"
"Why bother?" He said. "You've already placed me on the same societal plane with you. So for the sake of this discussion let's continue to pretend we are equals."
Jesus Christ, I thought. This guy's wound tighter than a Swiss watch.
"Again, my apologies," I said. "There are a lot of unknowns here. If I offended you, it was not my

intention."

Ducey cocked his head and looked at me. The manners were beginning to pay off. Or he was toying with me. I remained silent and allowed him to play his mind games. He seemed to be the type that enjoyed them.

"I believe in pecking orders, Mr. Dunham," he said. "I do not say this to be a snob. There are those above me as well as beneath me. But having a solid hierarchy lends itself to discipline and balance. I would not allow my servants to address me by my first name. Nor would I any man in my employ. Do you understand?"

"Yes," I said.

"This does not mean I think myself a better person, it's just that I happen to think a structured society demands no less. It ensures the trains run on time, wouldn't you agree?"

They sure thought so in Germany about eighty years ago, I thought silently. I decided not to respond with that.

"I can see where you're coming from," I answered. "I have a military background that adheres to the same principles. In order to maintain proper discipline, rank and station must be observed and orders must be followed."

"Precisely, Mr. Dunham," he nodded with a slight smile. "And I know all about your military background."

Cocky bastard, I thought. You don't know shit about me. I looked him over. He had the appearance of a decent guy. He might even be cool if he didn't wear that entitled, smug look of arrogance plastered all over his face. How the hell does a guy like this survive in here, I wondered?

"I read about your case, Randall," I said. "And while I won't pretend to know the details, I have had some experience with your previous employer."

"Some experience?"

"Yes. You could say that."

"You killed for him, correct?"

I whipped my head to the right where the closest guard stood. He didn't seem to be paying attention. I looked back at Ducey, my eyes widening a bit.

"I have no idea what you're talking about."

Ducey chuckled. I hadn't been sure that the tight ass was even capable of laughter but there he was, laughing at me. He shook his head and looked at me with condescension.

"If that's the way you want to play it, Mr. Dunham."

"Jesus Christ, would you please stop calling me that?" I was starting to get pissed off.

"You would prefer Mr. Simmons?" He laughed again.

"I would prefer that we cut through this bullshit and try to find some common ground. There may be a way we can help one another."

I was now annoyed and made no attempt to hide it.

"You're serious?" He asked. The smile fell from his face.

"You're goddamn right I'm serious. This man is trying to kill me. And I'm fairly certain he had a hand in ruining your life. I would think that a little payback might interest you?"

Ducey leaned forward. Placing his elbows on the small partition of wood, he interlocked his fingers and rested his chin on top of them. He had let go of the mirth and now looked at me with what can best be described as sadness.

"I'm sorry, Ryder. I truly am. William Kenealy is a monster. He is the closest thing to pure evil that I've ever encountered."

"Roger that," I said.

"But at the risk of sounding insensitive, you may want to consider just killing yourself."

"What?!" I said. It was louder than I'd intended. The guard to my left looked at me. I raised a weak hand in contrition and he looked away.

"Why would you say that to me?" I asked.

"Listen. You seem like a decent guy, a good man. And I was very sorry to hear about your family. What a horrible tragedy. We do live among vermin, do we not?"

I didn't respond. People don't talk about my family.

"How long have you known Mr. Kenealy?" He asked. It was a change of course.

I paused. There were several things I wanted to say but I had him talking. I kept it going.

"Not long, a few months. Not even."

"And did you ever spend any real amount of time with the man?"

"No, not really. We had coffee a couple of times but mostly it was phone calls."

"I see," he said. He clammed up. Pursing his lips he took in a deep breath and blew it out. He was weighing his next words. Weighing them carefully.

"Ryder, I worked for Mr. Kenealy for seven years. The last two years I was never far from his side. He liked me.

I was his right hand and he was grooming me to run the company someday. Under his son of course, but with more power."

"And what did his son think of that?"

"Well, he never would have known. He would have been more of a figurehead. He didn't want the responsibility anyway, only the perks. A seat on the board to wow his lady friends and all the Ferrari's he could drive. That type of thing."

"I read up on the son following in his dads footsteps," I said. "It didn't seem like that at all."

"Of course it wouldn't. Appearances, Ryder. Appearances are very important."

"You don't think much of the younger Kenealy I take it?"

He didn't reply.

"Why?" I asked.

"You haven't met him?"

I shook my head.

"You're not missing much. He's a cliché. A spoiled rich kid who will inherit the keys to daddy's company. But he has no clue how to run it. If left to that dolt, GSI would be bankrupt within a decade."

"Do you think Kenealy agrees with that assessment?"

"Of course he does. He knows that his son could no more run that global enterprise than a blue ass baboon. But, as I said, appearances are important."

"I guess."

A small light flashed in the number 7 divider. I hadn't noticed the small bulb.

"What's that?" I asked.

"Five minutes. And then we have to say goodbye."
"Seriously? That's it?"
"Next time, have whoever arranged the V Pass say that you're family. You get a full hour if you're family. They must have put you down as a paralegal or something similar. Somebody bringing me information."
"I sure as hell don't look like a paralegal."
"The guards have no clue what you're here for. Nor do they care. They set the timer according to the V Pass."
"Shit," I said. I leaned toward the window, my expression pleading for an answer.
"Why did you say I should kill myself?"
"I'm sorry, I shouldn't have -"
"Why?" I cut him off. My face showed the strain.
"Because he will catch you. And he will make you suffer in ways you cannot imagine."
"That's a pretty bold statement considering you don't know me."
"No, but I know him. As I said, the man is pure evil. And he is brilliant. You cannot out maneuver him."
"Is he smarter than you?" I asked. It was a blunt question.
"Well, let's see," he said. He spoke slowly, drawing out the words in a mocking fashion. "He's still walking around a very free, very wealthy and very powerful man."
He paused long enough to double down on his look of condescension.
"And I'm in here. What does that tell you?"
"Yes, but you weren't expecting it. He had the advantage of planning your downfall I'm guessing. Right?"

He remained silent.

"So it's not like he won a fair chess game. He sandbagged you. I'm putting my money on you in a fair fight."

"Don't suck up to me, Mr. Dunham. It's not your style."

"I'm not. Every battle I've ever seen this guy win is when he's double dealing somebody. I've met him and I've met you. You are smarter."

Ducey looked up and to the left. He was pondering this.

"Well," he said. "It really doesn't matter, now does it? I'm in here and he's not. Check and mate to Mr. Kenealy."

"Do you have anything at all I can use?" I asked.

"Have you met The Brit yet?"

The question surprised me.

"Who's the Brit?"

"No, I suppose you haven't," he said. "Those who meet him don't live to talk about it."

"Who's the Brit?"

"The Brit is a very scary man, Mr. Dunham. He's a serious psychopath and Kenealy's main enforcer. Avoid him."

"What's his name?"

"His name is Rothschild but in the inner circle we called him The Brit. Not to his face of course."

The light came on again. This time it stayed on.

"Time's up," Ducey said. He shot me a tight-lipped smile.

"Please. Is there anything else?"

His smile turned to a frown. And then he nodded.

"Yes, Mr. Dunham. Forget this madness. Run. Hide.

Change your identity. It's a small miracle that you're still alive."

"Why?" I was desperate. I could see the guard approaching.

"Do you honestly think you were the first? The first hard case he tricked into doing his bidding?"

"But don't you want some payback?" I asked. "A chance to get even?"

He took his time. And then he answered.

"Mr. Dunham, I have found a way to survive in this hellhole. And that is what I will continue to do. Survive. And, with any luck, in five years I will go home. I will hold my children and make love to my wife. And I will try to forget that I ever knew a man named William Kenealy."

It took me a second to respond.

"That's it?" I asked.

"Why Mr. Dunham," he said. "That's everything."

I looked at him in a whole new light. He was right. Absolutely right. It was everything.

"Let's go," the guard said. He was standing behind me. Ducey pushed back from the chair and stood. He began to turn and then stopped. He leaned towards the glass.

"Go and see if there remains a store in the San Fernando Valley named Coiled. Van Nuys I think. It's a gadgets and electronics shop. A guy named Joe Simpson owns it. Or did. He is another of Kenealy's play things. He is allowed a certain latitude because he provides things. He can build things. Anything. He might have what you're looking for."

"I said let's go," the guard said.

"Good luck, Kevin," Ducey said. He called me by my fictitious name.

"Thank you, Mr. Ducey," I said. I used his formal name. I knew he would appreciate the gesture. Raising my hand in farewell I nodded to him.

Offering me the same sad look once more, he turned and walked to the far end of the small hallway. The door opened from the other side. And just like that, Randall Ducey was gone.

I followed the guard to my own door. It was a very different door than Randall Ducey had walked through. He had a wife and kids waiting on the other side.

Raging Storm
30

The entire ride back to my safe haven, all I could think about was the look in Ducey's eyes. I'd seen that look before in combat. That vacant stare, that inner battle of a mind that's seen things that it never thought it would see. The guy was arrogant but I didn't sense any lying in him. He might be a pompous asshole but at the very least, he seemed honest.

I hated dishonesty. It was one of my biggest pet peeves. As far as I was concerned, you can go through life as a miserable prick, but at least do it honestly.

Ducey looked like a man who had battled fear for so long, that it no longer effected him. He seemed to have given up. Not completely, there was still a part of him that wanted to do his time and get out. Go home to his family. But you could see that he no longer worried about Kenealy. I guess the way Ducey saw it, all the man had to do was snap his fingers and he was dead. After a while, living with something like that forces you to put it away. To ignore it. Dealing with it every day was counterproductive to ones sanity. So you learn to compartmentalize out of necessity.

I eased into the right hand lane and took the exit which would lead me to Oxnard. The sky was a perfect blue as it is so often in Southern California. It didn't rain much here and what a lot of people don't realize is that this part of the country is a desert climate. People see the green lawns and perfect palm trees in the movies and think California is sub tropical, but it's not. It's drier than shit and one of the world's hottest locations, known as Death Valley, is not far from here. That seemed like a good name for the operation I was currently on, Death Valley.

I drove the rest of the way back listening to a classic rock station and zoning out. As I pulled into the driveway I was happy to see Rob's Jeep.

I walked through the front door and spotted my friend walking out of his bedroom.

"Hey, man."

"Ryder my man," he said. He looked happy to see me. "How did it go?"

"It was eerie, dude. Very strange."

"Did you get to meet this cat?"

"Yup."

I spent the next few minutes filling Rob in on exactly what had gone down. He laughed when I told him about the guards and how they'd bought my stoned surfer act hook, line and sinker.

His expression changed when I laid out the entire conversation. I told him about Ducey's advice to me.

"Man," Rob said. He searched in silence for the right words and I didn't interrupt his train of thought.

"I hate to say this Ryder, but maybe the guy's right. I was kind of keeping this to myself but why not just go live, brother?"

"After what Kenealy did?" I said? "Are you fucking serious?"

I hadn't meant to respond with anger. It just came out that way.

Rob didn't bite, he remained calm.

"Look man, he did it. It sucks. But it's done. There's no changing it."

My friend hesitated again, looking at the floor as he struggled with his words. And again, I remained silent, as I waited to hear him out. Straightening up, he looked me dead in the eyes.

"You're going to get yourself killed, brother. This is out of your league."

"Out of my league?" I laughed.

"Yeah, yeah," he said. He gave me a condescending smirk and tilt of his head. "I know you're a bad ass, Ryder. But it's little old you against a guy with an army of bad asses. A really smart guy who's connected on every level. How the hell can you beat those odds?"

I stared at Rob as I tried to think of a response. After a few moments I realized that my silence was winning his argument so I simply shrugged.

"Really?" He laughed in disbelief. "That's it?"

I turned and walked into the kitchen. Rob remained standing in place. As I walked to the refrigerator to grab a bottled water I knew he was right. I knew that the chances I could actually pull this off were slim. There was a better chance than not that I'd end up dead. So I had to ask myself, why did I care so much? Why the hell *couldn't* I just walk away? What was driving me? Too many thoughts were coming out, becoming a jumbled mess inside my head. I had to cut through the bullshit and take a direct path to the problem. Turning to look at my friend I found the words.

"Rob. I don't know what to tell you. I don't know how to describe to you what this feels like."

Rob returned my stoic gaze and allowed me to talk.

"After everything that happened with Debbie and the kids. To be used like that," I said. I spoke in broken sentences, blurting out different thoughts and feelings as I had them. "To have the most horrible thing that has ever happened to me, that ever could happen to me, twisted and used for evil. I can't let that go. I don't want to let it go. Kenealy is an evil motherfucker. The world would be a better place without him. Since I started down that path with him, it only makes sense that it comes full circle and ends with him."

I finished and we both stood without speaking. I stared at him with an almost desperate need that he understand. He had a look on his face that I couldn't read. For reasons I couldn't quite grasp, his silence was starting to annoy me.

"He's got to go, man," I said.

"Are you sure it's him that's got to go?" Rob asked. The question stunned me.

"What the hell is that supposed to mean?"

"You know damn well what that means, Ryder." He stayed calm, his voice level.

"The fuck I do," I said. I made no attempt to hide my

growing anger.

"You can get pissed at me if it helps, brother. But we both know what I'm talking about."

"No, Rob, why don't you enlighten me?"

"Okay. The truth is, you blame yourself for what happened that night. You're much angrier with yourself than you are with Kenealy."

More silence as we stared at each other. I was glad that we weren't in the same room. If we had been I would have knocked him on his ass.

"And deep down I think you know it," he said.

More silence and then he continued.

"So who is it you really want dead?"

"Man, fuck you," I said.

I was trying to hold it back, the anger which was fighting its way to the surface. And I wasn't even sure why. I hadn't expected this, it was coming from nowhere. I hated Kenealy, hated him. I wanted him dead. That much was true. But that wasn't what was going on now. What was causing me to feel this much pain, this much hostility towards one of my best friends? I lowered my head, remained silent and tried to process. And bit by bit, it started to come in focus.

Like the clouds parting and a ray of brilliant sunlight shining on my face, it finally hit me.

He was right. One hundred percent, dead on correct.

I looked up. Looked him in the eye. And understood exactly what he meant, what he was driving at. And although, I guess a part of me had known it all along, this was the first time seeing it clearly.

Rob saw the inner turmoil melt away as I confronted this

realization. He tightened his lips into a grim and somewhat sympathetic smile.

I felt the cleansing release of acceptance and came back from the dark corner into which I'd retreated.

"Okay," I said.

Rob stood in silence, having watched me wrestle with my demons. I nodded at my friend.

"Okay."

"It's cool, Ryder. It's completely normal. But it will put certain things into focus now that you know it."

I felt my eyes filling with moisture. Not now, I thought.

"And Ryder," he said. "I hate to steal a very corny line from every psycho babble movie ever churned out, but it's not your fault."

He smiled wryly at me.

"It's really not. You didn't kill Debbie or Hunter or Sasha."

Fuck, the tears fell down my face. I could actually feel them hitting my shirt. I was officially blubbering again.

"Some disgusting, loser junkie killed them. In your own house. And who in the hell could have ever seen that coming, brother?"

Rob walked over and placed a hand on my shoulder.

"Who?" He asked again.

I wiped my face with my right hand.

"You know what, Rob? Even as you say that, I know you're right."

"Well good," he said. "That's a good first step."

"But you know what else? I don't care. Because even if it wasn't my fault, I still want to be with them. I don't want to live without them. They're all I ever think about."

"I get that."

"And I don't want to wait for old age."

"Yup," he said. "That's normal too. But no matter how many Kenealy's you kill, or use to commit suicide, you need to ask yourself one question."

He paused.

"And what's that?" I asked.

"Is this what Debbie would want?"

"Jesus Christ man." I turned away. "That's dirty fucking pool."

"Maybe. But answer the question."

I put my hand to my forehead and closed my eyes. I felt tired. Tired and drained.

"How the fuck did I let this happen," I said. My voice choked with emotion. "How the fuck did I allow this?"

I turned back to face my buddy.

"Yeah, now you're getting it," Rob said. "That's what I meant, brother. Fuck this bullshit. Karma will take care of that dude. Go live. Forget this payback. Get off this suicide mission."

I took a very deep, cleansing breath and exhaled it loudly.

"I hear you, Rob. For real I do. And I appreciate you having the brains and the balls to help me face this."

He nodded.

"But there's one thing you are missing?"

"What's that?"

"I want this. I want this motherfucker dead. And I don't really think I want to die. Not really. It's just that I don't care. Or at least I didn't. I'm glad that I'm getting this shit sorted out but nothing changes."

"Are you serious?"

"Maybe I'll be a little more careful."

Rob looked at me with a blank expression. I walked over to the couch and flopped down.

"Look bro," I said. "I'm gonna clear out of here. It was wrong of me to dump this shit on you. I'll buy your dad's truck. I can live in it or in some shit box hotel room. It's not a big deal, you know I've roughed it a lot worse."

"Fuck you. You aren't going anywhere."

"Dude -"

"No, man," he said. "I didn't think I was going to be able to talk you out of this bullshit. I know how stubborn your ass is. But if you're hell bent on going through with it, then there's no way I'm letting you go it alone, asshole."

"Listen, Rob," I said. "As you know, this guy is well connected. If he finds me here then you are in deep shit too. What kind of friend would I be if I allowed that?"

"What kind of friend would I be if I said goodbye and good luck?" He answered. "This discussion is over. You are staying right here."

I started to respond but Rob shut me up with a look. Finally I allowed myself to chuckle. I raised a hand and he walked over and clasped it tight.

"Thanks, Rob."

"You got it, Ryder."

With that, he turned and walked out of the room.

Raging Storm
31

It was only an hour's drive south down Hwy 101 from Oxnard into the San Fernando Valley. The legendary basin, surrounded by mountains, is north of L.A. and Hollywood. And it is home to almost two million people.
Immortalized in the 80's movie Valley Girl and the song of the same name, the valley is iconic. Home to movie stars, street gangs, and every type of humanity in between, it is definitely a one of a kind place. I'd spent some time here years ago as Kurt, one of my platoon mates, was from Van Nuys. Every so often we would run up from Camp Pendleton on a weekend. It was nice to get a good, home cooked meal and get away from the cramped squad bay. And it was only about a hundred mile drive, no big deal. I smiled as I remembered those weekends. We would drink cases of beer and destroy his mother's lasagna.
Rob, who was Kurt's best friend, was always there as well and together we'd terrorize the seedy bars in Reseda. One night in particular we had a pretty serious

tussle with a group of bikers. They'd started it, but it didn't matter. We finished it, even though there were five of them and three of us. We laughed our asses off afterward but back then, we considered this fun.

Kurt had been killed in action years ago in Iraq during a sweep of some houses. After kicking in a door, he'd walked straight into an AK-47 leveled at his chest. He never had a chance. One of our guys tossed a grenade into the room and wounded the bad guy. Rob and I then breached the house and finished him. We both emptied a full clip into the piece of garbage. That had been a very bad day. Rob never got completely over it. He and Kurt were inseparable.

Now, as I drove the familiar streets, many bittersweet memories came rushing back. I gave some thought to dropping in on his mom but realized that might not be a good idea. Not with all things considered. I was a wanted man. Besides, I had business.

Coiled turned out to be in Northridge, a short distance from Van Nuys. Using the miracle of GPS, I found the place with no problem. Now the question remained, would Joe Simpson be there and better still, would he give me the time of day?

I parked the truck in one of the alley parking spots behind the shop. There was a back door leading into the store which sported a large Welcome sign. I walked through the door and into a high tech lover's wet dream. Every imaginable gadget, and some unimaginable, was either on a shelf or hanging from a wall. I didn't see anybody so I started going up and down the aisles. The dude sold some gear that I didn't even know was legal to own as a civilian. Military grade stuff, such as police scanners, tasers, tracking devices and more. This guy had it all and I was willing to bet his mind understood the inner workings of every piece.

As I turned up the next aisle I took a step and then froze as I felt a piece of steel pressed against the back of my head.

"Move and you die," a man said. The voice had a noticeable quaver. He was nervous.

"Whoa," I said. I remained motionless, making sure not to move. "Buddy, I am not looking for trouble."

I spoke calmly. I wasn't nervous. This guy was no pro. He had already made a colossal mistake. He had gotten way too close. Let's see if he would make another one.

"May I turn around?" I asked. "Please?"

"Very slowly," he said. His voice was shaky. I almost felt bad for him.

"Okay," I said. "Don't shoot me. I'm turning around now."

I did a slow motion half turn and got my first look at the man. At roughly five feet five inches tall, and grossly out of shape, he wore a pair of dirty jeans and a black Star Wars shirt. The shirt highlighted a silhouette of Darth Vader staring into the Death Star. His chubby face bore the look of man who ate six candy bars and a full bag of potato chips a day. But his eyes told the real story. He was terrified.

I completed the turn and smiled at him. It was a genuine smile. I liked the guy without knowing why. Part of it was because of what he had just done. It took a lot of guts to be this afraid and still make a stand.

"Now," he said. His voice shook. "Get to your knees and-"

I snatched the gun from his hand so fast that he didn't even have time to flinch. His eyes widened in shock and his lips quivered as he tried to control his fear. I pointed the gun at his head.

"Let's have a little chat, shall we?" I said.

"Oh my God," he said. He struggled to hold his tears back. "I'm going to die today."

I looked and him and chuckled.

"Why in the hell would you die today?"

"He told me. He said that if you showed up you were going to kill me."

"Who told you that?"

His eyes narrowed and he swallowed fiercely, his Adams apple bobbing like a cork in rough seas.

"Never mind," he said. "Nothing."

"No," I said. "I asked you a question."

I wasn't smiling anymore.

"He did."

"Who is *he*?" I asked. My voice had an edge which suggested I was tiring of this game.

"You know who!"

I looked into his eyes. I saw the fear. Okay, I thought, I'll play along.

"Yeah. I guess I do. But he's full of shit."

The man looked to his left and then to his right, his face a mask of panic.

"Shhhh…you can't say that!"

He spoke in a desperate hush, keeping his voice low. He didn't seem to be afraid of me anymore. "He hears everything!"

I studied him closely. Was this guy serious? He was either deranged or knew something I didn't.

"I know why you're here," he said. "So go on and get it over with!"

"Are you Joe Simpson?"

"You know damn well I am so do it already!"

What the hell, I thought? This was getting bizarre.

"You'll be doing me a favor," he said. He sighed with the soft resolve of a man who had accepted his fate and had given up the struggle.

Jesus Christ, I thought. This guy has more sides than the United Nations.

"Joe, I am not going to hurt you. Why the hell would I?"

He looked at me with suspicion. He didn't believe me.

"Why?" I asked.

"I-I don't know. I never know the what's and the why's. But whatever he says will happen always happens. Always."

"And he said what concerning me?"

"That you might come for me. And that if you did I should blow your head off because if not, you would do the same to me."

"No," I said. I shook my head. "That's bullshit. He lied to you."

He scanned the room again as if this was some sort of elaborate ruse. As if he was being tested and Kenealy would pop up from behind a counter should he say the wrong thing.

"Holy shit, man. Relax." I tried to calm him.

"No…I don't believe you. Stop torturing me and just do

it."

With obvious physical exertion, he lowered himself to his knees and bowed his head.

"Please make it quick," he said.

Now it was my turn to look around. I scratched my head and tried to figure out if I was being punked. This guy was nuttier than a fruitcake. But aside from that, he seemed harmless enough.

"What can I do to convince you that I'm not here to hurt you?" I asked.

"Nothing. There's nothing you can do."

"Ducey sent me," I said.

From his knees he looked up at me. I saw the light in his eyes. The name registered with him.

"Nice try but Mr. Ducey's behind bars."

"Yeah, I know," I said. "In Chino. I visited him yesterday."

He stared straight up at me. I could see all the possibilities racing through his mind. He was weighing different scenarios, running a full war game sequence in his head. Finally, he spoke.

"Why would you go and see Randall?"

I smiled inwardly as he used his proper name.

"Because Kenealy is trying to have me killed. And by telling you that lie, he was hoping to stack the deck in his favor and have you do his dirty work for him."

"Okay, he said. "But that still doesn't explain why you went to Chino."

"I did some digging and found the case that got Randall locked up. The fact that a smart cookie like Ducey took the fall didn't add up. It suggested that he may have come up on the losing end of something which Kenealy orchestrated."

Simpson shifted his weight from knee to knee. He grimaced as he put this tidbit in the computer program his mind was building.

"Can I get off my knees now?" He asked.

"I never told you to get on them." I said. I smiled and offered a hand.

He took it and I helped pull him to a standing position. It wasn't easy.

"So what do you want from me?" He asked. "Why come here?"

"Well, I was hoping that you could help fill in some blanks. Help me understand how to get to Kenealy."

"You're going to try and take him down?"

"Joe," I said. I emphasized each word to show him how serious I was. "I'm *going* to take him down. I'm just not sure how yet."

There was that suspicious look again.

"You're nuts. You have no idea who or what you're up against."

"So tell me."

"I can't."

"Why?"

He looked around the room again and took a deep, nervous breath.

"Because I don't know you. How can I possibly trust you?"

We stared at each other in silence for several seconds. He was right. I nodded and raised the gun to his head.

"This thing loaded?" I asked.

The man flinched and leaned backwards as though that extra few inches might save him. He nodded frantically.

"Good," I said.

I spun the gun around in my hand so that the barrel was now pointed at me. I offered to him.

"Take it."

"Wh-What?"

"Take it. Take the gun."

"Why?" He asked. A perplexed look crossed his face.

"Because you're right. How can you possibly trust me?"

"This doesn't make sense."

"Yes it does. I am going to give you my life. Take the gun and shoot me if you think that's the best way to get in Kenealy's good graces."

He swallowed hard and eyed the gun.

"But I'm trusting that you will understand the bigger picture. I don't know what type of sway Kenealy has over you, but I'm willing to bet you'd like to be out from under it."

His eyes left the gun to lock with mine. I saw the pressure he was under. The pressure that he lived under every day.

"Take it," I said. "I'm trusting you. So that maybe you can trust me."

Slowly, his hand went up. He hesitated as if this was a trick. Finally, his hand curled around the grip and he took the gun. I lowered my arms and stood in place. Simpson took two steps backwards so I was no longer able to snatch the gun as I had last time. He was a fast learner. I saw his hand tighten around the grip.

"You're for real?" He wanted to believe me. I could see

it.

"Yeah, Joe. I am."

He let out a deep breath he'd been holding and I saw his thumb move.

"Okay then," he said. He nodded. "Okay."

He pressed a button and caught the magazine as it dropped out of the gun. Then he slid the bolt back and forward. The 9mm cartridge exited the barrel and flew towards me. I caught it. The gun was empty.

"Well played," he said.

"Thank you. But this isn't a game."

"Oh but it is. And it's a game that this man loves to play. And he never loses."

"What do you say we change that?" I offered my best steely glare.

"Let's go back in my office. I'll tell you all I know."

He turned and walked towards the back of the store.

Raging Storm
32

Simpson led me to a small office located at the back left corner of the store. We entered and he hit a light switch. There was a small metal desk against the back wall and several shelves packed with various electronic parts and gadgets. Some I recognized as transmitters, others as receivers. Joe had an even more impressive array of cyber goodies in here than he did in his store. It started to dawn on me what Coiled was all about. It was a front. Joe Simpson was in the surveillance game, among other things.

He sat behind the desk, and although I could tell that he still wasn't completely at ease with me, he began talking. And once he started it only took me a couple of minutes to realize that he was one of those rare geniuses. There was nothing this guy didn't know about high tech. I couldn't even understand half the gizmos he described to me.

And holy shit did he have the goods on GSI. He knew the inner workings of pretty much every one of their shady operations. The knowledge he possessed was imperative as he supplied the surveillance. In essence, his computer savvy and know how helped Kenealy pull it all off. He had listening and tracking devices as well as cameras so small they would fit on a cuff link. This was shit that would have made James Bond proud.

Joe also gave me the low down on what happened in South America. The thing that had sent Ducey to prison for twenty years. It wasn't supposed to go down the way it did, but mistakes were made. Once the illegal operation had been exposed, Kenealy threw Ducey to the wolves.

Joe explained that Ducey had taken the fall without putting up much of a fight. He understood that if he crossed Kenealy, his life expectancy would drop to less than a week. So, he plead guilty to crimes he didn't commit and took a deal. Survival will make you do things like that.

Simpson had enough dirt on Kenealy to lock him up forever. That is, if he lived to testify. And even if he did testify and Kenealy got convicted, his life would be forfeit. He would die if he ever crossed the boss and he knew it. With this type of insurance policy, Kenealy trusted him with all sorts of needs. And Simpson obeyed his commands. He had no choice. He was a slave. No wonder Simpson was spilling his guts. He knew an opportunity when it dropped in his lap. I was that opportunity. If I was able to get rid of Kenealy, Simpson would be free. Free from the manipulative and twisted hand of a psychopath.

The more I heard, the angrier I became. Kenealy wasn't just dirty, he was as corrupt as they come. It became obvious that he was devoid of any conscience. Absent any sense of decency. He had a sick knack for using people. Using them and then throwing them away once he'd squeezed out every last bit of blood. And he did it with a sociopathic apathy.

Like he'd used me.

He'd searched me out when I was at the most vulnerable time of my life. He'd heard my story in the news and then he had listened in that meeting as I poured my heart out, as I bared my pain. He felt my anger while describing the murder of my family. He'd seen it all, drank it all in and then he figured out a way to exploit it. The cold, calculating son of a bitch played me. He'd moved me around his personal chess board like a pawn. And then he had tried to sacrifice me. But he'd failed. And now the king was being hunted. It had to be an uncomfortable feeling for the bastard.

I listened to Simpson and a lot of pieces fell into place. I'd thought that I'd known the inner workings of William Kenealy before but I didn't know shit. Before hearing what Joe laid out for me, I had no idea what kind of monster I was up against.

And another thing started to happen, I started to really like Joe Simpson. He was a damn good guy. He was being forced to dance to a tune that sickened him. And like me, he had been played. Kenealy kept him in check using the fear of death. He pulled him this way and that and there was nothing Joe could do about it.

I thought I'd wanted revenge before this meeting. Now I didn't care if it cost me my life or my freedom, I was going to rid the world of this malignant cancer.

When Simpson stopped talking, I started asking

questions. Where did Kenealy go for fun? On vacation? What were his favorite things? Favorite possessions? What did the man do with his free time? How much time did he spend in Malibu verses Florida? Where were his offices here?

I wanted inside Kenealy's head, to know every possible thing I could about him. With the right information I could formulate a plan. And as I heard Simpson's answers, I began to have an idea. A way to take the fight to him. But there was still one nagging thing.

"Tell me about the Brit."

Simpson's face turned ashen. He hesitated for a second.

"Randall told you a lot," he said.

"Not really, we didn't have a lot of time. But he did warn me about some British Special Forces asshole. Some guy who heads up Kenealy's security."

"Rothschild," Simpson said. He whispered it as the dark cloud remained over his face.

"Seriously? The guy's name is just Rothschild? No first name?"

"That might be his first name. I'm not sure. But that's what *he* calls him."

"Again with that *he* stuff. Why can't you say his name?"

"You do not want to mess with Rothschild," Simpson said. "He is a dangerous man."

I shot him a hard look.

"So am I."

"Yeah, I'll bet you are. But I'm also willing to bet you have a soul."

He stared at me in a way which actually made me pause. I filed that away for later use.

"What does he look like?" I asked.

"Tall," he said. "Tall and lanky. He has a brush haircut. Do you know what a marine haircut looks like? Like in the movies?"

I smiled.

"Yeah, I think I know."

"Well like that. But it's his eyes…"

Joe's voice trailed off as he went to a mental image in his head. I could see it haunting him.

"What about his eyes?"

"They're the darkest eyes I've ever seen. Like a sharks."

"Anything else you can think of?" I asked.

"I've told you everything. Enough to get me killed."

I nodded my head and smiled at the man who had more guts than he knew.

"I don't blame you for being nervous, Joe. And I can't tell you how much this means to me. You trusting me. I know you went out on a serious limb here. But stop worrying. I'm going to get him."

"I want to believe that," he said.

"Trust me, Joe. I'm not going to let anything happen to you."

He looked at me with a troubled expression.

"Listen," I said. I reached into my pocket and pulled out a burner. "This is a prepaid phone. If I need you I will call the store and ask if you have any vintage transistors. I will call myself Blake White. You simply say no and then call me back on this burner. I already put my number in it."

He reached out and took it.

"You didn't put your real name in it, did you?"

"No, of course not. And there's only one number programmed, Joe. That would be me."

"Okay," he said. He put the phone in his pocket. He hesitated and I could see a question forming in his mind. He dropped his eyes and shifted nervously.

"What's up?" I asked.

"If, for some reason," he said. He hesitated again. "If for some reason he gets a hold of you. If he captures you…" Another pause. I let him squirm until even I couldn't take it anymore.

"No, Joe," I said. I placed a hand on his shoulder. "No, I will not give you up."

"What if he tortures you?" His face was that of a child, imploring his father to explain away the boogie man.

"Joe. Relax."

"Easy for you to say."

I looked at him and realized that he was right. It *was* easy for me to say. I had lived my life as a warrior and was confident in my abilities. Not to mention I had little left to lose. But Joe Simpson had been the kid who never played sports in high school. He was on the chess team. He was the guy who went to the midnight Star Wars showings dressed as one of the characters. He had most likely spent his entire life being bullied. And yet here he was, facing up to his demon's knowing full well the consequences if Kenealy found out. My admiration for him grew. He was right. It was easy for a guy like me to be cool under pressure but what Joe was doing took real balls. To pull down on me with that gun took some serious guts, even if the execution had been poor. To risk his life to help me take down Kenealy took strength and courage. I held out my hand for him to shake.

"Joe, stop selling yourself short. You've got nerve, man. And I'm telling you right now that I will not get caught and even if I do, I'm willing to die. He will never know that I spoke to you."

Joe shook my hand but did not return my smile.

"You don't understand." His Adam's apple bobbed as he swallowed nervously. "He already knows."

Despite myself, I froze for a brief second. His words hit me strangely. Eerily. I stared at him.

"What the hell do you mean by that?"

"He knows everything. I don't know how, he just does."

"Then why did you spill your guts?"

"Because I can explain this away. I'll say you got the gun from me and then took off. But he can never know I told you all that stuff."

"Dude," I said. "You're being a little paranoid."

"Am I?"

That was my cue to leave. I offered my hand again and he shook it.

"Remember, Blake White."

"Vintage transistors. I got it."

"Ok. Take care, man." I turned and walked to the door of his office.

"You too," he said.

Before walking through the door I turned and looked at him. He stood there calmly but I knew his heart had to be racing.

"Thank you, Joe," I said.

He simply nodded.

I turned and left.

Raging Storm
33

By the time I got back to Oxnard, night was beginning to fall. I drove to the beach and parked. Getting out of the truck, I took a slow walk down the sidewalk that ran along the edge of the beach. The salt air smelled intoxicating and I breathed deep, filling my lungs with it. There were benches facing the ocean. Choosing one, I sat and watched the last remnants of a summer sunset. It painted the seascape a glimmering, orange. It was almost surreal that there was still this much beauty to behold in a world that seemed like it was pure evil. No, I had to tell myself. This wasn't the case. The world was not evil, not most of it anyway. My world might fit that bill, but only because I had brought it upon myself. I had to be true to that one fact. None of this would be happening if I hadn't agreed to dance with the devil.

I looked out in silent awe as the sphere of amber flame, many millions of miles away, turned into a half sphere. And then a quarter and then an eighth, finally sinking below the horizon of the Pacific. The ocean was calm.

Serene. With no wind it was almost glassy. A pair of old school long boarders finally called it a day and exited the water, boards under their arms. The last light faded. I made my way back to the truck, backed out of the parking spot and drove the short distance to my hideaway.

When I entered the kitchen through the garage door, Rob was there, standing in front of the stove, stirring a pot. The aroma of pot roast was intoxicating and only upon greeting it, did I realize how hungry I was.

"God damn, man," I said. "That smells good, Crawdog."

"Thanks, man. Almost ready."

"What are you doing away from base again? They'll put you in the brig for desertion, you know?" I laughed.

"Nah man, I had a bunch of leave saved up so I took a couple weeks."

"Why?"

Rob shot me a look that called me stupid. Then he went back to stirring the gravy which I could see bubbling near the top of the pot. There was a bottle of scotch on the counter. I didn't see a glass.

"No," I said. I glared at Rob having understood the implications of his look. "I don't want you to fuck your life up. Just hiding me is enough to get you in some serious trouble."

"That's a load of shit."

"No, Rob, it's not! I fucked up bad. Real bad. But you don't want this bullshit in your life. Trust me."

"Remember the day Kurt died?"

The question came out of left field and caught me by surprise. Kurt and I had been good friends, but as I said,

Rob had considered Kurt his best friend. They had been in Force Recon a couple years longer than me and had seen even more shit together.

"I was thinking of that earlier today," I answered. My voice was somber. "I was only a couple of miles from his mom's house."

"Yeah, I know. I guess that's why we both thought about it."

I allowed the silence to speak volumes as we were both transported back to that hot, dusty day in Iraq. It was something that neither of us would ever forget. Not ever.

"You know what?" He said. He didn't look up. "We didn't fight for the politics. Maybe we were there for political reasons but you know what I'm talking about."

"I know, man," I said.

"Yeah. Once the shit went down, we fought for each other. We fought for our brothers."

I remained silent and watched as he struggled with the dark thing. The darkness that all combat veterans dealt with when bad memories surfaced. The doubts, the fears, the second guessing, it can do a number on you. What we saw. What we did. Those we lost. We all wrestled with it, some better than others. One thing was for sure though, alcohol didn't help and once again I glanced at the bottle of scotch on the counter. Since I was feeling a little pessimistic at the moment, I saw it as half empty.

"It was my turn, Ryder."

"What are you talking about, man?"

"I was supposed to kick that door."

He had turned his back to me and I had to strain to understand his words. He breathed it in a hushed whisper.

I thought back to a time he'd said that to me once before, a long time ago when we were both very drunk. I didn't respond then. Didn't know what to say. I couldn't remain silent again.

"Rob," I said. "That's crap."

"No man, it was my turn."

"Dude, there were so many doors. We all kicked our share."

"That was my door, Ryder. It was my turn. I watched Kurt walk up to it. I was going to stop him, tell him it was my turn."

He paused and we both let the quiet moment envelop us. Rob turned to face me. His eyes were wet and red. I wondered how long he'd been drinking.

"But I didn't."

"Rob, come on, man."

He looked to the floor and I could see him choking back his emotions. He was trying in vain to hold it together.

"I don't know why I didn't. I don't know if I felt something or what. But I let Kurt kick that door."

"Don't do this to yourself."

"That's not true. I let him kick that door because I knew, Ryder," he said. He looked back up at me. "I let him die because I felt it. I felt it and I froze."

His gaze fell behind me and I watched him go to that distant place. He didn't cry, his face just froze and I knew that he was watching Kurt die again. For the thousandth time. His eyes were a vacant, glazed stare.

"We all had those feelings, man. Every fucking day in Fallujah. You're only remembering it like that because of-"

"It should have been me," he said.

He was back, locking eyes with me again.

"Man, that's bullshit. It should have been you my ass. It should have been me. It should have been Larry or Dave or Brad or Mike."

He took a deep breath and then cast his eyes back to the ground.

"But it was Kurt," I said. "War sucks, man. Don't try to make any sense out of it. It'll drive you nuts."

He cleared his throat and coughed. Then he turned back to the stove. The gravy was boiling over the edge of the small pot.

"Fuck!"

Rob turned the burner off and grabbed the pot. He hustled it over to the sink as gravy splashed onto the floors and counter top.

I laughed and the tension evaporated. He shot me that 'up yours' look. Playful Rob was back.

It was like that. Quick bouts of it and then nothing. Until the next time.

"You gonna offer me some of that scotch, asshole?"

Rob was smiling again. He had put his memories away. He was all right.

"I thought you were giving up booze for a while?" He laughed.

"Yeah," I said. "But I'm not gonna let a good friend drink alone either."

He grabbed the bottle from the counter and underhanded it to me. I caught it with one hand, unscrewed the cap and took a good long pull.

"One thing," Rob spoke.

I looked at him.

"No more of this shit about me not getting involved. Got it?"

The whiskey stung my throat. My chest caught fire as it made its way down to my stomach. I nodded and gave him a grim smile. What else could I do?

"We go through this fucking door together," he said.

I nodded again. I understood. I guess I had all along.

"Good," he said. "Now let's eat. I want to hear a plan."

We filled our plates with roast beef, potatoes and green beans. After five minutes of shoveling food into my mouth I took a breather and wiped my mouth with a napkin.

"Hey Rob," I said.

He looked up from his plate.

"How hard would it be for you get me some C4?"

Rob startle to chuckle. Smiling, he shook his head and then took another bite.

I began to explain.

Raging Storm
34

Lake Arrowhead is one of the world's most luxurious lake playgrounds for the super rich and famous. Notorious gangsters, business moguls and movie stars had summer homes here. 5-Star resorts dotted the coastline. Known as the "The Alps of Southern California" it is a breathtaking and beautiful place. An ideal location to get away from the stress of everyday life. That is, if you can afford it.

So, of course, Kenealy had a sprawling waterfront mansion along the eastern shore. The sunsets had to be magnificent as one gazed westward from the estate. According to Joe Simpson Kenealy did not spend a lot of time here. However, security was always tight. Armed guards protected the home and its contents including the prized jewel. Kenealy's number one possession. A 1939, 48 foot Burger yacht. The extremely rare yacht had been in the family for decades, first his grandfather's and then his father's. Now it was his and again, according to Joe, Kenealy cherished her like no other thing in his life. She held great sentimental value as the man had spent many of his childhood days upon her. It was even named Constance, after his grandmother. When his father died he'd moved the boat from Catalina Island off the Pacific Coast, to this fresh water home. No salt water would ever touch his baby again.

The vessel, although not large by yachting standards was breathtaking in every detail. Smooth, polished handrails and teak decks ran the length of the boat. Its wooden hull received the finest maintenance against leakage and rot. The exterior, a glossy white, sparkled in both the sun and moonlight. The interior was perfection, every fixture and accompaniment, the best money could buy. It was a gem. Featured in the most prestigious yachting magazines in the world, she was famous.

And she was Kenealy's pride and joy.

Men with means, men who collected such invaluable things, had stopped making offers. They knew that it was futile. It was, as a matter of fact, priceless to Kenealy. He had turned down sums much higher than the boats actual value. Kenealy viewed these offers with disdain, as if the buyers were asking him to sell one of his children. Some counter offers included thinly veiled threats. This was to dissuade a prospective buyer from ever insulting him in such a manner again. They never did.

The boat was, in a word, beautiful and it was exactly what I had been hoping to find.

It was perfect.

I'd spent the previous day researching everything I could find on the boat. I'd studied the Burger meticulously and had even downloaded the specs. God bless the internet where every piece of information one could ever want is at your disposal.

The layout was simple enough. Still, I pored over every detail of the schematics until the boat became mine. Rob, true friend that he was, had managed to secure for me a shape charged block of C4. This would direct the force of the blast whichever way I wanted it to go and I knew exactly where to place it. I would secure the charge to explode upwards through the hull, directly below the fuel tank. This would have the effect of hitting the boat with napalm and coat the entire hull in burning fuel. That would spread upwards into the cabin and consume the entire boat.

It was not enough to sink the Burger. A sunken boat could be retrieved and restored from such a shallow depth as the dock. I wanted it to burn to a crisp and then sink. A total loss from which there could be no restoration. The biggest *fuck you* I could possibly deliver to Kenealy.

I drove the F-150 to the San Bernardino Mountains and parked in a lot frequented by hikers and campers. In the back of the truck was my SCUBA gear and a bag with the explosive and the detonator. I had already rigged the detonator with a five minute delayed fuse. This would give me time to make my escape and watch the fireworks from a safe vantage point.

As I slung the gear over my shoulder I spotted an aging couple hike into the parking lot. They headed for an old woodie VW, giving me a friendly wave. I waved back, acknowledging them both with a big smile. I had shades on and a floppy recon hat. They wouldn't be able to describe me although it didn't matter anyway. Kenealy would know who had done this. And the last thing he would do is tell the cops.

The last slivers of sunlight cut through the trees to dance on the lakes mirrored surface. I had hoped there would be more wind. A slight chop on the water would have helped mask the bubbles from my scuba equipment. It was a minor detail but the devil was in those details.

I waited until dusk turned to darkness and then checked my navigation system. In the old days, we had to maneuver through dark water with a compass. Plotting an azimuth beforehand, we would maintain our bearing the entire swim. This got us to within a respectable distance from our targets. Small variations always meant you'd be a little bit off. The invention of GPS had made things a lot easier and a damn sight more accurate. As it was, I had gone shopping earlier this morning. I was now the proud owner of a fancy dive watch that had built in GPS. I programmed the boathouses exact coordinates into it. Easy as pie.

Walking through the dense forest, I broke through a thicket of trees on the lakes edge. I donned the wet suit, weight belt and buoyancy compensator from which hung my regulator. The regulator is what you put in your mouth to breathe. On my right leg I had a dive knife strapped and tied to my weight belt was an underwater power saw used by Special Forces. I placed my clothes in the dive bag and hid it under some scrub.

I estimated a two mph swim, which meant it would take me roughly twenty minutes to reach the target. Prepared for either wood or wire at the bottom of the boathouse, I gave myself ten minutes to cut through either. Five minutes to place the charge and then another five to get to a safe distance. I planned on heading out away from shore. I would fill my vest with air, float with just my head above the water and watch the fun.

I entered the water and standing knee deep, slipped on my fins. Then I spit in my mask, rubbed and rinsed it, and slid it over my head, fitting it snugly in place. I checked my regulator one more time. There was two hours' worth of air, which was more than enough.

As experienced divers wearing flippers do, I walked backwards until I was waist deep. Then I turned and submerged myself. Taking a few powerful strokes, I felt my way along the bottom towards deeper water. I then adjusted my buoyancy compensator until I had zero gravity. I would neither sink nor rise. Checking the illuminated GPS I began my slow and steady swim. The visibility was almost non-existent as I could not afford to use an underwater light. That would have made me visible to anybody on the shore. I monitored my GPS watch and sure enough, within twenty minutes, I arrived at the target.

As expected, the boathouse's wooden walls ran down to within three feet of the bottom. The lower few feet below the boards was wire mesh. It resembled a type of large strand chicken wire. My guess was that this free space allowed for some water flow. Lakes can have currents if the wind blows hard enough and this cuts stress on the boathouse.

I began cutting and wondered if there were any underwater motion detectors or sonar of some type. If so there was nothing I could do about it so I concentrated on the task at hand. It was important I get in and out as quickly as possible. If I did trip an alarm, I wanted to be long gone before Kenealy's men could respond.

Making short work of the fence, I soon had a hole that I could squeeze through with a fair amount of ease. After prying back the wire, I swam into the large boathouse. There she was. The rare and priceless 1939 Burger.

I placed my hand upon Kenealy's baby for the first time. Swimming down to the bottom of the hull, I placed both hands on the center. Then I pushed down until my feet touched the lakes bottom. I could touch, but barely. There was a good six feet of water between. It made sense. Chop or small waves could make the boat rise and fall, albeit slightly. Six feet of water was more than enough to ensure it never hit bottom. I wondered how often they had to dredge it.

Encased by the boathouse, no star or moon light was visible. It was pitch black as I dragged my hand along the hull and swam slowly backwards toward the stern. I arrived at the back of the Burger in moments and then repeated the process this time swimming back to the bow. I was getting a feel so as I could accurately pinpoint the middle of the vessel. The fuel tank was situated across the center of the hull to evenly distribute weight. After a few more passes, I knew exactly where I needed to plant the explosive.

It took only a minute to secure the charge using sharpened fasteners that dug into the wooden hull. Had the boat been steel I would have used magnets, which would have been easier. As it was, I enjoyed piercing the boats flawless hull. It felt like I was violating Kenealy himself. It felt good.

With the charge in place I needed only trigger the time delay and the job was complete. My thumb went to the blinking, red button. Pausing for a few seconds, I enjoyed the moment. With a rather large smile plastered on my face, I pressed the button and the red light went solid. No more blinking.

The countdown had begun.

Swimming towards the hole in the mesh wire, I squeezed my way through the opening. I needed to distance myself from the imminent blast. Although five minutes was plenty of time, one was never sure about those timers.

After making my way through the wire, I hugged the bottom of the lake. I kicked hard towards deeper water and heard a very loud metallic ping. Something slammed me in the back, spinning me around so that I was now staring up at the surface. It took me a full second to realize I had taken a bullet to the air tank. The water had slowed the bullet enough that it didn't penetrate the steel scuba tank. If it had, I would have been blown into so many pieces, that they wouldn't have found enough of me to bury. But it still hurt like hell. The force of it was so staggering that I actually felt dizzy. It felt like somebody had kicked me in the back with a frozen boot. Through the water, I saw brilliant flashes coming from the shore. They were shooting at me from less than twenty yards away. I could see the white trails in the water as they fired blindly towards the source of the bubbles. Another round slammed into my thigh with the force of a sledgehammer. The bullet had to travel through several feet of water plus a three millimeter wetsuit. Yet it still felt as if Mike Tyson had given me a Charlie horse. I knew the round had not entered my leg as I had been shot before. It is not a sensation one forgets.

My heart rate immediately doubled. I don't know how they knew I was there but I needed to get the hell out of their line of fire. The only choice I had was to try and swim around to the other side of boathouse.

I struggled to control my breathing as panic ran an icy finger down my spine. It was dark and I was alone and completely vulnerable. And I was under a full scale assault. The only thing in my favor was that I knew what to do. I unbuckled my buoyancy compensator vest. The scuba tank straps onto the back of the vest. And from the tank runs the hose which has the regulator on the end. With the vest floating beside me, and I kept the regulator in my mouth breathing long, deep breaths. I needed to build up a store of oxygen in my lungs because I would soon be without. Grabbing the knife from the sheath on my lower right leg, I prepared to cut the air hose. This would send a frenzy of bubbles to the surface and cause a diversion. That diversion would allow me to kick hard and distance myself from the dock. My attackers would focus on the bubbles, thinking that my equipment had been hit. I knew I could hold my breath for at least a minute and a half. I hoped I could get far enough away before they realized what I'd done.

Why is it that nothing ever goes to plan?

What came next was a complete surprise. From out of

nowhere a strong arm grabbed me from behind. I felt a forearm press into my throat. Things had gone from bad to worse. An iron grip closed around the back of my skull. The man pushed my head down into the forearm. He was trying choke me out and he was pretty good at it. I felt my Adam's apple being crushed as the man tried to kick and bring us both up. I knew that if he got me to the surface it was game over so I grabbed the mesh wire and hung on for dear life. The regulator was still in my mouth but as I was being choked, I wasn't able to draw any air. The only plus was that the shooting had stopped as I'm sure they did not want to hit their own man.

A single thought ran through my mind. I'm dead. There's no way I'm surviving this. I saw Debbie. I saw the kids. I started to relax as my oxygen depleted brain began to accept the situation. I would be with them soon. *And it looks like I'm losing this fight...*

A surge of anger flooded into me. I went from panic, to calm and finally to furious, in the space of just a few seconds. I wasn't going out like this my inner voice screamed. Think, I ordered myself.

With the fingers of one hand still firmly clinging to the wire, I turned the knife around in my free hand. The blade extended out from above my thumb. Whoever had a hold of me was holding me tight. I knew that his head was directly behind mine.

Bringing my arm up in a vicious snap, I stabbed dangerously close, behind my own neck. I felt the knife find its mark. Pulling back my arm, I repeated the thrust and once again the knife thudded into flesh. Even underwater I heard the man groan. I felt his grip go slack. The hand holding my neck released and the arm around my throat weakened as the man grabbed for his wound. With my throat no longer crushed, I took in a big gulp of air through my regulator. I spun to face him. Wrapping my legs around his torso, I held on to the fencing with a death grip to prevent him from surfacing. The man had a dive mask on but nothing else. He tried in vain to kick to the surface but I held fast. He let out a pitiful scream with the last of the air escaping from his lungs. Underwater it sounded garbled but the message was not lost in translation. He began to claw at my face so I decided to speed things up. With a vicious thrust, I jammed the six inch dive knife through the middle of his Adams apple. Yanking to the right, I severed his artery. The man blinked in shock. He stared into my face and then his eyes went dark and lifeless.

I held his limp body easily now as I took long, deep breaths. It felt as if an angel had given me a fresh lease on life as my brain received the badly needed oxygen. I breathed again and again and felt my strength return. Finally I pushed the man's body into the hole of the meshing, trapping him against the wire. This would prevent him from floating to the surface.

Now I could hear dogs barking and a large splash sounded from the shore. I didn't have time to worry about that. Taking one final deep breath, I cut the line. Air hissed out violently, the rubber hose whipping back and forth. The tank was emptying itself and I can only imagine what the mass of bubbles looked like from the surface.

Removing my weight belt, I pushed away from the dock

and kicked as hard as I could. I took powerful strokes with both my arms and legs as I hurried to distance myself from the boat house. The detonator was ticking down and I wasn't sure how much time I had left. I had to put as much water as possible between myself and - The water pressure changed causing a sharp pain in my ears. An invisible force thrust my body forward as if I had caught a wave while surfing. Even underwater the entire world was suddenly illuminated. I could see rocks and sand on the bottom of the lake as clearly as if it had been noon on a sunny day. The blast that followed was incredible and I swam even faster to get away from what I knew was coming next. Seconds later I heard the multitude of loud splashes falling all around me. Pieces of 1939 Burger and boat house, both large and small, began to rain down from the sky.

I wondered how many of those splashes were pieced of men. Those unfortunate enough to have been in or around the boathouse.

Fuck them, I thought.

My air was almost gone and having no other choice, I kicked to the surface. My head broke the water and I sucked in huge gulps of air as I waited for whatever might come to pass. I was out of options. I needn't have worried. The only men I saw were those running down from Kenealy's lake estate towards the blazing inferno. I could see what was left of the burning boat with no problem as the boathouse was no longer there. It was as if a giant hand had reached down and plucked it up from around the vessel. The remnants of the beautiful and rare yacht were completely ablaze. There wasn't an inch of it that wasn't on fire.

As I watched the thing burn, it occurred to me that my time would be better served making my escape. I checked my GPS and saw the line I had to take. Then I ducked my head under and started swimming as fast as I could. When I needed air I turned my head as an Olympic swimmer would and took a breath. It allowed me to swim and watch my handiwork. I did so with jubilation. The blaze wasn't letting up a bit. By the time the fire department got there it would be a charred skeleton. It was gone. I had done it.

I reached the spot where I'd originally entered the water and took one last look. Even from a distance it was beautiful. I stripped the fins from my feet and pulled off my wet suit. Looking at my thigh, I saw the ugly red welt the bullet had made. Fuck it, I thought. A small price to pay.

The bag was where I had left it and I quickly dried off and pulled on my clothes. I could hear the wail of distant sirens but it was far too late. The priceless and rare 1939 Burger was no more. Kenealy's baby was gone.

I had finally drawn blood. I was on the board.

Raging Storm
35

I slept like a baby, waking after 8am. Swinging my legs out of bed, I trudged to the bathroom, turning to look in the mirror. I had healthy bruising on the front of my throat and the sides of my neck from where that guy had tried to choke me out. I looked at my thigh and it was the same, an ugly purple bruise from that bullet smashing into me. But the smile on my face hadn't faded. Not a bit. And the best was yet to come.

I'd arrived back in Oxnard after midnight. Rob was waiting up and he listened in rapt silence as I recounted the entire nights work. Nursing a scotch, he pressed me for details. He made me repeat the events over and over. I understood. He was a combat veteran and it was a junkie's life. The adrenaline was something that crept into your being whether you wanted it or not.

He and I tried to make sense of why the guy who had jumped in the water for me had done so unarmed. He didn't even have a knife. The best we could figure was that I had sounded an alarm and he was most likely one of the guys shooting at me. And then he decided he'd be a hero and donning a mask, jumped in to drag me out of the water. I was certain that those men did not know who, or what, I was. Chances are they thought me some petty thief out to steal a few of the Burger's goodies. I doubt Kenealy would have warned them about me. He knew I was gunning for him in Malibu. The thought most likely never entered his head that I would go to Lake Arrowhead. Well, too bad for him and too bad for the others amassed around the boat house when it blew. Even I hadn't expected that big an explosion. The thing must have had a full fuel tank.

Rob and I toasted a successful op and, together, we finished the bottle of Dewar's. Rob drank the good stuff. On occasion, he drank a lot of the good stuff. But I'll say one thing for the son of a bitch. He could handle his scotch. I'd seen him drink enough to put me in a coma on many a night and he always wore it well. Unless the drink was tequila, he rarely lost control.

We'd both hit the rack after 2am. I awoke six hours later feeling good. In fact, I felt great. Because as much fun as last night had been, today would be even better. I brushed my teeth and grabbed a two minute shower. Getting dressed in a pair of beach shorts and a T-shirt, I walked into the kitchen to find Rob making a pot of coffee.

"What up, man?" I said.

"Yo."

I grabbed a coffee cup and stood behind him waiting my turn. Rob turned and filled my mug and then I walked over to the table and took a seat. My friend grabbed a box of Corn Flakes, filled a bowl and then grabbed a gallon jug of milk from the refrigerator. He managed to hold it all and walked over to join me at the table.

"No bacon and eggs this morning?" I asked.

"Nah, no time. Gotta run an errand."

"Need any help?"

"Nope," he answered. "Just dropping some papers off at my parent's attorney. Tax shit."

"Cool."

"So, when you gonna make the call?" He asked. Even Rob was smiling.

"Later. I'll let him stew all day then I'll ruin his evening. He's already got to be chewing nails, talking to me should send him over the edge."

Rob laughed and then tore through his Corn Flakes. We sat in silence, he eating and me deep in thought as I sipped my coffee. Finally, Rob finished his cereal and pushed back from the table. He bid me farewell and went to place his bowl in the sink. Then without another word, he took off.

I poured another cup of coffee and walked into the family room. Grabbing the remote control from the end table, I pressed a button and the TV screen flickered to life. I flipped around for the better part of an hour for an hour and saw nothing about the boat. I had thought that the deaths might have made the news but there was nothing. I wondered if somehow they'd covered it up. Maybe the surviving guards had concealed the bodies? Nothing seemed outside the realm of possibility where Kenealy was concerned.

The rest of the day I did more research. Looking for anything I could use to my advantage. I found the

Pasadena house that belonged to Kenealy. Joe had told me all about it. Like the yacht, it had belonged to his grandfather and then his father before him. It was where Kenealy had spent much of his youth. I started to form another plan. I would test my idea later when I spoke to Kenealy.

Then I had another idea. After a quick online search I found what I was looking for. Something for sale that interested me greatly. I called the number listed and closed the deal over the phone. Rob got home later that afternoon. I told him what I'd done and asked if he would complete the purchase later that evening. He agreed. I gave him the cash and some instructions. Finally it was an hour or so before dusk.

I jumped in the truck and made my way to Pacific Coast Highway 1. Heading north, I arrived at my destination in a little over an hour.

Stearns Wharf is an iconic landmark. Built in the 1870's it's an old, wooden pier located on the beach in Santa Barbara. With seafood restaurants, gift shops and other tourist fare, it's a popular destination. It is also an unbeatable spot if you simply want to walk out onto the ocean and take in the beauty of the Pacific.

45 miles north of Oxnard it was an ideal location to place the call I was looking forward to making. On the off chance that there was a way to trace this call, I didn't want to be anywhere near Rob's parent's house. I didn't think it was possible but after seeing Joe Simpson's store, I wasn't taking any chances.

I meandered out to end of the wharf. Taking my time to look in shop windows, I did my very best to blend in among the tourists. It didn't much matter, nobody was looking for me here, but I stuck to the protocol.

Finally, I walked out to the far end of the pier and leaned against a railing. I felt my throat tighten as I noticed a family posing for pictures. I swallowed hard as I saw the love and joy in their faces. They were together, most likely on a vacation, and life was good. It hadn't been too long ago that I had shared this joy. They could have been my family. Father, wife and two kids. My thoughts went back to that final day on the beach, watching Sasha and Hunter playing in the ankle deep water. Racing up the sand as small waves crashed and rushed towards them. They would shriek and try to outrun the foamy water that always caught them. As the water receded they would chase it back into the Gulf of Mexico. Then repeat the process as another small wave approached. Little did they know that they were living the last day of their lives. I swallowed hard for a second time, feeling my eyes growing wet.

And it's my heart that's breaking down this long distance line tonight...

That part of my life was over, I told myself for the thousandth time. And all I had left was to be thankful for it. Thankful for the time I'd felt what many people never get to experience. I tried like hell to convince myself of that but it was damn near impossible. I still felt the ache, the pain and more so, the simmering rage that bubbled beneath the surface. My soul was forever damaged. Not only by what had happened, but by what I had done since.

Earlier that afternoon, I'd called Kenealy's secretary

from a different burner. I told her to tell her boss that I would be calling that evening and that it would be in his best interest to answer. I knew he wouldn't be able to resist. Reaching into my pocket, I grabbed the phone and punched the number in. I knew it by heart. The phone rang three times and then he answered.

That voice.

The man.

"Speak," he said. Still giving orders.

"Hi Billy, how are you?" I spoke with a sincere smile, making no attempt to hide the enjoyment in my voice.

"If this is who I think it is then I must ask, why haven't you turned yourself in yet?" Kenealy wasn't taking the bait. He stayed in character. "I'm told they will go easier on you if you give yourself up."

"Oh fuck you and your bullshit act, Kenealy. It's just you and me on the line here."

"So I guess you're going to tell me that you're not recording this, right?"

"What good would it do?" I laughed. "It's inadmissible and even if it wasn't I know you're too much of a coward to ever take the real credit you deserve."

"Interesting choice of words, Ryder. Coward. That's rich. But I can see through your bullshit as well."

"Really? Please enlighten me."

"For starters, my family is alive and well. And do you know why?"

This was going to be his tact, to try and dig at me. I knew his game but played along.

"I'm sure you're going to tell me," I answered.

"Because I protect them. I protect them like a real man

does."

I didn't respond. Here it comes.

"So what's your excuse, tough guy? Mister big bad Special Forces marine." He laughed as he mocked me. Mocked my pain. Mocked my devastation. I focused on the bigger picture. I wouldn't give him the satisfaction of losing my temper.

"You let your wife and children die because you couldn't even stand up to a bunch of hopped up junkies. Pathetic."

I remained silent.

"Can you still hear them screaming? Begging you to do something? How is it you haven't killed yourself yet?" He asked. "Not enough guts?"

I hesitated before responding.

"No, I have the guts. The reason I haven't made that journey yet is that I've found another purpose in life. Something that gets me up in the morning. Something that pushes me day and night."

"Stop it," Kenealy said. He scoffed. "You're scaring me. You do realize what a pathetic attempt that was at my home the other night, don't you? You never even came close and your escape was sheer luck."

"Luck? Maybe. But I'd like to think of it as divine intervention. And speaking of missed opportunities, how about those three assholes you sent to kill me at *my* house. Like you said, jerk-off, not even close."

"Your house? You mean that little shack in Florida that wouldn't even be suitable as my servant's quarters?"

"Well, I do the best I can, Billy. I wasn't lucky enough to be born with a silver spoon up my ass. My grandfather didn't do all the heavy lifting for me like yours did for you."

I paused allowing him to respond. He didn't so I continued.

"Is that why you became a millionaire thug, Kenealy? Because you know damn well you don't have the brains your Grandpa had?"

"Don't talk about my grandfather, you piece of filth," he said. I could hear his tone change. He'd stopped laughing. "You aren't worthy to even speak his name."

Bingo. There it was.

"Now don't go getting all bent out of shape over a dead old man, Kenealy. It's not like you to lose your cool."

I laughed again and could almost hear his teeth grinding on the other end of the line.

"Tell me," I said. "Was grandpa a lowlife thief and murderer like you?"

"He was more a man than you'll ever be," Kenealy answered. His voice had a low growl. I could tell it was getting difficult for him to hold it together.

"I highly doubt it. What did he do? Run booze during prohibition? Prostitution? Did he sell our nations secrets to the Russians?"

Silence.

"And how about your daddy? Was he as much a scumbag as you are? Is being an outlaw the Kenealy brand? Your family's contribution to society?"

"Big words from a clueless nobody, Ryder. You don't have the brains to comprehend what we've accomplished. You try building an empire sometime."

I laughed.

"Coming from somebody who has never actually built one, I find that pretty amusing, asshole."

"I'll tell you what's amusing. That you think you have a future."

"Nobody lives forever," I said.

"That's a fact. But the difference is that I will enjoy my life. You will be on the run like a cockroach for the rest of your short days. I'll be living in my mansions and riding in my limos and flying in my Gulfstream. You will merely exist in misery."

"Not true, Billy. I'm having a grand old time these days. In fact, I went to a really nice bonfire last night. Sat on the shore watching the flames and had a tremendous evening. And I was thinking of you the entire time."

I paused and allowed him to react but he didn't bite.

"It was a lot of fun," I continued. "I only wish I'd brought some weenies to roast."

"Fuck you," he said. He spoke slowly, emphasizing both syllables.

"Oh no, Billy. Fuck you. That sure was a nice boat. What a shame."

"You're a dead man, Ryder. Even if the cops get to you first, you're a dead man."

"Now don't get so emotional, Billy. I didn't do it. I mean, I'm far too clueless to pull off something like that."

"You will pay a steep price for that."

"It was a really nice boat from what I hear. Grandpa's right? And a bunch of your men died too? Damn. That's a real shame. I'm very sorry for your loss."

"Speaking of losses, did you hear about your pal

Ducey?"

It was my turn to pause.

Noting my hesitation, he laughed. And then he dropped the bomb.

"It seems that one of my old employees hung himself in his cell last night. I guess he just couldn't live with the guilt anymore."

I froze.

"Such a shame," Kenealy said. "He had a beautiful family too. So much to live for."

"I don't know what you're talking about," I said. It was a weak response.

"You didn't think I'd find out about your little visit to Chino? I'm three steps ahead of you, scumbag."

Jesus, I thought. The news hit me like a punch in the stomach. I'd gotten the guy killed. I remembered Ducey's words. He had five years left. Five years. I bit my tongue, stifling the response I wanted to give.

"Doesn't mean a thing to me," I said.

"You honestly have no idea what you set in motion," Kenealy said. "You don't know who I am, do you?"

"Uh-oh," I said. "Is it your turn to try and scare me?"

"It's coming, asshole. It's almost upon you and you don't even know it."

"Hey Billy," I said. I changed the subject. "You interested in selling that house in Pasadena? That's a real gem you have there. I can only imagine the pride one would feel if they actually earned a home like that."

Kenealy said nothing.

"Yeah," I said. "But I guess you wouldn't know much about that now would you?"

He remained quiet, chewing on this unexpected turn of conversation.

"Yes sir, it's a really nice house. Also Grandpa's, right?"

"You're a dead man."

"I hope your insurance is paid up, Billy. You never know when an act of God can strike."

I waited. Nothing.

"But then again, it's not about the money when it comes to the Burger and that old house, is it? You really loved them didn't you?"

"Motherfucker."

"Oh, forgive me. I should have only used past tense for the yacht. You still have the house, don't you?"

"Please try," he said. "I want you to."

I could hear the quaver in his voice. It was taking every bit of the man's self-control to keep from going ballistic. He was not used to being talked to like this and certainly not from an underling like me.

I smiled.

"Sleep tight, now Billy. And feel special. Because you are the sole reason I live. And that, my friend, is a rare devotion."

"I'm talking to a dead man."

I laughed heartily, knowing full well it would send him over the edge.

"I'm going to watch you die you miserable scumbag!"

He finally lost the battle of wills and let loose his fury.

I laughed again. Right in his ear.

And then I did the worst thing I could possibly do to him at that moment. I ended the call with a click.

I gazed out at the moonlit ocean for another full minute.

Then I looked around to make sure that nobody was watching. Snapping the burner in two, I removed the battery. Then I dropped the pieces into the water. Turning to leave, I walked down the pier towards the parking lot. My laughter before hanging up had been an act. I wish it hadn't been. I wanted to laugh. To at least smile. I wanted to relish in Kenealy's anger. But the bastard had stolen that from me. I felt sick to my stomach about Ducey. It had to be true. He wouldn't have made it up. It was too easy to check. I had gotten the man killed. I was responsible.

It was a very long drive back to Oxnard.

Raging Storm
36

I woke up early and got a beach run in. 5 miles in 32 minutes. That's a pretty good clip, especially in sand, but I used to be faster. After showering, I ate a good breakfast. Then I went online and searched for news about Ducey. I couldn't bring myself to do it last night. Sure enough, there it was. The man had reportedly killed himself. Of course, I knew it was bullshit, but that was the official line. It was devastating. All I could think about was what Ducey had said to me about holding his kids. Making love to his wife. I had to tell myself over and over that I didn't do it. I wasn't responsible for the crimes of a monster. But I couldn't shake the guilt. But I would use it. Use it to steel my resolve.

I closed the laptop and went into the garage to take a closer look at the toy I'd purchased yesterday.

It was an older model Kawasaki Ninja with low mileage. The guy was asking two thousand dollars and the best part was that he lived here in Oxnard. Rob had completed the transaction for me right at the house. The owner had agreed to ride it over. He had a buddy follow to give him a lift back. When Rob asked about paperwork I'd instructed him to have the guy sign the title over to him. Hell, I told him, once this is over the motorcycle is yours. A thank you present. He'd laughed. Last night I'd given it a cursory glance but was too tired to give it a thorough going over. Now I inspected it. It looked well maintained and I knew it ran. Sitting atop the seat was the helmet with the black tinted visor the guy had promised me. It was perfect. I would be incognito. I could be sitting next to Kenealy at a stoplight and he'd never know it was me. It was perfect. There was a plastic clip for a phone mounted by the speedometer. I snapped my phone in place and punched Kenealy's Pasadena address into the maps app. With typical L.A. traffic it would take me roughly an hour and a half to reach the place. I grabbed a couple things from the house and headed out.

I hadn't ridden a motorcycle in a very long time and it felt exhilarating. Sitting atop an engine and commanding the type of thrust you felt on a fast bike was a great feeling. Unlike a car, you have to become a part of the machine. Want to go left, you have to lean left. Right? Lean right. Your weight is an integral part of the ride and if you know how to use it, the feeling is like no other.

I wove through traffic, feeling the warmth of the California sunshine. There wasn't a cloud in the sky and as I rounded curves, I took in the palm lined roads.
A car load of teenage girls sped by in the fast lane and they all smiled and waved as they passed. Cute girls. Kids, I thought. So innocent to the world. They lived

without the knowledge of the evil that permeates society. Monsters like Kenealy were still unknown to them, which is as it should be. I hoped they would live their entire lives only hearing of the occasional horror on the evening news. That they'd never have to confront it firsthand.

I took the 101 freeway straight from Oxnard to where it intersected with the 134 West. After zipping through Glendale, I breezed into Pasadena. Following the route on my phones GPS, I soon entered the wealthy neighborhood of Linda Vista. I made my way to Oak Grove Drive, passing several gated estates. It didn't take me long to find Kenealy's place and I motored by casually without turning my head. Using only my eyes to peek left I saw that in the driveway, beyond the gate, there were several men milling about. Security.

I laughed knowing that I had Kenealy on high alert. I was in his head.

Perfect.

I took the first left possible and followed the smaller streets that wound through the hills. Using the GPS for guidance, I found the spot I was looking for. I was on a hill behind Oak Grove Drive. From this angle, I knew that Kenealy's house would be below me.

I pulled to the side of the narrow road and turned off the motorcycle. Putting the kickstand down I got off the bike and walked through the bit of scrub brush. From here I could look down upon the different homes. And there was Kenealy's walled estate. There were large palms at the bottom of the hill. The trees ran behind all the properties. They provided privacy for the wealthy home owners. I maneuvered to a spot where I could see the front gate which was on the right side from my vantage point. Pulling a small, but powerful, pair of binoculars from my cargo pocket, I kept a close eye on the gate.

I settled in to wait. After what I did to his yacht, I knew that all I had to do was mention the old house and Kenealy would tighten security. And with that would come his head of security. It stood to reason that if I waited long enough, The Brit would make an appearance.

Joe Simpson had told me that Rothschild drove a convertible Bentley. I remembered seeing a Bentley parked outside the mansion on the cliffs the night I'd almost died. If that held true, it should be easy enough to spot him. While not uncommon in this area, I doubted that one of the hired goons that worked for Kenealy could afford one. Except for Rothschild of course. I was confident that he was very well compensated.

After two hours of boredom, I was beginning to give up hope. Cars had come and gone but none that fit the description I was looking for.

Finally, I got a break. The gate opened and in pulled a Bentley with its top down. Using the binoculars, I was certain that I'd gotten my first glimpse of the infamous Brit. As Simpson described, he had a very short brush cut and a strong jaw line. Even from behind the wheel of a car, I could tell he was in excellent shape. He wore an air of confidence. I lost sight of him as he pulled further down the driveway and the house blocked my view. But it didn't matter. I had him.

I jogged the tiny bit back to my motorcycle and hopped

on, firing up the engine. Wasting no time, I headed back the way I'd come. I got to Oak Grove Drive and pulled off to the side. Putting the kickstand down, I knelt in front of the bike, and pretended to look at the engine. Any passersby would think I was having mechanical trouble. I waited and watched and within fifteen minutes, saw the Bentley pull back out of the driveway. He made a right and drove off in the opposite direction. Jumping on the bike, I began to follow at a safe distance.

It was a lot easier to tail somebody on a bike because if need be, I could simply weave in and out between the cars. You couldn't do that in a car. Sure the people you cut off might honk, but it was a big city and people were always honking.

Rothschild was heading west, but I had no idea where he was going. For all I knew he was driving to Kenealy's mansion in Malibu. I had enough gas to get around for another few hours so I wasn't worried about that. After less than fifteen minutes, the Bentley made a right turned into a residential area. We were on the west side of Burbank. It was a nice surprise. Burbank isn't very far from Pasadena at all.

I slowed down and followed from a greater distance. There were fewer vehicles to hide behind going through these exclusive neighborhoods. My quarry made a couple turns. I assumed he was heading home. It was almost 5pm so that was a safe bet. His left turn signal came on in front of a very prestigious looking, gated neighborhood. I pulled the bike to the side of the road so as not to pass him. From a half a block away I watched as Rothschild approached a guard shack. Instead of driving to the right, closer to the guards, he stayed to the left. A gate rose and he entered the upscale neighborhood. Waiting a few moments, I finally drove up to look. The sign in front of the guard shack instructed guests to the right and residents to the left. Rothschild had gone under the gate labeled resident. Bingo.

The entire afternoon had been worth it. I now had invaluable information. I smiled and pondered the many possibilities. I would head back to Oxnard and figure out my next move. But I felt very good about the time spent. I had finally seen the infamous Rothschild.

And I knew where the bastard lived.

Raging Storm
37

"Hello?" The voice answering the phone sounded stress and tired. I felt an instant pang of remorse. I knew what this was doing to Joe. I had to remind myself that this was for him as much as me.

"Hi. My name is Blake White. I'm looking for some old transistors. Do you have any in stock?"

"I'm afraid that at present I don't, Mr. White."

"Okay, I'm glad I called before driving out. Thank you anyway."

"You're welcome."

With a click I ended the call and rose from the chair I'd been sitting in. I walked out into the back yard to feel the warmth on my face as I waited for him to call back.

After five minutes I was beginning to have my doubts when my phone finally rang.

"Hey Joe," I said. I hoped the sincere warmth I felt for him was evident in my voice.

"Hello, Ryder."

"Listen man, I know you're going out on a limb for me, but I need some information."

"Such as?"

"I did a little reconnaissance and I'm pretty sure I managed to get a look at Rothschild. Do you happen to know where he lives?"

"Burbank," Joe said.

I smiled.

"Well then I definitely made him. Can you give me anything else on the guy? Any small thing that I might be able to use?"

"Well," he hesitated. "I don't have a lot of facts. Just things I heard."

"I'll take anything," I said.

The line was silent for several seconds. Joe was nervous.

"Look Ryder, you don't have any idea what he is capable of. Why don't you cut your losses and get far away from here? You could just disappear."

I paused briefly and then answered.

"I'm past that Joe. Please, man. Help me get him. Help me and you'll be free."

"Did you say that to Mr. Ducey as well?"

The question came out of nowhere. Of course he would know. I hadn't even thought of that. There was that punch in the gut again.

"Joe, I don't have the words to tell you how sorry I am about that. But the fact is, that only strengthens my resolve. Somebody has to stop this psycho."

He let out a long, loud breath into the mouthpiece. I doubted he was even aware of doing it. My smile had faded. I felt horrible again.

"Ryder," Joe said. "My best advice is this. If you have a clean shot from a distance, take it. Do not try to fight

Rothschild head on."

"Why not?"

"Because he's not only dangerous, he's psychotic."

"Well," I said. "Like I told you the other day, I'm kind of dangerous myself."

"I don't doubt you are, Ryder. But as I told *you* the other day, it would appear that at the very least you have a soul. The Brit does not. I've heard some things."

"What kind of things," I asked.

More silence.

"Come on Joe, you know you can trust me."

He hesitated a bit longer and then spilled.

"Like he got kicked out of the British Special Forces for being too violent. Too violent, Ryder. What does that tell you?"

"Which branch of the British Special Forces?"

"I don't remember."

"British Commandos? Royal Marines? SAS?"

"That one," he said. "SAS. Are they good?"

Damn, I thought, they were England's elite guys, the best of the best. If that was true then Rothschild was for real.

"Uh, yeah," I answered. "They're not bad. What do you mean by too violent?"

"Well again, this is only what I heard but apparently, he liked to torture people. When he was in Afghanistan I heard he took a lot of pleasure in mutilating prisoners while he killed them. Like, mutilating them before they died. Get it? Some seriously sick shit from what I heard. I don't know if it's true or not. I don't even know if you can understand what I'm talking about."

I understood better than he knew. Having also served in the Special Forces I knew about the fringe element that you ran into every now and then. Real whack jobs who had found their calling in the gruesome art of war, these guys loved every second of it. They did shit that was unspeakable. The good news is, when caught, these psycho's would go to prison. But for most of us, it was a job. A violent, but necessary job. We were professionals. Still, shit goes down in a combat zone and a lot of it isn't pretty. War brings out the absolute worst in some men.

"How did he hook up with Kenealy?"

"I have no idea. He was already part of the organization when I first came aboard."

"And how did that happen anyway?" I asked. "If you don't mind me prying?"

"That's a long story. But I swear to you that I never knew what I was getting into. After graduating from MIT I needed a job and heard about an opening at GSI. I filled out an application and got hired in their R&D department. And over time, certain people noticed that I had a flair for electronics and surveillance."

"MIT?" I said. "That's impressive."

"Thank you."

"How big is GSI's Research and Development department?"

"Pretty damn big. There's a lot of competition for government contracts so we always have to stay ahead of the curve if we want to win them."

Yeah, I thought to myself, or just have the CEO's of your competition murdered by some idiot.

"But how did you end up as one of Kenealy's..."

I paused, searching for the right turn of phrase.

"...special people?"

"It just kind of happened. One day, out of the blue, I get called into Randall Ducey's office. He started asking a lot of questions. Personal questions. Questions that you wouldn't normally get asked by an executive."

"Didn't that send off any warning signals?"

"Well, at the same time he was being very complimentary. Telling me that Mr. Kenealy had taken notice of my skills and that I had a great future with the company. That I was being considered to head up an R&D division."

"So they played to your ego?"

"You have to understand, Ryder. At that point I had no idea what Kenealy was like or what GSI was capable of, and in fact doing, around the world."

"I get that, man," I said. "I'm not judging."

"They're a huge corporation with large defense contracts and conglomerates worldwide. I was young and excited to be getting noticed by their top people. I thought I had a big future. I thought my dreams were coming true, that I was going to matter."

It wasn't just an explanation, Joe was trying to get some things off his chest that he'd been holding in for a very long time. I could tell. I let him vent.

"How the hell could I have possibly known? How could anybody have known?! I mean, who in the world would suspect that the entire thing is pretty much a front for a criminal organization!? I started questioning everything! Is it all rigged?! All companies, our government?! Who the hell is clean?!"

He was getting worked up, his voice was rising.

"I get it, Joe," I said. I spoke with understanding, trying to back him down a bit. "Listen brother, he played me too. That's what he does. He finds emotional weak spots and he exploits them. He took the worst tragedy of my life and used it against me."

Neither of us spoke for a brief time. I was reflecting on how I'd allowed Kenealy to take advantage of me and I suspect Joe was doing the same. Finally he spoke. He asked me a question. A very direct question. It caught me off guard.

"Was that you in Washington? At the Ritz Carlton?"

I let my silence do the talking for me. How could I explain? How could I possibly justify murder? What could I say to this man that would help him to understand?

"It's…it's not how it seems, Joe," I said. My tone had changed. I spoke in a low voice. A distant voice. "It's not at all how it seems."

He must have heard the pain in my voice. He must have known that I'd just admitted my greatest shame to him. Joe allowed another brief moment of silence and then it was his turn to offer comfort.

"I'm sorry, Ryder. I shouldn't have asked. Like you said, it's what he does. He lies and manipulates. Don't be too hard on yourself."

I took in a slow breath and released it. Funny how emotion creeps up on you. A simple trigger and all the feelings come rushing back to the surface.

"Yeah," I said. "Yeah."

"What else do you need, Ryder?" He asked. He was

trying to end the phone call. He was right. It was time.
"That's it, man. I appreciate this more than you know and I will be careful, Joe. I promise you that."
"Good luck," he said.
"Thanks. Take it easy, brother."
He snorted an awkward laugh.
"What?" I asked.
"Nobody's ever called me that," he said. "It's what cool guys call each other."
"Listen to me Joe," I said. "I know we're just getting to know each other but I already consider you a friend. You're a hell of a decent guy and you've got guts. You don't know how rare that is, man."
"Thanks, Ryder," he said. "I mean, thanks, brother."
It was my turn to laugh.
"Take care," I said.
" Oh, one more thing"
"Yeah?"
"Nice job on the boat." He said it with a chuckle.
I broke into a heartfelt belly laugh.
"Thanks," I said. "He didn't take it very well."
"I'll bet."
"See you, man."
"See ya."
The call ended with a click. I was smiling again.

Raging Storm
38

I had just gotten off the phone with Joe when I heard a door close inside the house. Walking in from the back yard, I saw Rob digging in the refrigerator. He came out with a rotisserie chicken, some light mayonnaise and a bottled water.
"Hey man," I said. I walked over to the couch and flopped myself down.
"Hey brother."
I couldn't help but grin as he called me that.
Rob placed the chicken on the counter. Grabbing a loaf of wheat bread we keep next to the toaster oven, he slid it down the counter. He then pulled a plate from the cupboard and went into a drawer, coming out with a knife. Pausing, Rob leaned against the granite counter top to look at me.
"How'd it go?"
"Not bad," I answered. "Kenealy did everything but call out the National Guard. I've got him spooked pretty good."
Rob laughed. He straightened and began making his

sandwich. Removing the chicken from its container he carved out two good hunks of breast meat with the knife. Placing them on the plate, he opened the bread and grabbed four slices tossing them onto the plate as well. Reaching for the mayo, he used the knife to smear a disgusting amount onto two of the bread slices. Placing the chicken on those pieces, he crowned them with the other two slices and his lunch was ready.

He saw me frown.

"What? It's light mayo," Rob said.

"Yeah, but when you use three times the normal amount it kind of negates that, don't you think?" I laughed.

"Well I was going to ask if you wanted one but now you can kiss my ass."

I laughed again.

Rob took a healthy bite that left a big glob of mayo in the left corner of his mouth. He wiped it away with his hand.

"So what else did you get today?" He asked with a full mouth.

"Well," I said. "I got my first good look at this British asshole I told you about."

"No kidding? The mysterious Brit?" Rob smiled.

"Yeah, but there's more. Turns out the dude was SAS."

The smile faded and Rob's face now wore a very serious, tight lipped grimace. SAS earned instant respect in our world.

I spent the next few minutes relaying the telephone conversation I'd had with Joe Simpson. Rob listened intently as he wolfed down the rest of his lunch.

"What happened today?" He asked.

"I spotted him at Kenealy's and then followed him on the Ninja. Perfect stealth vehicle by the way. The tinted helmet is like hiding in plain sight. I shadowed him to his neighborhood but it's gated so I couldn't follow."

"That's easy enough once it gets dark."

"Yeah, but I want to take it slow. I need solid intel on this guy before I make a move."

"Why?" Rob asked. He shot me a stern look. "I think you're making a big mistake, Ryder. I agree with the computer geek. Why not just take him out?"

"Don't know. He kind of intrigues me. I think I might be able to use him to get to Kenealy. Just a gut feeling."

"Fuck that," Rob said. He grimaced, shaking his head. "If it's true that this guy is SAS then just snipe his ass. Why risk it?"

"It might come to that. I don't know," I said. I stood and walked towards the kitchen. "Hey, leave that stuff out, man."

Rob cleared the way as I commandeered the chicken and bread. He chugged his water and trudged into the family room to fall back into the spot on the couch I had vacated. I started fixing my sandwich taking care to show Rob that I was foregoing the mayo.

There was that ever familiar finger gesture.

"Listen man," I said. I spoke as I put the food away. "Would do something for me."

"That's why I'm here. What do you need?"

"Kenealy's oldest son. The guy who stands to inherit the company. Can you find out if he has a place out here? My guess is it wouldn't be too far from daddies house."

"Okay, but wouldn't the guy live in Tampa?"

"Yeah, but if Kenealy has a place out here, I'm willing to bet that the heir to the throne has one too. They have a research plant close by so it makes sense."

"Why his kid? What's the angle?"

"No angle. I just want to know everything. I hope it never comes to this but if I have to, the guy might come in handy."

"Yeah, okay. I'll see what I can find out."

"Thanks."

"So what's your next move?"

I gave this some thought as I chewed. Rob allowed me time, grabbing the remote and turning on the television. As it crackled to life, I swallowed the bite and smiled down at my friend.

"I think I'm going to get up early tomorrow and spend the day with my new British pal."

"Well all righty then," Rob said with a laugh. "You kids have fun."

I chuckled as I took another bite.

Raging Storm
39

There seems to be about a four hour window in the Los Angeles area where traffic isn't brutal. From roughly one in the morning to five in the morning, otherwise it's varying degrees of a snarled mess. One of the few benefits is that it makes tailing somebody a lot easier. If you were trying to follow somebody in a small Midwestern town it would be a difficult task. You would most likely get spotted before they finished driving down Main Street. But here in Burbank one can take cover behind any number of frustrated commuters. Especially on a nimble little motorcycle like my Ninja. Waking up at zero dark thirty, I'd gotten out of Oxnard well before the sun came up. Now, sitting a block away from the gated entrance to Rothschild's neighborhood, I waited. I figured him to be an early riser as are most military people by sheer habit and repetition. Either way it didn't matter. This was what I was doing today.
Sure enough, the man did not disappoint. As the first rays of sunlight were peeking over the low mountain range to the east, I spotted his Bentley. He pulled

through the gate and turned right, heading in my direction. I waited for him, and a few others, to pass and then pulled the Ninja into traffic and began tailing him. His first stop was a strip plaza. He parked the Bentley and was walking into a Smoothie Queen when I pulled into the lot. I pulled behind a Chevy Suburban and watched the front of the store through the tinted windows of the large SUV. It was ideal cover.

Within ten minutes he exited, carrying a large, Styrofoam cup. I was willing to bet that Rothschild had ordered the healthiest drink in the place. I would double down that he'd added a protein shot. People with military backgrounds tend to be somewhat predictable.

I waited until he pulled out of the strip mall and then eased back into traffic. I kept a good hundred yards between us. It was easy to keep an eye on him. His luxury car stuck out among the normal domestic and foreign cars on the road. Bentley's have a very distinct look.

I could tell where he was heading next by the route he chose. Sure enough, within ten minutes, he eased his car into the driveway of Kenealy's Pasadena mansion. I couldn't help but chuckle as I watched several sentries come out to greet their boss.

I was in Kenealy's head. He was certain that I'd try to do to his home what I did to his precious yacht. The truth is, I never had any intention of touching this place. But it sure drew the cockroaches out of the woodwork and tied up a lot of his resources.

And as I figured, it led me to The Brit.

After passing the house, I did a slow U-turn and stayed

way back, parking on the side of the road. I was a good ways from the driveway but would be able to see when my quarry left. Another advantage the motorcycle has is that it is very fast. If I needed to catch up to Rothschild, I had the horsepower to do it.

He wasn't there long, not even five minutes. He'd most likely wanted a situation report and to keep his men focused. As the Bentley pulled out of the driveway it turned towards me. I pulled out my phone and pretended I was texting. The car sped past me on the opposite side of the road. I watched in my small, side view mirrors as it made a right on a residential street. I knew this would lead back to downtown Pasadena.

Doing another U-turn, I rode to the street he'd turned down. I spotted him and increased my speed to narrow the distance. As we got into heavier traffic it was easier to hang back and hide among the other vehicles. After a few moments, the Bentley turned into another, larger, strip mall. I held back and when I finally eased into the parking lot, I could see his car parked in front of a Whole Foods. Rothschild got out and walked into the store. It didn't surprise me that he was into health food. Special Forces goes hand in hand with fitness. Most of us tried to stay in top physical shape.

After approximately fifteen minutes, he exited the store pushing a shopping cart. Several bags were in the cart and I watched as Rothschild unloaded them into the trunk of his expensive car.

He pulled out of the strip mall, crossed three lanes, and immediately got in the left turning lane. It would have been too obvious to follow so I waited.

When the left turn arrow changed to green, I watched as he made a U-turn and headed back the way he came.
Was he buying groceries for the troops, I wondered. Not likely. I doubted he would ever show subservience to his men. Plus, any mercenary worth his salt would come to work prepared.
Instead of doing what Rothschild had done, turning right and then making a U-turn, I waited for an opening. I then tore across the road, against traffic, to resume my tail. In about a mile, I watched as the Bentley made a right onto Hwy 210 heading east.
I sped up, getting on the freeway myself, and weaved through cars until I was close enough to keep him in my sights. The freeway was thick with morning commuters and I wondered how long I would have to stay in this mess. After close to an hour of stop and go traffic, the Bentley finally took the Rancho Cucamonga exit.
He was too far ahead of me. If I stayed in the bumper to bumper mess I was in, he'd get away. I maneuvered to the shoulder and gunned the bike. Zipping towards the exit, I ignored the angry commuters who honked and flipped me off. When I finally got to the off ramp, the Brit was nowhere in sight. And I had no idea which way he'd turned.
Shit, I cursed myself. How the hell could you lose this guy?
Once again I got on the shoulder and sped down the ramp. When I got to the light I stopped and stood, feet on each side of the bike. I looked to my left and right. There he was. He had made a right and was only a couple blocks up the road.

Breathing a sigh of relief, I made a quick right in front of a motorist who had waited his turn. He did not appreciate my cutting in line and sat on his horn until I waved an apology. That seemed to placate the man. Within a few minutes, the Bentley left the main road and turned into a residential area. Keeping a safe distance, I followed and after a few blocks Rothschild made a right turn. I approached where he had turned and saw that it was the entrance to another gated development. There were a pair of large ponds on each side of the approach. In the middle of the grand entrance, in front of the guard shack, was a three story high, faux mountain. A bronze eagle sat atop the craggy peak. Water trickled down the rock mountain.

Nothing says swank like a bronze eagle, I laughed to myself.

This time Rothschild had pulled up to speak with a guard. I pulled off to the side and watched as the two men exchanged a laugh. They seemed plenty familiar with one another. The gate then rose and Rothschild drove off with a friendly wave. The gate dropped as the Bentley disappeared into the neighborhood.

That was it. End of the road.

I had a gut feeling that whoever he was seeing here would take up some time. The fact that he had brought groceries suggested this. There was no point in waiting. I'd gotten the intel I needed and the gold nugget was the Smoothie Queen. I was willing to bet that it was a morning ritual for him.

I thought about what Joe had advised and gave some thought to taking him out from a distance. I could set up in the hills across the road. Although it would be simple enough, there were other factors to consider. One of these was that blowing the top of his head off would traumatize any witnesses and some of them might be kids. I wasn't about to do that to a child or anybody else. I could also drive up next to him and simply unload a clip into his Bentley but there were also risks with that. A guy with his training would more than likely see that coming. The last thing I needed was to end up in a gun battle on the streets of Burbank. These were possibilities. Nothing more. I would figure out my next move later. My mornings work over, I turned the motorcycle to begin the long drive home. All in all, it had gone well. I knew a little more about the enemy and had discovered what might be a pattern. I would figure out a strategy soon enough but for right now I was happy to be making progress. I wasn't in a hurry.

I had nothing but time.

Raging Storm
40

After battling rush hour traffic, I made it back to Oxnard around lunch time. Walking through the back door I found Rob beaming at me from over his laptop which he'd set up on the kitchen table. Next to the laptop sat a full bottle of Budweiser and two empties.

"Hey man," I said. I returned his broad smile. "May I assume from your shit eating grin that you found something?"

"You know it," he answered. "That was too easy."

"Sweet, let's hear it." I opened the refrigerator and grabbed a water.

"Well, young William Kenealy Jr. has a freaking sweet place in St. Petersburg, Florida. It's over seven thousand square feet on the Intracoastal Waterway. Swimming pool, guest house, dock with two different boat lifts. If I didn't hate the little bastard before, I do now."

We both laughed.

"How did you get all that?" I asked.

"The address was easy, I got it from tax records which

are public domain. All I had to do next was type the address into Zillow and voila, Richie Rich's house. Simple."

"Cool, good work, man. What about here?"

"Even better. The prick has a beach house in Pacific Palisades. Not as big as the Florida pad, but right on the damn sand overlooking the Pacific."

"That's not too far from Malibu I think."

"Nope, it's not far at all. And it's only about an hour from here."

"Very cool. You got the address?"

"Right here," Rob said. He slid a piece of paper across the table.

"Dude, you're the man," I said. "I can't tell you how much this means to me."

"You thinking of snatching the kid? I'm pretty sure that would draw out daddy."

"Nah man, I'm not going to hurt anybody who doesn't have it coming. It's just good to know I have a hole card to play in case things get hairy."

"Nobody said anything about hurting him. Just grab him. What better way to flush out the big fish?"

"I hear you man, but I can't do that. Not yet anyway. After Washington, I won't involve somebody if I don't know they're actually dirty."

I paused as the shame of Bradley Wakefield swept over me yet again. The vivid memory of his widow haunted me for the umpteenth time. I cast my eyes downward and felt the hollowness in my chest that always accompanied the guilt.

"I hear you man," Rob said. He understood.

"For all I know this kid is clueless about his dad," I finished. "He may be completely in the dark."

Rob saw my pain and offered me a simple, tight lipped nod.

"I get it, Ryder. I do. But I doubt it," he said. "The apple never falls far from the tree."

I turned back to the fridge, opened it, and surveyed my options. There were a couple pieces of chicken left. There was also a plate with three slices of pepperoni and sausage pizza.

"You mind if I finish this pizza?" I asked.

"Go for it," Rob answered.

Grabbing the plate, I ripped off the cellophane. Shoving a piece in my mouth I took a bite. Damn, I thought, is there anything better than cold pizza? I remembered when I was a young boy, running downstairs the morning after my parents had thrown a party. My brother and sister and I would go from pizza box to pizza box looking for the uneaten slices. We would fight over the good ones until dad came down to straighten us out. When dad got pissed off, everybody got real quiet, real fast.

"So how did it go today?" Rob said. It brought me back to reality.

I chewed the rest of the piece, swallowed, and then answered.

"Not bad. The Brit likes smoothies in the morning and is a health food nut. He made a stop at the Pasadena house but wasn't there very long."

"Anything you can use?"

"Well," I said. I paused, pondering the possibilities. "If

the smoothie thing is a regular morning ritual, which I suspect it is, I could take him out right there. Or maybe even take him alive if I had a van."

"I still say you should listen to Joe's advice. Why mess with a guy like that?"

"Maybe," I said. "But he may come in handy later. Anyway, he ended up going into some other gated neighborhood so I couldn't follow. I'd love to know who he was going to see."

"Could be anybody. Who knows?" Rob answered.

"Yeah. Well I'm going to take my time. No need to rush this."

"Just kill him, bro."

"Dude, I'm not a marine anymore. My answer to every problem isn't to kill it.

"Bah," Rob answered. "Once a marine, always a marine."

I chuckled and went to the sink to wash my hands. The pizza was good and had filled me up. After drying my hands on a dish towel, I walked towards my bedroom. I entered and came out a few moments later with a bag containing one of my disguises.

"See you later," I said.

"Where you heading now?"

"South. I'm going to do a little recon on the Kenealy brat. Want to come along?"

"No thanks. Got some plans tonight."

"Okay." I grinned at him. "Should I ask?"

"Just some chick I see every now and then. She's driving up from Oceanside. Might catch a movie."

"Make sure that's all you catch, devil dog." I laughed.

"Up yours, she's not like that."
"Kidding, Robert. Kidding. Have fun."
"Will do. Be safe, Ryder."
"Always," I answered.
Walking out the garage door, I headed for the Ninja. I was looking forward to my little beach excursion.

Raging Storm
41

It had been a slow ride down from Oxnard. Not only had I hit rush hour traffic, but all the departing beach traffic as the sun prepared to go down. The sun worshipers were packing up and heading home. Arriving in Pacific Palisades, I drove along the beach and found the parking lot I'd been seeking. Before leaving I'd used the map feature on my phone and found what I was looking for just north of Kenealy Jr.'s beach home. Pulling into the lot I noticed a group of bunch of teenagers hanging around some vehicles. I parked as far from them as I could on the other end of the lot.

I took my helmet off and strapped it onto the back of the seat. Looking around to see that nobody was watching, I went into the side bag and came out with my fake beard. The glue strips were already in place and I pasted the thing to my face in one quick motion. I looked in the motorcycles small, circular mirror and made the necessary adjustments.

I had on flip flops, tattered shorts and a grimy shirt. I'd worn a scraggly, dirty blonde wig under the helmet. Now it had a disheveled and matted look, which was the appearance I was after. I wanted to be invisible and one of the best ways to do that was to look homeless. People tended to tune them out, often looking the other way when they approached.

There was a small, boarded cut which led from the pavement to the sand. I walked down it, shuffling my feet and doing my best to appear uninterested in my surroundings. I was a drifter, going whichever way I felt at the moment with no general purpose or destination. Not a tough stretch, I thought with a frown.

I knew that once I hit the beach, Kenealy's home would be the fourth one if I headed south.

Making my way to the water's edge, I stood briefly and watched a pair of surfers carving up some right breaking waves. They were good, shredding and cutting with what had to be years of experience. I'd always found surfing to be a spiritual thing and just watching it made me feel grounded. But now was not the time.

I turned to my left and started south. The homes on this stretch of beach were large. They all sported wide, lofty back decks elevated high above the sand. Worth a fortune, they belonged exclusively to the upper crust.

As I approached the homes, I left the water's edge and angled my way up the sand for a closer look. I gazed up onto the deck of the first house and saw some of the beautiful people staring down at me with disgust.

Clearly, they had no problem looking at a vagrant when he was out of reach. I could imagine what they were saying to each other about me. Turning away, I did my best to avoid eye contact. I was still going for invisibility.

I made it to young Kenealy's house and continued my wayward shuffle doing my best to look like a harmless vagrant. His place was stunning, at least from my vantage point. The entire back side of the house was glass. The deck, painted a modern white, had a polished, nickel chrome railing. I could see an outdoor grilling kitchen and several overstuffed deck chairs. I kept my head down as I ambled, using only my eyes to look upon it. After passing the house by a good hundred feet, I turned around, switching directions. I headed back to make another pass. The sun was almost down and the light was fading. Once it was dark I planned on getting a lot closer, but right now I needed to know if anybody was home.

I was almost parallel to the house, when a light came on. It startled me.

The windows now glowed a soft yellow. Almost immediately after that, a couple appeared on the back deck.

Unbelievable.

I looked up and into the face of the young Kenealy. My heart jumped. I recognized him from his pictures. There was no doubt. It was him. He was standing at the rail, drink in hand and gazing out at the sunset. The woman by his side looked familiar but I couldn't place from where. She had the stunning, drop dead good looks of a super model. The last remnants of sunlight sparkled off her diamond necklace. Her smile was ivory perfection

and she had on a pretty sundress cut above the knees. She balked as she saw me staring up at her. Moving her hand down to her dress, she pressed it flat against her legs. I watched her say something and then Kenealy himself stared down at me. He looked pissed off.
Fuck me, I thought. They think I'm some pervert trying get a cheap thrill. Shit. I hadn't meant to stare and I cursed myself. I did not need this guy's radar up. Averting my eyes, I turned away and staggered a bit as I made my way back down to the water's edge. Nothing to see here, just a drunk staggering down the beach. Don't even think twice about it.
I continued north, intentionally passing the parking lot in case they were watching. There was no need to let them see me climbing atop a motorcycle. That would have raised a few questions.
I reevaluated my plan then and there. It was pointless breaking into the house tonight. Just knowing he was here was worth the trip. The Kenealy bastard was actually here. Several thoughts ran through my mind. Some of them not so nice. I could have taken him out if I'd wanted to. I could still take him out. And why not? This was a war which I didn't start. Kenealy had tried to kill me more than once. Taking out his number one son would be quite a coup. Maybe it would let the bastard know what it felt like to have a family member murdered. To have a child murdered. He had mocked my families death. I could let him experience what that pain felt like. I could do it right now.
Even as I had those thoughts, I knew I was incapable of it. The kid might be innocent. It was possible that he had

no idea what a scumbag criminal his father was. And as I'd told Rob, I couldn't kill him in cold blood. I had murdered one innocent man, I wasn't going to make it two.

My work done, I turned to walk a swaying, uneven line back to the parking lot. The kid would be a hole card I would draw upon only if absolutely necessary. I hoped it would never come to that. As it was, I felt a pang of guilt because I was going to make him fatherless. It sucks having a conscience sometimes.

As I was now a good distance away, I looked back towards the house. I could still see them. They were standing side by side, looking out over the ocean. They looked happy and why shouldn't they be? They were young, rich and by the looks of it, in love. Did they have plans for a family? Who knows? It was all ahead of them. Just as assuredly as it was all behind me.

Debbie flashed into my mind and I swallowed hard, feeling that all too familiar lump in my throat. Fuck me, not now I thought.

Stop it, I told myself. Stay on task. But it was impossible. I saw her face, I could smell her hair. She was with me again.

And it's my heart that's breaking down this long distance line tonight...

It's funny how many times your heart can break. The moment you start thinking the worst of it's over, it comes back with a vengeance. Just when you think that the worst of your pain is behind you, it hits you like it happened yesterday. The scars rip, tear themselves open and the wound is as fresh as it ever was.

I steeled my jaw and forced myself to stop looking at them. It wasn't easy.

As I headed into the parking lot, I wiped the moisture from my eyes.

Raging Storm
42

I walked back through the cut in the sand and made for my bike. The streetlights had come on and the parking lot was fully illuminated. My Ninja was the lone vehicle on this far end of the lot. On the opposite side, the teenagers remained, mingling and talking among themselves. The last trace of the suns amber glow was darkening the horizon and bronzing the cloudless sky. The wind had died down and it promised to be a warm evening.

I made it to my bike and was about to remove the fake beard when I heard the rumble of another motorcycle pull into the lot. I looked up and felt my chest tighten. There is no mistaking a California Highway Patrol bike. As there was still a nationwide APB on me, I left the beard where it was. I fiddled with my bike and tried to act as casual as possible although my heart rate had doubled. The cop's powerful Harley Davidson Electra Glide rumbled and I watched as he scanned the lot. Shit.

I mounted the Ninja, pulling the key out of the front pocket of my shorts. Inserting it, I depressed the clutch and pressing the red button, my bike fired to life. At that exact moment, the cop spotted me and turned my way. As there was nobody anywhere around me, I was pretty sure he was coming for me. I had two choices. I could run and hope to outmaneuver the more powerful motorcycle as he got on the radio and called for backup. Or I could sit still, smile, and try to talk my way out of whatever this was. I liked my odds better with the verbal option so I placed both feet on the pavement. Keeping my hands in very plain sight, I waited. And I smiled. The cop pulled his bike to a stop in front of me, blocking my path. Standard police tactic and completely expected. I smiled and did my best to look like an innocent civilian, and in no way a wanted felon. But, the hamster inside the tread wheel of my brain was running at heart attack pace.

Shit, I thought a second time.

Why is it that once cops pull you over, they like to take their time? It's like a curtain gets drawn and they go into their act. I like cops, I respect them. They have a dangerous and thankless job and they take a lot of shit from a lot of assholes. But this guy was a peach. His body language told me as much. The way he glared at me while removing his helmet and dropping the kickstand on his bike. Something told me that he was not going to be sweet talked. I did the only thing I could do. I waited patiently and let him run his show.

Throwing a leg over his bike the cop stood, and having already removed his helmet placed it on the seat of his bike. His right hand went to rest on the butt of his gun and I swear he cocked his hip as he turned to address me. All he needed was a cigarette or a wooden match stick hanging out of his mouth. A real cowboy.

"Kill the engine," he said. He spoke loud and with authority over the noise of my bike.

I twisted the key and the motor died. I began to climb off my bike.

"Stay seated, sir!" He commanded. His eyes widened and his hand closed tighter around the pistol grip. He bent slightly at the waist, his feet spread apart lest I attack. It was ridiculous.

"Sure thing, officer," I said.

I lowered my leg back down and showed him my hands. The best thing I could do to relax this guy was to remain as placid and as submissive as possible.

"What seems to be the problem?"

"You stay right there and keep your hands where I can see them." He spoke with authority, ignoring my question.

"Okay."

Looking me up and down, he took a step to the left, and examined my motorcycle. My calm demeanor had the desired effect because he seemed to relax, albeit slightly.

"What's your business here?" He asked.

"Here in this parking lot?" I offered a reassuring smile. "Absolutely nothing, officer. I took a sunset stroll and now I'm leaving."

"A sunset stroll?"

"Yes, sir."

"Do you live around here?"

"No, sir. I live in the valley."

"Where in the valley?"

"Van Nuys."

He took a few seconds and seemed to ponder this. Finally he got down to it.

"License, registration and proof of insurance, please."

I hesitated and then shook my head as I rolled my eyes. I gave a short laugh.

"You know what's crazy, officer? I keep all that in my wallet, and when I got home from work today, I just threw on these shorts and dashed out the door. I'm afraid that I left my wallet in my jeans."

He didn't respond, only stared me down as his eyes narrowed with mistrust.

"Officer," I said. "I work construction and had a really bad day. I came down here to chill out and watch the sunset."

"So you do not have any ID?" He said. He eyed me suspiciously.

"Well of course I have ID, sir. I left it at home is all. I guess I wasn't thinking. Sorry. I got blown up by an IED in Iraq and sometimes my brain is a little scattered. I forget things."

I hoped that the guy was a veteran and would warm to me with this information. His next sentence told me otherwise.

"The law states that you carry these documents whenever operating a motor vehicle. Forgetting is not an excuse."

All righty then, I thought, so much for the veteran angle. This guy was a serious by-the-book dude. Okay. I decided to try a different angle.

"Sir, I have done nothing wrong. It is illegal for you to stop me without reason or probable cause."

The cop glared at me.

"I have been nothing but courteous and respectful and followed all instructions. So please tell me what law I've broken or let me be on my way."

He shot me a serious fuck you look and then answered.

"Some of the residents reported a suspicious person walking the beach. Looking into their homes. You fit the description so there's my probable cause, smart guy."

"You've got to be kidding me," I said. "Since when is it illegal to look at the homes along the beach? I don't get to see how the other half lives very often. These places are gorgeous. It's impossible not to notice them."

"Or it could be that you're casing them. Either way, you made a lot of people nervous. They thought you were up to no good."

"Well sir, if it was me they were referring to then they were wrong. I'm just an average tax paying citizen. I have a small house in Van Nuys and I work construction. Like I said, I had a really miserable day and thought that watching the sunset would help me relax. Some guys get high, some guys drink, I like to take walks. It was stupid to forget my ID but it was not done intentionally."

The cop whipped out a notepad and pen from his left breast pocket.

"What's your social security number?"

It was my turn to look at him with mistrust. I was getting very anxious. This was not going well. With every passing second, the guy was forcing my hand.

"For the second time, officer, I have done nothing wrong. I understand that some people may have gotten nervous but this is a public beach and I am a part of that public."

"I asked you for your social security number. I'm going to call it in and if you check out, you can be on your way."

"I don't have it memorized."

"You served in the military, correct?"

"Yes."

"Well I know for a fact that they make you memorize your social security number."

"Yeah, and like I said, I got blown up in Iraq and it messed with my memory."

The cop looked at me with a scowl. He wasn't buying it.

"Why are you wearing a disguise?"

Uh-oh.

"What are you talking about?" I answered. It was weak but I couldn't think of anything else.

"That's a fake beard or I'm Santa Claus. Why the hell are you wearing that?"

"So now there's a law against trying to look cool? Why the hell are you hassling me? I've done nothing wrong."

I glared at him and felt my temperature rise. I was getting pissed.

Sensing the shift in my demeanor, the cop reached for his shoulder mike and thumbed the button.

"Dispatch, this is Patrol five-niner-seven requesting immediate backup."

The radio crackled to life.

"What is your 10-20, five-niner-seven?"
"Beach parking C in Palisades."
"Roger that. Back-up on the way."
"Jesus Christ, man, I haven't done anything. What the fuck is this?"
The cop took two steps backwards and drew his gun.
"Sir," he said. "Step away from the motorcycle and lay down on the pavement with your arms spread to your side."
And that was the ball game. The situation had gone code red.
I quickly weighed my options. If I got belligerent or acted threatening, he would keep his distance. Might even shoot me. I needed him close.
"Fine," I answered. I swung my leg over the bike. "Look, I'm sorry I got upset but like I said, it's been a shitty day."
"Lie down on your belly and spread your arms," he commanded. "I'm not going to tell you again."
"Yes, sir."
I spoke meekly and complied, dropping to my knees and then, using my arms, lowered myself to the pavement. With my head turned to the side, I noticed the teenagers on the other side of the parking lot. They were gawking and whispering among themselves as they watched.
"Interlock your fingers and place your hands behind your head."
This was what I'd been hoping for. He was going to cuff me himself. I did exactly as he instructed.
His footsteps crunched on the asphalt as he approached me. A knee dropped into the middle of my back and

none too gently. I heard the sound of his gun sliding back into its leather holster. Then the sound of him going into his cargo belt for a pair of cuffs. A hand grasped my left wrist and the cold, hard steel clamped down. He clicked the cuff closed with a loud snick and pulled my arm behind my back. Since I hadn't resisted at all he relaxed and let go of my left wrist. He held the handcuffs and grabbed for my right wrist.

Now or never.

I yanked my right arm away and jammed it under my body, between my chest and the pavement. Acting instinctively, the cop reached under me, trying to grab my arm and regain control. Pushing my chest off the ground with my right arm, I reached under my chest with my left. My hand closed around the cop's wrist. I had him. Clamping down on his wrist like a vice, I rolled to my right. With his arm locked, the cop had no choice but to roll with me. It was a basic wrestling maneuver. The entire move had taken less than three seconds and now the cop was on the bottom, my back pressing down on him.

He screamed and I felt his free arm moving. He was going for his gun.

Tightening my stomach muscles, I did what's best described as a half sit up to free some space between us. I then slammed my body back down, snapping the back of my head into his face. It connected with a meaty thud. His body shuddered. Letting go of his arm, I spun around so that now I was not only on top, but facing him as well.

"Stop!" He screamed.

His nose was bloody and his face wore a mask of terror, mouth turned down and eyes wide like saucers. I'm sure he saw his life flashing before his eyes.

"I'm not going to kill you," I said.

Out of the corner of my eye, I saw two of the young men taking choppy, uncertain steps as they headed towards us. Good Samaritans looking to help the officer. But they were nervous. Normally I would have applauded that type of courage. Today was not normal.

Turning my attention back to the cop, I grabbed his hair with my left hand. I leveled two hard punches at his chin with my right, pivoting my shoulder to put my weight into them. With the cop squirming, the first punch missed and hit him in the front teeth. I heard one of them snap in half. The second one landed squarely on his chin and he went out, his eyes rolling back in his head. I shook the pain from my hand, blood spraying from a gash across my knuckles.

And then I turned my attention back to the parking lot. The two heroes were only twenty feet away and closing fast. Grabbing the cops 9mm, I yanked it from the holster and turned, leveling it at them.

"Who's first?!" My face was a mask of fury.

Both men skidded to a stop and then turned on a dime, slipping and sliding from the quick change of direction. Getting their feet under them, the two set a Palisades C parking lot speed record in their haste to get away.

There was no time to lose. I grabbed the cop's second pair of cuffs from his belt and flipped him over. Pulling his arms behind his back, I had him cuffed in no time. From the leather pouch, I grabbed the key and shoved it in my pocket. I would free my left wrist later. Using the corner of my shirt, I wiped down the cuffs I'd just placed on him as best I could. I didn't have time to wipe down the gun so I made sure the safety was on and shoved it into my pocket alongside the key. I hadn't touched anything else. I gave him a last look.

"I'm sorry," I said.

Leaping to my feet, I looked across the parking lot and saw the terrified crowd watching me. A young woman screamed. The group decided they seen enough and scattered. Some of them headed for the sidewalk. Some of them onto the sand. But all were putting some distance between themselves and me.

Good idea, I thought as I placed a solid kick against the side of the cop's bike, knocking it over.

Jumping on the Ninja, I twisted the key. For the second time, the engine roared to life. Edging around the police motorcycle, I gunned the throttle and made a beeline for the exit. Peeling out of the lot, I lowered my head and raced north on the Pacific Coast Highway like a bat out of hell. When I was a good mile or so down the road I finally slowed to a normal speed. I made the first right turn possible and started winding my way through the hills and back roads.

By the time I'd worked my way back to Oxnard, my heart rate had finally returned to normal.

Raging Storm
43

"Holy shit, Ryder!" Rob stood in front of me, a look of disbelief on his face. "Did you really take out a cop?!"
"I didn't take him out," I said. I took a good pull from my second beer. "He'll be fine after a bit of dental work."
The moment I'd arrived home I headed straight to the refrigerator and grabbed a long neck Bud. My frayed nerves needed it. If that had gone the other way I would be in custody right now facing
murder charges and probably the death penalty.
"Dude," Rob said. He gaped at me and shook his head.
"You weren't there, Rob. It was an impossible situation. I had no choice. I got goddamn lucky that his back up didn't show."
I chugged the rest of my beer and walked over to the couch. Grabbing the remote, I turned on the TV and found the 24 hour local news channel. They were airing a story on the drought and its effect on farming but I

knew it wouldn't take long to see if I had made the news.

"Why in the hell did you wear the drifter disguise? Wrong part of town for that shit."

"Yeah, I know. It was a mistake. I thought that with all the homeless people in California, I'd fit right in."

"Ryder," Rob said. "There are no homeless people in Pacific Palisades. In fact, I don't think there are even any middle class people."

He laughed.

"Okay, I got it." I shot my friend a sour look. "I fucked up."

"Should have gone with the surfer disguise. That wouldn't have stood out at all."

"Yeah, but I was on the bike. Couldn't exactly tote the long board."

"Should have taken the truck," he answered. He wore a large smile. Rob was enjoying himself.

"Okay, asshole. I get your point."

He laughed again and walked into the kitchen. Grabbing the bottle of Dewar's that was on the counter, Rob unscrewed the cap and poured himself a drink.

"So," he said. After a brief pause he continued. "Did you forget the part of recon training that dealt with blending into your surroundings? I mean, why didn't you just wear a ski mask and carry a big sack with a dollar sign on it?"

"You're a funny guy," I said. "You should really think about doing stand up."

Rob snorted with laughter. He was in a particularly good mood.

"What's going on with you, man?" I asked. "Didn't you have a date tonight?"

"Nah, she blew me off. Made some excuse about not feeling well."

"Sorry."

"Not a biggie. We're not serious, just friends with benefits mostly."

"Well," I said. "At least that's something."

"Anyway, been doing some thinking about my future. Got some ideas about it."

"What the hell are you talking about?" It was my turn to laugh. "We both know you're a thirty year man."

"Well," Rob said. He took his time. And another swig of scotch. "Maybe you don't know half the shit you think you do."

I looked over at my friend. There was a trace of hostility that I couldn't help but notice. Rob was still smiling but for some reason he looked a little pissed off as well.

"How much have you had to drink, bro?" I asked.

"Oh, about enough," he said. He gave me a playful smirk. "But that ain't gonna stop me from having some more."

Another laugh.

I turned as I heard the television mention Pacific Palisades. Grabbing the remote, I turned the volume up. There was a news crew in the C parking lot amid the flashing red and blue lights of different cop cruisers. A local surfer was being interviewed.

"I couldn't believe what I was seeing," the long haired, young man said. He spoke with a wide grin, enjoying the attention. "This dude was on the ground being cuffed by this cop and all of a sudden he just went totally ballistic and next thing you know he was like, on top of the cop and the rest of us were like whoooooa…"

"And were you able to get a good look at the man who assaulted the police officer?" The pretty blonde reporter asked.

"Totally! The guy was like a bum, you know? Like, he had a beard and stuff and dirty clothes and he looked like, homeless, right? But then he pulls a gun and points it at us and we all started booking, you know?"

"Can you tell us what happened next?" The reporter shoved the microphone back in his excited face.

"Well, then the dude jumps on this motorcycle and hauls ass. And that was it. It was crazy!"

"And at any time did you fear for your life or for the life of the police officer?"

"Oh, for sure! We all thought the dude was gonna waste this cop and then when he pointed the gun at us we all totally shit. Oh, sorry!"

"It's okay," the reporter said.

"I've never been so freaked out in my life! It was completely wigged!"

The reporter shifted to the young woman who stood next to the surfer.

"And can you add anything to that, Miss?"

"No, it's like he said. It just happened really, really fast. One minute we were all just hanging out and the next thing you know I hear somebody scream and we all looked over and saw this cop fighting this guy. I couldn't believe it. Next thing you know somebody yells gun and we all ran. I'm still freaked out!"

The surfer put his arm around her and she leaned into him.

The reporter turned back to address the camera. She grimaced and gave her best, rehearsed serious look. "There you have it, terrified witnesses and a police officer very lucky to be alive. Reporting from the beach in Pacific Palisades, this is Claire Duncan. Back to you, Larry."

"Very lucky indeed, Claire. Thank you," Larry the anchorman said. He then went on to another story.

Rob had watched, grinning from ear to ear and emitting a low and steady chuckle. Now that the story was over he threw his head back and let loose a belly laugh.

"I'm glad you're having a good time, buddy."

I glared at him. It wasn't amusing to me at all.

"You know Ryder," Rob said. He wiped his eyes as his laughter subsided. "Most people come out to L.A. to get discovered and never end up doing shit. You came out here to *not* get discovered and you're an overnight sensation."

He resumed laughing. Rob was having a grand old time.

"Good one, good one," I said. "Keep 'em coming, asshole."

I stood up and began walking towards the refrigerator for a third beer when one of the phones in my pocket rang. It was the burner I used exclusively for Joe Simpson.

I answered immediately.

"Hey man, what's up?"

"Ryder," Joe said. It sounded like he was out of breath. "I need you to come out here tomorrow."

"Whoa. Slow down, man, What happened?"

"I can't talk. Just get here as soon as possible tomorrow morning," he said. There was an almost frantic edge to his voice.

"Joe, calm down," I said. I spoke in a calm and soothing manner, hoping he would relax. "Tell me-"

The phone clicked in my ear.

"Joe. Joe!" It was pointless. He was gone.

Rob was no longer laughing as he read the look on my face and had heard my end of the short conversation.

"What's up?" He asked.

"I don't know. That was Joe Simpson, the guy I told you about from The Valley."

"Okay. What's up?"

"I don't know. But he sounded like he was in trouble. He wants me to come out there tomorrow."

"Why?"

"You heard the call, he didn't say why. Hung up on me."

Rob stared at me in silence. Gone was the mirth, he was all business now.

"Well, you can't go. You know it's a trap."

"Maybe."

"What the fuck do you mean maybe? It's a trap."

"If they'd wanted to trap me why not have him call casually and ask if I could stop by tomorrow, I have something to show you? Why make it sound like he was in trouble?"

"I don't know," Rob said. His frustration was evident. "Because they're smart?"

I paced the room and thought. If it was a trap then there were bound to be a lot of guys waiting to jump me. I don't think that Kenealy would want me killed outright. I was pretty sure he'd want to see me face to face, maybe even do it himself. There was something else in Joe's voice. It sounded like fear. He was afraid. Maybe he'd learned that they were on to him? Maybe he was just being paranoid? Either way the guy was stressed out about something. I made my decision.

"I'm going."

"What?!" Rob yelled in disbelief.

"Look, man," I said. "I'm not going to just walk in the front door. I will check the place out and I will go in ready. Like Fallujah, brother."

"Yeah, but in Fallujah you had a platoon of jarheads covering your six. I'm going with you."

"No you're not. I need to do this alone."

It was one thing for me to allow my friend to hide me out. It was another thing to have Rob walk into an ambush with me. This wasn't Iraq. Rob and I had belonged there. But all this shit I had caused. I wasn't going to live with Rob's death on my hands too.

"Fuck you, Ryder. I'm going."

"No, man. Please. You're already risking enough."

"Hey Ryder," Rob said. He walked over to me. "I'm fucking going and that's that."

He put a hand on his hip and squared his jaw. I knew this look. He wasn't going to back down. I shot him a smile and then shook my head at the crazy bastard.

"Okay. But you're gonna hang back. If any shooting starts, I want your field of fire to be ninety five degrees."

He simply stared at me.

"Got it?" I said. I matched his stern expression. This

wasn't a game.

"Yeah, okay," he finally answered. "I got it."

I knew he was full of shit, telling me what I wanted to hear.

"Cool. Be ready to go at zero seven hundred hours, devil dog."

"Oh seven hundred. See you then."

Rob slammed the rest of his scotch, placed the glass on the counter and walked back to his bedroom. I killed the TV, turned out the lights and headed to my bedroom.

Tomorrow was going to be an early day.

I planned on leaving the house at six.

Raging Storm
44

It had been easy enough to sneak out of the house. I woke before six in the morning. After throwing on a pair of cargo pants and a t-shirt, I grabbed the now infamous vagrants wig and beard, stuffing them into the big pocket on my left thigh. In the right pocket I placed my small CZ .40 caliber pistol. It had a full clip. I dropped a second full clip next to it and buttoned the flap to ensure neither would fall out.

After tip-toeing out of the bedroom, I'd exited through the back door which was farthest away from Rob's room. The Ninja sat in the driveway so it was a simple matter of pushing it a block down the street and then firing it up. Rob would be pissed off but I didn't care. He knew Joe's store was in the Valley, but I never gave him an address or even the name of the place if memory served correct. He couldn't follow.

I made it to the valley in less than an hour and worked my way toward Simpson's store. It was too early to meet with him but I wanted time to do a little reconnaissance. I had to make sure the place wasn't being surveilled. Parking the bike a few blocks away, I donned the disguise. The same disguise that had almost gotten me arrested twelve hours earlier. I didn't have to worry about sticking out in this part of town. The San Fernando Valley is a world apart from Pacific Palisades. Homeless people are a dime a dozen here.

I thought back to the conversation I had with Rob last night. He was right. I should have gone with the surfer disguise. That wasn't like me, I knew how wealthy that area was and yet I chose to stand out. Was it a subconscious decision? Was I trying to get caught? I remembered Rob suggesting that I had a death wish. I hadn't thought so, but now I began to wonder how close to the truth that was.

I thought about the cop. I'm sure he was back in his home. His only real injury had been his chipped front tooth. Maybe a broken nose. I felt terrible about it, the guy was only doing his job. I have nothing but respect for law enforcement and fire fighters. Those guys are the everyday heroes. Most people can't even imagine having a job where you face real danger on a daily basis. I wished I could find him and explain. Apologize. But that was an impossibility.

As I walked towards Joe's store, I shuffled my feet and kept my head down. I stopped to look in trash cans and picked up the occasional cigarette butt. It was important to remain tactical. When I was a block away I turned left and started heading away from the shop. It was crucial that I looked like I had no destination, that I was wandering. I expected eyes on me. I had to assume the worst.

I kept this up until well after the shops had opened. From time to time a police cruiser would motor past and look my way. I found a friendly wave usually netted the same in return. As many times as I'd circled Coiled, it was pretty obvious that nobody was staking the place out. Not from within shouting range in any case. If there was a sniper placed somewhere in a distant building then so be it. Not a lot I could do about that if they saw through the disguise. Still, my gut told me that Kenealy wouldn't be satisfied with just clipping me. No, after what I'd done he would want to look in my eyes. I was certain of that.

I hadn't seen Joe enter the store but he may have gone in the back when I was out of that particular line of vision. Either way, it was time. I had to get in there and see what he wanted. I would enter through the back, gun drawn, ready for a fight.

I made my way towards the back alley, keeping in character all the way. Although I saw nothing out of the ordinary, I stayed on full alert. It was so quiet. I almost wished there had been something amiss. This was creepier.

I made my way to the rear entrance. The closed sign was hanging in the door which didn't seem like a very good omen. Either Joe was too afraid to open up or he'd taken it on the lam. I didn't want to consider the third possibility. I half expected a locked door and gave a soft push. It opened a crack. Unlocked.

I took in a large breath of air and exhaled. As I did so, I

went into my right cargo pocket and wrapped my hand around the .40 caliber. Keeping low and in a shooters stance, I pushed the door open and froze, expecting anything.

Silence. Nothing.

I pushed the door open the rest of the way and stepped into the store. It was dark. No lights were on. That was good for them if they were lying in wait, but it was also good for me.

Now inside the store, I let the door swing back, guiding it with my left hand. Along the narrow corridor leading into the store, I could see a light switch. Staying on the balls of my feet I made my way down the hall. I wanted to call out for Joe but knew that would be a very bad idea if there was a team lying in wait. Noise discipline was very important.

My left hand went for the light switch as my right hand trained the pistol down range. I had thumbed the safety off and was ready to rock and roll should the occasion call for it.

I flipped the light switch and the stores fluorescent lights flickered to life. I could see down the middle row of shelves. Nothing seemed out of the ordinary.

My heart was pounding out of my chest. I expected a full frontal assault at any second. Having already decided that I would not be taken alive, I prepared to go down in a blaze of glory. I was not going to give Kenealy the pleasure of watching me die after his sadistic enforcer did God knows what to me.

I steadied my breathing and continued my slow creep. Moving to my right and keeping low, I scanned the next aisle. Again there was nothing. I continued as far right as I could and each aisle was the same, merchandise on shelves. Nothing else.

Okay, I thought to myself. Empty. I looked to the left side of the store and noticed Joe's office door. If he was in there he sure was being quiet. I was going to give him a heart attack popping up out of nowhere. Fuck it, I thought. He should have been out here to greet me instead of making me go through this bullshit.

I made my way to the office door and put my hand on the knob. I considered the fact that the ambush might be in here but dismissed the thought. Tactically it would have been foolish. There's no way that professionals would set up in a small office with only one entrance. Nobody with any training would make such a mistake. I turned the knob and pushed. The door swung wide.

There are certain times, especially in combat, when you freeze in shock. A roadside bomb goes off and you watch a guy you were talking to five minutes earlier, get blown to hell and back. You're on patrol and a fellow marine's head comes apart as it catches a snipers bullet. You watch as a good friend kicks in a door and catches a hail of bullets in the chest.

You quite literally freeze. Your mind races to process what you've seen. It's called shock and no amount of training can prevent it. The brain needs a few moments to catch up with reality.

This was one of those moments.

Joe Simpson was here. Joe Simpson was all over the small office.

The walls dripped blood. Each wall. It looked as if

somebody had taken red paint and applied a crimson splash and drip pattern.

In the surreal haze of the moment, something caught my eye. Upon the shelf closest to the door, only two feet from my head, lay one of Joe's arms. Placed at eye level, the arm extended, hand towards me. The fingers broken. Broken and manipulated so that they lay flat against his palm. All except the middle finger. It pointed upward. Facing the door. Intended for me.

Joe's legs sat stacked against the far wall. Stacked as somebody might put away their boots in a closet, neat and placed together. Sawed off below the knees.

I felt my stomach lurch.

Joe's other arm lay propped up on some books to the right of his desk. The fingers on this hand were also broken. Also bent inwards. A lone digit, the pointer finger, was sticking straight out, pointing to the wall behind the desk. There was a crude message written in blood.

RYDER WAS HERE

I stood rooted in shock and then lowered my eyes from the message to lock eyes with Joe Simpson. His severed head sat atop his desk, eyes wide and staring at the doorway. At me. He was looking at me. They had pried his mouth open so that it was in a perpetual scream. His tongue, cut out, lay on the table in front of his chin.

But his eyes. His eyes said it all. They told the story. The horror of the torture he had endured. I didn't have to ask myself what sick bastard could do something like this, I already knew.

I felt a wetness roll down my cheek and it was only then

that I realized I was crying. Silently crying, as I stood looking at my latest victim. I had done this to him. I had killed him. I had involved him. Joe Simpson would be open for business, selling his gadgets and living his life if I hadn't involved him.

I jumped in shock as a car door slammed outside the front of the shop. Seconds later the front doors rattled as somebody tested to see if they were open.

"Go around the back," a commanding male voice said.

In the distance I heard a siren wail.

Holy shit. A setup. My blood froze.

I took a last look at Joe Simpson.

"I'm sorry," I said. My voice, soft and low, cracked with emotion. "I'm so sorry, Joe."

I couldn't think of anything else to say.

My inner voice screamed at me. Get out!

I tore for the back door, pistol still in hand. Yanking the door open, I dashed out into the alley, running smack into a uniformed officer. His gun was still holstered.

I shoved him backwards and pointed my gun at his head, pulling back the hammer with my thumb.

"Freeze!" I growled it in a low voice, hoping his partner wouldn't hear.

The cop, who looked no more than twenty years old, went pale. He froze.

I put a finger to my lips and shushed him.

"Take off the belt and do it fast," I said.

He complied and with nervous, fumbling fingers, undid his utility belt. The belt held, among other things, his weapon. His eyes were wide and pleading. He wanted no part of me.

"Toss it to me."

He did and I caught it.

"Now run!" I hissed the command.

He looked at me with a mixture of fear and confusion.

"Run!"

I thrust out my arm and leveled the gun at him.

The young cop turned and sprinted down the alley as fast as his legs would carry him. I watched as he rounded the corner and ran out of sight. I then tossed the belt aside and pocketed my own pistol. With five quick strides I crossed the small alley and hopped the brick wall that opposed the back of Joe's store. I landed in a back yard. I continued running, bolting to the next wall and vaulting it with adrenaline fueled ease. I leapt wall after wall. There were more sirens now, a lot of them, but they had no idea where I was heading. I ripped the wig and beard off and dumped them in a trash can. Making a quick right I headed down a side street that ran parallel to my bike. After three blocks, I made another right. A cop car flew past, its lights flashing. I forced myself to slow down. To walk. I crossed the street, strode to my bike and with trembling hands, donned the helmet and put the key in the ignition. The Ninja came to life with a rumble. Making a slow U-turn, I tried to control my breathing as I drove away. Away from the lifeless, dismembered body of Joe Simpson. Away from the scene of incredible carnage. My arms shook as I held the bikes grips. I swallowed hard and imagined what Joe must have endured. The nightmare he'd experienced. It was too much. I'd promised him he would be safe. I had told him to trust me. He did trust me. Like my family had trusted me to keep them safe. Tears fell again.

I tried to clear my head. To tell myself it wasn't my fault. But it was no good. Nothing would ever be good again. There were too many thoughts now. So many different things running through my mind that it was difficult to focus on any of them.

The miles ticked by and the trembling finally stopped. My head began to clear. As the pain gave way to something much darker, I knew only one thing. And I knew it with absolute certainty.

I was going to kill that British psychopath.

Raging Storm
45

I made it back to Rob's place, my mind still reeling. I'd seen brutality in the war but the mutilated corpse of Joe Simpson blindsided me. I hadn't expected it at all. And the fact that he had suffered that unspeakable horror because of me was almost too much to bear. I felt overwhelming guilt. If I hadn't been so goddamn stubborn this wouldn't have happened. Because of my private crusade against Kenealy, two people had died. Randall Ducey and Joe Simpson. Both killed because I had reached out to them. It was a bitter pill to swallow. And even worse, I had involved one of my closest friends. Using his parent's home as a safe house had been selfish. I was not only putting Rob in the cross hairs of this lunatic, but his parents as well. Well, I was going to fix that. Tonight would be my last night here regardless of what Rob said to me.

I parked the motorcycle in the driveway, behind Rob's Jeep, and walked into the house. I knew I would have to take a load of shit for ditching him. I didn't care. I was

way past that.
Walking into the open garage I entered the house through the door leading to the kitchen.
"Rob!"
No reply.
"Rob!"
I walked into the family room and towards the back door. Looking through the window, I checked the backyard. Not there.
Doing a one-eighty, I made my way back through the kitchen to his bedroom. The door was slightly ajar so I knocked. No answer. I pushed it open. Rob wasn't there. The house was empty.
Okay, no big deal, I thought. But it was strange that his Jeep was in the driveway. I knew Rob wasn't into walks or even running, aside from what he had to do in the Corps. But there was something going on that I couldn't put my finger on. The other night when he was getting drunk, there seemed to be some hostility behind his good mood. It may have been my imagination I felt something. This entire episode was most likely beginning to gnaw at him. Hiding me made him an accomplice to murder and Rob was no dummy, he had to have been thinking about that. Maybe he was beginning to feel used. The fact is, Rob was acting out of loyalty and friendship. He felt honor bound to help me but I knew it must be placing a tremendous burden on him. I couldn't blame him if he felt put out. For Christ's sake I had involved him in multiple felonies. Some friend I was. This did nothing but cement my decision to leave. I had to make this right. I had to act, to feel some sort of

forward motion. I had gotten both Joe and Randall killed. I wasn't going to allow something to happen to Rob. No fucking way.

Walking into my bedroom, I grabbed my duffel bag from under the bed. I walked to the dresser and began emptying it, placing neat stacks upon the bed. Then I went to the closet for my shirts.

As I packed, my mind went into overdrive. I had to come up with a next move. My train of thought broke as one of the phones in my pocket buzzed. It was the phone in my right pocket.

A chill ran through my body.

Joe's phone.

Holy shit, I realized. What had I done? The enormity of my mistake came crashing down upon me. After getting the call from Joe last night, I hadn't given a thought to the phone. Even when I knew that he may have been compromised, I hadn't turned the burner off. I didn't take the fucking battery out if it. I didn't destroy it. Not even after finding Joe's mutilated corpse had it crossed my mind. I'd been in shock finding his body. And then the frenzy of having to escape the police. I hadn't even thought about the goddamn phone. They could trace it. With all Joe's expertise and electronic wizardry, they could pinpoint my every move. I felt an icy dread wash over me.

I spun to face the door and instinctively dropped to one knee as I grabbed the CZ .40 caliber from my cargo pocket. The only thought that raced through my panicked brain was dear God, there couldn't be a worse scenario. Things could not have been more fucked up.

I was wrong about that too.

The burner continued to ring. There was no voice mail set up. It would ring forever if I let it or if the party calling me didn't give up. And whoever was calling was not giving up. There was somebody who wanted very much to speak to me and the only thing I knew for sure is that it wasn't Joe.

I put the pistol in my left hand, keeping it trained at the doorway. Fishing the phone out of my pocket with my right hand, I brought it up to stare at the screen for a moment. I hesitated, thinking for a second that if I didn't answer, none of this would happen. It was a foolish thought born of panic. Everything felt like it was moving in slow motion.

I pressed the green button and somehow got the phone to my ear. I said nothing. I listened to the silence. It didn't last.

"Now, now Mr. Dunham," a male voice said. The condescending British accent left little to the imagination. "Don't tell me you're the shy type?"

The Brit. The lunatic who had dismembered Joe. I felt my fear turn to anger.

Still I remained silent.

"Mr. Dunham, I can hear you breathing. I must say that you are being extremely impolite."

"You motherfucker," I said. My tone was low and ominous. It wasn't an act, I was feeling very dangerous.

"Well now, that's not very nice. I would expect better manners from a fellow serviceman."

"I'm going to kill you," I said. "Do you hear me? I am going to end you."

"Wow," he said. "Unexpected. You are much ruder than your friend, Mr. Dunham. Robert is a perfect gentleman."

I remained silent as the mention of Rob's name punched me in the gut. What have I done, I thought? What have I done? This wasn't happening. It wasn't possible. What was left of my world caved in on me. There is a point of no return and this was it. I felt my sanity slipping away. The only sound was my heartbeat.

"Hello? Are you there, Mr. Dunham?"

I was catatonic. I couldn't find words. And if I could I wasn't sure that I'd be physically able to speak them.

"Hellllllo. Mr. Dunham?"

"Where?" It was all I could think to ask. My tongue felt so thick I wasn't sure it came out right. I felt like I was going to pass out. This was too much.

"Right to the point I see. Good. Well, your friend decided to spend the weekend at the lake with us. We would be ever so pleased if you could come and join us."

"I will trade my life for his," I said. My voice was on auto-pilot. It was a statement of truth. No forethought. I meant it.

"My, my, my," the Brit said. He paused and laughed. "How very dark of you, Mr. Dunham. Why would you think the worst of this situation?"

"Fuck you and your games, Rothschild. Make the arrangements. Once Rob walks free, you can have me."

"Hmmm, you know my name. Certain people sure do like to talk, don't they? Or should I say didn't they."

He laughed again.

"Make the arrangements you psychopathic piece of

shit."

A pause.

"Well now that hurts my feelings, Mr. Dunham. Why would you resort to name calling? I have done nothing to you, good sir. As a matter of fact I hold you in high esteem. You are a fellow warrior with some very obvious skills. And I am a man who appreciates and respects talent when I see it."

"Don't you fucking lump me in with your kind you twisted freak. You and I are nothing alike. Nothing!" I yelled, losing the battle for my emotions.

"If you say so, Mr. Dunham, but having seen some of your handiwork in the past few months, I am inclined to disagree. Still, let's not argue."

"Why did you have to do that to Joe?" I hadn't meant to ask the question. It popped out of my mouth. I could still see Joe's eyes, staring at me. I could see him. I couldn't stop myself. "Why didn't you just shoot him. He was a damn good man. Why? Why would you do that you sick fuck?"

Rothschild chuckled. I lost it.

"Why?!"

"You seem greatly disturbed, Mr. Dunham. And I'm not sure what you're referring to, sir. But getting back to the matter at hand, you are formally invited to a very exclusive party on Lake Arrowhead. I'm sorry that we didn't have time to mail proper invitations but I believe you know the address."

"Rob's life for mine. He didn't do a fucking thing. He's innocent," I said. It was pointless. This guy didn't give a shit. But it was my only play.

"If you leave now, you can make it in time for dinner. We are having a barbecue out on the back lawn. We're thinking of having a pig on a spit. All in your honor."

"My life for his. I will be there by six o'clock."

The only hope Rob had was if I could get a couple clean shots off. One for Kenealy and one for this British motherfucker. If I could somehow, creep up undetected there might be a chance. Even as I thought it, I knew it was an impossibility.

"Excellent! I look forward to finally meeting you in person," Rothschild said. He sounded jubilant.

I breathed into the phone and fought the urge to vent my rage. I knew it would be futile. I had to stay calm, stay focused.

"Six o'clock," I repeated.

"Drive safe now, Mr. Dunham. I'd hate for anything to happen to you."

"I'll be seeing you soon, Rothschild."

Click.

The call ended.

I stood in place for a solid five minutes. Breathing. Staring at the floor and breathing. I felt worse than I ever had in my life.

Almost.

Raging Storm
46

As I stood in stunned silence, I thought back on the past few months. Every job I had done for Kenealy. Every decision I had made. Every single thing I'd done since that horrible night I'd lost my family had been a foolish miscalculation. I had destroyed countless lives. I had failed my wife and kids. Innocent men had died because of me.

I felt like putting a bullet in my head.

You don't know how desperate I've become and it looks like I'm losing this fight...

I stood mute and struggled with the unbearable burden. And then the angst, the dread, the internal breakdown began to act as a catalyst. Something brooding and dark grew and it was not foreign to me but had never felt so magnified.

Yes, nothing would ever match the fury that I had experienced watching that meth head kill my family. But that was madness. Blind, maniacal rage. This was different. This I controlled.

Bubbling anger, like hot lava from a fissure, seeped out of me. I turned to walk into my bathroom. Placing my palms on the edge of the sink, I stood and looked into the mirror, staring into my own face. Into my own eyes. I didn't like what I saw. What I felt.

"Enough."

I spoke to my own reflection. My voice menacing. I was beyond angry. And not at Kenealy or even The Brit. The anger was all for myself. It was time to end this bullshit. It was time to stop feeling sorry for myself. Time to put it all behind me and start doing things right. This was getting old. I done with the tears. Done with the self-pity. I stared into my own bloodshot eyes and thought about Debbie, Sasha and Hunter. As painful as it was, it was time to bury them, to stop living as a crazed demon chasing their ghosts. I was at my breaking point.

I would do everything possible to save Rob. I would give them a fight they wouldn't believe because that was the only thing I could do. The only thing I knew. There was no way they would trade him for me. He was now involved. Thanks to me. They would kill him even if I surrendered. That much I knew with certainty. I knew that the only chance I had of saving my friend was to take out Kenealy. That was the only play. Without their employer, nobody would even think about Rob again. Why would they if there was no longer a paycheck involved? I knew it was a long shot, but my advantage was that I was ready to die. I was willing to bet that Kenealy's men weren't.

And with these thoughts came a sobering realization. I

was most likely going to die within a very short period of time. I was most likely living my last day. There might be tomorrow but nothing beyond. I was ninety-nine percent sure of it. That was okay. I accepted it. I didn't care anymore.

I walked through the house and into Rob's room. Looking in his closet, I found his sniper rifle and a box of ammo. Grabbing both, I walked back to my room and lay it on the floor. I bent down and pulled the box out from under my bed to inspect my own arsenal. I still had the Val which I'd used to take out the 3 mercenaries who had broken onto my home in Florida. I also had two flash bangs as well as a few fragmentation grenades that Rob had brought me. And I had my the .40 caliber CZ pistol.

It was enough. It was all I needed.

They would expect another water approach. I would. But I had a few surprises in store for them. Distraction, diversion and then a shock and awe entry. Kenealy would be there, he had to be. The cocky bastard would feel safe with his army around him. But I was sure he would be there. I had no doubt that he would want to witness my demise from a front row seat. If there was one thing I could depend on, it was that asshole's ego.

I loaded everything into the F-150 and went back in the house to write a letter. If things went bad, the police would come to Rob's house as part of their investigation. I wanted the chance to explain. It was the last thing I could do to try and bury Kenealy if all else went wrong. What started as a quick note became three scribbled pages as the words came pouring out of me. Before finishing, I took a few extra minutes to write about Ducey and Simpson. I knew that it would never be enough to arrest, much less convict, but I had to get it out, to let somebody know.

I signed the bottom of the letter and then took a step back to take a final look around the house. It had been my bunker, my sanctuary. I couldn't help but wonder whether Rob would ever see it again. The thought steeled my resolve.

Turning to walk towards the garage, I stopped in my tracks as a sudden thought occurred to me. I stopped in place. And froze.

Of course.

The solution smacked me in the face with the subtlety of a baseball bat. It had been there the entire time. I felt like an idiot for not thinking of it earlier. Why was my initial instinct always to rush into battle? It was the training. Fight force with stealth or an even greater force.

Okay, I thought to myself. Okay. The plan came together in seconds. It was so obvious, and in fact, was an option I had considered before. The unexpected conversation with Rothschild, hearing of Rob's abduction had rattled me. I hadn't allowed time to process. But I was thinking straight now. And it became crystal clear what I would do.

I felt a growing excitement. I could save Rob. I now realized that I actually had a very good chance of actually saving him. It was the way I was going to fix this. The plan came together without effort.

Right now the Brit was massing his troops, preparing for the attack that he knew I would launch. He'd most likely cover all possible entry points and his men would be on high alert. I'm sure that every possible soldier they could muster would be there. Every mercenary with any combat experience at all would be at the lake house. Rothschild would stage them in an impenetrable 360 degree perimeter. They were going to stack the deck so far in their favor that I would never stand a chance. Kenealy would hole up in a safe room waiting for my capture or death. Waiting for Rothschild to bring him his prize.

Me.

They were all gathering there, awaiting my arrival. They knew I was going to come in guns blazing.

Well screw Lake Arrowhead. They could wait until hell froze over.

I was going to Pacific Palisades.

Raging Storm
47

Wearing black fatigues, I sat on my haunches by the water's edge. Thankfully, because of rare cloud cover, it was a very dark night. I brought the small, but powerful, binoculars to my eyes and looked up into the glass walls of the beach house. There was a light on somewhere near the front of the home. I had no idea which room was lit, but it blanketed the back deck in a soft glow. Other than that, the area was dark. That was a stroke of luck as I planned on breaching the house through the back.

This time I brought the truck, leaving it in the same parking lot in which I'd fought the cop only two days earlier. It was strange being back there. There was still a few strands of fluttering, yellow police tape wrapped around two palm trees. Only two other vehicles were in the lot as night had fallen and the beach goers were gone.

I backed into a spot that was the closest to the path leading to the beach. Once I made the grab, I didn't want to have to haul Kenealy's son across a parking lot. After I left Rob's, instead of driving down the coast, I'd jumped on Highway 101 and headed south into Thousand Oaks. I exited on the cheaper side of town and found a place called the Blue Moon Inn. It was a seedy, low rent motel located off the freeway. Frequented by the homeless as well as junkies and prostitutes, it was perfect. The occupants minded their own business and were not the type to call police. This was where I would implement phase two of my operation. I'd chosen a room on the backside of the motel. Here, the parking area backed up into woods and was dimly lit. I proceeded to make it even darker by taking out a few of the light bulbs near my door. Once I returned from Pacific Palisades it would take mere seconds to get my prisoner into the room.

The plan was simple. I would breach the beach house, locate and subdue. Although I had no idea what Kenealy's son was capable of, I wasn't worried. Growing up rick and pampered, I was pretty sure that he'd never been in a fistfight in his entire life. My biggest problem was likely avoiding the splash of urine when he pissed himself.

Once I made the grab I would render him unconscious, get him to the truck and then to the hotel room. At that point I would call Kenealy and arrange a swap. The Brit would want to negotiate but I would insist upon speaking to daddy himself. Under the circumstances, I was pretty sure I could get him on the phone. They would both demand to see the kid alive but that was their problem. I would be holding all the cards so they would have to dance to my tune. If Kenealy wanted his son back, I would need proof that Rob had been released.

Period. No debate.

From my distant position I saw a figure, a lone shadow, pass in front of the soft, yellow light.

Perfect. He was home.

Although it sickened me to think about, I knew there was a chance I would have to get physical with his lady friend. I hoped not, but there was no way around it if she got in the way. If possible, I would apply a sleeper hold to avoid having to strike her. The effects were not permanent and the victim is usually unconscious for less than a minute. But if that wasn't possible I would do what I had to do. Rob's life hung in the balance.

I looked down both sides of the dark beach. There was nobody present.

It was time.

Keeping low, I sprinted towards the house. I made it to the overhanging deck in seconds. It was too high to reach from the outer edges. However, as the sand rose up the hill closer to the house, it would be within reach.

First there was the security fence to deal with. Under the deck and in the shadows, most people never noticed it. The fence prevented people from wandering up between the houses. Wire cutters made short work of the chain links and I soon had a long, vertical cut through which I could squeeze.

Once on the other side, I climbed the soft sand of the dune and peeked over the bottom of the deck. It was all clear. I pulled myself up and over, quietly dropping to a crouched position. Pausing, I knelt beside a chaste lounge chair and took the time to survey the inside of the home. From my vantage point I could see the kitchen which spilled into a beautiful living area. There were a pair of couches and three easy chairs arranged around a beautiful, glass table. The large, flat screen TV was off. Down a hallway, which led to the front of the home, I could see the glowing light which I'd noticed earlier. As one approached the hallway, there was also a staircase on the right.

I crept on the balls of my feet, keeping low. I had to move fast as there was no cover other than the deck furniture. The entire downstairs of the beach house was glass. There were no windows. There was no need for them. The walls were windows. The doors were windows. It reminded me of the house on Hilton Head. I wondered how long my luck would hold as I reached out to grab the doorknob. Moving as fast as I dared, I twisted the knob. Unlocked. I voiced a silent thank you in my head. This was going as well as I could have hoped for. If I'd needed to pick the lock it would have left me exposed much longer. Once again, I wondered how long my luck would hold.

I pushed the door open and prayed the hinges didn't squeak. Remaining motionless, I listened. The faint sound of a symphony orchestra were wafting through the home. Very good. I waited and watched, happy to have this little bit of noise cover. There were no shadows in play, no sounds of movement.

Keeping as low as I could, I placed a wary right foot over the threshold and entered the house. The first thing I had to do was locate the man. Once that happened, the rest of the story would write itself. I thought about simply waiting in a darkened corner off the kitchen. He would most likely come for a drink or a snack at some point. But I realized that could mean a long wait and I wasn't prepared to be that patient, or that exposed. No, I would find the him and attack. I had no doubt I could overpower him in short order. And if something went sideways, I could always take him at gunpoint.

I pushed the door back towards the frame. Then I crept to the kitchen and positioned myself against a wall and in the shadows. Peeking down the hallway, I could see the open door of a room from which the light was being produced. Classical music continued to float throughout the homes built in speakers.

From the lit room came the sound of a chair rolling on the tile floor. Following this, the unmistakable sound of typing on a keyboard. I had him. Kenealy Jr. was in his study. There would be no better opportunity. It was time to move.

Taking a deep breath I stepped into the hallway and made for the door. I almost made it.

The footsteps came rushing up behind me. Startled, I attempted to spin around, to cover myself. Too slow. Feeling a soft, dull thump against the right side of my head, I found myself floating in an empty void. I no longer had legs or arms. A surreal sense of detachment came over me. Although I was still conscious, my body felt nonexistent. There was no pain. I felt as if I was falling into a deep chasm and time slowed to a crawl.

I didn't feel the second blow land.

My world simply went black.

Raging Storm
48

My eyelids fluttered open. A nuclear flash of light blinded me and it felt as if a railroad spike had pierced my ears. I immediately slammed my eyes back shut. I tried to focus as my brain attempted to come back online. The burning in my pupils screamed like a banshee through the rest of my head. A wave of nausea struck as I struggled to make some sense of my situation. I tried moving my hands to my aching head but my arms didn't work. If not for the excruciating pain, I would have sworn this was some bizarre dream sequence. I need to slow down, to focus.

I was sitting. Sitting in a chair. The realization struck me. My hands were bound behind me. Now came the panic. The nausea grew stronger and I felt an odd rolling sensation. My body rocked from the left to the right. I was either very ill or not on land. That was it. I was on a boat. I knew it now, I could feel the motion as we swayed to and fro. That would explain the nausea. That and the concussion I knew I had.

I needed to see, needed to know. Once again I forced my

eyes open and endured the second jolt of pain as light burned into my retinas. And then, slowly, my triple vision turned to double. Shapes started coming together. The world came into focus. I looked up and saw a face that I hadn't seen since Florida.

William Kenealy sat on a bar stool. He was smiling ear to ear. Tucked into pressed, tan khakis, was an expensive, yet casual, canvas short sleeve shirt. The top two buttons were undone. On his sock-less feet was a pair of docksiders. The arrogant bastard looked like he was on his way to a regatta.

Next to him sat Rothschild, dressed in black pants and a black, long sleeved, turtleneck shirt. Always the mercenary, I wondered if he dressed this way to look the part or was it for real. Was he really this tactical. Completing the look was a brown, leather shoulder holster housing what looked to be a 9mm Beretta.

There was a man to their left whom I did not recognize. He was also dressed tactically. Most likely a bodyguard. A menacing brute, he wore a brush haircut and a very serious demeanor. He was one of the biggest men I'd ever seen and looked as if he could bench press a Volkswagen. Like Rothschild, he also wore a pistol in a shoulder holster.

They were all staring at me. While the large bodyguard glared, both Kenealy and Rothschild wore mocking smiles. They were grinning and enjoying both my confusion and my rude awakening.

I remembered.

I'd entered the young Kenealy's beach house. I was creeping towards the front of the house. That was my last memory. They must have been there. They must have been waiting for me. But how? How the fuck had they known? I struggled to think as my head spun. Did they have that base covered all along? If that was true then I never stood a chance. I had underestimated Kenealy yet again and I knew that this time would be my last. There would be no escaping this. I was a dead man. With great effort, I moved my head to the left and then to the right taking in the surroundings. I was in the salon, or living room, of a boat. I strained to look behind me and through a sliding glass door saw a short back deck. There was a fighting chair in the middle of a rectangular space. I was aboard a sport fishing boat. I had been deep sea fishing before and knew. This looked like a big one judging by the width of the beam and the depth of the salon.

A clear, plastic sheet covered the deck beneath my chair. It ran half the length of the floor back towards my captors. Looking behind me I could see that it also ran all the way to the rear door leading out to the deck. I was in the middle of at least ten square feet of plastic sheeting. It was also secured to the walls.

Shit, I thought. This wasn't good. They planned on this getting bloody. I thought about Joe Simpson and felt my chest tighten as I struggled against the mounting panic. At the other end of the room, Kenealy and Rothschild sat in front of a very nicely furnished bar. There were six comfortable bar stools and a brass chair rail ran the entire length. To the right of the bar was a staircase which would lead to the bridge.

The two men sat smiling at me, as they enjoyed the

moment. I felt anger replacing the pain and used it to tamp down my fear. I locked eyes with Kenealy.

"You motherfucker," I said. It came out as a growl. It was all I could think to say.

Kenealy's smile faded. He said nothing, only grimaced and then shot his British enforcer a quick look.

Rothschild paused for a moment. Then he rose. He took long, slow strides towards me. When he was in front of me he stopped. Standing close, towering over me with his arms crossed. The smile was gone. All I could do was return the glare. And then, with speed too fast to follow, the back of his right hand fell across my face with a loud and heavy smack.

The pain I had endured earlier was nothing. A thunderbolt erupted between my ears. The experience was so intense that I lost vision for several seconds. I also lost my hearing, save for a single high, shrill note that bounced around inside my skull for me alone to hear. As my options were few, I did the only thing I could do and rode it out. When the pain mercifully faded, I looked back up into Rothschild's eyes and once again, glared at him. His smile had returned.

"Mind your manners, lad," he said.

His British accent made it sound charming, almost endearing, and it struck me as funny. Despite myself I began to chuckle. It was heartfelt. And although I knew it was most likely my brain's defense mechanism kicking in, I did nothing to try and rein it in. With the knowledge that I didn't have much time left, I chose to enjoy it. It was one of the few choices that I still controlled.

Rothschild watched me with a curious expression.
"Mind my manners?" I asked. My laughter faded.
"Why? Because otherwise you'll do nasty things to me?"
I chuckled again. I had little to lose. I knew it. They knew it.
"You have no idea, Mr. Dunham," he answered. He had put the serious face back on. This guy ran hot and cold in the space of a second.
"Well, actually I do," I said. "Don't forget that I saw what you did to Joe."
His smile returned. Jekyll and Hyde.
"Why yes, I know. I rather enjoyed watching you find him," he said. "Your feeble apology made me feel warm inside. Very touching, sir."
Jesus, I thought. They'd been watching me.
He saw the realization on my face and nodded, giving me a tight lipped smile of condescension.
The sick bastard.
There was no rationalization for what they had done to Joe. There was no way that any sane man could have performed such an act. I felt my fury returning. And although I had no illusions of getting out of this alive, at the very least I could take my pride with me. I smiled back at the grinning son of a bitch. I would go out letting him know that I wasn't afraid of him. Even if it was a lie.
"What went wrong in your life, mate?" I asked. I adopted a British accent hoping it would offend him. "Did you catch your mumsy giving the postman a good rogering?"
Rothschild smile drooped and I noticed a twitch in his

eye. I pressed on.

"Or did daddy sneak into your bedroom to pay you late night visits after enjoying a few pints at the pub?"

I beamed up at him.

"The thing is, I really want to know." I dropped the accent and looked at the man with disgust. "What turned you into such a self-loathing coward?"

A second explosion of bright light followed and there was that high, shrill ringing in my skull again. I wondered what the note was. C sharp? E Flat? I never did have an ear for music. And, I never even saw that one coming. The guy was fast.

"I give you full marks for bravery, Mr. Dunham," Rothschild said. "But rest assured, you have absolutely nothing to gain with such petty insults."

"Right O then, Governor," I said. The accent was back and I laughed through the pain. I wasn't going to give him an inch. "Duly noted. Pip pip, cheerio."

I laughed out loud and waited for the backhand. Instead, Rothschild merely smiled back. The bastard actually let out a small chuckle. Okay, I thought. Interesting.

He turned and walked back to the bar where he took his seat next to Kenealy. It was now my turn to grin at both of them. I did my best to smile through the fear and waited for what would come next.

The two sat in silence. Staring. Saying nothing. They were playing mind games with me and I realized that they wanted to make this last. Fine, I thought. More time to fuck with them too. Finally Rothschild broke the silence.

"You're most likely wondering how we caught you," he said. "How we knew that you'd go for Mr. Kenealy's son."

I remained silent. I wasn't going to give him the satisfaction.

"Would you care to know?"

"I don't give a shit about anything you have to say you twisted fuck. So why don't you just get on with it and kill me?"

"Me?" Rothschild asked. "Do you think it's going to be me who kills you?"

I stared at him, my breath coming short as I realized the end was approaching. I wasn't going to answer. Whatever game they were playing, I wasn't going to be a willing participant.

"No, Mr. Dunham, no. It will not be me. Although I wish it were otherwise, Mr. Kenealy has different plans for you."

Different plans, I thought? What the hell was he talking about?

"Let me take this opportunity to introduce you to our newest employee. Your demise will be something of an initiation for him. A way to prove his mettle, so to speak."

I felt my heart rate quicken. It was coming. I thought of Debbie. Almost there, honey. Hold on.

"He's been looking forward to it," Rothschild said.

I said nothing.

"We're ready for you now," Rothschild said. He raised his voice and turned his head to call up the flight of stairs.

The room fell silent as footsteps sounded from atop the bridge. I saw feet and then legs come into view as a man walked down the stairs. He was taking his time. Next his midsection. Then his chest.

When his face finally appeared it came as a huge relief. I let out the long breath I'd been holding. I knew now that this was not reality. This was a dream. A very bad dream but none of it actually happening. It was a nightmare. There was no other answer. I would wake up shortly. The truth was not possible. It simply was not possible.

"Hello, Ryder," he said. The familiar voice snapped me out of my delusion.

He stood now at the bottom of the landing and locked eyes with me. I was still unsure what was reality and what was not.

Dumbstruck, I looked into the face of Rob Crawford.

Raging Storm
49

I sat bound to the chair. I was their prisoner. Helpless and held against my will, my death was imminent. Yet none of that mattered anymore.

My mouth hung agape. I was close to catatonic as I stared into the eyes of my closest friend. I blinked over and over. It was involuntary. I couldn't stop. It was as if my brain was telling my eyes that they were mistaken. To clear the absolute horror of the betrayal, I needed only refocus.

Kenealy sat beaming, a huge smile plastered on his face. He looked like he might start running around the room high-fiving the others. Rothschild wore a shit eating grin. He chuckled as he watched me struggle with this inexplicable twist of fate. The large bodyguard never changed his expression. He stood off to the side and continued to glare at me with open hostility.

To his credit, Rob didn't smile. That would have killed me. I don't know why, but it would have. He fixed me with a look that can be best described as disappointment. Disappointment with a touch of hostility. I locked eyes with him and did nothing to hide my shock.. My mouth continued to hang open as I struggled to accept the reality that had just walked into the room. I felt as if I was losing my sanity. I could accept capture. I could even accept dying. I'd played the game and lost. But this was too much, the final blow. I was completely and utterly crushed. Nothing made sense. Nothing would ever make sense again. I didn't even want to try and figure it out. I didn't want the effort it would take to wrap my head around it. I felt only intense sorrow. Bewilderment and sorrow that my friend would sell me out. I felt the same pain as I did losing Debbie and the kids. This was another death. The death of a close friend. The death of a loved one. It simply wasn't possible. We'd fought together. We'd bled together. He had been my brother. I stared at him and felt nothing but pain. There was no anger, I didn't have the strength. There was only pain and the hope that it would all be over soon.

I tried to talk. To say something. My mouth moved. I could feel my vocal cords tense. But nothing came out. I stopped trying.

"Cat got your tongue, buddy," Rob asked. He cocked his head and offered me a subtle look of concern.

Kenealy and Rothschild laughed.

Rob took a few steps towards me and stopped. Standing in the middle of the room, he placed his hands upon his hips and stared down at me. I looked at him and then to the others. My eyes were wide and begging the question. I looked back to Rob.

"You want to ask me something?" He said.

I swallowed hard before answering. My throat was

sandpaper.

"How?" I managed to squeak in a weak voice. "How is this possible?"

"Well," Rob said. "To be honest with you, it's a little complicated."

He paused and allowed the silence to fill the room.

"I-I thought they had you," I said. "I was going to give my life to save you."

"And I appreciate that, Ryder. It means a lot to me."

"Rob," I said. It was almost a stammer. I was still in shock. "Why?"

"It wasn't an easy decision, I want you to know that. But in the end, I did what I had to do, my friend."

"You joined the enemy? That's what you had to do?"

"Mr. Kenealy is not the enemy, Ryder," Rob said. He made a sweeping gesture with his arm, turning to his new boss. "He is a brilliant man who knows how to reward those who are loyal to him. You had that chance and you threw it away."

"This is not happening," I said. I sat in stunned disbelief as my eyes glazed over and I looked down at the floor of the salon. "This is a bad fucking dream and I'm going to wake up any second now."

Laughter erupted behind Rob.

I looked back up to lock eyes with my friend.

"When?" I asked.

"I reached out to Mr. Kenealy two days ago. He offered me an opportunity and I accepted."

"What about the Marine Corps, man. You swore an oath."

"An oath?!"

He paused to look around the room. Then he lowered his voice and continued.

"Don't make me laugh. We are nothing more than cogs in a machine that chews us up and spits us out. We're nothing but puppets. Go to this country and kill these people. Now go over here and kill these people. Oh, you lost a bunch of friends? Sorry about that. Here's a shiny bauble to pin on your chest so you'll feel better. Okay, time's up. Now go to this land and kill these people. And the process keeps repeating itself. It's all a fucking lie, Ryder."

"So get out!" I yelled. "Just get out! Why would you sell me out to join up with this murderer?!"

"Murderer?!" Rob said. He laughed. "Did you honestly just say that? How many people have you killed lately you hypocrite?"

"That was different! I thought I was doing some good! Ridding the world of scum and predators! You know that!"

"So as long as you're cool with it, killing people is no big deal? Do you even hear yourself, man?"

Rob began to laugh. He turned and shared the laugh with his new pals. Now I was starting to get angry. Really angry.

"You gutless coward," I said. I had reached my breaking point. "You fucking gutless piece of shit."

"Me gutless?" Rob spun back to face me. His face screwed up in unexpected mask of anger. "Why don't we have a little chat about being gutless, Ryder?"

He strode to me and bent at the waist to make direct eye contact. His breath was short and I could see that he was doing his best to contain himself.

"Why didn't you kick that door, Ryder!?"

Against my will I gasped, the question knocked me for a loop.

"Are-are you serious?" I couldn't believe what I heard.

"Why didn't you kick that door?!" He repeated.

"Fuck you!"

A smack landed across my face and for the third time my head exploded in pain.

"You knew!" Rob yelled. "You knew there was somebody on the other side so you let Kurt do it! You killed him!"

My chest heaved with anger. I said nothing, only ground my teeth and wished to God that I could reach his throat.

"So that's what this is about?" I asked. "After all these years you finally tell me the truth? Those times you were drunk, blaming yourself? What was that bullshit about?"

"Like I said, Ryder, it's complicated. That's only one small, but important, piece of the puzzle."

He turned and walked back to the bar where Kenealy and Rothschild stood. I couldn't see the expression on his face but his words sent a chill down my back.

"Anytime you want, gentlemen. I'm ready to do it."

I saw Rothschild reach behind his back and produce a pistol. He handed it to Rob and then smiled at me.

"No, Mr. Dunham, regrettably, It's not I who gets to kill you," Rothschild said. "He does."

Rob turned back to face me.

"Are you serious?" I shouted at Kenealy. "You're going to have my best friend kill me? Are you really this fucking twisted?"

Kenealy and Rothschild said nothing. They looked to Rob whose left hand went to rest on the top of the gun. With a rapid motion he'd performed countless times, he slid the top housing unit back and forth. He had chambered the round that would send me to my family. And then, after sitting on that bar stool, saying nothing the entire time, Kenealy stood. Preparing to speak, he paused as if searching for the perfect words. He smiled. And then he began.

"You know, I liked you, Ryder. I really did," he said. "And you were right up there with Rothschild when it came to garbage disposal. You were one of my favorite operators, and I was growing quite fond of you, until you turned on me. But, your impressive skill set aside, you lacked the one thing I demand in all my people."

"What's that?" I asked. "Being soulless?"

"Why no, son," he said. "Loyalty."

Kenealy paused briefly for emphasis and then he smiled and continued.

"And my soul is just fine. So is Rothschild's and every other operator in my employ. We only engage those who are in the game. I could not, and would not, ever intentionally harm an innocent person."

He turned and walked to go behind the bar. Grabbing a crystal carafe, Kenealy poured himself a drink. He took a sip and walked back around the bar, returning to his stool. He placed his glass on the bar and sat.

"What you had no way of knowing was the man you took out in D.C. was trying to have me killed. There were two different teams hunting me."

"Bullshit!"

"No, it's not bullshit, Ryder. And if you had remained calm, and above all loyal, I would have explained that to you. But instead, you flew off the handle and thus became a liability."

"You used me to commit a cold blooded murder," I said.

"Son." He paused to emphasize his point. "Do you know of any murder that isn't cold blooded?"

"Don't call me son you arrogant, sociopathic prick. You're a thug and a killer. Nothing more."

Kenealy narrowed his eyes and glared at me. The smile disappeared. Men did not speak to him in that manner.

"Coming from a man who killed at the behest of your government, I find that rather hypocritical," he said. "If you can tell me the difference between the leaders of our country and myself, I'll let you live."

"Our leaders don't commit to war unilaterally! And it is never for personal gain!"

Kenealy began a slow chuckle. It was infectious and both Rothschild and Rob joined him. The chuckle grew to a laugh as the three enjoyed the moment. I was beginning to think the large bodyguard was a robot as his expression never changed. When it subsided, Kenealy just shook his head.

"Well, son, I knew you were a bit of an idealist, but I guess I missed the fact that you were also a fool. My mistake."

"It's the same thing, Ryder," Rob said. "There is no difference."

"Fuck you, Rob," I said. "I never want to hear another word come out of your mouth you traitorous piece of shit."

"Ouch," he said. Rob traded a look with his new boss. He then turned back to face me. "That stings buddy and I don't think you quite understand the position you're in. I have requested this be quick and painless for you. And Mr. Kenealy has agreed to that in light of services rendered."

"Too bad, son," Kenealy said. "I had such high hopes for you. You could have been a very rich man."

"I'll see you in hell, scumbag." It was cheesy but it was all I could think to say.

Kenealy simply snorted and smiled. He looked to Rob. "Time to earn your way in, Mr. Crawford."

"Yes, sir," he answered. His expression turned to stone, all business he faced me.

"Go ahead and do it, friend," I spoke boldly. "If you can."

Rob walked slowly, menacingly, towards my chair. He tapped the gun against the side of his leg as he made his way to me. I raised my chin and glared at him defiantly. If I was going out, it would be as a man. They wouldn't get so much as a whimper out of me.

Rob walked at a leisurely pace. He circled behind me. I felt the gun press against my temple as he squatted down, directly behind the chair, bending at the knees. His face moved to the right side of my head until his mouth was almost touching my ear.

"It's better this way, Ryder. If you'd kept up the insults, I'm afraid that Rothschild would have gotten much more close and personal with you."

"Fuck you and fuck him," I said.

"There it is. There's that Ryder Dunham moxy. But be

careful what you say or this might last a good hour rather than me just shooting you in the head."

What happened next was so unexpected that it was surreal. I thought my mind was playing tricks on me. There was a subtle tapping on my right hand. The tapping of a metallic object.

"But before I do this, Ryder," Rob said. He remained behind me, squatting down, my body shielding the others view of him. "I want you to apologize to both Mr. Kenealy and his distinguished English colleague. Apologize for your vulgar insults."

The tapping stopped and I now felt the metal object pressed against my right hand.

Rob was trying to give me something.

I sat in shocked silence trying to sort out this unexpected event. And then I understood.

My karambit.

As it dawned on me, I grasped the play and extended my fingers. The cold metal moved up my hand. Rob pressed the gun against my head. I stuck out the ring finger on my right hand and felt the hard steel loop slip into place. Using my fingers and thumb, I worked the steel ring down into place. My other fingers wrapped around the handle. I secured my grip on the knife. I knew the game. Exactly what I had to do.

"Rob," I said. "Fuck you. And fuck both this British coward and little Billy Kenealy."

"Ryder, I'm warning you," he answered. He feigned anger as he stood and walked to my side. I felt the barrel of the gun press into my temple. "Apologize."

The karambit was now in place and I grasped the handle.

By bending my wrist I was able to lay it across the ropes that bound me. I began a simple back and forth motion and could feel the razor sharp blade slicing through the bonds. As I did so I made a show of moving my head to the right, pressing it up harder against Rob's gun. It would attract attention away from any movement they might have noticed behind me.

"Hey Kenealy, you filthy piece of shit," I said. "Have you ever had the balls to actually kill a man yourself?"

The son of a bitch, I thought as I continued to cut the rope and bark at Kenealy. Rob's bullshit had been an act. Every bit of it was a plan. Executed without my knowledge. If it wasn't for the dire circumstance we were both still in, I would have been speechless. But I knew that there would be plenty of time to sort this out later if we survived. Right now I had to be at my best.

"Watch your tongue," Kenealy said. "Before I cut it out."

I could see he was becoming agitated. I pressed on.

"You mean before your limey lapdog cuts it out. We both know you don't have the balls to get your own hands dirty."

I laughed. Then I looked at my friend and continued.

"If it wasn't for this piece of shit turning traitor I would have killed both of you. You know it and I know it."

Rob kept up the charade. He pressed harder with the gun, pushing my head sideways.

"Some people never know when to shut up," he said.

I felt the rope loosen. I was through. As it begin to slip down off my wrists I grabbed it with my left hand so it wouldn't drop to the floor. I was free.

"There is one thing I can't quite figure, Billy," I said. I grinned and smiled at the man as he glared at me from his bar stool. "I saw a picture of you and your wife at a charity event. She doesn't look like a typical money grubbing whore. I'm assuming you married her before you became a low rent thug like your Grandpa. Is that about right?"

Rob thumbed the hammer back with a loud click.

"Say the word, sir," he said.

I snorted, laughing in Kenealy's face.

"But my guess is that she's the best money can buy," I said. "What other type of woman would want a pathetic worm like you?"

"I can't allow any more of this," Rob said. He took a step back and pointed the gun, a foot from my head. He prepared to shoot. "Say goodbye, Ryder."

I smiled triumphantly and grinned like a drunken monkey. I was daring Kenealy to do something. I could see that he was struggling to control himself.

"I'm actually surprised you even like women. I'll bet that you and Rothschild -"

"Stop!"

Kenealy's face was red. But he wasn't speaking to me. He was speaking to Rob.

The room fell silent. I breathed a sigh of relief. It was working.

"I'm sorry, Mr. Crawford," Kenealy said. He took a second to compose himself. "I truly am. But I have to break a promise I made to you."

Rob exhaled loudly. I could only imagine what was going through his head. He looked at Kenealy and nodded.

"I understand, sir," Rob said. He looked back at me and continued. "Can't say as I didn't warn you, pal."

Kenealy stared at me with pursed lips, his eyes ablaze with anger.

"I was ready to let you leave this world as a soldier, quickly and without pain. I attempted to show you mercy," he said. "But since you saw fit to bring my family into the matter, we will now go another route."

Rob lowered the gun and I turned my head to look at him. He shrugged.

"You brought this on yourself," he said.

"Fuck you." I looked him in the eye. "I'll show you how a man dies."

"Well," he said. He gave me a smile and a private wink. "I hope you're ready. Because it's coming."

"You just worry about yourself, asshole," I answered.

Kenealy turned to look at Rothschild. He gave a slight nod. A green light. Rothschild returned the nod and then looked back at me. He stood, pushing back from the bar stool.

He began rolling up his sleeves. Slow and deliberate. Grinning like the Cheshire cat, he fixed me with an almost maniacal smile. I realized how sick the man was as the pure joy he had for his twisted craft was written all over his face. Rothschild was in his element. Thrilled by this unexpected development.

He walked behind the bar and I heard a drawer open. There was a jangling of silverware. It was obvious what he was looking for and sure enough, when he walked back around the counter, he had a knife in his hands. It

was a not a very long knife but it looked plenty sharp.
I braced myself for what was to come

.

Raging Storm
50

Rothschild turned to the right to face his employer. He smiled.

"Sir," he said. He spoke with exaggerated courtesy. "With your permission I would like to find out exactly how tough our ferocious friend truly is."

"He's all yours," Kenealy said. He gestured with an open palm towards me. "You have carte blanche."

He was serving me up on a platter.

"Very good, sir," Rothschild answered.

He beamed and rubbed his hands together. I wondered how much of it was an act or if the guy was actually this sick?

"Okay, Mr. Dunham," he said. He stepped towards me. "Let's play a game, shall we?"

"Sounds good old chap, but we'll have to hurry," I said. "I have a rather pressing engagement later this evening."

"Cut the shit, Ryder!" Rob yelled. It surprised everyone and we all cast our gaze upon him as he stood to the side of the room and glared. "What the fuck are you trying to prove?"

"I told you never to speak to me again you cowardly piece of shit."

I scowled at my friend as I played along. "You go ahead and wet your pants over this limey prick if you want, but he doesn't scare me."

"Do you want this to last an hour!?" He asked. "Shut your mouth and make it easier on yourself!"

Good old Rob was having fun with the role. I could tell. He was also trying to ease some stress. This was going to get very ugly, very quick. And we both knew it.

"That's quite enough, Mr. Crawford," Rothschild said. He addressed Rob with a slight frown. "You have proven yourself, but do not allow mercy to cloud my opinion of you. I will take it from here."

Rob nodded and then looked to the floor.

Kenealy's top enforcer, former SAS elite British commando and all around nut job, advanced on me. His smile had grown more devilish. The psychopathic bastard was truly giddy.

Brandishing the knife at chest level, Rothschild began to explain.

"So this is how it will work, Mr. Dunham. I am going to start operating on you. Removing unwanted body parts and such. Are you with me?"

"I'm all ears, psycho."

"Ha," he laughed. "Yes, for now. Well played. However, back to the point, the game is to see how long you can keep up this amusing charade."

He paused for emphasis. I was beginning to realize that the man was also a showboat.

"If, at any time, you decide that you aren't quite as hard

as you thought you were, you may call out for clemency. And the louder you call out the more I shall expedite these procedures. Are you following me?"

"Sounds like a hoot," I said.

I was putting on a good act, but even though I knew what was coming, I was still pretty freaked out. To be absolutely frank, I was shitting my pants. Any man ever tells you they aren't afraid before combat, that man is lying to you. Or he's insane. And although I knew that there was no other way, I didn't look forward to what was coming next. There were so many things that could go wrong, so many ways that this could go sideways. Most of which would result in my being butchered by this maniac. Not to mention what they would do to Rob. I was certain that would be equally gruesome.

"Yes," Rothschild said. "Also, the more contrition you show, the more you beg Mr. Kenealy for forgiveness, the more things will go your way. Do you understand the rules?"

"Yes. Yes I do. But that's only because you're explaining them so well."

I held fast to the severed ropes with my left hand. My right hand quivered and flexed around the karambit. I had a plan but I needed him closer. Much closer. I was happy to see that he also held the knife in his right hand. It would matter.

The Brit pivoted to smile at his boss. Shaking his head in amusement he turned back to smirk at me.

"I will give you this, Mr. Dunham, you are one cheeky bugger. I dare say that it would have been a privilege to have fought beside you in combat."

I laughed out loud.

"You know what, asshole? I thought the very same thing about one of your old buddies. Good looking, clean cut British fellow that broke into my house and tried to kill me."

Rothschild blinked several times. I saw his eyes darken as his mood changed in a split second.

"But at least I'll give those guys points for taking me on like men. I mean, sneaking into a house and shooting up a guys bed won't win any medals for valor," I said. "But it's a damn sight braver than the way you're going about it. But then again, judging by what you did to Joe, I'd say you specialize in cowardice."

The smile was gone from his face. He leaned towards me.

"If you bring up my colleague again, I will start by cutting your tongue out. It is a small miracle that you were able to beat him. A one in a million chance."

"Ah, but I did beat him," I said. I smiled right back in his face. "What was his name anyway? I figure you must know him since he has the same queer accent as you. Oops, sorry. I meant had."

Rothschild froze. He stared at me in silence and I watched him consider his many options. I could see that he was about to lose it.

And then the bastard straightened and smiled at me. I could read his thoughts. He knew that I was trying to bait him. And that he'd almost bought it. Shit.

"I know the game you're playing, Mr. Dunham," he said. The smile grew broader.

My heart skipped a beat. This wasn't going to work. He

wasn't going to get close enough.

"Really?" I asked. Ignoring my fear, I attempted to match his smugness. "Please enlighten me."

I took the opportunity to look behind him to where Kenealy was sat watching. He was waiting for the show. I doubted that this was the first time he'd watched his assassin work. The large bodyguard's expression still hadn't changed. He seemed like a real asshole. I was counting on Rob to take him out.

"It's so sadly transparent," Rothschild said. "You're trying to get me to lose my cool so that I will kill you quickly in a fit of rage."

He chuckled and looked around the room with a wide grin, proud to have ferreted out my plan. Turning back to me, he finished his brilliant analysis.

"But it won't work. In fact the angrier I become, the slower I will go. And, you are forgetting one very important thing. If you force me to cut your tongue out, you will be unable to beg for mercy. You will be unable to apologize to Mr. Kenealy. This could end up being a very long and horrible night for you, Mr. Dunham."

"Jeeeez," I said. "You're right. I hadn't thought of that."

"And seeing as it's your last night on earth," he said. "I do not think it's in your best interest to continue this tact."

"My, but you do like giving speeches, don't you?" I laughed. "Your friend didn't talk as much. But he did cry like a little girl while as I questioned him."

Rothschild stared down at me. He was close enough to cut me if he swung the blade, but I needed him closer. I pressed on.

"You wouldn't have any way of knowing this but after I killed the other two, your man lay there on my floor groveling. He started begging for mercy and pleading with me to let him live. It was pretty damn embarrassing."

"Oh, Mr. Dunham," Rothschild said. He moved closer as once again his mood grew darker. "You are only proving to me what a fool you are. You are accomplishing nothing else. And this is your final warning. If you mention my colleague again, I will remove your obscene tongue."

"Well, it may help you to hear that he didn't suffer. I finally put one between his eyes because, quite frankly, I couldn't take it anymore. Him lying there, crying and pleading, was becoming awkward for both of us. I almost wanted to give him a hug before I shot him."

"I am going to enjoy this," Rothschild said. The blade quivered in his hand. He was on the brink.

One more good push.

"Goddamn, man. If you guys are the best that the crown can come up with then it's no wonder you need America to bail you out of every conflict."

Rothschild sprang and almost knocked us both over backwards as he slammed into me. He was practically sitting in my lap as he pushed my forehead back with his left forearm. His knife went under my nose, pressed flat against my skin. He pushed up so that the tip tore into my right nostril. It was extremely painful and I felt blood run down my lips and onto my chin.

"Fair warning was given, lad. Now, open your mouth," he said. His eyes sparked with tempered rage. He twisted the blade so that it tore the skin deeper.

"Open it! Or I will start with your bloody nose!"

It was now or never.

"I have a better idea, asshole," I said.

I came up quick as lightning with my left hand, keeping it close to my body and forced it between us.

His face registered alarm. But I was too quick.

Using my forearm, I knocked his arm to the left which took the knife from my face. Without breaking momentum, I went over and then back under his arm. Snapping my elbow down to my side, I pinned his arm. He tried to stab me but with his right arm immobile, he could only move his wrist and was barely able to slice the skin. The blade did not penetrate.

And then Rothschild did exactly what I had hoped he would. He reached across both our bodies with his left hand to try and free himself. It was instinctive. His entire left side was now exposed. I whipped my right arm around and plunged the karambit into his rib cage with all the force I could muster. It sounded like a boxer hitting a heavy bag.

His eyes widened and he shuddered as the blade entered between two ribs and punctured his lung. I held him fast and watched him struggle as blood bubbled in the corner of his mouth.

As this was happening, I saw Rob drop to one knee in a shooters position and take aim at the large bodyguard. I hear two gunshots ring out.

I withdrew the blade and thrust again, this time six inches lower, into his kidney. The curved steel sunk in to the hilt and I twisted it with a snap, doing even more internal damage.

Checkmate. I knew it and he knew it.

His eyes remained wide and transfixed, staring into mine with disbelief. His mouth opened to scream only no sound came forth. He tensed up, his body going rigid as he went into shock.

"You lose, motherfucker!" I hissed it through clenched teeth, my face an inch from his. "This is for Joe."

I ripped the blade out of his side and then thrust it in a third time.

Rothschild gasped as his eyes rolled back in his head. He slumped forward, falling against me and I could feel his dying breath, foul and warm.

Looking around his lolling head, I saw the large bodyguard scrambling for cover. He had his gun drawn and as he made for cover, fired another round at Rob. Not hearing any return fire, I looked to the right and saw my friend in a crumpled heap on the floor. My heart stopped. Time slowed to a crawl.

Through the surreal haze of the moment, I heard a voice yell. I turned to see Kenealy, scrambling from where he had dove to the floor. He was on the move and heading for the staircase. My focus and fury now turned to him. Rothschild, seconds away from death, was out of the fight. I let go of the karambit and grabbed for the 9mm in his shoulder holster. Wrapping my hand around the grip, I pulled the gun free and fired a shot in Kenealy's direction. The large bodyguard dove over the bar, desperate for cover.

Kenealy was almost out of sight, only his legs were still visible as he dashed up the steps. I steadied the gun and placed another shot up the staircase.

I heard a sharp cry from the top of the landing.

The bodyguard popped up from behind the bar and aimed his gun towards me. I heard another loud boom and felt a round slam into Rothschild's back. The force of it threw us both backwards as the chair toppled over. That worked in my favor and as we hit the floor, I rolled behind Rothschild's lifeless body, using it for cover. I raised the pistol and fired in the direction of the bar. The bodyguard ducked low. Now that I had time to steady myself, I grabbed the weapon with both hands and looked for a clean shot.

Several seconds passed as each of us waited for the other to make the next move.

From the bridge atop the stairs I heard Kenealy scream out for help.

Nothing.

Kenealy screamed again, this time with more anger and desperation.

The bodyguard then did a very foolish thing. With his loyalty larger than his brain, he made the fatal error of leaving his secure position. Firing a blind shot over the top of the bar, he left his cover and made a frantic dash up the stairs towards his boss.

Unfortunately for him, at roughly forty feet, I was a surgeon with a 9mm. I placed two quick shots into the center of his back. One of the rounds must have hit his spine as the large man's legs folded under him. He crumpled, falling like a sack of cement. Rolling back down the steps to the floor, he lay on his back staring up at the ceiling. His chest was heaving and he gasped like a fish out of water. In a slow, jerking manner, the man rolled his head to the side. We locked eyes. His breathing continued in short, raspy huffs, his chest rising and falling. He was struggling to comprehend what had happened to him. I watched his confusion turn to realization as the truth finally caught up with him. He was going to die. And then, in a commendable display of perseverance, he made one last attempt. His trembling arm tried to move. To point the weapon that he still clutched in his right hand. He strained, brow furrowed, forehead creased in palpable determination. The arm dragged along the floor, desperately trying to line me up. The closer it got, the more his arm shook as he willed the gun in my direction one inch at a time.

I'd seen enough. Taking quick aim, I squeezed the trigger once more. The round caught him in the forehead and the large, surly man was out of the fight.

I stayed behind Rothschild's corpse and remained still. Gun pointed down range, I waiting for any action. I didn't know how many people might be on this boat or if Kenealy was going to rush back down with an AK-47 banging away. So I did what my training had taught me, I kept behind cover and waited.

I listened intently, trying to make out any noise. It was eerie. The boat had fallen silent. After the chaotic and frantic fight that had taken place, it was off putting. Although it had seemed like a lengthy battle, in actuality it had lasted less than a minute. Now it was quiet, the only sound being the lapping of the small waves against the hull of the sport fish. I took slow, deep breaths and tried to let my nerves settle.

Looking over to Rob's body which lay roughly ten feet from me, I strained to see if there was any movement. I could see only his back as he had fallen facing away from where Rothschild and I had been. He lay completely motionless. Staring at his still form, I experienced every emotion possible. Choking back tears, I waited, watching both Rob and the staircase. I half expected Kenealy to make a valiant charge, or to toss a grenade down into the room. Something. I didn't know. I expected everything and nothing. There was only utter stillness. The boat may as well have been empty.

When I couldn't take it anymore, I began to edge closer to Rob's prone body. Keeping the gun in front of me, I low crawled towards him until I was able to place a gentle hand on his shoulder. I wanted to turn him, to roll him towards me so that I could look at him. But I didn't want to see his face. I didn't want to see his face now that he was gone. I couldn't. So I held on to his shoulder with my free hand and tried to control my emotions.

"I'm so sorry, Rob," I said. It came out as a whisper. I flashed back to my final words to Joe Simpson. This felt similar only much, much worse. "I'm so fucking sorry, man."

Giving his shoulder a soft squeeze, I moved my hand to rest it on the top of his head. It was too much, I couldn't bear it. Stroking his scalp as one would a child, I felt tears running down my face. This pain eclipsed any other feeling I'd experienced tonight. It was devastating. I struggled to control my emotions as I ran my fingers through his hair.

"Dude," he said. "What the hell are you doing?"

I almost jumped out of my skin.

"Are you fucking kidding me?!" I hissed it. I yanked my hand from his head.

"Holy shit," he said. He groaned. The pain he was experiencing was evident in his voice. "That fucking hurt."

"What the fuck!" I whispered. "I thought you were dead!"

"Yeah, so did I," he said.

"How?" I asked.

"Kevlar man," he said. He tapped the body armor on his chest. "And that big fucker only caught me with one round. It knocked me for a loop though."

With a painful grimace, Rob hoisted himself to a sitting position. Looking down at his chest, he put a finger through the hole in his shirt where the round had passed. He scanned the room and smiled when he saw Rothschild. Then he noticed the big bodyguard with half his head blown off.

"You do that?" He asked. He gestured towards the man with a sideways bob of his head.

"No," I answered. "He committed suicide, dumb ass."

Rob gave a low laugh as the tension evaporated. We exchanged a look that said it all. We'd done it. Against all odds, we'd done it.

"Where's Kenealy?" He asked.

"He made it up those stairs. I think I hit him."

"That's the bridge," Rob said. "The only way down besides those stairs is a ladder to the back deck."

"Then he's up there, because I would have seen him come down the back ladder."

Both of us sat in silence, plotting our next move. We looked from each other to the staircase and back again.
"What the fuck, Rob. How the hell did you not drop that big guy?" I asked. "His fucking weapon was holstered."
"I had him but my gun wouldn't shoot," he said.
"Blanks?" I asked.
Rob grabbed the gun from off the floor and pressed a black button on the side of the grip. The magazine popped out and he did a quick scan.
"Nope, unless these rounds have the primer removed."
"Too much trouble," I said. "They probably took out the firing pin."
Rob slid the upper housing back and did a quick examination. He nodded at me. The firing pin was gone.
"Unbelievable," he said. "Where's the trust?"
I laughed.
"Don't take it personal, man."
We fell silent again. Finally Rob asked the question.
"What's the play, Ryder?"
"I'm going up."
"We're going up."
"Okay," I said. I wasn't about to argue. "Grab his gun."
I pointed to the piece that was still clutched in the dead bodyguard's hand.
Standing, I did a cautious creep to the bottom of the landing. Rob fell in behind me, first grabbing his new weapon.
"Me first," I said. The look on my face told him there would be no discussion.
He nodded.
I took a deep breath and started up the stairs.

Raging Storm
51

"Mayday, mayday..."
Kenealy's voice sounded pained, short of breath.
"This is the Never Enough in dire need of assistance. I repeat, this is an urgent mayday from the Never Enough. Please acknowledge."
I crept up the stairs, my own breathing rapid and shaky. I was doing by damnedest to control the adrenaline that coursed through my veins. I noticed that the gun in my right hand was shaking. This was, at least partially, due to the blow I'd taken to the head inside the kid's beach house. My skull was still thumping but other than that all I felt was excitement. Minutes earlier I had given myself up for dead. Kenealy had won, beaten me. And when I thought that Rob had betrayed me, it was one of the lowest moments in my life. I had been ready to die. Now I was on the verge of taking Kenealy. I was going to get the son of a bitch and finish this once and for all.
I turned and threw up a halt sign to Rob who was a couple steps behind me. He froze.
"Mayday, mayday, mayday," Kenealy said. The stress in

his voice was telling. He was panicking. "This is the Never Enough, seventy-seven foot sport fish out of Marina Del Rey. We are under attack. I repeat, we have been boarded and are under attack."

I made it to the top of the stairs and took another deep breath. Exhaling slowly, I prepared myself for the confrontation. I had no way of knowing whether Kenealy had a weapon aimed at the top of the landing. He may have been waiting to see my head come into view. Although it was dark upon the bridge, the glow of the control panel offered light. I crouched low and peeked my head around prepared to pull it back should Kenealy take any type of shot.

What I saw was perfect.

Kenealy had his back to me. He stood on one leg, leaning against the control panel of the bridge. Bent at the waist, he used his stomach to help take the weight off of his one good leg. The other leg dangled with a bullet in the meatiest part of his hamstring. The light khaki trousers he wore had a large blood stain a few inches below his buttocks. It spread downward and fanned out as he bled. I did hit him. I knew it.

I stepped to the top of the landing, and straightened to my full height. Thumbing the hammer back on Rothschild's 9mm, I took a deep breath.

"Drop the mike, asshole," I said.

Kenealy spun around, hopping on one leg to face me. His face was a ridiculous mask of terror, eyes wide as saucers, mouth agape. I almost laughed at him. We stared at each other, saying nothing, I enjoying the moment, he dreading it.

A static filled response broke the silence.

"Never Enough, this is Chief Petty Officer Landow of the United States Coast Guard. Please repeat. I say again, please repeat."

Kenealy froze, his hand tightened around the mike. I raised the pistol.

"I said drop the mike."

I took a step closer.

"Never Enough, please repeat. This is the United States Coast Guard," the man on the other end of the radio said. He hesitated and then added. *"Did you say you were under attack?"*

Kenealy's eyes blinked rapidly. He looked at the mike in his hands and then back to me as he wrestled with his next move.

"Never Enough, do you copy? Never Enough, this is the United States Coast Guard. Please respond."

Kenealy made his decision. He raised the mike to his mouth as fast as he could.

"This is the Never Enough! We have been boarded by Ryd-"

The small, enclosed space of the bridge echoed the loud blast of the 9mm.

Rob dashed up the remaining steps and burst onto the bridge. He took in the scene as he stepped to stand by my side.

"Why the hell did you do that?" He asked. He leaned to the right to admire my handiwork.

I looked at Rob, my teeth grit in controlled fury, and then back to Kenealy.

"Because shooting him would have been way too quick

and much too humane for this murderous prick."
Kenealy stood frozen, the mike still clutched in his hands. His eyes left mine and he turned his head to look behind him. The radio, built into the large control panel, was shattered, smoke wafting from the hole I'd blown in it. There would be no further transmissions.

Kenealy turned back to face me, dropping the useless mike. His face showed both fear and loathing.

I kept the 9mm leveled at his chest and weighed my options. The three of us stood still. We stood and waited for somebody to make the first move. Finally, Rob broke the tension.

"So, what do you think?"

"Don't know," I answered. "Got any suggestions?"

"Uhhhh, yeah. Kind of."

I heard the humor in his voice and turned to look at my friend.

"They were planning on a sea burial for you. There was even talk of sending you to Davey Jones locker while you were still breathing."

"I never would have allowed that to happen!" Kenealy shouted. "I was going to let your friend finish you quickly! Painlessly! I swear on my children!"

"Is that why you gave him a useless gun?" I asked. I looked at him with disgust.

"We had to do that! We had to be sure we could trust him! If he had pulled the trigger we would have known!"

"You're a sick fuck," Rob said.

"Goddamn it, Ryder! Don't you do this!" Kenealy screamed. He struggled to control his fear as panic gripped him. He looked to Rob and then back to me.

"You were threatening everything I'd worked for! Everything I devoted my life to! What was I supposed to do?!"

"You had me murder a man in cold blood," I said. I glared at him. I too struggled. To control my anger and not shoot him then and there.

"I was acting in self defense! That man was trying to have me killed!"

"Bullshit! If that was true you would have had Rothschild or one your other goons take him out! You needed a patsy! You set me up to take the fall, you son of a bitch!"

"No! It's not true!"

"And then you sent a team of mercenary's into my house to murder me in my wife's bed! You didn't even have the decency to respect my wife's bed!"

"Rothschild planned that! I knew nothing about it! I never handle the details!"

"Speak the truth for once in your miserable life! You tried to set me up for Wakefield's murder!"

"No!"

"Admit it!" I took another step towards him and raised the pistol high.

"Oh my God," Kenealy said. He dropped to his knees and placed his head in his hands.

"You killed Ducey!" I yelled.

"No, he killed himself," Kenealy answered.

"And you butchered Joe Simpson!" I was close to losing it. "Admit it!"

The tough, hard as nails, William Kenealy did not respond to this. He was weeping like a frightened child, his head hanging down, his shoulders shaking. I should have enjoyed it but instead it sickened me.

"Get up!"

Kenealy gave a frantic shake of his head. Wiping at his eyes with his fingers, he remained on the floor and looked up at both of us. And then his face lit up with an idea. He pointed a finger at us.

"I will make you both richer than you ever dreamed! Ten million dollars for each of you!"

His eyes implored. He nodded up and down, an old sales trick to get your prospect agreeing with you. I couldn't believe the transformation in the man. He had gone from being a strong, authoritative leader to a sniveling worm in the space of ten minutes. But then, bullies tend to do that when you bloody their nose.

"Fuck you and your money," I said.

"Well, now hold on a second partner," Rob said. "Let's hear the man out."

I turned my head to glare at him.

"Kidding!" He laughed and showed me a toothy grin. "Just kidding, buddy."

"Twenty million each!" Kenealy shouted. "I have it in gold bullion in a safe back at the estate in Malibu! I can have it brought out by boat right to where we are! Right now!"

I watched him grovel. He wet his lips, nervous eyes darting between the two of us. He elaborated on his blossoming plan.

"One of my men comes out in a small boat with the gold! We load the gold from that boat onto this boat and then I go away and I never even think about you again!

You have my word! And you can keep the Never Enough! It's yours! I'll even sign a bill of sale!"
"This beautiful boat?" I asked. "All mine?"
"I swear it!"
I remained quiet, basking in his desperation. It hung in the air as his eyes begged me to take the deal. I could almost smell it.
I turned to Rob.
"What do you mean a burial at sea?"
"They have cinder blocks on the back deck. Along with some chains and padlocks."
"Fucking Rothschild!" Kenealy screamed. "I would never have let him do it!"
"By the way, Ryder," Rob said. He took on a serious tone. "The Coast Guard might be able to triangulate that call. We may want to step this up a bit."
I nodded at him.
"Get your ass up, scumbag," I said. "It's time for you to pay."
"No! Please!"
I took two large strides towards him as he rolled away to shield himself. Grabbing his arm, I began dragging him across the bridge to the top of the stairs. Rob gave me a wide berth. He let me handle this, watching as I dealt with the man who had brought such utter chaos into my life.
"Get your ass up!"
"No, please don't do this! Do you know how many people depend on me?! Do you know how many people's lives this will ruin?!"
"Since when have you ever given a shit about other

people?" I asked. "Now stand up!"

He refused to move. It pissed me off. Putting the sole of my boot against his back I shoved. Kenealy tumbled down the stairs, bouncing all the way.

Behind me, Rob laughed. I turned to my friend and whispered a quick directive. He smiled and nodded, understanding immediately. I then hustled down the stairs in case Kenealy tried something unexpected. This was his boat so Lord only knew what surprises he had hidden throughout.

I needn't have worried, the man never moved. He lay on the salon floor whimpering and clutching the back of his wounded leg.

Again, I grabbed him by the arm and dragged him. Through the plastic sheeting and past Rothschild's body towards the back of the boat. I opened the door with one hand and pulled him through with the other.

Sure enough, situated on the back deck was everything Rob had detailed. There were three cinder blocks, three long lengths of chain and three padlocks, all with the keys in them.

"Don't tell me," I said. I spoke gruffly as once again I put a foot on Kenealy's back and pushed him towards the back of the deck. "This was all Rothschild's doing, huh?"

Slamming against the transom, he banged his head on the gunwale and let out a small cry of pain.

"Gee, sorry about that," I said.

Kenealy looked up at me in stark terror. H shook his head and desperately tried to appeal to my greed.

"Think about it, Ryder," he said. "Twenty millions

dollars! Even if you don't trust me, you could disappear. With that type of money you could go anywhere. You could buy a small palace on a tropical island under an assumed name. I would never even think of you again I swear it!"

"What's he babbling about," Rob asked. He walked through the door and onto the deck. I turned and raised my eyebrows, asking the question without speaking. He smiled his answer and gave me a quick nod. I smiled back.

"Shithead was describing the tropical paradise we could buy if we let him live," I answered.

"Nice," Rob said.

"Okay," I said. "Let's get this show on the road."

I grabbed one of the chains and threaded it through a cinder block. I then grabbed a padlock and tossed it beside Kenealy's feet. Bending down I grabbed his right ankle and started to loop the chain around it. Kenealy, more out of hysteria than bravado, lashed out at me with his other foot. I was ready for it and leaned back so that the kick missed me. All the same I felt inclined to respond so I leaned forward and drove my fist into his nose. Blood flowed down over his mouth and chin. Kenealy cried out and covered his face with his hands.

"This is happening, Billy. You can go about it the hard way, like you just did, or you can fucking sit there and let me finish."

Kenealy began weeping. He looked up to Rob.

"Please stop him. Please!"

"How?" Rob asked. "He seems pretty intent on doing this, pal. I'm not even sure what I could do."

"Shoot him! Shoot him and I'll make you rich!! Forty million dollars for one bullet!"

I started laughing and Rob joined in. Kenealy didn't get the joke but he soon would. I finished up, getting the third cinder block chained tightly around his ankle. I removed the keys from each padlock and held them up for Kenealy to see. Then I tossed all three into the ocean. He wasn't getting loose without a hacksaw. I rose and turned to my friend.

"Robert," I said. I spoke in a dignified, upper crust tone. "Would you please fetch me the late Sir Rothschild?"

Rob chuckled and walked back into the lounge to retrieve Rothschild's body. As it was only a few yards away, he was back in no time, his arms wrapped around the late enforcer.

The back of the boat had a small door for hauling large fish aboard. It was much easier to pull them onto the deck through this door than to lift hundreds of pounds over the transom. I opened it as Rob dragged the lifeless body over. Only then did I notice the small rubber raft lashed to the back of the boat.

"What's this?" I asked.

"That's how we brought your ass aboard," he said. "You think we carried your unconscious body down the gangplank at Marina Del Rey?"

I shrugged.

"We took you right from the kid's house to the raft. Then motored out about half a mile to where this big bastard was waiting."

"Wait a second," I said. "Don't tell me that you were the guy who knocked me out!?"

"Nope. It was Rothschild. He insisted." Rob laughed.

I shook my head in wonder as Rob grinned ear to ear. He was proud that his plan had worked.

"All right," I said. "But you still owe me a good fucking explanation."

"Later, man. The clock is ticking here."

Rob grabbed Rothschild's right arm and stooped low to get under his armpit. I did the same on the left side and together we lifted.

"Hold on a second," I said. The karambit was still stuck in Rothschild's side. I yanked it out. "Almost forgot this."

"I have the sheath tucked in the back of my pants if you want it."

"Yeah," I said. I offered him a sour glance. "I'll get it later."

"In you go!" Rob said.

Giving a heave, we flung Rothschild's corpse into the Pacific. It missed the inflatable raft by a few inches. He floated for half a second and then sank under the surface.

"What the hell are you doing?!" Kenealy screamed. Red-faced, he was on the verge of losing it. "He's already dead!"

"Uhhh, what do you call this, Rob?" I asked.

"This is called chumming," he answered.

"We're chumming," I said. I gave Kenealy a broad smile.

"For what?!"

"Why, sharks of course. These waters are full of sharks. Trust a couple guys who have done a lot of diving not far from here. Sharks will come for miles once they catch a whiff of Rothschild."

"Dear God," Kenealy whispered. "No."

"Ahhhh, you're catching on," I said. "Stand up."

Kenealy shook his head and pushed back against the transom.

"Stand up."

"No," he said. He whimpered. I almost felt sorry for him.

I took a very deep and very noisy breath, and then exhaled it just as loudly.

"Really? Do you really want to do this the hard way?"

"For God's sake! Don't throw me in alive! At least have the decency to shoot me!"

"Funny you should mention that. As it turns out, I'm going to give you a sporting chance. A chance you never gave me. But first I need you to stand up."

Kenealy looked from Rob, back to me and then to Rob again.

Rob nodded, giving him a grin, and motioned for him to rise.

Slowly, Kenealy got to his feet, favoring the leg with the bullet in it.

I looked to Rob and extended my hand. He handed me his gun and I turned back to show it to Kenealy. Then I popped the magazine out. Holding it in my hand, I used my thumb to push the rounds out of the magazine one by one. They hit the deck in a steady rhythmic pattern.

When the magazine was empty I bent and picked up one of the cartridges. I held it up, making sure Kenealy got a good look. Slowly and deliberately, so as there would be no doubt, I fed the round into the magazine. Then I slid the magazine back into the gun until it clicked. I pulled the bolt back and released it, chambering the round. I then pushed the small, black button again and the now empty magazine dropped into my hand. I showed it to Kenealy and then tossed it aside.

"So here it is, old pal," I said. "One bullet and it's all yours."

I paused for emphasis as Kenealy's eyes darted back and forth between the gun and me.

"Once I give you this you will have a choice to make. You can take the easy way out and put a bullet in your own head, or you can shoot me."

"Are you fucking crazy, Ryder!?" Rob yelled. "That wasn't part of the plan!"

"Shut up, Rob! I know what I'm doing!"

Kenealy swallowed hard but kept his mouth shut.

"Now," I said. "I'm counting on your cowardice to save me, because you have just the one bullet. If you choose to shoot me, then bravo, we both die tonight. But know this, after you do it, Rob is going to toss you into the ocean. You will sink like a stone and become dinner for some big, nasty fish."

"Ryder, don't you fucking give him that gun!" Rob screamed.

"Dude," I said. I turned my head to lock eyes with him. "This twisted fuck was going to have my best friend kill me! Well, with his massive ego, I know that he's his own best friend so I'm going to have him kill himself. Poetic justice I think."

"And what if he shoots you?!"

"Fuck it. Then I get to be with Debbie and the kids

again. Either way he dies. That's all I want."

"Please don't do this, man," Rob said.

"Don't worry." I said. "He doesn't have the guts."

I extended the gun. Kenealy hesitated for a second and then snatched it from my hand. He turned the gun and pointed it at me.

"The safety's off. All you have to do is pull the trigger."

Kenealy wet his lips and debated silently. He looked towards Rob who took two steps back and one to the left. He wasn't going to get both of us with one shot.

"You shoot him and I swear to God I'm going to cut you into ribbons before I toss you in," Rob said. "You'll be bleeding so much that the sharks will be on you before your head goes under water."

"Come on Kenealy," I said. "Just put the gun against your temple and pull the trigger. This will all end. You won't feel a thing."

Kenealy's breathing came in short, labored huffs. His face bore the stress of a man who knew that he was close to death. He was terrified. I was ninety-nine percent certain what his decision would be.

"I wonder?" I asked. "Will you drown before you feel the first shark tear into you?"

Kenealy nerves firing, blinked repeatedly as I mused over the possibilities.

"Hard to say." I said. "Personally I'd prefer drowning. I can't even imagine the horror of getting eaten alive by those mean fuckers down there."

"Ryder," Rob said. "Why are you doing this?"

"Don't worry, man. He's too much of a chickenshit to shoot me. I doubt he's ever even killed a man himself."

Kenealy thrust the gun forward, pointing it at my head. The fear was gone from his eyes, replaced by a steely resolve. He had made his decision and it appeared as if I'd guessed wrong.

Oops.

"You know what," he said. He paused, a crazed look on his face. The upper hand was now his and he savored it. I honestly hadn't expected him to find the courage.

"Since I'm going to die anyway, I don't give a fuck how it happens. It may be horrible but at least I get to send you to hell first."

"You don't have the balls," I said.

Kenealy's eyes narrowed. I extended my arms out wide, like Jesus on the cross, all the while mocking him with my smile.

And then Kenealy surprised both Rob and me.

He pulled the trigger.

Raging Storm
52

Click.

Kenealy, who a split second before had worn a wild eyed mask of supremacy, now looked dumbfounded. He tried to squeeze the trigger again but it wouldn't budge.

"No, no," I said. I instructed him in a calm and soothing voice. "You have to pull the hammer back with your thumb."

Kenealy looked at me with a blank stare.

"You see, the gun firing sends the upper housing unit back and forth. That not only chambers another round, but also cocks it."

He continued to stare, his face ashen.

"But seeing as how the gun didn't fire and the round is still in the chamber, all you have to do is cock it yourself."

Rob chuckled and Kenealy turned his head to the left and gave him the same, stunned look.

"Like this," I said. I mimicked the motion with my own thumb.

Kenealy followed instructions this time and thumbed the hammer back.

"Excellent. Now go ahead and try again, Billy."
Kenealy thrust the gun forward again and desperately pulled the trigger.

Click.

My shoulders shook as I began to laugh. And the more I laughed, the stronger it grew. Before long I was holding my sides. It was one of the greatest, most genuine laughs of my life and I enjoyed it to its lengthy fruition.

"You dumb fuck," Rob said. He shook his head and mocked the man with a look of disgust.

I looked Kenealy in the eye as my laughter slowed to the point where I could speak.

"Well, this does answer a lot of questions about you," I said. I wiped a tear away. "I knew that you were nothing more than a cheap thug in an expensive suit."

Kenealy stood there with the same blank look on his face. He was in shock, having had the tables turned on him so completely. He didn't even plead for mercy. He was beat. And he knew it.

"This is the gun we gave him," he whispered as he looked down at the weapon.

"Well no shit, dumb ass," I said. "Did you really think I'd be stupid enough to gamble with my life?"

I snatched the gun from him and with a flip of my wrist, tossed it into the ocean.

"Dude!" Rob shot me a pained look. "That was a nice fucking 9mm! I could have gotten another firing pin for like twenty bucks!"

"Sorry, man," I said. "You can have the one I took off Rothschild."

"Oh." His chipper demeanor returned. "Cool. Thanks."

The time for games was over.

Taking a step forward, I grabbed Kenealy by the throat. He gasped and pried at my hands but I was much too strong. Holding him easily, I stepped, pushing him to the edge of the open door.

"Rob," I said. "Grab those cinder blocks and put them on top of the transom."

"You got it."

He did just that, the chains rattling as he set them on the edge of the boat by the door.

Kenealy's mouth turned downward and it appeared as if he might start crying. He shook his head in quick back and forth motions, pleading with me. His eyes said it all.

"Rob," I said. "Please push them in."

"With pleasure."

"No," Kenealy whispered again. He could barely speak. All the fight was out of him.

"I'm just doing what we set out to do, Billy. I think the world will be a hell of a lot better place without a piece of shit like you in it."

Using both hands, Rob shoved two of the blocks in the water and then the third one immediately after. The three landed with loud splashes in the dark water. Kenealy grabbed the sides of the boat, hanging on in desperation as the weight tried to pull him over. I still had him by the throat but before letting him go, I moved forward so that our faces were almost touching.

"You lose," I said, repeating my earlier words to Rothschild.

"Please," Kenealy said. "Don't."

With a push I sent him back towards the gaping hole of

water. His arms flailed as he clawed the air looking for a handhold. It was no use. He went into the water with a huge splash.

I expected his head to surface. For him to give me one last pleading look as he struggled to tread water. But that didn't happen. The water swallowed him up. He disappeared into the darkness.

It was finally over.

I stood there for a moment, looking at the water, chest heaving, trying to process what had just transpired. The entire evening had been so surreal that I was having a tough time distilling it. To experience such intense emotions, from one end of the spectrum to the other, had left me on empty. I was spent.

I wasn't sure how long I stood there. I felt a hand on my shoulder.

Turning my head to the right, I stared into the face of my best friend in the world. If that status had ever been in question before, it was an iron clad fact now.

"We need to go, brother," he said.

I didn't respond. I couldn't. I looked at him and tried to control the different emotions that flooded my senses. All this madness had started with Debbie and the kids. With Kenealy's death it felt like a chapter in my life had finally come to an end. But as with many endings, it was bittersweet. I retreated to a private area of my mind and although I was looking at Rob, I wasn't seeing him.

I saw them. My family.

"I know man," Rob said. He gave my shoulder a squeeze. "But in all seriousness, we're sitting ducks out here."

I snapped out of the fog and refocused, taking a second to clear both my mind and my throat. He was right. Now was not the time to shut down. I took a deep breath and exhaled.

"You got any ideas about what to do with this boat?" I asked. "Because I'm fresh out."

"Yeah, man. Actually I have a really good one."

Rob smiled at me with that devilish, care-free grin. And then he explained.

Raging Storm
53

The next day I woke up late. Very late.
But then again we didn't get back to the house until after three in the morning. Still, it was strange to wake up and see my clock read 11:30am.
Rob had suggested that I stay awake as I was most likely suffering from a concussion. But I couldn't. It was not even in the realm of possibility. Upon arriving back at his parent's house, we'd toasted a successful operation with a shot of scotch. And then I'd all but passed out. It had been the end of a very long day. The end of a very long few months.
I had no remorse about killing Kenealy. He was a rotten, murderous bastard and the world truly was a better place without him in it. I also had no problem with the way I killed him. Truth told, I enjoyed the fact that he suffered. Perhaps I would have done things differently if I hadn't seen the mutilated corpse of Joe Simpson. Kenealy could lay that off on Rothschild all he wanted, but he knew. He'd known exactly what had happened and in fact, had most likely sanctioned it.

I lay in bed and stared at the ceiling as I recalled the evening.

After deep sixing Kenealy, we'd dragged the big bodyguard to the back door and sent him down to join his friends. Then we went back up to the bridge and moved the boat, heading inland. It turned out that Rob knew a thing or two about GPS navigation systems. As we'd been drifting about 10 miles off the coast, the first thing Rob did was erase the existing trail. If the authorities ever got their hands on the boat we weren't sure whether they could trace its movement. But at the very least we could erase the memory. Even if they could figure out where we'd been, the odds of finding Kenealy's body were slim to none. I doubted there would be anything left of it. The other two might wash up on shore somewhere, but I doubted that too. With all the blood in the water there would have been plenty of sharks. And they don't tend to waste much.

After erasing the memory, Rob had set a GPS plot towards Japan. Straight out into the middle of the Pacific Ocean. Once we engaged the boats auto-pilot, it would steer itself. The gas tank on this beast held an astonishing thirty-one hundred gallons. Neither Rob nor I knew the fuel efficiency of the boat, but it didn't matter. Even if it got one nautical mile to the gallon, three thousand gallons would put it a very long way from home. Not to mention that if the boat motored into a storm, or even large swells, it would most likely swamp and sink. I've been in the middle of the Pacific. It gets very big and very rough.

After completing these tasks, we make our exit by way

of the small rubber raft. Being Special Forces, this was old hat for us. So as we motored back towards my truck, the Never Enough began its unmanned, Pacific voyage. We'd set the boats speed at a leisurely ten knots per hour. This wouldn't arouse any suspicion if the Coast Guard took a look at it on radar. Nothing to see here, just a big, expensive boat filled with rich guys heading out to deep water and large game fish.

I'd made Rob explain to me several times why he thought that selling me out was a good idea. And why he hadn't thought to mention it to me. He did his best to convince me that if the entire thing had been an act which we were both in on, they would have smelled it. Kenealy and Rothschild had to be one hundred percent convinced that he had flipped.

Seeing as how things had gone I had no choice but to forgive the son of a bitch. I did remind him at every given opportunity how bad my head hurt. Of course, instead of making him feel guilty, it only served to amuse him so I soon stopped. Rob had been right, but it was one hell of a gamble he'd taken with both of our lives.

I swung my feet out of bed and made for the kitchen to find my friend sitting at the table, reading the paper. As always, a steaming cup of coffee was in front of him.
"Hey man," I said.
"Hey bud," he answered.
"How long you been up?"
"About twenty minutes or so. Sorry if I woke you."
"You didn't."
I walked over the coffee pot and poured myself a mug.

"That was some serious shit, huh?" Rob asked. He grinned at me.

I nodded without returning the smile. Taking a sip from my cup, I leaned into the counter.

"Dude, we got lucky," I answered. "Very lucky."

"Fuck that. It was brilliantly planned and flawlessly executed. You're welcome."

I couldn't help but chuckle. The bastard could always make me laugh. I looked at my friend and felt a bond that defied explanation.

"Dude, I owe you my life."

"Yeah well," he said. "Saving your ass is what I do best."

"I'm serious, man. What you did took balls. If it hadn't gone down like it did, they would have killed you too."

"I know. And that's why I had to let them take you at the kid's house. Like I told you last night, they were sure that you were going to race up to Lake Arrowhead and launch a one man assault. I convinced them otherwise. I explained how you'd already scoped out the beach house and that it was your emergency plan. Rothschild wasn't sure about it but once they nabbed you there, I earned instant trust."

"Yeah, just enough to give you a gun without a damn firing pin."

Rob shrugged.

We both fell silent and I sipped my coffee, staring into nothing.

I waded through the different thoughts and emotions I'd dealt with in the past twenty-four hours. It was pretty messy but I knew one thing with absolute certainty. It was time to leave. I'd made my decision and knew it was the right one. Rob would try his best to talk me out of it but there was no chance.

"Listen, Ryder," he said, "This calls for a celebration. I say we go grab some steaks, a couple lobster tails and some more good tequila."

He looked at me and paused, weighing his next words. "And hear me out on this bro, but I know this chick who has a friend and they would love to come hang out with us."

It was like this after a dangerous mission and particularly after combat. You could be in the nastiest, ugliest firefight of your life. People could be getting killed all around you, but once it was over, you went on with life. In fact, the next day you felt an incredible rush of energy, almost a youthful exuberance. I knew it was the minds way of dealing with stress. But it was always the same. The urge to get drunk or go grab a woman was never as strong as it was the day after combat. After my first couple battles I'd found it strange. I'd felt guilty for feeling that rush. There were guys we lost. People we killed. I thought I was supposed to be down or morose about it. But as a warrior, you come to realize that not only does life go on, but it's a very normal reaction to survival. You'd faced down death and had lived. It was all very primal. Of course you mourned your own fallen, but you put that on the back burner. You dealt with that later.

"What do you say, buddy?" Rob snapped me out of my haze.

"Dude..."

I hesitated, searching for the right words.

"…you know that I -"

"Yeah, man, I get it," he said, interrupting me. "I know it might be too soon for a chick but you don't have to do shit with her. Just talk and hang out. Chill and enjoy the company of females for a change. I'm telling you brother, it's exactly what the doctor ordered."

"I've got to go, Rob."

I'd ripped off the Band-Aid and now stared at him with a pained expression.

"Go where?" He asked. Rob wasn't connecting the dots.

"I don't know where," I said. "But I've got to leave. Today."

"What the fuck are you talking about? It's over, man."

"Over? Rob, I'm still a wanted man. My face has been on the national news. I'm a fucking fugitive."

"But you're innocent!"

I looked at him and said nothing. He understood.

"Well, okay. Maybe not innocent but you know what I mean."

"I hear you, man. And I owe you my life. But you know that I have to leave. This is not my home. I don't have a home anymore."

"That is complete bullshit, Ryder!" Rob yelled. He was getting upset. "You will always have a home as long as I do! I'll rent a damn house with you in Oceanside if you want! At least until you figure out your next move!"

"Rob," I said. I stayed calm. "Every day I stay here, every day I spend around you, increases the chances of you taking the fall with me. I am still wanted for murder. You are now an accessory."

"That's crap and you know it! What the hell are you going to do?! Wander the fucking country?!"

I shook my head and cast my eyes to the floor. How could I make him understand?

"I've got to, man."

"Look, Ryder," Rob said. He took it down a notch as he tried to reason with me. "You're just freaked out about what happened. I get that. But give me one night. Stay one more night and tomorrow we can figure out your next move. Okay? Tomorrow?"

I remained silent.

"You said you owed me. Will you at least give me that?"

Listening to my friend's desperate plea, I felt a wave of emotion sweep over me. I loved him. He was more of a brother to me than if we'd had the same parents. And he was right. I did owe him. Everything.

"Okay, buddy," I answered. "One night."

"Awesome!" He clapped his hands together. "So here's the deal. I'm going to run out and grab the supplies and you clean up a bit. This place looks like a couple marines have been crashing here."

He laughed and went to grab his keys.

"Hang on," I said. I walked into my bedroom and came back with two hundred dollars. I handed it to him.

"Here," I said. "It's my turn."

"Okay, thanks Ryder."

I appreciated him not fighting me on that.

Rob scooped up his keys and gave me a salute. Then he dashed out the garage door.

I heard his Jeep fire up and listened as he pulled away.

Standing in place for a full minute, I downed the rest of my coffee. Then I walked to the bedroom and threw everything I owned into my duffel bag and suitcase. I hauled them both into the kitchen and grabbing a pen and piece of paper, I wrote two notes.

I'm sorry, Rob. I do owe you. That's why I'm doing this. I hope one day you'll understand and forgive me. I'll be in touch. Love you, bro.

The second note I wrote was to Rob's father. I told him I was buying his truck and that Rob could take care of the title and registration. Then I went into my bag and removed ten thousand dollars.

I left the notes and the cash on the kitchen counter top, picked up my things, and walked out the garage door. Getting in my truck, I started the ignition and then sat and took a long last look. I thought about everything that had happened. How upside down and hectic my life had been the past few months, the past few weeks in particular.

Kenealy was gone.

It was over. It was time.

Backing out of the driveway, I squared my jaw and steeled my resolve. As difficult as this was, it was the right thing to do.

I put the truck in drive and pressed down on the accelerator.

The last several years of my life I'd spent in some pretty hot climates. From the Middle East to Florida and Southern California, it was always hot. I was sick of it and wanted a change. Needed a change.

I headed north.

Don't Miss the Exciting First 2 Books

Of The

JAMES HARRIS SERIES

GOOD COP BAD COP

&

MOB RULES

By

Richard Nesbitt

98000637R00224

Made in the USA
Columbia, SC
19 June 2018